THE BALFOUR TWINS

*Betty McInnes titles available from
Severn House Large Print*

All the Days of their Lives
Collar of Pearls
MacDougal's Luck

THE BALFOUR TWINS

Betty McInnes

Severn House Large Print
London & New York

This first large print edition published in Great Britain 2007 by
SEVERN HOUSE LARGE PRINT BOOKS LTD of
9-15 High Street, Sutton, Surrey, SM1 1DF.
First world regular print edition published 2006 by
Severn House Publishers, London and New York.
This first large print edition published in the USA 2007 by
SEVERN HOUSE PUBLISHERS INC., of
595 Madison Avenue, New York, NY 10022.

British Library Cataloguing in Publication Data

McInnes, Betty (Elizabeth Anne), 1928-
    The Balfour twins. - Large print ed.
    1. Twins - Fiction 2. Domestic fiction 3. Large type books
    I. Title
    823.9'14[F]

    ISBN-13: 978-0-7278-7616-4

All Severn House titles are printed on acid-free paper.

Printed and bound in Great Britain by
MPG Books Ltd, Bodmin, Cornwall.

To David Winterburn,
with thanks for his help and support.

One

19th September 1919

Annette and Lisette Balfour stumbled over ruts and potholes on a farm track, holding tight to their father's hands. They were only four years old, but they did not complain, though they glanced up at him anxiously from time to time because the surroundings were unfamiliar. James Balfour's little twin daughters were accustomed to walking upon smooth Edinburgh pavements.

Identical dark-brown eyes mirrored their apprehension.

The date was 19th September 1919, and Annette looked upwards, trying to gauge Papa's mood. He seemed sad, she thought, as if his thoughts were far away with Maman, who died and went to Heaven seven weeks ago. The little girl wished her father would smile. A smile would be reassuring on this momentous day, when their lives were changing forever.

She remembered Papa had seemed more cheerful during the long train journey from Edinburgh to their final destination, a little town called Kirriemuir in the county of Angus, Scotland.

'I liked the train, Papa,' she ventured.

'Did you, darling?' he said absently.

The trees all around were old and very tall, hedgerows and undergrowth unkempt and shadowy. Lisette hung back a little, dragging at his hand.

'Papa, I don't like this place.'

James Balfour glanced down compassionately at his small daughter. Lisette was a cautious child, afraid of the dark, scared of being alone. Like himself. Annette was the sturdier twin, full of mischief, ready to make the best of any situation. Like her mother. He sighed.

'Remember now, Maman told us to be brave.'

'If we're brave, will we have medals like yours?' Annette asked.

'Maybe. We'll see.'

He smiled briefly at his girls, but mention of Maman's last whispered breath had saddened them. They wore black mourning bands on their sleeves, a constant reminder of their loss. The twins plodded on, weary and silent. It had been a long day. After the train journey from Edinburgh, a slow chuffing train had brought them to a small red sandstone town, tucked into the foothills of the Grampians. Leaving the station, they had climbed a steep brae and boarded a bus heading out into the countryside, alighting at a rough farm track sign-posted Kilmuckety.

As they walked and stumbled along, Papa had explained that the Kilmuckety estate had been owned by the Balfour family for many generations. The house where he and his older brother Robert had been born lay just ahead, hidden by trees.

The twins looked ahead eagerly but could see no end to the rough track, which seemed to wind on forever.

'Aren't we there yet, Papa?' Lisette asked plaintively.

'Not far now, my pet.'

James Balfour didn't know how he would have survived his wife's untimely death, without their daughters. He had been forced to contemplate a lonely future, to think and plan ahead, for the sake of his motherless twins.

His heart gave a painful lurch as they looked up at him with trusting dark eyes so like their French mother's. Seven weeks ago, Suzanne Balfour had succumbed to the virulent strain of influenza raging throughout Europe. So-called Spanish flu had reached Edinburgh that summer, and tragedy had struck just as the Balfours were looking forward to a happy future together, now the Great War had ended.

James had spent the war years in the engine room of a large Merchant Navy ship, carrying stores and military equipment to Gibraltar, Gallipoli and other wartime destinations. In port in France, he had met and married his lovely French wife, Suzanne Lefevre. A love

9

affair cut tragically short, five years later.

The ship's sympathetic captain had given James generous leave of absence when Suzanne died, but now his ship was back in her home port of Leith and James was due aboard within the next few days. By then, the twins' future would be settled.

He smiled down at them with forced cheerfulness.

'You'll love living on a farm with Aunt Connie and Uncle Bob and four big boy cousins. Your aunt writes that she and Uncle Bob can hardly wait to have two little girls to care for.'

'Don't they like big boys?' Annette asked curiously.

He laughed. 'Oh yes, the bigger the better! There's plenty work on a farm for big boys. I should know! Your uncle and I worked very hard on this farm when we were lads.'

'But you didn't stay, did you, Papa?' Lisette said.

Children can ask awkward questions at times, he thought ruefully.

'No, I didn't stay. My father said I must, but I wanted to go to sea, so off I went. My papa was not happy, bless him, neither was my big brother.'

'But you sailed to France and married Maman, and that made everyone happy,' Annette said.

He nodded sadly. 'Yes, my dear. Very happy.'

★ ★ ★

10

They came upon Kilmuckety House with startling suddenness. The twins stopped and stared. They had not imagined anything quite so grand. The tenement flat Papa and Maman had rented near Leith docks had been small, but cosy.

The front door was flung open at that moment and a buxom woman came rushing to meet them. She was followed by a tall man who was an older version of Papa. Four big boys of varying age and size appeared, lining up in the background.

James hugged the smiling woman.

'Connie, my dear, it's wonderful to be home again!'

The two brothers shook hands and clapped one another awkwardly on the shoulder, then the entire family turned attention to the twins. Papa introduced them.

'As you can see, Annette and Lisette look so alike you may have difficulty telling them apart at first, but there are differences of temperament, which you'll soon recognize.' He looked at his daughters and heaved a sigh. 'You'll maybe find identical twins can attract unwelcome attention. People stop and stare, as if the girls were a sideshow at the fair. Suzanne was determined to encourage our girls to develop as individuals. For example, they need not be dressed alike.'

Connie Balfour wiped away a tear.

'Poor wee motherless lambs! You can rest assured we'll respect your dear wife's wishes, James.'

11

Recovering her good spirits, Connie usher-ed everyone out of the cold into a gloomy hallway as big as a barn, and just about as badly lit.

'We'll have high tea tonight, in honour of the occasion,' she announced.

She opened a door into a passageway lead-ing to a huge cavern of a kitchen, shooed four barking dogs and goodness knows how many cats into a back yard, then rolled up her sleeves, threatening dire consequences should any family member dare cross the threshold while cooking was in progress.

Uncle Bob smiled at the startled little girls. 'Never you mind your auntie, her bark's worse'n her bite. Come and see your bed-room. It's pink. Your Aunt Connie's been working on it for days. How that woman's enjoyed herself!'

They all clattered upstairs to view the feminine apartment, big boys included. The smallest big boy spoke up shyly.

'That's my old teddy bear on your bed, wee lassies. You can share him till the new baby comes, then I 'spect the baby will want him.'

News about the baby thrilled the twins. They had dolls, of course, but they loved babies.

'Is a real baby coming?' they chorused.

The boy nodded. 'Yes, it's on its way. Can't you see my ma's expecting?'

'What's she expecting? Is it baby clothes?' Annette asked breathlessly.

All the big boys laughed, being well versed

in the facts of life.

'No, you daftie, Ma's expecting a baby, of course!' the smallest one grinned.

Everyone sat around the large kitchen table for high tea. There were wonderful smells of cooking and baking, and heat pulsed from a gleaming black stove. The twins sat side by side on seats elevated to adult level with cushions. Papa sat beside them to lend a hand, and there was laughter, the first they'd heard for weeks. Even Papa laughed when he saw the food.

'What a grand spread, Connie! Ham, eggs, sausages, apple pie, cream, your famous scones, and more butter than I've seen in years!'

Connie beamed modestly. 'Och, that's one advantage of living on the farm.'

Robert Balfour smiled faintly. 'Don't imagine we live like lords all the time, James. Farm produce usually goes to market in Kirriemuir and Forfar to make ends meet. We survive on porridge and broth.'

James was startled.

'I'd no idea money was tight, Bob!'

Connie threw her husband an exasperated glance. 'Och, farmers are aye moaning, James. We manage fine.'

She turned to the twins.

'I never introduced you lassies to your big cousins, which was remiss of me.' She nodded across at her brood. 'Starting with the biggest, that's Matthew, Mark, Luke and

13

John. You can't beat the Bible for names.'

'Will the baby have a Bible name too, Aunt Connie?' Annette asked.

'Yes, lovey. It'll be Benjamin, because it'll be the youngest – and last, God willing.'

'What if it's a girl baby?'

'If only I were so lucky!' Connie sighed, piling food on plates.

The twins studied their biblical cousins with interest. Annette pointed.

'Who's that boy? He's not one of them.'

Connie glanced at the interloper.

'Oh, that's Fergus McGill. He comes from the neighbouring farm.'

Annette studied the tousle-haired boy. He certainly wasn't a Balfour. He had carroty hair, a freckled nose, and a ferociously angry glare. She frowned.

'What's *he* doing here?'

'He's in wee John's class at school,' her aunt said. 'Fergus has five sisters older than him, so he much prefers to stay around our boys.'

'I hate girls. They're bossy,' the boy said.

Annette bridled. 'No, they're not.'

Eyeing Annette warily, he took a deep draught of milk, which left a white moustache on his scornful upper lip.

'Why are there two of you, 'zactly the same?'

''Cause we're twins!'

He made a rude, retching noise. 'Yuk! One of you's enough.'

Sternly, Uncle Bob turned upon the visitor.

'Any more o' your lip, my lad, and you'll be

14

out the door!'

There was not another cheep from Fergus McGill for the remainder of the meal. Wisely, the boy had decided a feed like this was not to be missed.

Soon after, Connie took the twins upstairs to bed. Denied the joy of daughters of her own, Connie had been looking forward eagerly to this moment. The rambling farmhouse boasted a large bathroom, complete with impressive bathtub, basin and water closet, relics of more affluent times. Connie had made Bob's life a misery before the twins' arrival, till he'd been forced to pay a plumber to restore hot and cold water to the system, rendering tin baths and outdoor privy things of the past.

With two little girls splashing happily in a warm bath, two heads of shining dark hair to be brushed and small white nightgowns trimmed with lace warming by the fire, Connie Balfour felt as if she'd arrived in paradise.

Meanwhile, men and boys tended to farmyard chores by lantern light, before retiring thankfully to the living room. A blazing fire and paraffin lamps made pools of light around the large room. Bob explained that the two biggest boys had left school at the age of fourteen to help him on the farm. They were working together, building a model sailing ship, while the two younger ones struggled with school homework.

15

The two Balfour men relaxed by the fireside, James dressed in borrowed working shirt and trousers. Thoughtfully, he eyed the two lads engrossed in building a ship. Did they have dreams of leaving the farm to see the world? If so, he pitied his brother, but couldn't blame the youngsters. James's hands were blistered and sore, every muscle aching after barely an hour of pitchforking fresh bedding into the byre.

'I'd forgotten farm work was so hard,' he said.

Bob smiled, leaning forward to light a pipe. 'Maybe it's you that's soft.'

In the firelight, James took note of deep furrows lining his brother's face, and hollows in the thin stubbled cheeks. Robert Balfour was like an old man, long before his time. Looking around with sudden concern, James could see that the old family home had grown pitifully shabby and threadbare over the years, much of its fabric sadly in need of repair. Leaving the twins in the Balfours' care had seemed the best option, but now James wasn't so sure. Guiltily, he wondered if he'd added more weight to his brother's burden of work and worry.

'Should I have stayed on the farm, Bob? Would it have helped?' he asked uneasily.

His brother looked up in surprise. 'No. We lost so many farm workers in the war, it's not a question of manpower any more, James. In my opinion, using more machinery is the way ahead, if we could afford it.'

'I'd offer to pay for the girls' keep, but Suzanne's last illness took all my savings, and I've no option but to go back to sea,' James said awkwardly. 'But we could make alternative arrangements for the twins, if Connie finds she can't cope once the new baby arrives.'

Bob brushed the suggestion aside with a laugh. 'Och, she'd be affronted if you even mention such a possibility! I assure you, James, looking after your wee lasses will be pure joy for my bonny wee wife, after dealing with a husband and a houseful o' lads...'

The last few days of James's leave passed all too quickly. On the night before his departure, he came to the twins' room and sat down on the pink quilt. There was a smile fixed on his lips and a fierce ache in his breast.

While his daughters sat up in bed listening solemnly, he explained he would be leaving very early next morning, long before they were awake.

Their dark eyes were too bright, but they were not in tears.

'Why don't you stay, Papa?' Lisette said.

'I'm a sailor, darling, and not much of a farmer. Uncle Bob and the big boys work hard and I'd just be in the way.'

'Will you come home soon?'

He hesitated. He'd been warned the ship would be trading around Africa and Asia, and would not return to Britain for at least two years.

'Not too soon, I'm afraid,' he said gently. 'This time we're sailing to the Far East.'

'That sounds awfully far away, Papa,' Annette said in a small voice.

'It is, darling, but I promise I'll be back one day.' He kissed them fondly. 'Meantime, I've something for you to keep for me, till we're together again.'

James reached into a pocket and took out the three medals he'd gained during the Great War. The two little girls stared wide-eyed, the oil lamp casting golden light upon silver, bronze and brightly coloured ribbon.

Their father laid the medals on the quilt. He touched one with a fingertip.

'This one's for you, Annette, the British War medal. It's silver, with King George's head on one side and an impression of Saint George on the other. You can see the ribbon is golden yellow in the centre, with stripes of white, black and blue.'

He pinned the medal to the yoke of the little girl's nightie and turned to Lisette.

'Yours is the Victory medal, Lisette.'

'Mine's gold!' she breathed. He laughed.

'Hardly! It's bronze. The lady shown on the front is Victory and the writing on the back reads – *The Great War for Civilization.*' He pinned the medal to her nightie.

'Annette, look!' Lisette cried delightedly. 'My ribbon has lovely colours, like two rainbows.'

Her twin looked, and glowered sulkily.

It's not fair! Annette thought. *My ribbon's*

18

black an' blue. She pointed truculently to the third medal.

'Who's having that?'

'That's mine.' James picked up the remaining medal. 'This one's rather special. I saved a shipmate's life.'

'Maman *told* us you were a hero!' Lisette said proudly. Her father smiled.

'Not a real hero, dear. I just happened to arrive on the scene at the right time.'

'Were you scared, Papa?'

'Absolutely terrified. My knees turned to jelly, otherwise I might have run away.'

The twins looked sympathetic.

'We had jelly knees when we saw the big house and the big boys, but we didn't run away, did we, Papa?' Annette declared stoutly. Their father hid a grin.

'No, you stood your ground bravely. You deserve a medal.'

He hugged and kissed his little daughters, but couldn't bear to say goodbye. The word seemed so final, somehow. Instead, he laughed shakily.

'Night night, my darlings, don't let the bugs bite.'

'Oh, there're no bugs in Aunt Connie's beds, Papa!' the twins chorused.

'She boils 'em alive in the washboiler,' Annette added, gleefully...

The twins settled quickly into a new way of life. Their names were soon shortened to Annie and Lizzie, Connie having decided foreign names were not advisable, because of lingering prejudice after the war. The girls helped their aunt in the house and followed their uncle around the farm with fascinated interest.

Two of the big boys were so big they were nearly men, but all the boys, including Fergus, played football in the paddock at weekends. Sometimes they let the twins join in, and Fergus felled them with a tackle whenever the opportunity arose.

On weekdays there were kittens and pups for the girls to play with, and acres of mud which squelched beneath their stout new boots. The twins' pale city faces grew round and rosy.

In the daytime they did not miss their father, but at bedtime they took the medals out of the drawer to admire, before Connie came upstairs to tuck them in, kiss them goodnight, and light the nightlight candle to dispel fear of the dark.

The medals formed a comforting link with their absent father, but were also a source of jealousy.

'Mine's nicer than yours,' Lizzie observed one night.

Secretly, Annie shared the same opinion, though plough horses would not have dragged it from her. She scowled.

'No, it's not.'

'Yes, it is! Mine's just like a golden sovereign.'

''Tis not! It's like a dirty penny!'

Lizzie was on her knees in the rumpled bed, red with fury.

'My ribbon has two rainbows, yours is black an' blue like bruises!'

That did it. The twins fell upon one another, kicking, punching and screaming.

Connie came panting upstairs and stood in the doorway, hands on hips.

'Is there murder in this room? I thought you were wee ladies, but you're wilder warriors than my laddies.'

The little girls howled with misery.

Connie sat on the bed and gathered them in her arms. Patiently, she reached the reason for the squabble.

'Och now, your daddy wouldn't be giving out medals to start another war, would he?'

They looked shame-faced. Guiltily, Lizzie knew she'd started the fight. She'd been boasting, and Papa never boasted, even though he'd saved somebody's life. She tried to make amends.

'Annie's medal has King George on it, mine only has a lady in a nightie.'

Annie smiled magnanimously.

'Your ribbon has a rainbow, though.'

'*Two* rainbows,' Lizzie said...

The Balfour family went to church every Sunday in nearby Kirriemuir. Uncle Bob drove them there in a vehicle called a charabanc. This was used on weekdays to ferry pigs to market, and to collect berry pickers in summertime and schoolchildren in autumn to harvest potatoes from the fields during the holidays known as 'tattie holidays'.

Bob had haggled successfully for the old charabanc with its owner, a farmer living in the glens. The hill farmer had been keen to get rid of the troublesome mechanical monster, which stuck fast on wintry roads, grinding to a stubborn halt when faced with icy conditions which horse and cart traversed with ease.

Respectable churchgoers eyed the battered old bus dubiously – none more so than the Balfours' wealthy neighbours, the McGills, who arrived at the kirk in a gleaming black landau with brown leather upholstery.

The Balfour children made a point of lingering behind in order to watch the McGills walk into the kirk. The mother and five daughters led the way, dressed to the nines in velvets, silks and flowery hats, but the sight the Balfours waited to view eagerly was the boy Fergus.

Fergus slunk along behind his parents and sisters, dressed in full Highland outfit, topped by a tam o' shanter with cock o' the north feathers. He wore a black velvet jacket with silver buttons over a white shirt with a frothing lace jabot and frilly cuffs, a red Royal Stewart tartan kilt, tartan hose, red garters and shiny black silver-buckled shoes.

The twins and the big Balfour boys cheered him into the kirk.

Fergus scowled at them all horribly.

★　★　★

Annie had become friendly with Fergus McGill, because she admired his nerve. It was exciting to follow the boy around to see the mischief he got into. With remarkable tolerance, ten-year-old Fergus did not seem to mind her tagging along.

Lizzie was more wary than her twin, but did admit to admiring Fergus's undoubted good looks. His hair was rich auburn, his skin clear and pale, and his eyes the colour of the whisky Uncle Bob drank to welcome in the New Year.

One rainy Saturday afternoon, Lizzie begged paper and crayons from cousin John, and settled down to commit Fergus McGill's attractive image to paper.

Connie paused in her constant sock-knitting to glance over her niece's shoulder.

'Why, that's Fergus McGill to a T. Very good, Lizzie dear!'

Annie admired her sister's drawing, then reached for pencil and paper. 'I'll draw Fergus being naughty. That's more like it.'

Quick as a flash, she had sketched an apple tree, with Fergus in the topmost branches, stealing apples. A figure recognizable as Uncle Bob waited grimly below, along with a bad-tempered old sheepdog that had good reason to loathe small boys.

The sketch harked back to a recent incident, when Fergus was caught stealing Bob's prized eating apples and fled with the dog snapping at his heels. The twins howled with mirth.

Studying the two drawings, Connie was impressed. She'd had very little schooling and was no artist, but she had brought up four boys and considered herself a fair judge of a child's ability. She could not fail to see that these were talented wee bairns, able to read, write and draw beautifully, already far in advance of her own dear lads at that age. Her boys' strengths lay along more practical lines and Connie was proud of her sons, but the twins' ability seemed outstanding.

It worried her. How on earth could she and Bob ensure that these clever girls realized the full potential their poor dead mother had planned for them? What chance would their intelligence have to flourish in the harsh environment of this rundown old place? Connie studied her own red hands, coarsened and calloused after many years of hard, unrelenting toil. She'd hardly had time to open a book, all her life. She could offer these bright girls boundless, generous love, but would that be enough?

Connie did not attend church next Sunday. This was so unusual the twins were restless and out of sorts. Their aunt kept a supply of peppermints, called 'granny sookers', in a coat pocket. They would sit on either side, drowsy and soothed with peppermints, while the minister droned away in the pulpit above their heads.

They complained loudly when the sermon began.

24

'Why isn't she here?'

'Shh!' whispered big cousin Matthew. 'The baby's on its way.'

'Will it be sitting at the table when we have dinner?' they yelled excitedly.

Heads turned, people stared.

'No, 'course not. Shush!' Matthew growled, scarlet with embarrassment.

The sermon seemed even longer and more tedious than usual that morning, but when the bus returned to the farmhouse and the twins dashed inside, the baby wasn't there.

Connie had expected an easy time with this one, especially as it was a little before its time. She'd had no bother with the others and had no reason to expect a long, difficult labour, but it took the combined efforts of midwife and doctor to deliver Bob and Connie's frail, tiny daughter as dawn broke that Monday morning. Connie was desperately ill, and the delicate premature baby gave cause for concern. Worried Uncle Bob did his best to cope in the anxious days following her birth, but the house was disorganized, the twins neglected, and meals scanty and badly cooked.

Annie complained bitterly to Fergus McGill. They were halfway up a tall sycamore tree, perched on a stout branch, one of Fergus's favourite haunts. He had hauled her up there with some difficulty.

'Everything's horrible since the baby came,'

she told him mournfully.

'It's 'cause it's a girl. They're always trouble,' he said idly.

'I'm not trouble!'

'You will be, when you're older.'

Actually, Annie had been quite a pleasant surprise to Fergus. Being much younger than him, she could be bossed around. She had a mind of her own occasionally, but mostly did as she was told. She'd torn the knees out of long black stockings, her dress was ripped and filthy, but she didn't seem to care, which he found admirable. He knew her sister couldn't stand him, but Fergus didn't mind. One twin was quite enough.

'It's not fair. I'm not allowed to hold the baby, 'cause she's too small,' Annie grumbled.

He yawned, settling himself more comfortably on the branch.

'Piglets are much nicer than babies, anyway. I could let you hold a piglet, if you want.'

'When?'

Fergus hesitated. The sow was a huge angry beast, fiercely protective of her litter.

'When can I hold a piglet, Fergus, will it be soon?' Annie persisted eagerly

'... Um – maybe. We'll see,' he hedged, praying that, given time, the stubborn wee wretch would forget the rash offer.

Robert Balfour sat by his wife's bedside, holding her thin hand. Connie was a little better, but still too weak to leave her bed, and the baby's pathetic cries were not much louder than a kitten's mew. Husband and wife looked at one another in despair.

'We can't go on like this, Bob,' Connie said. 'The doctor's never out of the house at a shilling a visit, and the potato crop's a disaster this year. How can we survive the winter?'

'We'll pull our belts tighter, love.'

Connie sighed. 'Oh yes, we can do that, but it's not what your brother and his poor wife wanted for their wee girls, is it?'

'No. It's not,' he agreed heavily. There was a solution to the problem of the twins' well-being. He wasn't sure if Connie would agree to it, yet something had to be done. He took a deep breath, and went on, 'James was concerned about us, wondering how we'd manage with a new baby on the way, Connie. I reassured him, but I didn't see this crisis looming. However, before James settled on us, I know he considered asking Suzanne's older sister to look after the twins. Dr and Mrs Gregory are a childless couple, not short of a shilling or two. Maybe they'd jump at the chance to take the girls.'

'But the Gregorys live in London!' Connie cried.

He nodded.

'I have the address. I could write and see what they decide.'

The suggestion struck Connie like a blow to the heart. If the twins went to stay with this wealthy London couple, chances were she'd never see them again. She would be heartbroken, but this was no time to consider self. She agreed with Bob that they must do what was best for the twins' future.

'Write to Dr and Mrs Gregory, Bob,' she told him steadily. 'Explain the situation and tell them we'll abide by their decision.'

One month later, Fergus McGill swung down like a monkey from the lower branches of his favourite tree and dropped at Annie's feet.

'So you really are leaving?'

'Yes. Aunt Madeleine and Uncle Dermot will look after us now. They're rich people. I bet their motor car's bigger'n better'n yours.'

Fergus let that pass without argument, a fair indication of his state of mind. There'd be nobody to play with when Annie went. Fergus and John Balfour were the same age and in the same class at school, but they were far from being friendly and fought most of the time.

'I thought you wanted to hug a piglet?' he said sulkily.

'I can't. Aunt Madeleine's coming for us tomorrow. We've to wear red dresses and shiny shoes.'

'Oh – *yuk!*'

Fergus turned on his heel and stalked off in disgust. Annie watched him go, tears welling up. He hadn't even said goodbye.

Despite Fergus putting a damper on things, the prospect of living in London was still exciting. The twins had never met the

Gregorys, but Annie imagined Aunt Madeleine would be an older, wealthier version of their dear dead Maman, which was comforting.

The delicate baby had clung to life and was growing and putting on weight. Connie was a shadow of her former self, but sufficiently recovered to supervise every detail of the twins' wardrobe. The girls' new outfits from Jarvis of Forfar had nearly bankrupted Bob, but family pride would stand for nothing less than perfection.

On the day of departure, the twins were bathed and scrubbed, and their hair washed, curled and brushed till it shone like black satin.

Connie's heart uplifted a fraction as she studied the results of all her efforts. The little girls looked a picture in red velvet dresses, white stockings and black patent shoes.

She hustled them downstairs into the old drawing room.

This room was large, chilly and seldom used, its walls lined with portraits of bygone Balfours and furnished with the faded relics of better days. Connie sat the twins on a sofa beside a modest fire and gave them picture books. She wagged a finger.

'Don't you dare move. I broke my back ironing those petticoats. Your Aunt Madeleine will be here soon. Stand up when she comes in and answer nicely when spoken to. I don't want the woman to think you've been living with heathens.'

She left them sitting together, looking like angels.

It was an uncomfortable sofa. Horsehair prickled the backs of the twins' legs through threadbare plush. Minutes passed, old clocks ticked and Balfour ancestors looked down dolefully on the twins. Annie flung the picture book aside and stood up.

'You'll crumple your dress,' Lizzie warned.

'No, I won't. I'll walk to the window.'

One of the windows reached right down to the ground, like a door. Annie pressed her nose against the glass. Outside, the wind blew the last of the fallen leaves into golden drifts which would rustle crisply underfoot. She wished she were out there.

Fergus appeared suddenly out of nowhere, which indicated he'd been watching the house. He shoved his face close to the glass, hot breath forming a hazy circle of steam

'There's a new litter of piglets. It's your last chance to see them. Come on!' he said.

'How can I? My London auntie will be here any minute.'

'There's no sign of a car on the Forfar road yet. There's plenty time, if you hurry up!'

There was a bolt on the door and a handle that turned. Annie had it open in a jiffy. Alerted by a sudden draught, Lizzie looked round.

'Annie, come back!'

'Won't be long,' she promised blithely.

Fergus grabbed her hand and they ran off together, scuffing through drifts of leaves. A brisk breeze blew and Annie laughed, heady with the joy of sudden freedom.

They arrived at the pigsty and peered in at the pig family, through the bars of the metal gate. Fergus was relieved to find the sow lying peacefully. This was a younger mother than the bad-tempered old sow and nine tiny piglets were lined up neatly alongside the mother, suckling.

'Oh, they're sweet!' Annie breathed.

'Thought you'd like them,' he said nonchalantly, hands in trouser pockets.

Annie in red velvet had aroused strange emotions. He'd never noticed before how black and shiny her hair was, nor how her eyes sparkled when she smiled. His eyes went uncomfortably prickly and even though she was a girl, he was sad she was leaving.

Fergus roused from his reverie to find her grumbling, bottom lip out, glowering.

'This is my last chance, and you promised, Fergus!'

'What?'

'You promised I could hold a piglet.'

Fergus eyed the sow nervously, but the big recumbent beast hadn't opened an eye since they'd arrived. She was a picture of motherly bliss, piglets suckling peacefully.

'OK. I'll get you one,' he said.

He eased the gate open and crept in, Annie at his heels. He laid hands gently on the nearest piglet.

At the touch of his chilly hands the piglet rent the air with an ear-piercing squeal.

Fergus grabbed it as the angry sow heaved herself speedily upright, the squealing litter dropping off her teats.

'Run!' he yelled.

Annie obeyed as Fergus reached the gate seconds before the enraged mother and slammed it shut. He shoved the squealing piglet into the little girl's arms.

'Hold it, and mind you don't step in the pigshit!'

She struggled with the wriggling little animal, her dress ripped by its wildly flailing trotters. She staggered, feet slipping and slithering, lost her balance and fell backwards into a midden of filthy straw mucked out from the pigsty. The piglet escaped, squealing.

'Now you've done it!' groaned Fergus, and took off after it.

Annie picked herself up. She was in a pitiful state, and the smell was awful. Miserably, she turned and trailed back home.

Meantime, Madeleine Gregory and a nursemaid had arrived by taxicab from Forfar railway station.

'You will wait, please,' she said casually to the driver, stepping down outside the farmhouse to greet Connie with a smile and a kiss.

The visitor's careless extravagance with the taxi driver had rendered Connie almost speechless. She pointed the nursemaid towards the kitchen to keep an eye on the sleeping baby, and ushered the lady into the drawing room.

Only one twin was present. Connie looked around wildly.

'Where's Annie gone, Lizzie?'

Madeleine winced. She laid a hand on Connie's arm.

'My dear, what is this Lizzie and Annie? My sister gave the children beautiful French names.'

Connie hesitated. She could hardly tell a lady of foreign extraction that foreigners were suspect in these parts.

'It's ... um ... easier for Scots folk to say, Mrs Gregory,' she improvized lamely.

Madeleine smiled, amused. 'You Scots will accept no language but your own!'

She crossed the room to where Lizzie stood, and studied the child, entranced. The little girl was beautiful, the image of poor Suzanne. Madeleine almost wept. How many years had she and Dermot waited in vain, longing for a child just like this to call their own?

'Ah, Lisette, *ma petite*, I am so glad I am to be your new Maman!' she said softly.

The stylish lady dazzled Lizzie, who could see a resemblance to Maman, although her mother had never dressed so finely, nor worn so many beautiful rings. A delightful perfume clung to her aunt. It scented the whole room.

'Where's Annie?' Connie demanded with a grim light in her eye.

'Er ... out, Aunt Connie,' Lizzie said, with dread.

She'd had a premonition of disaster ever

33

since she'd watched her sister romp off with Fergus McGill. Sure enough, Annie chose that moment to open the glass door and rush in. A playful wind slammed the door shut behind her, trapping the most awful stench inside the room.

Madeleine took a choking breath.

'What is this dreadful smell?'

'Pigshit!' Annie announced tearfully, provoked beyond the limit of her endurance.

'*Mon Dieu!*' Madeleine recoiled in horror. She could see a likeness, but surely this coarse and filthy child could not be the little angel's twin?

Connie closed her eyes and swayed a little, before recovering manfully.

'Don't worry, Mrs Gregory, I'll make sure Annie is washed and changed.'

She grabbed the culprit by the slack of the bodice and ran her out of the door. Safely outside in the hallway, Connie pointed upstairs.

'To the bathroom at once, miss. Into a hot bath to wash away that stink, while I restore that poor woman's nerves wi' a strong cup of tea. Don't dare come down till you've changed every stitch of clothing and are smelling of roses, d'you hear?'

In tears, Annie obeyed. Despite her best efforts, Lifebuoy soap could not get rid of the powerful odour altogether. She dressed in a skirt and jumper considered not good enough for London and sat on the windowseat to sob while she towelled dry her wet hair.

Annie seethed with shamed misery and bitter resentment. Nobody could understand how much she'd wanted to run free through the leaves, nobody would listen if she explained how she'd longed to hold the little piglet.

That was a bad mistake, admittedly, but at first sight it had seemed so quiet and sweet! And now Aunt Madeleine couldn't stand sight and smell of her. A hot tear ran down the little girl's cheek.

A shower of gravel hit the bedroom window with a suddenness that made her jump.

Fergus stood below. He called up to her cannily.

'I saw the London woman arrive. Are you all right?'

'No, I'm not. I don't want to go to L-London with her, Fergus!'

Annie began crying in earnest. Fergus was seriously disturbed.

'You shouldn't go, if you don't want to,' he declared stoutly. He paused, frowning, then made up his mind. 'Come down. I'll show you where to hide so she won't find you.'

It was an appealing thought, but Annie hesitated.

'She'll take Lizzie away.'

'Not if it's twins she's after.'

Annie could not argue with that. She tiptoed downstairs and a few minutes later scrambled out of an open window and was holding Fergus's hand. The two children fled into the bushes, making for the highest branches in the concealing bulk of an ancient pine tree.

The whole household turned out to hunt for Annie. After two hours of frantic searching without any trace of the child, Madeleine Gregory lost patience. There was a train to catch, and very annoying complications to face if they missed it.

'Enough!' she said firmly. 'Annette has made it clear that she does not want to leave the farm, and I would never force her to live in the city against her will. If Lisette will agree to come, Dermot and I will be very content with one little daughter.'

She smiled down at the little girl, but Connie had serious doubts.

'They're twins, Mrs Gregory! They should not be separated.'

'My dear, I'm well aware of that!' Madeleine said soothingly. 'I'll make sure the girls keep in touch, and Annette will be very welcome to join Lisette should she change her mind.'

'But it's not right...!' Connie began, nearly in tears.

Robert Balfour intervened. He was sick and tired of all the fuss. If Annie loved the farm so much, why not let the lassie stay and take her chance?

'Connie dear, you must remember James said that poor Suzanne had wanted the twins to develop as individuals. If one lass remains here and the other goes to Mrs Gregory, surely that will grant their mother's dying wish? I'm certain my brother would approve.'

'Aye, well, I suppose...' Unhappily, Connie could think of no objection.

A little later, she kissed Lisette and wept as the taxicab carried the little girl away from her down the farm track, to disappear onto the Forfar road.

Yet Connie's heart was a good deal lighter than it might have been.

She tried not to smile, recalling poor Madeleine Gregory's horrified expression as filthy little Annie burst into the drawing room, and the awful stink spread throughout.

Pigshit? Connie pondered. God certainly moved in mysterious ways!

Whatever the way of it, she thought, the outcome was that when Annie decided to creep out of hiding, Connie would still have two little girls to care for – her own longed-for baby girl, and Annie, her dear, naughty, little niece...

High in the pine tree, Fergus shook Annie awake.

'You can wake up. It's safe now. They've been gone for ages.'

The hiding place was one of Fergus's most secure places. He'd fitted a platform of planks spanning two of the higher branches. Thick evergreen growth shielded the hiding place from anyone down below who happened to look up.

Annie had fallen asleep, curled up like a

kitten while he'd kept an alert watch. She sat up, rubbing her eyes. He looked at her triumphantly.

'Good show. You've won.'

'Aunt Madeleine's gone?'

'Yes, and taken your stuffy wee sister with her.'

Annie sat up suddenly. 'No! Lizzie wouldn't leave without me.'

'Well, she did. I watched her climb into a taxicab with the woman, and off they went.'

Fergus had been quite sorry to see Lizzie go. He'd admired her for not liking him.

Annie was totally devastated. It had never entered her head that her twin would leave without her. They had been inseparable since birth, and Annie had confidently expected Lizzie to make a stand and refuse. But she hadn't. Lizzie had gone, and something vitally important had gone with her, leaving a cold and empty space within her twin sister.

'When will I see her again?' the little girl wailed.

'Probably never. London's thousands of miles away,' Fergus answered comfortingly.

Lizzie had enjoyed the taxi drive to Forfar station and the thrill of travelling first class to Edinburgh. She'd sat close to her aunt on the plush seat. The nursemaid helped unbutton her coat. For once in her life Lizzie was centre of attention, not one of a pair. It made her feel really special.

'Where will we stay in Edinburgh, Tante

Madeleine?' she asked.

'In an hotel, darling.'

Madeleine glanced down fondly at the pretty child, so polite and well-behaved. She was thankful she had not been obliged to accept the other rude little ragamuffin.

'Lisette,' she ventured, 'I know you can never forget your own dear Maman, but perhaps you would prefer to call me Mummy, rather than Tante Madeleine? But of course, it's up to you, my dear.'

Lizzie considered the suggestion. Mummy *did* sound cosier. She smiled shyly.

'I'd like that ... Mummy.' And was rewarded with a scented hug.

Lizzie had never been inside a large hotel, and its luxury took her breath away. Soft lights shone down on beautifully dressed people relaxing in sofas and armchairs. A uniformed attendant whisked Madeleine, Lizzie and the nursemaid upwards in a gilded lift. Lizzie was shown into a large bedroom dominated by a huge, high bed.

Her new mummy issued orders to the nursemaid.

'The child is tired and will go to bed now. She will have warm milk and sandwiches brought to the room after she has been bathed.'

'Yes'm!' The nursemaid bobbed a nervous little curtsey.

A bathroom leading off the bedroom was for

Lizzie's own personal use. It was green and white marble and brass taps shone like gold. Lizzie and the nursemaid were so shy and awestruck they hardly exchanged a word during the bathing ritual.

Afterwards, when she'd drunk warm milk and eaten small sandwiches with the crusts cut off, Lizzie discovered that she was tired. The nursemaid helped her climb into the high bed.

'When will my mummy come to kiss me goodnight?' Lizzie asked.

The girl looked surprised.

'She won't. Mrs Gregory's dining with friends tonight.'

'But who'll tuck me in?'

'Me, miss.' the nursemaid said, tucking the quilt tightly round her charge. She looked at the little girl, frowning. 'What's that you got pinned on your nightie?'

'It's my papa's medal.'

'It's got a pin. That's dangerous.' She unpinned the medal and put out the light.

Left in darkness, Lizzie yelled with panic.

'I hate the dark, we always have a night-light!'

The nursemaid hesitated. She was sorry for the bairn, but much more scared of her new employer.

'Mrs Gregory never said nothing about a nightlight, but there's a light in the corridor outside, miss, and you can see it shine under the door, if you look.'

The door closed, and Lizzie was left alone

in the dark. Annie wasn't there any more. The twins couldn't huddle together for comfort in a huge strange bed. The frightened little girl buried her face in the cold white pillow, in case someone heard her cry.

With the knowledge that identical twins share, Lizzie sensed that her sister was lying alone in bed too, heartbroken and crying. But Annie was lucky, she thought. Aunt Connie was there to give comfort with hugs and kisses. Aunt Connie would make sure the candle nightlight was lit, burning brightly to chase away the dark.

Two

Annie was lost and miserable without her twin. Winter had arrived early, but it was not a winter which filled crevices behind the dykes with white, blown snow. Wet sleet made farm life a misery and turned farm tracks to rivers of muddy slush.

The little girl moped around the house, bored and lonely. Her aunt understood the problem, of course, and normally Connie would have given the child support and sympathy. But Connie had not fully recovered from the baby's birth and the frail infant's health was a constant worry. She had no energy to spare for anything else. When Annie pleaded to be allowed to help with the baby's care, Connie refused.

'She's sickly, lovey. Maybe when she's older, but not yet. She must be handled gently, she's so small.'

'I can be gentle. I held a tiny piglet,' Annie protested.

'Don't I know it! If it hadn't been for that piglet, you'd be in London with your sister,' Connie said grimly.

Which led Annie to believe, mistakenly, that Connie didn't want her.

42

1 Deeply hurt, the little girl put on boots and mackintosh and ran outside, to be met by sleety rain and a cutting north wind whistling through bare trees. She'd intended to run away to London, then they'd be sorry! But the miserable weather changed her mind.

2 She went in search of Fergus McGill. It was Saturday afternoon, and her big cousins had gone off to Forfar to a cinematograph show, but she guessed where Fergus could be found. Sure enough, he was in the barn, nestled in a secret burrow he'd made behind bales of straw.

3 Fergus was reading a book by the light of a round bulls-eye of glass set in the wall. He had recently enlarged the secret burrow to accommodate Annie, because he felt some responsibility for her obvious misery. She rolled aside the old wooden tub guarding the entrance and crawled inside.

4 Fergus lowered the book. 'I came here for a bit of peace, far away from females.'

5 'I'm not a female, I'm a girl,' she said. 'What're you reading?'

6 '*Treasure Island*. I'm going there when I'm bigger.'

7 He put the book down and looked at her. 'You look awful. What's wrong?'

8 Bursting into tears, she poured out the whole sad story.

9 'But you didn't *want* to go to London with your swanky auntie, did you?' Fergus asked.

10 'No, but if I *had,* I would never have gone without Lizzie,' she declared loyally. 'I'd have

43

kicked and screamed and made a terrible fuss, b-but Lizzie didn't and Auntie Connie says twins should stay together.'

'Why?' He yawned, his attention wandering back to the enthralling page.

'Because...' Annie paused. Fergus did not even like his own sisters. He would never understand how close the twins were. Though they were far apart, Annie could still tell if her sister was glad, sad, hurting or even ill, but Fergus would only laugh if she told him. Tears trickled down her cheeks. He looked exasperated.

'Oh, turn off the waterworks, for heaven's sake! Why make such a fuss, just because you're not allowed to hold a stupid baby? What's its name, anyway?'

'She's called Leah. It's a Bible name. The Bible says Leah was tender-eyed.'

'Sand storms in the Holy Land made 'em tender, I expect.' Fergus said sagely. 'I named your piglet Lizzie, by the way, to make up for losing your snooty sister.'

Annie's sudden smile was radiant. 'Oh, Fergus, thanks! Can I go an' hug my Lizzie piglet now?'

'No fear!' he declared emphatically.

Lizzie Balfour had been bombarded with so many new experiences in the bustle of journeying to London, there was no time to feel homesick.

After leaving the hotel, Lizzie, her aunt and the nursemaid had travelled first class to

44

London. When they arrived at King's Cross station, Madeleine Gregory summoned a porter and had their baggage transported to a large black limousine waiting outside. A chauffeur in green uniform took charge, opening the car door and seating Lisette and her new mummy with a rug draped over their knees. Then he motioned the little nursemaid into the passenger seat beside him and drove off into a frantic hurly-burly of traffic.

Lizzie had been getting to know her nursemaid. That morning while the nursemaid washed and dressed her, Lisette had learned the girl's name and something of her background. She was called Ruth McGibbon, and had been brought up in an Edinburgh orphanage. Ruth explained that from the age of twelve she had been trained by the orphanage staff with a view to becoming a children's nurse. She was now fifteen and had been recommended to her future employers as honest, clean and reliable. Lack of family ties had been an added recommendation, in Madeleine's opinion. There would be no unwelcome fuss from relatives, should the girl prove unsuitable.

'Mrs Gregory wants a Scottish girl to look after you, Miss Lisette,' Ruth said.

'Why?'

'Because they say we Scots are a' Jock Tamson's bairns, I s'pose.' Ruth smiled.

'I'm not! I'm a Balfour, and my Maman was French.'

The little nursemaid looked wistful.

45

'You're lucky, miss. I never knew my ma. Matron chose my name off a gravestone.'

Lapped in luxury in the car, Lisette's eyes soon closed and she slept, head resting against her aunt, who glanced down fondly at the sleeping child. Madeleine was a confident woman, called upon to serve on committees and make speeches at various gatherings in aid of charity, but she knew nothing about bringing up children. The little girl lay fast asleep, body twisted at an uncomfortable angle. Nanny was not handy and Madeleine experienced a moment of panic. She did not want to disturb the child and make her cry. *Mon Dieu*, what do I do? she wondered anxiously.

Hesitantly, she slid an arm around Lisette and eased her gently into a comfortable position. The little girl sighed and nestled closer. Madeleine swelled with loving pride. She really was a mother now, caring for a child's comfort. My own little girl! *Mine*, she thought fiercely. Just let anyone try to take her from me!

Lisette stirred in her sleep.

'Maman, is it you?' she whispered urgently, and again softly, 'Maman, I love you!'

Not 'Mummy' as instructed! Madeleine felt chilled. So Lisette still clung to her dead mother in her dreams. Madeleine wondered uneasily if it could be possible to fight the ghost of a much-loved mother, to win the heart of a little girl.

$\star$ $\star$ $\star$

A few miles farther on they left city streets and entered quiet avenues lined with large houses. She roused Lisette gently.

'We're home, *chérie*, wake up!'

Lisette sat up, rubbing her eyes. Ahead of them in the darkness lay a large white house beside a short driveway. The house blazed with lights and Lisette smiled in delight.

'It's fairyland, like the story Ruth told me on the train.'

Madeleine frowned.

'Lisette, you mustn't call your nanny Ruth.'

'Why not? That's her name.'

'Perhaps. But she is called Nanny in my house. Do you understand?'

'Yes, Mummy.' Lisette nodded dutifully.

'Good girl.' Madeleine hugged her foster-daughter thankfully. The last thing she wanted was rebellion, cheek, and a battle of wills, like the dreadful twin sister.

Kilmuckety House had been rambling and badly lit, but Lisette had never found its dark corners threatening. The furniture was old and shabby, every room in need of a lick of paint, but that had made the old house seem more homely and comfortable. It didn't matter if ancient chairs and tables suffered yet another scuff, or inkspots landed on a threadbare carpet. Aunt Connie might sigh and tut-tut ruefully, but it wasn't the end of the world.

Life in the Gregory household was very

different.

Bermuda House was square-built and orderly. There was nothing shabby or faded about it. Madeleine Gregory took Lisette's hand and led her into a white hallway lit by two dazzling chandeliers. The large space was very warm and echoed to the soothing sound of cascading water. Lisette stared in disbelief.

'Is that a real fountain, Mummy?'

'Only a very small one!' Madeleine laughed and waved a hand at many exotic orchids growing in urns around it. 'These plants are delicate, and need plenty of heat and humidity, but aren't they pretty?'

Lisette agreed, but why would anyone go to such lengths to grow plants you couldn't eat? Uncle Bob grew vegetables in the kitchen garden to feed the family or sell at market for a few pence, and moaned bitterly when the crops failed in unpredictable weather. She stared at the fragile hothouse beauties, and tried to make sense of it.

A maidservant appeared to whisk away outer clothing.

'Has Dr Gregory returned home yet?' Madeleine asked.

'Yes, ma'am. Master's in the study.'

'Why isn't he in the drawing room? You know I prefer it!'

'Begging your pardon, ma'am, but his slippers were in the study. Doctor wanted supper in front of the study fire, cosy-like.'

'Oh, did he?' Madeleine frowned her annoyance and ordered maid and nanny off to the servants' quarters.

She had looked forward to her husband having a memorable meeting with their daughter in the beautiful drawing room where special guests were received. Now they would meet in an untidy book-lined study, the atmosphere hazy with pipe-smoke. Sighing, she took Lisette by the hand.

'Come and meet your daddy.'

Lisette followed obediently, although she didn't want to meet this man. She could remember her own father perfectly well, and knew how much she missed him. Only that morning she had made a fuss when her nursemaid flatly refused to pin Papa's medal to the bodice of Lisette's dress.

'Your mummy wouldn't like it, miss!' Ruth had said.

So in the end they had compromised and Ruth had pinned the precious medal to the little girl's vest, unseen under the dress. Lisette could feel it there, close to her fast-beating heart, as Mummy led her into the room to meet her new daddy.

Dermot Gregory had been dreading this moment, though he'd given his dear wife no hint of it. Of course he wanted children. But their own! He doubted if he could accept his brother-in-law's twins as substitutes.

The door opened and Madeleine came in holding a small girl by the hand. He was struck by how beautiful his wife looked, positively glowing with happiness.

'*Voil*á, my darling! Here is Lisette, our

49

daughter!'

'Where's the other one?' he asked.

Her expression changed.

'Oh, Dermot! She is not like this little one. Annette is cheeky, dirty and very rude. She would not come with us, so we left her behind.'

It bothered him to hear the twins had been separated. 'My dear, was that wise?'

Madeleine shrugged.

'It was unavoidable, darling. The child made it very clear she would never leave the farm. She hid herself and couldn't be found, but Lisette was very eager to come to us. Truly, Dermot, she is an angel!'

She urged the little girl forward.

The doctor's trained eye took note of the child's nervous exhaustion. There were dark smudges under the remarkable dark eyes. This little girl had lost mother, sister and close relatives all within a tragically short space of time. The poor little soul must be devastated! He couldn't help but pity her, though pity seemed a cold emotion far removed from love.

He realized with a start that the intelligent child had been studying him intently. He smiled kindly.

'Well, what do you make of me, Lisette?'

'You are very tired and sad,' she said.

Madeleine had been expecting a pretty little speech. She gasped in dismay.

'Lisette! What a way to greet your daddy!'

But Dermot was startled by the child's

50

perception.

'She's right, Madeleine. I *am* very tired.'

'But not sad, my darling!' Madeleine cried tearfully. 'How can you be sad, when we have all we ever wanted now?'

Ah, but at what cost? he longed to say. He'd had high ideals when he'd worked for a pittance in city slums as a newly qualified young doctor. Now he tended the rich and famous in a Harley Street practice and was a very wealthy man. He loved Madeleine with all his heart and had worked tirelessly to give her everything she could ever want, but he couldn't give her the children they both longed for. He'd agreed to foster his nieces to keep his wife happy, but he doubted if he could love this little girl as he might have loved his own. Maybe the child sensed it, judging by the way she studied him. He knew from past experience as a doctor that small children are much more perceptive than adults are led to believe. So he smiled cheerfully.

'Tiredness and sadness go hand in hand, you know. I'll be right as rain tomorrow,' he promised.

As months went by on Kilmuckety Farm, baby Leah thrived and grew into an engaging toddler. To Connie's relief, Leah's winning ways had helped Annie to recover from the loss of her sister, and Lizzie's name was rarely mentioned. Annie was totally engrossed, helping her aunt and uncle in the house and around the farm.

Connie's vigour had been restored. She was in her element now with two little girls to look after, her own cherished little daughter and Annie the remaining twin. But as Annie's sixth birthday approached, Connie's conscience began troubling her.

She raised the subject of Annie's schooling with her husband one evening.

'It's time the wee lass started school, Bob.'

He yawned lazily, slippered feet stretched out to the fire.

'Annie's a great help with the farm animals. To be around birds and beasts is the best education a bairn can have, to my way of thinking. Time enough for reading and writing later.'

'But she's clever, Bob! She should be at school. It's what James would want.'

Bob's expression darkened.

'But James isn't here to attend to his bairns, is he?'

'He's at sea!'

'Aye, he's at sea, where my brother has always been when the going gets tough.'

Connie leaned forward earnestly.

'I'll bet Mrs Gregory has put Lisette to the best school money can buy. Do you want Annie to be the loser?'

Bob Balfour pondered a minute in silence, then sighed.

'Connie my dear, you're right, as usual. We can't let our wee lass down, can we?'

* * *

52

Annie Balfour started school in Kirriemuir at the beginning of term. She had been looking forward to the experience, because she was longing to write to Lisette. Connie sent picture postcards regularly to London, but that wasn't the same as her own personal letter.

So Annie set off happily one morning with schoolbag on back, hand in hand with Luke and John. She was so excited she could hardly spare a backward glance for Connie, sobbing forlornly on the doorstep with Leah in her arms.

Cousin Luke was thirteen, a big boy longing for the day he could leave school and do as he pleased, which did not include working on the farm. Cousin John was eleven. School reports had marked him as average, but what John lacked in learning he made up for in determination. John's secret ambition was to grow rich. He envied the Balfours' neighbours, the McGills, and was determined to find a way to become twice as wealthy. Merrily, the three Balfours boarded the bus taking them to school, all three harbouring different expectations, dreams, and aims in life.

Annie's morning did not go well. It was a large class and little ones were expected to sit quietly at rows of wooden desks. She was an active child used to running about outdoors. Soon she was feeling hot and cramped. Her head ached as she laboriously copied rows of capital As, Bs and Cs from the blackboard. She could read quite well but hadn't realized writing would be so tedious. When the bell rang for playtime she was close to tears.

Outside, Annie found herself lost in a sea of strangers and wandered around unhappily, searching for a friendly face. To her delight, she spotted Fergus, at the centre of a group of boys playing marbles by the railings. She took to her heels and ran towards him, shouting at the pitch of her lungs.

'Fergus! Fergus, it's me, Annie!'

The little girl burst into the midst of the group, scattering marbles and toppling Fergus, who had been carefully balanced, ready to play a winning shot. The other boys gathered round, grinning broadly.

'Who's your wee sweetheart, Fergie?'

Fergus glowered at Annie. 'Never saw her before in my life!'

John shouldered his way to the front. He had no love for Fergus McGill and no time for liars.

'He knows who she is! She's my cousin Annie Balfour and he plays at making houses with her in the bushes round our farm. He's a big girlie!'

Fergus doubled his fists.

'Who're you callin' a girlie?'

The fight soon involved every boy in the playground and went down in the school annals as the biggest and best battle ever. Annie slipped quietly away and lined up with the little ones to march smartly indoors out of the fray. The first day at school went better after that, and lessons ended with a story.

But afterwards, Fergus avoided Annie and

refused to speak to her. Worse still, he never set foot on Balfour land again. She soon realized she had lost her dearest playmate, and though she soon made many girlfriends, a hurt and empty space remained.

Madeleine Gregory gave much thought to her foster-daughter's education and had decided Lisette would learn to write and speak French fluently and to mingle gracefully in high society. She could imagine her daughter as a beautiful debutante in the presence of the King and Queen. That was Madeleine's dream for Lisette, a brilliant marriage the ultimate aim.

She selected Miss Dora Kingsley's Preparatory School for Girls to teach Lisette the basics. Miss Dora had a reputation for finding places for her pupils at schools patronized by nobility. Madeleine did not dwell much upon her own background, for she, her sister and older brothers had been brought up in a French village and had shared an education with onion-growers' children. She planned a very different start in life for her adopted daughter.

Lisette had spent hours wandering around looking at the treasures in Mummy's house. There were beautiful pictures, carpets and delicate ornaments in every room. Shining silver and delicate porcelain lay beyond reach in locked display cabinets.

Lisette could look, but she had been ordered never to touch, or run in and out to the garden. Valuable ornaments might be toppled, muddy shoes would soil priceless carpets. The obedient little girl kept her hands behind her back in case she was tempted to touch anything. Her slippered feet stole through silent rooms so softly she could have been a tiny ghost. Sometimes in her loneliness she would pretend Annie was with her. What fun they could have had! She could almost hear her sister speaking...

'Go on, silly! Touch their precious old ornaments, if you want to. The nursery's full of toys, and the garden has bushes to play hide and seek in and trees to climb. Enjoy yourself, cowardy-custard! I would!'

Then Lisette would sob in a sad little whisper, 'I daren't! Mummy and Daddy won't love me if I'm disobedient and dirty. I'm so scared, Annie! I'm not brave, like you...'

Times were hard on the Balfours' farm when Annie Balfour was approaching her tenth birthday. The harvest failed in torrential downpours and potatoes rotted in the pits. However, Connie made sure there was no shortage of love and laughter in the house. There was always food on the table – plain fare, mind you, but beautifully cooked and tasty.

Heaven alone knew how she managed it! Bob Balfour thought, tears of gratitude almost choking him. Connie gave strength to her exhausted husband, and comfort to the failing fabric of the old family farm. But how long could they go on like this? Bob wondered despairingly.

Leah had started school, still small and slight, an elfin little creature. Not so bonny as her cousin Annie, as her mother was first to admit, but with a smile to warm your heart. Annie looked upon Leah as a sister, and Connie had long since adopted Annie as a daughter. Memories of Lisette had grown dim.

Lisette and Annie wrote four dutiful letters to each other every year. Easter, summer holidays, birthday and Christmas. Connie dreaded the arrival of Lisette's letter. It never failed to provoke an angry scene.

'Why does she write most of it in French? I can't understand a word!' Annie grumbled.

Neither could Connie and she felt guilty. French was not taught at Annie's primary school.

'You'll learn the language when you go to Forfar Academy, lovey,' she said soothingly.

'*If* I can win a bursary. *If* we can find cash to buy a uniform!' the girl said bitterly.

'I'll make one, if I have to.'

'Auntie Connie! You can't make a school blazer!' Annie wailed in horror.

Connie sighed. 'In the meantime, my dear, reply to your sister in the King's English. Your writing's better than hers, in spite of her fancy education.'

The twins hadn't set eyes on one another since Lisette walked out of the door, which Connie thought a crying shame, especially since their father had now left the sea, and she'd hoped the wee lasses might be reunited at last and living with him. But James Balfour hadn't come home to the farm. He had written that he'd left the ship at Singapore and found a job working on a rubber plantation in Malaya, living in accommodation not suitable for children. So his little girls hadn't set eyes on their father either, since he'd left Scotland. Connie wasn't complaining, because she loved Annie and didn't want to lose her, but it was a sad state of affairs.

Of course, Madeleine Gregory had made promises and planned duty visits many times over the years, but these were always cancelled at the last minute with plausible excuses. Easter was party time at Lisette's school and weekends were fully occupied with lavish parties in friends' houses. Summer holidays were spent on the French Riviera to improve Lisette's French accent. Autumn meant a return to school, where Lisette was now a weekly boarder. Christmas and New Year brought another hectic round of festivities and a skiing holiday in Switzerland. Letters remained the only link between the twins.

Annie settled down to write to her sister on pages torn from an old jotter. She wrote that she'd helped Uncle Bob birth a cow and the wee wet calf had stood up shakily soon after it was born. It was a miraculous sight. She wrote proudly that she had been given a puppy as a birthday present. She'd named it

Barney and Matthew was helping her to train the clever pup to herd sheep. Yesterday, she added, she'd helped Uncle Bob whitewash the byre and earned a whole sixpence. Later, she'd bought sweets from the Co-op van and shared them with all the family, for a treat. Annie did not mention Fergus McGill. She longed to tell her sister how sad she felt when he passed by without a word, but she didn't think Lisette would be interested.

Annie paused thoughtfully and chewed the end of the pencil. She supposed she still loved Lisette, but it felt like trying to love a stranger...

'Disgraceful!' Madeleine declared angrily, throwing Annie's dog-eared pages down on the breakfast table. 'To think my dear sister's child has attended an animal's birth and painted a filthy stable! The poor girl accepts a dog as a gift and is pathetically grateful. And you will notice, Dermot, that she writes not one word of her mother tongue!' She frowned at her husband, hidden behind the morning paper.

Lisette wished she hadn't shown Mummy the letter, but it was expected of her. Annie's news had affected Lisette strangely, evoking wistful longings and a hint of rebellion.

'I would like a dog,' she said.

Madeleine gave her a startled glance.

'Darling! London is no place for dogs. It would be cruel to keep a dog in the city!'

'Not if it is a very small dog,' Lisette argued.

'I would feed her and look after her and Nanny and I would take her for walks in the park.'

'No, Lisette!' said Madeleine firmly. 'A dog is out of the question. Who would look after it while you're at school?'

'Nanny would.'

'We do not pay Nanny to look after dogs!'

'Then you should pay her more!' the girl snapped angrily.

Madeleine was shocked.

'That's enough, Lisette! Go to your room, and no more talk of dogs, if you please!'

Dermot Gregory lowered the paper when they were alone.

'Well, well! Our little angel has quite a temper!' he remarked.

'Her sister's letter upset her, darling. She imagines farm life to be idyllic.'

Madeleine remained lost in thought for a minute or two.

'You know, Dermot, it is high time Lisette saw for herself how her poor sister exists on that awful farm. I shall arrange to visit Scotland for a week or two, before we leave for Antibes...'

When Connie received notice of the proposed visit she detected a ring of truth this time, and was thrown into panic.

'Where'll the woman sleep?'

'Calm down. She says to book all three of them into a Kirrie hotel,' Bob said, studying the letter.

60

'So our beds are not good enough!' Connie sniffed, relieved, but offended nevertheless...

Annie was excited but, after so many disappointments, resolved she would not get her hopes up till her sister walked through the door. Anyway, she expected they would have little in common by now.

But nothing could have been further from the truth. The moment Lisette stepped from the taxi, Annie rushed forward with a glad cry, shouldering Madeleine aside. The twins hugged ecstatically with tears and laughter, while the grown-ups watched with lumps in their throats. It was a reunion to wrench the heartstrings, as Connie remarked to Bob afterwards.

The girls went into the house, arm in arm.

'Look! I'm wearing Papa's medal!' Annie displayed it, pinned to the bodice of her dress.

'Me too!' Lisette giggled. 'But mine's pinned to my vest!'

Annie was puzzled.

'Why?'

'Because this is my best dress, and besides, Mummy hates to be reminded of the war.'

'Mummy?' Annie felt sickened.

Lisette could not meet her twin's accusing stare.

'Aunt Madeleine likes to be called Mummy. It ... it pleases her.'

'What about Maman? Have you forgotten Maman?'

Lisette lifted her chin and looked her sister

straight in the eyes.

'Annie, Maman is dead!'

To Annie's dismay, the twins discovered differences in their upbringing which seemed almost insurmountable. But Annie persisted.

'Would you like to take Barney for a walk, Lisette?'

'I can't. I'll ruin my shoes.'

Annie swallowed impatience.

'Oh, come on! I'll lend you galoshes.'

Gingerly, Lisette donned the clumsy rubber overshoes. She was not dressed for walking, and knew Mummy would not be pleased. Fortunately, Madeleine was resting from the rigours of country life back at the hotel, and Nanny was in charge. Nanny Ruth was spending a relaxed afternoon in the kitchen with Connie and Leah.

The dog Barney was in his element, romping on the hillside in sight of quietly grazing sheep. As the two girls leaned over the fence, Annie decided to show off her skill as shepherdess. She opened the gate and children and dog went into the field. Unfortunately, Barney was still little more than an eager pup, more accustomed to Matthew in command. He made straight as an arrow for the startled sheep at full pelt.

'Barney! Come by!' Annie yelled desperately.

But the dog continued to race around, sending the flock stampeding downhill towards the girls. Lisette kicked off the galoshes and ran screaming for the gate. Annie braved the stampede and grabbed Barney, dragging him out and swinging the gate shut before the flock could escape.

Lisette was in tears.

'My shoes are ruined and my good dress ripped! Mummy will be angry!'

'Who cares? Stop blubbering, Mummy's girl!' Annie yelled furiously.

The dog suddenly remembered his training and returned smugly to Annie's heel, pleased with his performance, but the twins walked home in silence, far apart.

All was not lost, however. The visit was not over yet and there was a surprise in store.

It rained heavily next day, and Madeleine remained at the hotel.

Lisette was eager to make up for yesterday's disaster, and had thought of a way to delight her twin, sharing a mutual interest. She and Nanny turned up in the taxi armed with a wooden box. Lisette burst into the kitchen and opened the box on the table to reveal a set of artist's materials that made Annie's jaw drop.

'Look, Annie!'

Inside were paints, crayons, pencils and two large pads of drawing paper. Annie had dreamed of such luxuries. She was forever drawing and scribbling when she could find a scrap of paper. She gazed at the wonderful array on the kitchen table and a tide of envy and bitterness threatened to overwhelm her.

She felt deeply humiliated. Bob and Connie Balfour could never afford to buy any of this, not in a thousand years. And I would never ask them to! she thought, outraged.

Lisette had noticed nothing amiss, and was smiling happily.

'Come on, Annie, let's draw. I brought these specially for you!'

'Specially so's you could show off and let us see how rich your precious Mummy is, you mean!' Annie said deliberately.

Lisette was astounded. She had only wanted to share her greatest pleasure.

'Of course not! What a horrid, ungrateful girl you are!'

'If it's gratitude you want, you'll get none from me!'

They were screaming angrily at one another by now, and Connie came hurrying in to see what the fuss was. She stopped in the doorway in horror. Annie had seized paints, paper and crayons, flung them on the floor and was stamping on them vigorously, while Lisette wrestled with her, kicking and punching.

Connie flung herself into the fray.

'Stop it, the pair of you!'

'She started it!' Lisette yelled, red-faced with rage. 'Mummy's right. She has the manners of a pig!'

'Pigs are better than London snobs!' Annie screamed, trying to reach her sister with a flailing fist. Connie struggled to keep them apart.

It was at that fraught moment the back door opened and James Balfour walked in. He stopped and stared at his screaming daughters in astonishment. Connie and the two girls were even more startled. They froze.

'James!' Connie gasped, releasing the twins. 'Why on earth didn't you tell us you were coming?'

'There was no time,' he said. 'I went to London when the ship docked, and Dermot told me Madeleine and Lisette were in Scotland, visiting you. That was a stroke of luck! I caught the early morning train, and here I am.'

'Aye. Here you are, James, after all these years! And your bonny twins parted and at odds, all because their father wasn't there to care for them!' Connie said reprovingly.

'I know.' He sighed. 'I was broken-hearted when Bob wrote and told me what had happened, Connie, but there was nothing I could do about it. I'd just left the ship and found a job in Malaya and had very little money.'

James studied his daughters. He'd never stopped loving them but they were big girls now, and hardly knew him. Would they forgive his neglect?

Annie recovered first. She ran to her father and hugged him joyfully.

'Papa, look! I'm wearing your medal.'

'So you are, my dear!'

James smiled with relief. This twin was Annie who'd elected to stay on the farm, judging by rosy cheeks and home-knitted jersey and skirt. The other twin hadn't moved. She was pale, with a city pallor, but beautifully dressed, her glossy dark hair tied back with white ribbon. There was no sign of a medal on her dress. He held out a hand.

'Come here, Lisette.'

She approached obediently. He hugged her, but there was little response. It was as if the child was not accustomed to such warm displays of affection. It saddened him. Annie slipped a hand into his.

'Have you come home to Scotland for good now, Papa?'

James hesitated. He studied the two children, so alike, yet with very different backgrounds. His fault for abandoning them to the care of others. He shook his head.

'No, dear. Circumstances have changed, and my home and workplace will be in Malaya from now on. That's why I've come back to see you both. I have something important to tell you.'

Their quarrel forgotten, the twins looked apprehensive. Lisette did not welcome her father's sudden appearance. Memories of Papa were hazy and she hardly knew him. Besides, she had a kind daddy she loved, in London. She found the situation confusing.

'It ... it sounds serious,' she remarked uneasily.

'It is, Lisette.' James nodded. 'But I hope you'll both agree it's happy news. I work on a rubber plantation, as you know, and there I met Teresa, the owner's daughter.' He smiled, his thoughts far away. 'We fell in love and were married a year ago. Last month Teresa gave birth to our beautiful baby boy.'

James paused. His daughters were staring at him, and for a startled moment it was as if his dead wife looked at him with reproachful dark eyes. It had not occurred to James that marrying Teresa could be interpreted as a betrayal of Suzanne's memory, but what did her daughters think? He put the thought hurriedly from his mind, and went on joyfully.

'So now, my dear daughters, you have father, mother and baby brother, waiting for you to join us in a new home in Malaya. We can be a real family once more! What do you say to that?'

Three

The twins exchanged a glance. The squabble forgotten, they had moved closer together and joined hands. James Balfour was encouraged.

'You understand, don't you?' he said patiently. 'This is a fresh start for us all in beautiful surroundings, and you can be together again at last.'

Annie spoke up first. 'Of course we understand, Papa, but ... but it's too late.'

He frowned. 'What do you mean?'

'I can tell you!' Lisette burst out. 'She means we have good homes, with people we love. We don't want to live in a strange land with strangers!'

'Lisette dear, I'm not a stranger, I'm your father!'

The twins were silent. James found he could not meet their eyes.

He had abandoned them to the care of others six years ago. He'd had good reasons for doing so, but children don't attach much importance to reasons, only reality. He had never stopped loving his twin daughters and had worked tirelessly towards the day they could be reunited as a family. Now the day had come, and he found that he was a stranger to his little girls, taking them away from settled homes and people they loved.

Annie broke an awkward silence tentatively.

'Besides, Papa, I don't think Lisette and I *want* to be together. She hates farms and I hate cities. We aren't twins any more, we're two completely different girls.'

Lisette nodded agreement. 'She's right. We wouldn't be happy, living with you and those others.'

All the same, she couldn't help feeling sorry for her father. He looked devastated. She remembered the night he had presented the twins with his medals. Although hers was little more than a lucky charm to her now, Lisette was suddenly overcome with grief. How different their lives could have been, if only Maman had lived!

James sighed.

'Well, thanks for telling me where we stand. I do appreciate your honesty. I just want you to be happy. That's all that matters.'

His rosy dream of life with his daughters was over. They don't need me, he thought sadly. The twins had made it clear they didn't need each other either. Which was a tragedy.

James felt close to tears.

Connie's heart had nearly failed her when she'd heard what her brother-in-law was proposing. She'd kept quiet however, not wanting to influence Annie's decision.

She'd come close to losing her, but now the offer had been turned down Connie was weak with relief. James Balfour looked so dejected her heart went out to the man. She laid a hand on his arm.

'You'll stay with us a wee while, James? There's plenty room since Matthew and Mark followed in your footsteps and went to sea.'

He shook his head.

'Thanks, Connie, but I should go. The girls have made their feelings pretty plain.'

'Well, maybe, but that's no reason why you shouldn't stay to see Bob and become acquainted with your wee niece. Leah's a darling and your nephews Luke and John are grown lads, helping their father on the farm. They have their own interests, of course – football and lassies, mostly!' Connie smiled.

James was tempted. He was weary and disheartened and a few days' rest seemed just the ticket before he headed back to Malaya. Besides, he wanted to find out how his brother was faring, though he couldn't help him financially at the moment. James had invested his savings in the rubber plantation and the house he'd had built in pursuit of his shattered dream. He wanted to make sure Annie's future was secure, living with Bob and Connie...

'No need to worry. Everything's fine!' Bob insisted, when he and James were seated round the fire later that evening, enjoying a dram of whisky. Connie was with them, knitting busily, but the two lads had gone off to town to see to their own affairs and Leah was fast asleep in bed. Annie, unusually subdued, had retired early to her room with sketchpad and pencil, gifted to her by her twin as a token of solidarity.

The adults could speak freely.

Pride would not permit Bob Balfour to reveal the true state of his affairs. He could barely scrape a living from farming in these hard times, but Annie had made it plain she wanted to stay with the farm. Quite right too, he thought, since it was part of her Balfour inheritance. Besides, he loved the lassie dearly and didn't want to lose her, and it was always possible his luck might take a turn for the better.

Connie gave her husband a quick look and went on knitting.

'Bob and I are delighted you've married again, James,' she remarked.

Bob nodded.

'Aye, and now you have a son. Another Balfour!'

'Yes.' James smiled briefly.

Connie glanced up, and wondered.

'Tell us about your wife. Is Teresa bonny?' she asked.

'More than bonny. Beautiful!'

'Teresa's an unusual name in these parts. Is she English?'

He hesitated.

'No. Her father's Malaysian, her mother's Japanese.'

There was silence for a minute or two, then

Bob grinned and leaned across to replenish his brother's glass.

'Well, James my lad, here's to you and yours, whatever the blend.'

The brothers laughed, and clinked glasses, sealing the toast.

Madeleine Gregory arrived at the farm next morning. She arrived alone, ordered the taxi driver to wait, and entered the house like a whirlwind. Startled, Connie met her in the hallway.

'Mrs Gregory! What's wrong?'

'Where is James Balfour?'

'In the kitchen at his breakfast, but—'

The angry woman swept her aside and stormed into the kitchen, kicking the door shut in Connie's face. James looked up.

'Why – Madeleine!'

'I'm surprised you remember, James Balfour! It is so many years since we met.'

'Yes, indeed. When I married your sister. I'll never forget that happy day.'

She crossed the room furiously.

'But already you have forgotten poor Suzanne! You and this other woman have a child ... yet after years of neglect, you come to steal my daughter!'

'Madeleine, please, listen—'

But she was much too angry. She shouted at him.

'No, you will listen! I will fight for Lisette, drag you through courts of law and make your name mud because you abandoned my sister's children. My husband is a respected doctor and I assure you we will win the custody. You will never take Lisette from us. *Jamais!*'

By now Madeleine had broken down and was sobbing uncontrollably. She was bitterly ashamed of such weakness, but try as she might, she could not stop it.

She would have been surprised to learn that tears revealed a gentler side to her nature, which impressed James much more favourably. On the few occasions they'd met, he had thought her a cold, selfish woman. He had been dismayed when he'd received Bob's letter telling him the twins had been separated, and that gentle little Lisette had gone to live with the Gregorys. Since the letter had taken months to catch up with him on his travels, James had decided regretfully it was too late to raise objections.

But today he was confronted by a weeping woman fighting desperately for a much-loved child, and his opinion of Madeleine Gregory as foster mother had changed. Gently, he took her by the arm and persuaded her to sit down. He sat opposite.

'Didn't Lisette tell you what the twins had decided?'

Madeleine wiped her eyes.

'Not really. She tries not to offend me, the dear child. She stammered and faltered and I cannot understand what she decided. So I lost patience and shouted, and then she cried. I was sorry and said no more, but I resolved to speak with you, because I am so frightened...' She paused, biting her lip to check fresh tears.

He smiled.

'You, frightened? That's hard to believe!'

'I have good reason, James. She wears your medal.'

'I'm touched. I know Annette wears hers.'

'Ah, but Lisette hides the medal from me! The nanny is an honest girl, and she told me. I was hurt, but I said nothing to Lisette.' She smiled faintly. 'How could I blame my daughter for concealing love, when I myself am adept at hiding my feelings? So now I am in torment, wondering if Lisette loves you enough to go with you. No wonder I'm frightened!'

He sighed.

'Madeleine, the twins told me they don't want to live in a strange land with strangers; they want to stay at home with the people they love. Those were their very words. You needn't be afraid. They don't want to live in Malaya with me.'

She stared at him.

'They say that to you, their father? Ah, children can be cruel!'

He smiled sadly.

'Cruel to be kind, Madeleine! Now I can stop dreaming, and get on with life...'

After the emotional upset of Madeleine Gregory's appearance James decided to cut short his visit. He thought it would make his departure less of an ordeal for all concerned.

The twins were in tears when a taxi arrived next day to take their father to the station.

'When will we see you again?' Annie asked woefully.

'When I come back to claim my medals, my dear. Look after them for me!'

He laughed and kissed them both fondly before climbing quickly into the car. Looking back as the taxi moved off, James saw his daughters standing close together, holding hands. The sight reassured him, although his eyes suddenly blurred with tears.

Connie believed in the curative powers of a good long walk, after distress. The two girls were given no time to mope after their father's departure. She ordered them off to walk the dog, who was getting under her feet in the kitchen.

Lisette was better shod this time. With one pair of town shoes already consigned to the bin, Madeleine had bought Lisette stout walking shoes to supplement a plaid skirt and white jersey, topped by a smart red jacket and matching tammy.

Annie trudged along at her sister's side wearing usual dog-walking gear, wellington boots, an ancient pair of John's outgrown trousers and a favourite old mud-coloured jersey which bore traces of Barney's enthusiastic paws. She had also grabbed a terrible old green beret, pulling it well down over her ears. The twins walked arm in arm. Recent events had united them and the companion-

75

ship felt warm and wonderful.

'You know, Lisette,' Annie remarked thoughtfully, 'you're rich and I'm poor, but I think we'll always love each other, no matter what.'

Lisette nodded.

'Yes, of course we will. We'll always be sisters, even though we're quite different girls. And guess what? Last night Mummy said she may let me have a dog. A poodle, she thinks.'

Annie grinned.

'Poodles are French dogs, aren't they?'

'Yes, but don't worry, I'll teach it to bark in English.'

'With a French accent?'

The twins burst out laughing.

Barney the sheepdog had been ranging freely ahead, investigating scents and sounds along the way. A rabbit went bounding off under Barney's nose, and after a moment's startled surprise, he went after it. Annie took up the chase, yelling orders. The dog paid not the slightest attention.

The surrounding woodland was crisscrossed with paths and the dog leapt out of the undergrowth in hot pursuit of its quarry in front of a cyclist who was pedalling quietly along the track towards the main road. Fergus McGill swerved, skidded, and landed swearing in the mud.

He was scrambling to his feet when Annie appeared. She grabbed Barney, who had lost sight of the prey and looked chastened.

Fergus scowled.

'Oh, it's you! Can't you control that blasted dog? And you're trespassing on McGill land, you know!'

'Is that so? Wait a tick, while I wipe McGill dirt off my boots.'

Fergus was a tall fourteen-year-old. His hair was auburn and wavy and he was very good looking when he smiled. He was not smiling now.

'You've no business to be walking your dog on my father's estate, you cheeky wee tyke. I've a good mind to...'

He broke off suddenly.

Lisette had followed her sister onto the path. The pretty, dark-haired little girl stood quietly surveying the scene. Fergus recognized her at once

'You're Lisette, Annie's twin!'

She walked forward, studying him curiously.

'And you're Fergus McGill! You were a horrid little boy. I hope you've improved?'

'He hasn't,' Annie said.

He ignored her. Fergus was intrigued. Looking from one twin to the other reminded him of advertisements he'd seen, labelled 'before' and 'after'. He smiled at the beautifully dressed child. She looked so clean she almost glowed.

'So you're visiting Annie. How long are you staying?'

'We leave this Saturday.'

'So soon?'

She smiled ingenuously.

'Yes. Are you sorry?'

Fergus blinked. He'd forgotten the charm of the Balfour smile. Annie hadn't smiled at him for years. He grinned awkwardly.

'I'm sorry if I was a horrid little boy, Lisette. I do remember you didn't like me, which is rather unusual. Girls usually do, you see.'

'Well, I don't!' Annie snapped.

She clipped on Barney's lead and grabbed Lisette's arm.

'Come on! We're trespassing on his dad's rotten land. He just ordered me off.'

Lisette obeyed, but glanced back over her shoulder.

''Bye, Fergus. You've improved. I like you better now!'

They heard him laughing as Annie dragged her off. Out of sight, Annie turned on her twin furiously.

'Don't be nice to him!'

Lisette stopped, wide-eyed.

'Why not? He's a boy, isn't he?'

'That's no excuse!'

Her sister laughed.

'Oh, Annie, don't be silly! I love meeting boys. The girls at my school talk about nothing else, and Mummy doesn't mind me having boy friends, so long as they go to good schools and their parents are well-to-do. Of course I was nice to Fergus. The McGills are rich!'

Sickened, Annie shoved her away.

'You're disgusting!'

'And you're jealous 'cause you're ugly and

78

dirty!' Lisette retorted angrily. 'No wonder Fergus ordered you off. You'd frighten the birds, dressed like a scarecrow!'

Annie backed away, wellingtons squelching mud. The two little girls stood facing one another, painfully hurt and sadly bewildered.

It's all very well talking about loving a sister no matter what! Annie thought tearfully. *Love can turn to hate in an instant, when boys are involved.*

Annie turned and ran, the dog racing beside her. She kicked the filthy boots off in the scullery and fled past Connie to the sanctuary of her room.

Connie stared after her. She'd been encouraged by the twins' behaviour now the bickering had stopped. They had been quite chummy when they'd set out and Connie had felt optimistic. She sighed. Optimism had been premature, obviously. There had been a serious falling out, and she winced as Annie's bedroom door slammed shut.

Annie flung herself on the bed in a flood of tears. *Ugly, dirty, a scarecrow!*

'I hate Lisette, I hate her!' she howled into the pillow.

She cried for a long time, only stopping when Connie's snow-white pillowcase was dampened and crumpled. Then Annie sat up and caught sight of herself in the mirror.

It was a terrible shock.

She looked awful. Red-eyed, face streaked with dirt, greasy hair a tangled mess, and none too clean. The dreadful clothes looked even worse.

Ugly, dirty, dressed like a scarecrow...!

Mortified tears rolled down Annie's cheeks. It was true, and she couldn't go on hating her sister just for telling the truth. She would have to do something about this.

She went to the bathroom and bathed. She washed her hair, towelled and combed it dry, and tied it back with red ribbon which matched a red jumper Connie had knitted her for Christmas. Black skirt, black woollen stockings and highly polished school shoes completed a transformation.

Annie studied the result in the mirror. It was a startling improvement, but there was still something missing. You're growing as fussy as Lisette, she thought, smiling at her reflection.

A smile. That was it!

Next time she strayed onto McGill land, nicely turned out and smiling, she hoped that Fergus would not be in such a hurry to send her packing ...

Fergus McGill's mother had intended sending him to an Edinburgh boarding school but Fergus dug his heels in and refused to go. He wanted to be a farmer, he declared, and his delighted father had dared to stand up for him, in opposition to his formidable wife. So it was agreed that Fergus would finish schooling at Forfar Academy then go on to agricultural college in Fife, to learn estate management and the latest farming methods.

John Balfour, meanwhile, was learning to farm the hard way. His brother Luke had shown little interest in farming and was now working in a garage. The family's fortunes had not improved and Connie was pregnant again – at the age of forty-four.

Her last boy was born as Bob and John were struggling to bring the harvest in before the rain came. They called the baby Benjamin, but right from the start he became Benny, for short.

Annie left school at fourteen despite Connie's protests. Annie could see she was needed to help her uncle and John on the farm, and besides, her aunt would welcome a helping hand, caring for a lively little toddler on top of everything else.

Bob Balfour was still struggling to plough the land with two old horses, unable to afford the tractor which would lighten the load. But singling turnip seedlings was the most monotonous and wearisome task of their farming year. A field of sprouting seedlings in need of thinning can seem endless. Annie and John hated the tedious work, but there was no escape. Everyone lent a hand, even Leah when she wasn't at school. Benny was usually around their feet also, happily hauling up everything green within sight, while his mother wielded the hoe.

This year, John worked with his father ahead of the others. To add insult to boredom, he rested on the hoe for a minute to watch the McGills' new tractor roar past, driven by Fergus, waving cheerfully. The injustice made his blood boil.

'Beats me how the McGills are so well-off, Da!'

Bob smiled.

'Alec McGill married a very rich woman, that's how.'

John heard this with mounting excitement.

'So that's how it's done!'

His father glanced at the young man with amusement.

'Aye, that's how! But just you mind, son, you've to spend the rest of your life with the woman. I married your mother for love, and I wager I made a happier bargain than poor hen-pecked Alec McGill!'

But John's thoughts were far away.

Marry a rich wife! Why hadn't he thought of that before?

Luke followed his older brothers to sea in the spring of 1930, when Annie was fifteen. He'd taken odd jobs here and there, helping occasionally on the farm and hating every minute. Now he seemed to have found his niche. He'd reached Australia on the last voyage, and judging by enthusiastic letters home, seemed certain to settle. Matthew had married a Canadian lass and was living in Canada with his wife and young family, and Mark had found employment in Brazil. Connie was saddened. Her family was scattered far across the globe. It made the younger ones seem even more precious to her.

Farming in Scotland being the way it was, Bob couldn't blame his sons for leaving, though he was forced to employ a retired farm worker to help out. He, John and Annie struggled on as best they could.

Fergus McGill graduated from college in 1932 with a useful degree in agriculture, and his parents decided to celebrate their only son's coming of age with a magnificent party on their estate. The Balfours were not invited.

As darkness fell, the celebrations continued with a huge bonfire and firework display the like of which had never been seen in Kirriemuir, not even on Guy Fawkes night. Annie took full advantage of the amazing spectacle, creeping through the woodland and hiding in the bushes surrounding their neighbours' house.

She had never seen so many beautifully dressed young people. They were dancing on the stone terrace in front of the house. Dancing frantically to the crazy beat of a seriously loud jazz band. The dancers screamed and yelled madly every time a rocket exploded in a starburst of glittering colour high above their heads, then went on dancing with renewed abandon, heels and toes beating clattering rhythms from the stone.

Annie wasn't sure whether to be deeply shocked or madly excited.

Lisette wrote often, describing similar

83

events with great enthusiasm. Dancing was such fun, and it could be so romantic, to be held in someone's arms, she wrote.

Annie left the bushes to have a closer look. Standing in the darkness she felt safe from detection. The revellers were oblivious to everything but the wild beat of the music, but Annie had never felt so lonely in her life, watching young people not much older than herself enjoying themselves, without a care in the world, it seemed...

'Caught you!'

She hadn't noticed Fergus stalking her. His sharp eyes had caught sight of movement down by the bushes and he'd decided to investigate the gatecrasher. He was intrigued to find it was Annie.

He was laughing as he grabbed her and held her. This was the old mischievous Fergus she remembered from childhood. Only they weren't children any more, and closeness roused strange new emotions.

Fergus was startled. He'd watched Annie grow up, given her a casual wave as she worked in the fields, passed the time of day in friendly fashion on the farm road, she on foot wearing overalls, he seated above on the tractor.

But tonight she wore a simple blue dress with white lace at the neck. Her shining black hair was bobbed and framed her face. Her eyes were dark and glowing in the firelight.

Fergus caught his breath. Was this lovely girl Annie? Or could it be Lisette? Was she a confusing blend of the two, conjured up by the wine he'd drunk?

'Why were you hiding?' he asked unsteadily.

'Because I wasn't invited.'

The sky lit up, bathing them in uncanny silver light. The dancers shrieked.

Fergus laughed.

'Don't be silly. Come and join the fun.'

'You call that fun?' she cried, glancing upwards at a cascade of silver stars far above. 'I call it shocking extravagance! It makes me so angry when...'

'Oh, don't be so pompous, girl!'

He bent and kissed her on the lips, silencing the outburst for several long, startled seconds. She broke away and stared at him.

Fergus felt dizzy, confused.

'I – I'm sorry, Lisette—'

'So that's it!' Annie said bitterly. 'You thought you were flirting with my sister! I'm Annie!'

'No, it was a mistake—'

'Yes, a bad mistake! Lisette is well brought up and knows how to behave in polite society, Annie is a farm worker who tends pigs. That's why I wasn't invited to your beastly birthday party, wasn't it?'

'No, of course not! Annie, please listen...'

But she had already pushed him away and fled into the woodland.

Lisette left school that year, aged seventeen, having passed all her exams. She was a clever girl – not that academic prowess was necessary for her future, Madeleine thought. Lisette's striking dark looks were already attracting attention and no doubt she would marry soon and brilliantly. There were plans for a splendid coming-out ball next year, and Madeleine's beautiful adopted daughter would also be joining the ranks of debutantes presented at court.

Meantime, Lisette and her foster mother settled down to enjoy the pleasures of the 1932 summer season.

Madeleine yawned and stretched luxuriously as she wakened on the morning of her forty-eighth birthday that August. It was quite true what they said, she thought. Being with young people makes one feel young. She didn't feel a day over thirty-eight.

Madeleine Gregory had mellowed remarkably over the years, thanks to Lisette.

A dear little white poodle called Blanche commandeered drawing-room chairs and sofas these days. Madeleine took the dog for walks in the park sometimes, when Lisette was out enjoying herself at a tennis party and Ruth had the day off.

Yes, 'Ruth' now, not Nanny!

Madeleine smiled. Another concession wheedled out of her by this much loved daughter!

But who could deny the darling anything, when she had brought such joy to a lonely childless couple? The house was filled with beautiful young people and the lovely airy rooms echoed to music and happy laughter.

Lisette was popular and generous with invitations to her friends. Pretty girls and fresh-faced young men down from Oxford for the summer vacation danced to the strains of the gramophone in the music room, the girls beautifully groomed, the men swaggering in the baggy trousers they called 'Oxford bags'.

The boys flirted innocently with Lisette, and were not above flirting courteously with Madeleine, attempting to curry favour with the mother. Of course, she saw through their naughty schemes, but how adorable these handsome, well-bred young men were! How *drôle* and charming it all was!

The young men thought Lisette 'absolutely spiffing', but Lisette was a wise girl. She laughed, teased and flirted, but made sure she stayed safely out of reach.

'Happy birthday, Mummy!'

Lisette drew back the curtains and put the breakfast tray down before kissing her mother.

Madeleine sat up and reached for a bed-jacket.

'Breakfast in bed! Darling, you're spoiling me!'

Lisette laughed.

'It was Daddy's idea. He was up at the crack of dawn to visit a patient, or he would have done it himself, the romantic old dear!'

Madeleine's eyes were misty.

'Bless him. He works so hard!'

Lisette sat on the bed. Forty-eight was middle-aged and quite old, yet her mother was still very attractive, even without make-up.

'You look beautiful today, Mummy, a true daughter of France!'

Madeleine paused. 'Why do you say that?'

Lisette laughed.

'Because you are French to the fingertips! One day we must visit the town where you were born. We might even find French relatives. Wouldn't that be fun!'

'No, darling! There is nobody. How many times have I told you so?'

'We do seem rather short of relations,' Lisette sighed. 'Maybe we should ask Annie to my coming-out ball. We haven't met for ages.'

'No, my dear, that's not a good idea,' Madeleine said firmly. 'The poor girl wouldn't know anyone. She would just be a fish out of water.'

'I suppose so.' Lisette sighed a second time.

She wanted her sister to meet Freddie Asherwood. Freddie was eighteen, and so handsome and amusing. His father, Lord Asherwood, had a private airfield on the estate, and Freddie was learning to fly. He had promised to take her up for a spin soon. Life was so exciting, and she thought she was falling in love. She would have liked to ask Annie's opinion, but—

'Mummy knows best, my darling!' Madeleine smiled, and kissed her cheek.

Annie Balfour's attention was focused on dancing that autumn too, but that had more to do with her cousin Leah. Leah Balfour was fourteen and Annie loved her like a sister. She was small and fragile-looking, but actually much stronger than she looked. Leah did not shine in the classroom, but she was very talented in another direction. She could dance!

Her talent had been discovered at the age of three, when she'd escaped Connie's vigilance while shopping in Kirriemuir and wandered into Miss Elsie Petrie's dancing class. The tiny tot had given such a stunning performance to the music of a Highland Fling, Miss Elsie had sought out Connie and offered to teach the child, free, gratis and for nothing. When Connie's pride intervened, Elsie had laughed.

'When you've been teaching clumsy bairns with two left feet for as many years as I have, Mrs Balfour, it's a miracle to come across a wee lass wi' such potential!'

So Leah danced, and more than fulfilled her early promise. By the age of thirteen she had passed exams and performed Highland dances before judges, winning rows of silver cups, medals and certificates which now adorned Miss Elsie's walls and shelves. Connie insisted that the teacher keep the silverware, as recompense for the good woman's kindness. The gesture also helped to salve Connie's pride.

But now Elsie Petrie had decided to hold a dancing display in Reform Street Hall that autumn, and her star pupil would be performing a solo ballet. Elsie had asked Connie to make Leah's costume and the Balfour household was thrown into turmoil.

'A tutu?' Connie said. 'What sort o' beast is that?'

'If it's a dog, can I have it?' Benny asked hopefully. He'd be going to school soon, and was usually to be found in the midst of any activity, getting in the way.

Leah and Annie laughed and explained. Connie pondered thoughtfully.

'We've butter muslin left over from cheese-making to make a frilly skirt, and my white satin petticoat would do for the bodice, I suppose...'

So Leah became a magical little ballet dancer, thanks to Connie's ingenuity and the patient hours Annie spent sewing on sequins. At the final fitting the delighted youngster performed a twirl on pointed toe in front of the mirror.

'Thanks, Ma! You're a genius!'

Connie was too emotional to say a word.

On the evening of the display, the Balfours waited nervously for the taxi Miss Elsie had ordered to bring the star of the show and her family to the hall. John had set off earlier on his bike to help behind the scenes, but Bob had to stay home to tend to the farm animals.

'I wish you would come and see me dance, Da!' his little daughter sighed.

'Not in these mucky boots, love!' her father joked and kissed her cheek. 'But don't worry,

Leah dear, you'll dance in my dreams while I put the pigs and horses to bed.'

Benny thought this very funny. He was dressed in Sunday best ready to go to the show, but now he rolled on the floor, laughing.

'Och, Da! Horses in bed!'

'Benny, stop your nonsense, here's the taxi!' Connie cried. She shook her head at her husband. 'Now see what you've done, Bob! The boy's suit is all dusty!'

She grabbed Benny with one hand and the cardboard box containing the precious costume with the other and headed out of the door.

At last Connie, Annie and Leah were seated in the back of the car, the box balanced safely across their knees, and the little boy sitting in front beside the driver. Bob slammed the door and stood clear. Smiling, he watched the car lurch down the uneven track, his wife hanging onto the precious box for dear life. Annie, bless her, stuck a hand out of the taxi window and gave him the thumbs up. Bob laughed, and turned away to get on with all the many tasks needing to be done.

Miss Elsie's show was well attended. She was known to be a fine teacher and something of a perfectionist. She had not displayed her pupils' talents in a public hall before, and anticipation was high. Every seat in the hall was occupied.

Connie and Annie sat near the front with

Benny, and as the display progressed Annie grew nervous. The other children danced so beautifully, Leah must have a special quality which Miss Elsie considered outstanding, Annie thought. But what if Leah was nervous, and didn't do herself justice? she wondered anxiously.

And then the lights dimmed.

Leah whirled onto the darkened stage, glittering like a small white flame as the spotlight followed every move.

Annie caught her breath. She knew Leah could dance, but she had never imagined she could dance like this. She floated effortlessly above the boards, leaping high, spinning and twirling, light as a feather, yet Annie knew that the strength and discipline required to create the illusion of ease was quite incredible. Annie watched enthralled till the dance ended, and Leah sank down in a curtsey, to rapturous applause.

The Balfours were proud and excited. Annie was already planning wild schemes to raise funds to let this much-loved little genius have the training she deserved. Not surprisingly, the mood in the taxi heading homewards was jubilant.

Connie had spoken at length with Miss Elsie in the dressing room, and was beaming.

'She says you're the most promising pupil she's had, Leah. There's plenty hard work ahead, but she's sure you could win a scholarship to a school where they train ballet dancers. What about that, lovey?'

'I'd rather stay at home,' Leah yawned.

Dancing came as naturally to her as breathing. She couldn't understand all the fuss.

The car had reached Kilmuckety road end and the driver slowed to negotiate the bumpy track. Connie could hardly wait to tell Bob about Leah's success. It would be a bit of cheer for her hard-working man. Oh, he'd be so proud! She stared eagerly ahead, and frowned.

'The house is in darkness.'

'He'll be round the back in the kitchen, putting the kettle on, I bet.' Annie smiled.

'But he promised he'd have the front lights on, dear, to welcome us home. It's not like Bob to forget.'

'Well, John's helping to clear the hall and we're earlier than we expected, so we've caught Uncle Bob on the hop, that's all.'

But Connie was on the edge of her seat.

'No, Annie. Something's wrong. I know it is!'

Connie flung down the box containing Leah's triumphant tutu and ran into a dark and silent house.

'Bob!' she cried. 'Bob! My dearest...'

She paused abruptly in the doorway of the lamplit kitchen. Bob Balfour lay peacefully in his favourite armchair as if asleep, but even as Connie called his name, she knew in her heart that he would never waken.

Four

Once the funeral was past, Connie faced a daunting situation. Her three eldest sons would have been a great support to their mother at this sad time, but they were well established abroad, and she had no intention of demanding their return. Instead, she relied more heavily upon John and Annie.

John was out in the fields from dawn till dusk, keeping the land ploughed and stock fed, while Annie helped Connie make sense of their finances in the following weeks. Leah and young Benny attended school, although Leah's classwork, never brilliant, was suffering. The talented youngster had no heart even for dancing lessons, and to Miss Elsie's dismay had stopped attending classes. What was the point, thought Leah sorrowfully, now that her da's pride in her achievement was no longer the incentive?

'More bills!' Connie cried despairingly one morning, leafing through the fresh batch of brown envelopes which had thudded on the doormat. 'The postie must be sick and tired of beating a track up our path.'

Annie stacked them with the rest. Her uncle's creditors had panicked after his unexpected death and were clamouring for payment. Unfortunately, Bob Balfour had been trading with firms who gave extended credit. Now a host of merchants and feed firms were demanding immediate settlement of their accounts, and the bank was threatening to foreclose on quite a hefty loan.

It didn't need a mathematician to work out that their situation was critical. Connie reached a momentous decision.

'We must sell the farm, Annie!'

'No! It's our home!' she said in utter dismay. 'Why not contact my father? Surely he'll help you? He must! He's part of this family too.'

Her aunt shook her head. 'Your father needs every penny to run that plantation of his in Malaya. Besides, even if he could raise enough cash in time to save the situation, I couldn't in all good conscience ask him to ruin his own chance of success.' She sighed heavily and patted her niece's hand comfortingly.

'I know how you feel, lovey, but I won't have my honest hard-working husband remembered as a man who couldn't repay his debts.'

There was nothing more to be said. Connie had made up her mind, and Annie was devastated.

John had been up since dawn repairing fences, and his expression was grim when told of his mother's decision.

'The McGills have had envious eyes on our farm for decades, Mam. I bet they'll jump at the chance to grab it now.'

'Aye well, their patience could be rewarded,' Connie said grimly. 'At least they have the cash to make improvements your father could only dream of.'

Annie had a hollow ache inside. The thought of losing the Balfours' much-loved family home was unbearable. Especially if the McGills bought it.

'What will happen to us?' she asked unhappily. 'Where will we go?'

'I'm not going anywhere,' John declared. 'I'm staying right here on Balfour land, even if it means working as a paid hand for McGill.'

Connie glanced at her niece.

'At least your future's settled, Annie love. Your father'll welcome you to his home in Malaya. It's what he always wanted, and a grand chance for you to get to know your brother and stepmother.'

But Annie found this suggestion ludicrous.

'I've no intention of deserting you now, after all you've done for me, Auntie Connie!'

There were tears in Connie's eyes.

'Heaven knows it'd break my heart to lose you, Annie love, but you must be sensible. There could be hard times ahead.'

Annie laughed. 'I am being sensible! I'll do what Uncle Bob would expect. I'll stay with you for as long as you need me.'

* * *

John's prediction proved correct. When Kil-muckety Farm came up for public auction, the McGills' bid topped the lot. It was whispered that the wealthy Mrs McGill had her eye on the farmhouse, a larger, more imposing dwelling than the McGills' present residence. She was rumoured to have plans to modernize and refurbish the rambling old property to the highest standard, no expense spared.

The sale gave Connie enough to settle Bob's debts, but with not much left over for a fresh start. John Balfour swallowed his pride and went to Alec McGill to ask for a job as a farmhand. The older McGill was not keen to take on the former owner's son, anticipating difficulties ahead, but surprisingly Fergus spoke up for John and won the day. It was agreed that John would have six months' trial as stockman, and if he proved satisfactory would be taken on permanently. Meantime, he was granted use of a vacant cottage adjoining the steading, rent free.

Connie and the rest of the family did not feature in the new owners' plans.

'So where will we go?' Annie wondered. 'Maybe we could rent a wee cottage in Kirrie-muir. I'll soon find myself a job!' The idea appealed to her, but Connie shook her head.

'Definitely not! It would turn my stomach, watching the McGills lording it in my ain house. I want to be as far away from here as possible, so...' She hesitated a moment.

Connie had spent sleepless nights agonizing

over their future and was quite clear in her own mind what should be done, but wasn't sure how Annie would take it.

'I had a letter from my cousin Agnes when she heard the farm had been sold, Annie,' she went on. 'Agnes lives in Fife, but her son works for an Edinburgh landlord. If we fancy moving to the city, she says he'll find us a flat to rent.'

Annie's spirits plummeted. She loved the countryside. To live in the crowded bustle of a city was her worst nightmare. She would feel trapped. She opened her mouth to protest, then saw the pitiful plea in her aunt's eyes, and closed it again. Her own feelings were not important. If Connie wanted this, then she must help her to make the best of it. Annie forced a smile.

'Edinburgh sounds fine to me.'

Greatly relieved, Connie hurried off to write the fateful letter, while Annie went on preparing for tomorrow's roup, the traditional Scottish auction of unwanted farm implements and household goods. Most of the farmhouse's contents would go under the auctioneer's hammer next day. The furnishings might fetch only a few shillings, but each piece carried priceless childhood memories. She was in tears as she went from room to room, but she cried alone. Nobody must know how heartbroken she was.

Annie made herself scarce while the sale was in progress. She could not bear to watch as the well-used family items went under the hammer. Whistling up Barney for company, she walked as far as the old stone footbridge over the burn, then paused and leaned on the parapet while the dog splashed about in the shallow water, hunting for water rats.

Sunk in thought, she was startled when Fergus rested his arms companionably on the parapet beside her.

'Boycotting the sale?' he said.

'So are you!' She wiped away a surreptitious tear, pretending to be engrossed in watching Barney snuffle in the riverbank.

'I hate endings, especially this one,' Fergus remarked.

'It's not the end for the Balfours, Fergus, it's a fresh start.'

'Brave girl!' He looked at her sideways. 'Your nose is red.'

'I have a cold.'

'There's a lot of it about,' he said mildly. 'So what are *your* plans?'

'As soon as the sale's over I'm leaving for Edinburgh with my aunt and the children.'

Fergus looked shocked.

'Edinburgh?'

'Yes, the country bumpkin is heading for the city, Fergus. I bet you're glad.'

'Actually, I'm not. You could never be a city girl. I thought you'd stay nearby.'

That proved infuriating.

'So I'm to wear wellie boots and overalls and get my hands dirty all my days, am I? Are you telling me I'll never match up to Lisette? Do you think I care?'

Coldly, she turned away, but he grabbed her arm and pulled her round.

'Wait a minute!'

They stood close together on the narrow footbridge. For a moment time stood still, and Annie forgot to breathe.

'Annie, please don't go to Edinburgh,' he said softly.

Her breath escaped in a sigh.

'It'd be ten times worse staying here, with you living in my home and your family strutting about on our land. I have to go, Fergus! I might end up hating you.'

He understood perfectly. The Balfours' farm had been an important haven when he was a lonely small boy swamped by a large family of older sisters. He'd always loved the shabby old house, but with Annie far away, something vital would be missing. He *must* keep in touch.

'Listen, Annie, I visit Edinburgh regularly to take orders from hotels and restaurants for farm produce. We could arrange to meet,' he suggested eagerly.

'What good would that do?'

'I can make sure you're all right.'

'As if you care!'

'Of course I care, you idiot!' he cried in exasperation, and pulled her into his arms.

'Let go!'

She struggled, a token protest, since she was curious to find out what might happen this time if they kissed. Last time had been in a garden lit eerily by fireworks, and had been a total disaster.

Perhaps Fergus remembered too. His kiss was wary at first, but soon he was throwing caution to the winds.

Barney had been alerted by raised voices from above, and interpreted the couple's odd behaviour as an attack upon his helpless mistress. Growling, the dog came bounding from the riverbank to the rescue, sinking its teeth into the young man's trouser leg.

Fergus yelled, promptly released Annie and hopped around madly, trying to loosen the snarling dog's fierce grip.

'Let go, you brute!'

Annie came to her senses. She shouted indignantly.

'Stop kicking the poor dog!'

Grabbing Barney's collar, she hauled him off with an ominous rending of cloth.

Thankfully, Fergus was unhurt but the flannels were ruined. He surveyed the damage furiously.

'Look what your horrible hound's done!'

'It's your own fault! You assaulted me!'

'What absolute rot! You didn't even struggle.'

It was humiliating but true. 'Ohhh, you beast!' she cried tearfully.

From the age of four this turbulent friendship had always ended in tears. Repentant, he took a step forward, ignoring the dog.

'Annie, I'm sorry...'

She backed away. 'Stay away from me, Fergus McGill! I never want to see you again!'

'No, Annie, please—!'

But she turned and ran before she had a chance to succumb to his dangerous charm.

Fergus made a desperate move to follow her, but the dog growled a menacing warning and bared its teeth. Fergus paused. Barney, duty done, bounded off after Annie.

The farm sale completed, Annie, Connie and the two children left the district without telling anyone. Their sudden departure was intended as a clean break, but left Fergus feeling cruelly rejected. To make matters worse, when he asked John Balfour for Annie's address, he was told politely to mind his own business. The dog Barney, now comfortably installed in the cottage with John, raised its hackles and growled...

Lisette Balfour had been saddened when told of her uncle's sudden death, though Uncle Bob was little more than a fond childhood memory. The decision to sell the Balfour farm had much greater impact.

When Dr Gregory arrived in the Bentley to drive her home after a visit to Asherwood estate, she learned that the farm had finally been sold. The news spoiled the pleasure of what had been a wonderful weekend.

Freddie Asherwood had kept his promise, and taken Lisette up for a short flight. He was a fully fledged pilot by now, and Lisette had found the experience thrilling. After Freddie landed the plane, he'd stolen a kiss. It was so romantic! Lisette was sure she was in love. She only wished she could discuss the symptoms with Annie, but news that the McGills had bought the farm caused her concern for her sister's future.

'Oh, Daddy! What will happen to Annie?'

'Your aunt has moved to Edinburgh with the younger children and your sister went with them.'

'But Annie loathes cities!'

He laughed.

'She's never really lived in one, my dear. She'll soon fall in love with Edinburgh, you'll see!'

'Couldn't Annie come and live with us, Daddy?'

Dermot hesitated. Originally, he had disapproved of separating the identical twins, but after fourteen years, attitudes had changed. Gentle little Lisette had stolen his heart, and now he loved her like the daughter he and Madeleine had always wanted. But what if Lisette and her naughty twin had come to them at the start? How would a childless couple, set in their ways and living in luxury, have coped with two high-spirited little girls? Life with twins would be twice as demanding. Dermot had no doubt that his dear wife would have been driven to distraction.

He sighed and changed down a gear for a hairpin bend. Sadly, he feared that to reunite the twins at this late stage could only lead to unhappiness for all concerned.

'No, Lisette, I don't think Annie would be happy living with us. It's too late.'

He gave her a quick, concerned glance and found she looked astonished.

'That's just what Annie and I told our father, when he asked us to go to Malaya!'

'Then you'll understand why it wouldn't work. I'm so sorry, my dear.'

'I still love Annie though, Daddy,' Lisette said sadly, after a pause.

'Of course you do. She's your sister.'

'Yes. My own special sister,' she said quietly.

She hadn't appreciated how precious the relationship was till it could never be resumed. She stared ahead through a blur of tears, and hoped her foster father hadn't noticed...

The tenement flat Connie's relative found for them was three floors up in Candlemakers Close, not far from Edinburgh castle.

Annie could understand why candle makers had once plied their trade in that particular area, since it appeared to be the darkest alleyway in the district. The city was in the grip of frost when they arrived, which did not help, and every chimney reeked thick yellow smoke into a freezing blanket of rime.

Auld Reekie was living up to its reputation.

Connie took one look at the flat's interior, rolled up her sleeves and began scrubbing every surface with Annie's help. After they had cleaned the four small rooms and tiny scullery from floor to ceiling, they rearranged the few items of furniture they'd saved from the sale. Connie put her hands on her hips and surveyed the scene.

'It still doesnae look much like home to me!'

'Give it time,' Annie said.

All that could be seen through clean windows were stone walls, grey slate roofs and rows of belching chimneypots. Even three floors up, Annie could detect no sky, and not a single branch or patch of green was visible. She didn't think she could stand it.

Leah burst into tears.

'I hate this awful place. I'd rather walk the streets. I'm going out.'

'Leah, no!' Connie cried in terror. Goodness knows what dangers lurked in city streets for a fourteen-year-old lass!

Annie searched hastily in a pocket and found her last half crown.

'Leah, love, there's a fish and chip shop on the corner. Go and buy four large portions. Bring them back here and we'll have a rare old feast!'

'Salt an' vinegar on mine!' Benny whooped.

That brought smiles and laughter, and Leah set off happily. Connie listened to her daughter's dancing step on the stairs, and looked at Annie with misty eyes.

'Bless you, my dear!' she murmured softly.

Benny had been chesty since he was a baby. Colds went straight to his chest, and he wheezed. Fresh air had been good for him, but city smog was a different story. Benny caught cold in bitter February weather, and the breathless wheezing became so alarming Connie was forced to call the doctor. It was then she heard the dreaded word.

Asthma!

'It's my fault, Annie,' she wept after the doctor had left. 'I should never have brought my bairn to this unhealthy place. The doctor says dust and fog are bad for him.'

Annie hugged her.

'There's not a speck of dust in this flat, and the fog will vanish when the weather's better. Didn't I hear the doctor say Benny's condition could improve when he's older?'

'Yes, love,' Connie wiped her eyes. 'But meantime he's to have steam inhalations and plenty good food. That costs money, and there's not much of that about.'

'That's easily fixed.' Annie smiled confidently. 'I'll get a job. I'm used to keeping farm accounts, and they're sure to need plenty of office workers in a city.'

But she soon found there was no office work available for an eighteen-year-old lacking a school leaving certificate.

Leah was more fortunate. She turned down Connie's suggestion of schooling and found work in a nearby florist's shop, where she tied loose flowers in attractive bunches for display, and appeared happy and contented. The few shillings she earned proved to be a godsend.

Annie grew more depressed, tramping the streets daily looking for work without success. She missed working with John, and the long walks on the hills with her beloved dog. According to John's letters, he and Barney were coping admirably with herding duties on the hill, but for some odd reason the dog couldn't abide Fergus McGill.

There was a newsagent's round the corner from Candlemakers Close, and inside the shop was a board with local advertisements pinned to it. These were mostly for items to sell or buy, or lost and found pets and property. Occasionally there were job offers of such a menial nature Annie had passed them by. But as time went by without any luck, she could no longer afford to be choosy. Studying the board one cold March day, her attention was drawn to a typewritten card standing out from among the handwritten ones.

Woman required for kitchen duties
WHYTE HOUSE HOTEL
The Pleasance
Apply to: Conrad Whyte, Proprietor

The venue sounded promising. But – she wrinkled her nose doubtfully. Kitchen duties? How cunningly vague! That could mean anything from cooking meals to washing dishes. Still, it was the most promising prospect she'd found so far, and she was growing desperate...

The Pleasance had once formed part of ancient gardens around Holyrood Palace, and Annie detected traces of past glory as she walked through the area. To the south she caught glimpses of parkland through gaps in the buildings. She could see rugged hills in the background, and her spirits lifted.

She paused outside when she reached the hotel. The big building might once have housed a large prosperous Victorian family, but was now rundown and shabby, with only traces of faded grandeur left. Annie stood at the entrance, eyeing it critically.

A brass plate with **WHYTE HOUSE HOTEL** in bold letters adorned the portico, and above the doorway was a colourful sign:

A WARM WELCOME, GOOD FOOD,
A KIND WORD.

Cheered, she went inside.

Early March is not renowned for the tourist trade and the hallway was dark and cold. A notice on an empty reception desk ordered *Ring for Attention*. She clanged the bell loudly.

Presently a middle-aged man appeared. He frowned.

'What do you want?'

Annie smiled.

'Mr Whyte? I've come to apply for the job.'

She held out the card the newsagent had given her. The proprietor glanced at it briefly.

'Sorry. The advert calls for a woman.'

The man's manner annoyed her.

'I *am* a woman.'

'I meant an older woman. You're much too young!' He stared at her for a moment, then relented. 'Oh, very well, I suppose you'd better see what's involved, now you're here.'

She followed him through a spacious dining room filled with bare tables and empty chairs. It smelled faintly of stale fried breakfasts. He pushed open one half of a wide swinging door and stood aside to let her enter a kitchen stacked with filthy pots and piles of dirty dishes. There were no kitchen staff to be seen, and sculleries and storerooms beyond hinted at even more mess and chaos. Annie met the proprietor's gaze. It was dark and fathomless.

'Your chef is a messy worker, Mr Whyte.'

He shrugged.

'Chefs aren't paid to clean up. Why do you think I advertised for a capable woman, not a flighty young flibbertigibbet?' He held the kitchen door open, dismissing her. 'Well, anyway, thanks for your interest, Miss ... er ... er...'

'Balfour. Annie Balfour.'

'I have a busy day ahead, Miss Balfour, so if you wouldn't mind seeing yourself off the premises...'

Annie stood her ground.

'Are you telling me I'm not a capable worker? That's not fair. You haven't even bothered to give me a trial.'

He paused and gave her a long, hard look.

'Very well, then. You have three hours to clean and tidy the kitchen, Miss Balfour, before the chef and his staff turn up to prepare dinner this evening!'

★ ★ ★

At least there was piping-hot water, and plenty of soap and scouring powder, Annie found. She piled pots, pans and dirty dishes in the sink and set to work. When that was done and the clean items stacked neatly on the shelves, she set to work to scrub grease and spilled food off floor, work surfaces, ovens and hobs.

By the time the proprietor returned, the kitchen and storerooms were clean and tidy, and Annie was exhausted but triumphant.

'Hmm.' He ran a finger lightly along a shining work surface and examined it closely. 'You can return at six-thirty for the evening shift. Don't be late. You should be finished around ten-thirty and I'll decide then whether to give you the job or not.'

She was sure he was hiding a grin. He'd had his filthy kitchen cleaned for free, and probably thought he'd seen the back of her. Well, she'd show him how wrong he could be!

She nodded icily and turned to go. She'd be back that evening to receive payment in full from Mr Conrad Whyte. Besides, she really needed his awful job, for Connie's sake.

He called after her.

'Kindly use the staff exit, Miss Balfour.'

She pointedly ignored the order, marching from the hotel through the front portico under the cheerful sign.

So much for the warm welcome and the kind word! she thought.

Lisette blossomed during the winter season,

and had never looked more beautiful, her foster mother thought. Most weekends promised excitement, with perhaps an intimate house party with friends, who made sure Freddie was invited. Or there could be some glittering evening event in ballroom or theatre, demanding her most glamorous gowns and the diamond jewellery which Mummy and Daddy had given her on her eighteenth birthday.

Madeleine Gregory's ambition for her adopted daughter was realized in 1934, when with a host of other debutantes, Lisette was presented at court.

Queen Mary was a gracious and regal lady, not renowned for idle chat when greeting lines of curtseying young women in white gowns. However, Lisette's dark eyes caught the Queen's attention. Her Majesty smiled and exchanged a few pleasant words with the striking dark-haired beauty. This was such a rare occurrence that Madeleine's pride knew no bounds.

Royal approval would be noted by the aristocracy, and greatly improve Lisette's marriage prospects. Madeleine had kept quiet about her adopted daughter's origins. If asked, she hinted at a family tragedy and a large Scottish estate. Lisette was competing for a wealthy husband with titled young women and small white lies were permissible.

Lisette's romance with Freddie Asherwood showed no signs of cooling as the season wore on, and Madeleine was delighted. Freddie was an amiable darling who adored Lisette and was an excellent catch. Freddie's parents, Lord and Lady Asherwood, approved of Lisette as a suitable girlfriend for their son and heir, and were already very fond of her.

Madeleine had high hopes that Freddie would pop the question, and that a sparkling society wedding could be arranged next year, in the summer of 1935, which was, opportunely, the King and Queen's Silver Jubilee year.

Lisette had never been happier as she walked arm in arm with Freddie towards the hangar where his plane was housed on his father's private airfield. She adored him. He was sweet and amusing, but she had discovered there was also a serious side to Freddie Asherwood. Today he seemed preoccupied, and she hung onto his arm and smiled teasingly.

'Penny for them, darling?'

Freddie glanced at her, and, as always, his heart beat faster. He'd had girlfriends before, but Lisette was unique and special. When they had met at first he'd found her attractive, but apart from her beauty there had been nothing to set her apart from the others.

Then one day, quite by chance, he had come across Lisette and her mother together, speaking fluent French. He had stood watching them unobserved, charmed by Lisette's vivacity, enchanted by the graceful gestures of her hands and arms, the laughing shrug of

112

her slender shoulders. It was a transformation that had taken his breath away. He saw beyond the pretty debutante in beautiful gowns and glimpsed a highly intelligent, passionate woman. From that moment, Freddie knew he would love Lisette Balfour faithfully till the end.

But recently, Freddie had begun to wish this all-consuming love had never happened. There was so much to lose now!

'I was wondering if there'll be a war,' he answered seriously.

She stopped dead. 'Darling, of course not! The last horrible war put an end to all that stupid nonsense.'

'I'm not so sure, my sweetheart. Pa tells me the German Chancellor's recruited a massive army and has rearmed the whole German nation. I can't help wondering what this chap Hitler is up to.'

Lisette smiled knowingly. 'My father's heard those rumours too, Freddie. He thinks a strong Germany could keep Russian Bolsheviks in their place.'

'Maybe, but where will it stop? Some of us are hoping for the best and preparing for the worst, Lisette. I've volunteered for training on fighter aircraft.'

It was a calm, beautiful morning, but she felt as if a shadow had crossed the sun.

'You'll join the Air Force if there is a war?'

'Yes. They'll need all the trained pilots they can get.'

She hugged him in sudden terror. She had

her father's medal to remind her of how dangerous wars could be.

'Freddie, stop scaring me! I love you so much!'

He laughed. 'OK, my darling, so let's forget war and talk love. There's something I've been meaning to ask you.' He went down on one knee. 'Miss Balfour, I absolutely adore you! Will you marry me and make me the happiest man in England?'

The formal proposal made Lisette laugh, she was so deliriously happy.

'Darling man, of course I'll marry you! But you really ought to ask Daddy's permission, you know. Oh, do get up, Freddie, the grass is soaking wet!'

She tried to haul him to his feet, but lost her balance. Laughing helplessly, they rolled on the grass, sealing the engagement with ecstatic kisses. The grass was wet, glistening with a dew heavy as teardrops, but they were too much in love to heed small details like that...

Madeleine was overjoyed when Freddie came to ask Dermot formally for Lisette's hand in marriage. She reached for pen and paper and settled down to discuss wedding plans. Lisette protested.

'Freddie and I don't want to get married till next year, Mummy. He has some training to finish and we haven't decided on a date.'

'Well, do hurry, darling. The best hotels get booked up so quickly. June would be best.

That gives plenty time to have your dress and the bridesmaids' dresses designed and made.'

But Lisette had her own plans for this wedding.

'Only one bridesmaid,' she said.

Madeleine frowned. *'Mais, chérie!* You have dozens of beautiful friends.'

'But only one sister. I want Annie to be my bridesmaid.'

'No!' Madeleine stared aghast. 'It is much too difficult. How could it be arranged? You tell me she lives in an Edinburgh slum. How can she have a suitable dress?'

'That can be arranged, if one uses kindness and tact, Mother,' Lisette said coldly. 'There are good shops in Edinburgh. You could open an account with one of the best, and Annie can choose a dress she likes.'

Madeleine gave a wail of horror. 'But the girl has straw in her ears and dirt under her fingernails. How can she be trusted to choose something so important? It will be a disaster!'

Lisette leapt to her feet. 'She is my twin sister, and she will not let me down!' she cried furiously. 'You parted two little sisters once! You did it smoothly and craftily, and that was cruel! But I want the sister I love beside me on my wedding day, do you hear?'

She stared at Madeleine with the anger and hurt kept hidden for fourteen long years. Her foster mother shrank back, as Lisette went on with deadly calm. 'Or there will be no grand wedding for you to organize, Mother. There

115

will be just Freddie and me and Annie, in a registrar's office.'

Annie had worked all summer in the Whyte House Hotel's overheated kitchen, but the approach of winter gave hope of some relief. An ancient extractor fan struggled to remove heat, smoke and smell from the area. The volatile chef cooked in an atmosphere of heated argument. Dishes were spilled, contents splattered on floors and walls in anger. Service was desultory and poor and customers complained.

Annie kept silent and did her best to make order out of bedlam, but it was almost impossible. The hotel was third rate. It was only the view of trees and hills from a window halfway up the stairs that kept her working there.

The first and second floors consisted of ten shabby bedrooms and one bathroom, perfunctorily cleaned and dusted by Minnie, a passionate devotee of Hollywood films. Whyte House Hotel survived upon its reputation for cheap bed and board, and was patronized mainly by commercial travellers. Few chose to stay more than a night or two.

Which was a pity, Annie thought, because the hotel had potential. Her work done, she sat one morning on the stairs, enjoying her favourite view. There were lots of attic rooms up above, Minnie reported, all packed with old rubbish. The views over city and parkland from up there must be even more spectacular, Annie thought. A shadow fell across her reverie.

'You are not paid to laze around, Miss Balfour,' Conrad Whyte warned.

Blast! Her employer was usually out at this time of day.

'You'll find everything in order in the kitchen, Mr Whyte. I believe I'm entitled to relax and enjoy the view, once my work is done.'

'Not up here, you're not!' He frowned. 'You're a country girl. Why not go back where you belong?'

'Are you giving me the sack?'

'No, kitchen staff are difficult to find. I just wonder why a girl like you ended up in a hotel like this.'

She wrinkled her nose. 'This place is not up to much, is it?'

'I don't claim to run the Dorchester!' he retorted icily.

She smiled. It was fun, baiting him. 'Funny you should say that. My twin sister's wedding reception will be held in the Dorchester in June. There'll be hundreds of guests and I'm to be bridesmaid. I warn you – I'll be taking a fortnight off this summer, Mr Whyte!'

'What a lot of absolute nonsense!' he scoffed. 'I don't believe you have a twin sister, let alone one who can afford a reception at the Dorchester. It's pure fantasy. You tell lies, Miss Balfour!'

She stood up angrily.

'It happens to be perfectly true, Mr Whyte.

But why should I bother to waste my breath, since you're already convinced I'm a liar!'

She turned and ran lightly down the stairs. He called after her.

'Please confine yourself to the kitchen quarters in future, Miss Balfour, and kindly stop mooning around my hotel airing delusions of grandeur. Customers don't like it.'

Annie was in angry tears when she reached the empty kitchen. Talk about a kind word, she thought miserably, she'd never heard one spoken here!

She was tempted to walk out right now and never come back.

Five

Annie stormed back to Candlemakers Close, fully intending to leave Whyte House Hotel forever. She had been mocked, had her word doubted, and although the family needed the wage, she decided to look for work elsewhere.

Expecting to find a sympathetic ear when she reached the tenement, Annie was taken aback to find the flat empty. Connie was not there.

This was such an unusual occurrence it threw her into a panic. She ran from room to room fearing the worst, but the beds were made, the dishes washed, not a speck of dust anywhere.

Of course, there was no reason why Connie shouldn't go out if she wanted to, Annie told herself. Benny's asthma had improved with the weather, and he had begun school at a nearby primary. The school provided dinner for a few pence weekly and Connie had opted for it, though it stretched her budget to the limit. She had reasoned it would be less bother for the little boy to stay for school dinners, rather than running home in all weathers for rushed meals. Leah had already decided to make a meal of sandwiches eaten in the backshop. Lunchtime was the florist's busiest hour.

When the castle gun boomed one o'clock and Connie still hadn't returned, Annie lit the gas under a pot of broth sitting on the stove, foraged in the larder for bread and cheese and ate a lonely meal. She had no idea where Connie was and the flat seemed dismal without her.

'Where have you been?' she demanded, when her aunt turned up two hours later.

'Working.'

Connie sank into a chair. She looked tired out and Annie was immediately concerned.

'You never told me you had a job!'

'The offer came out of the blue this morning, dear. The lass downstairs is expecting a bairn, and asked if I'd take on her job cleaning in the cinema. The work's too much for her now she's eight months gone.'

'Cinema?' Annie said. 'You don't mean the Olympia, that fleapit down the road?'

'That's the one. Of course I jumped at the chance. It's the perfect job for me, Annie. Cleaning's all I'm good for.'

Annie's heart softened. 'Nonsense. You're pure gold through and through.'

Connie glanced hopefully at the stove.

'Any tea left in the pot, Annie dear? You wouldn't believe the dust, dirt and rubbish in that place. Give me a byre to muck out any day!'

Annie boiled the kettle and made a fresh brew. She kept quiet about her own problems, which seemed petty. There was no question of handing in her notice after this unexpected development. Jobs were hard to find, and she could not risk putting an extra load on Connie's shoulders. Besides, to give Conrad Whyte his due, he paid his employees a fair wage with meticulous regularity, every Saturday.

He seemed surprised when Annie turned up for work as usual that evening. He had noted morning storm signals and had probably expected her to walk out. Well, she couldn't, not now! she thought bitterly.

Connie had cooked a beautiful meal for the family that evening, but Annie noticed how weary she looked. Her aunt was a perfectionist, and Annie knew she would not rest till every nicotine-stained nook and cranny in the shabby old cinema met her exacting standard of cleanliness.

Mr Whyte raised an eyebrow as Annie stalked past, rolling up her sleeves in preparation for the evening shift, but otherwise made no comment. She was sure he'd hoped to get rid of her in order to employ the older woman he'd wanted in the first place. Maybe that was why he was being so objectionable.

More cheerfully, she piled dishes in the sink, taking renewed pleasure in the work. It must be infuriating for him to be unable to find fault with her. She took great care to ensure that kitchen and storerooms were sparkling clean after every shift. She sighed resignedly as chef and kitchen staff arrived and settled down to create more noisy mayhem, in preparation for dinner that evening...

Annie and Lisette had been engaged for months in happy correspondence concerning the forthcoming wedding, scheduled for June 1935. Lisette had sent Freddie Asherwood's photograph for Annie's inspection, and it had met with approval. The handsome young man had kind eyes, Connie remarked, combined with strong chin and firm mouth which indicated pleasing strength of character.

Annie was genuinely delighted her sister had found such great happiness. Lisette loved a fine young man who obviously adored her. All the same, Annie found that a wistful little twinge of envy disturbed her, occasionally. Falling in love was another experience Annie had not shared with her more fortunate twin.

'Lisette's sent details of her wedding dress and my bridesmaid's dress,' Annie announced excitedly one chilly February day, reading a letter newly arrived from London. She and Connie were relaxing that afternoon, having finished their morning shifts.

'Don't tell me!' Connie held up a hand. 'I bet Madame Gregory's made sure the wedding dress is fit for a princess, and the bridesmaid will be drab.'

Annie laughed. 'Not a bit of it! The Balfour twins will stun the swanky congregation. Lisette is to be glorious in white satin with a bouquet of red roses, and my dress will be red.'

'Mercy on us!' Connie gasped. 'What's the bride thinking? Red's your colour, Annie. You'll steal her show!'

Annie lifted her chin. 'No, I won't! This wedding day will be the happiest of the Balfour twins' lives, to make up for the bad times.'

Lisette's letter went on to add that an account had been arranged with one of Edinburgh's leading ladies' outfitters. All Annie had to do was choose a dress, shoes and gloves, but the very thought threw her into blind panic.

'I've nothing good enough to wear to even set foot in that shop, Connie!'

Her aunt looked indignant.

'Nonsense! Your clothes are clean and paid for, which is more than can be said for some gentry folk, in my experience.'

So Annie entered the exclusive store a week later with head high and knees knocking. To her surprise, heads turned as she sailed past, and there was no mistaking the admiring glances. The shop mirrors revealed a striking young woman, simply but elegantly dressed, plain court shoes highly polished. Annie's confidence grew.

The choice of a suitable dress proved easy, thanks to heightened telepathy between twins on this momentous occasion. Annie recognized the perfect red dress the moment it slipped over her head. She and the shop assistant studied the dazzling reflection in the mirror in silence. A very simple perfect fit, and the colour absolutely stunning.

The assistant let out the breath she'd been holding.

'Wonderful, madam, quite superb!'

And Annie had to agree.

Lisette had thought of tactful ways to avoid embarrassment. The shop had instructions to send the bridesmaid's dress and the matching satin slippers to the Gregorys' London address. Annie could hardly hide a grin. An address in Candlemakers Close would certainly have raised eyebrows here.

She left the shop in a happy daze, a uniformed commissionaire bowing her out. On the doorstep, she returned rudely to earth, bumping straight into Conrad Whyte. Her employer steadied her, and cast a quizzical glance at the palatial doorway.

'Carrying fantasy a bit far, aren't we, Miss Balfour?'

'On the contrary, Mr Whyte! And I will expect an apology,' she said icily. Turning her back on him, she walked away. He called after her in ringing tones.

'Compliments on the outfit, Miss Balfour. A vast improvement on the greasy overalls.'

Leah Balfour had been quite content with a job in the local florist's, but when her mother started work in a cinema, Leah was green with envy. She did not fancy dusting, sweeping and picking up someone else's sweetie wrappers, but Leah loved going to the pictures on the few occasions she had enough time and money to attend a Saturday matinee. She watched enthralled as glamorous dancers danced on fantastic Hollywood film sets.

Once her sole ambition had been to dance, but that girlish dream had died with her much-loved father. All she craved now was to watch Ziegfeld's musical dancing Follies and Fred Astaire and Ginger Rogers' polished performances. The golden celluloid world was far removed from Edinburgh in the depressing month of March, and Leah longed to be even a small part of it.

A job in a cinema would go some way towards satisfying the craving. Any job, except cleaning. Leah began nagging her mother relentlessly.

'Please help, Ma!'

Connie frowned. 'I thought you liked working at the florist's?'

'There's no future in it,' Leah said. 'I'll be out of a job soon. Her daughter's leaving school at Easter and joining the business.'

This was a worry, though Connie was not keen on the idea of her fifteen-year-old daughter working at the cinema. Leah had blossomed recently, and her mother felt protective. Rough elements frequented the Olympia, with a roguish eye for pretty girls.

'Finding work at the cinema's easier said than done, lovey,' she hedged.

'The manager's pleased with your work, Ma. You could ask him, couldn't you?'

It was true – the cinema manager had been

complimentary about Connie's efforts with soap, water and elbow grease. He might go out of his way to do her a favour if she asked. He had indicated he'd hopes of attracting a more superior audience than the usual scruff, now the place was clean and shining.

Connie sighed. What with transforming the cinema to meet her own exacting standards, and caring for Benny when he wheezed, she had no strength left for argument.

'I'll see what I can do, Leah love,' she promised weakly.

Problems were mounting at Whyte House Hotel. Customers complained of stomach upsets. Conrad blamed the illness on a bug going the rounds, but the hotel's steak pie remained the chief suspect. He decided to have a quiet word with the Belgian chef.

But quiet words were a forlorn hope. The confrontation involved angry shouts and dishes of macaroni crashing to the floor. Annie kept her head down, washing dishes.

'So! You accuse me of poisoning peoples, monsieur!' the chef was yelling.

'No. I only said the meat was bad.'

'I could tell you! Meat is tough and needs much cooking.'

'That's not my fault.'

'I cook meat you order from market!' The chef threw up his hands. 'Is it my fault meat goes rancid in filthy kitchen?'

Annie jerked upright indignantly. To her surprise, Conrad Whyte leapt to her defence.

'This kitchen is spotless till you walk into it.'

The fiery chef let out a wild howl of rage. 'You are saying I have the dirty habits?'

'Too true.' Conrad nodded. 'Look at the mess on this floor!'

'I will not stay, Mr Whyte. I will leave you lurching!' the chef warned tearfully.

Conrad Whyte shrugged. 'OK. The choice is yours.'

Conrad walked out, while the kitchen staff gathered round to comfort the weeping man. Annie dried her hands thoughtfully and followed the proprietor. She found him sitting in the office, staring moodily at the wall.

'Thanks for standing up for me,' she said.

'It's time that wretched man learned some home truths. I've been much too lenient.'

'Is the meat as tough as he says?'

'Every bit.' He sounded tired and disheartened, and Annie's kind heart relented.

'If I found you a supplier of high-quality farm produce, Mr Whyte, what would you do?'

He looked up with sudden interest. 'Probably hug you, Miss Balfour.'

She backed away. 'Mr Whyte, to be quite frank, the sign above the entrance is misleading. Your hotel is not welcoming, the food is not good, and I've yet to hear a kind word.'

He grinned. 'You haven't been listening, Miss Balfour. This evening I warned customers, very kindly, not to touch the steak pie.'

Annie went home later that night knowing

that she was embarking upon a perilous course. She had made up her mind to write to Fergus McGill, without divulging her whereabouts, of course, and suggest that he paid a visit to Mr Conrad Whyte, proprietor of a select hotel in the historic Old Town, with a view to securing an order for farm produce.

This was a purely business approach, but she felt a buzz of dangerous excitement at the prospect, although quite determined to avoid another painful meeting with Fergus, much as she might have enjoyed seeing him, for old times' sake.

On the Kilmuckety estate, John Balfour had been watching the transformation wealth could bring to an ailing farm. The farmhouse had been gutted, then redecorated and refurbished to satisfy Mrs McGill's demanding taste. Bridge parties, tea parties and dinner parties were constantly on the go. When a tennis court planned for the summer was complete, no doubt there would also be tennis parties.

Half a dozen tractors and an American combine harvester made light work on the land, large new poultry sheds and a modern milking parlour replaced the tumbledown steading. Last year on the 12th of August the crack of shotguns on the hillside spoke of ample supply of grouse for lucrative shooting parties. The down side was that John was forced to swallow his pride and line up on Fridays to collect wages from the McGills.

There were compensations, though. John was in love.

Davina Williams was a new maidservant at the big house, and the moment John set eyes on her pretty face he dreamed of little else. One day he waylaid her on the washing green.

'Come to the pictures with me on Saturday, Davina?'

She gave him a glance and went on pegging sheets on the line. 'Sorry. I don't know you well enough for that, John Balfour.'

'Then you should get to know me better, shouldn't you?'

She smiled. 'Well, I may consider it. But not the back seats, mind!'

'That'll save a bob or two. I'll wait by the gate this Saturday and every Saturday, for as long as it takes.'

She was amused by his impudence. 'Proper little Douglas Fairbanks, you are!'

'No resemblance, miss. He's in America, I'm right here, and available.'

With a grin, he went back to the farmyard. Davina watched him go. He was a handsome lad, and if truth be told she'd been hoping he'd ask her out. She wouldn't appear too keen at first, but she'd probably accept the invitation.

John was quite certain she would, and the future seemed bright. He whistled as he walked up the hill with the dog at his heels to attend to the sheep. It was good to see the Balfour estate thriving, but so sad to know that his da hadn't had the money to do it himself.

John and Fergus McGill worked together remarkably well. They shared a love of the land and the determination to make Kilmuckety Farm the finest in Angus.

John paused frowning on the breast of the hill. The sheep were on the move and restive, which was not good for pregnant ewes. A hollow thudding shook the ground beneath his feet. The dog growled uneasily.

Horse and rider jumped a fence and came cantering across the field, scattering sheep right and left. John grabbed Barney's collar and stood his ground as the rider reined in her mount beside him in a scatter of muddy turf. The young woman dismounted.

'I was hoping I'd see you, Balfour.'

'Oh yes?'

He recognized her of course. This was Marigold McGill, youngest of Fergus's five sisters and the only unmarried one. She was frowning.

'What's your cousin Annie up to?'

'I have no idea,' he said blankly.

'Fergus had a letter from her this morning and is moping around the house. I hate to see him so unhappy. I thought that childish infatuation had ended ages ago?'

'So did I. The thought of McGills in the family home made Annie sick.'

'Charming!' Miss Marigold gave him a look. 'It seems she may have had a change of heart, though. Fergus won't confide in any of us, of course, but maybe you could find out from Annie what's in the wind, and pass it on?'

'Maybe. But it's really none of your business, Miss Marigold.'

Flushing, she remounted the mare and sat looking down at him.

'You may have four brothers, John Balfour, but I have only one, and I care about him!'

She swung the horse's head round, dug in her heels and galloped off down the hillside.

John dodged the clods of earth flung up by the horse's hooves and stared after her. His father's words came whispering back to him.

'Marry a rich wife, son, that's how it's done!'

But now he'd met Davina the advice would be hard to follow.

Fergus could hardly believe Annie Balfour had such power to upset him, after the effort he'd made to forget her. Since she'd gone off without a word, Fergus had worked hard on the land, falling exhausted into bed every night. There was plenty to be done to prepare for the summer of 1935, but with John Balfour's help the farm was already showing a profit. Maximum production of a high quality was Fergus's aim. He bought the best cattle, sheep, poultry, grain and grass seeds that money could buy, and expected rich rewards. The plan was working and Fergus had been reasonably happy – till Annie Balfour's letter arrived.

The businesslike note offered a potential

client for Fergus's lucrative hotel trade. It shouldn't upset him, but it did. The note showed no warmth, no friendship, said nothing about herself, how she was, what she was doing, where she could be found. The terse, impersonal words hurt Fergus more than a slap in the face.

It was very cruel revenge for a stolen kiss.

Annie arrived in London in June, a fortnight before her sister's wedding. This suited Madeleine, who had hoped for time to improve the girl's provincial manners and appearance if necessary. She was agreeably surprised when her niece stepped off the train. The girl was smartly dressed, and lovely.

Madeleine remained in the background while the twins rushed to greet one another with hugs, tears, laughter and kisses. Watching the girls' unrestrained joy affected Madeleine more than she had expected. She wondered if she had allowed her own longing for a child to cloud her judgement, when she had separated her dead sister's twins. If only she had shown some patience and compassion, despite Annette's mud and mischief! How much happier life might have been for both Suzanne's little daughters!

'Come and meet Mummy,' Lisette said cheerfully.

Annie advanced cautiously, recalling previous disasters. 'I'm very pleased to be here on this happy occasion, Aunt Madeleine.'

'And we are delighted to see you, my dear!'

Madeleine would have kissed Annie on both cheeks in the French fashion, but Annie hastily dodged the unusual greeting. Her aunt laughed and made light of the awkward incident, but it was an unfortunate start.

London was still in party mood after King George and Queen Mary's Silver Jubilee celebrations in May. Madeleine had planned a series of parties in the days ahead to give Lisette's friends a chance to meet the Scottish sister.

Annie panicked at the prospect.

'I can't go, Lisette! I don't possess a party frock!'

'Borrow one of mine!' Lisette opened a wardrobe door and selected an emerald green gown. 'Try this on. You can keep it if you want.'

Annie touched the silk gown with a fingertip. 'Lisette, I couldn't!'

'Oh, go on!' her sister laughed. 'I shan't need it again. I'll be a married woman living in a country cottage, wearing jerseys and tweeds all the time.'

Lisette sat on the bed watching Annie try on the dress. It had been one of Lisette's favourites once, and it felt odd, watching a dark-haired image of herself. This would be how others saw her, yet it was not her true image. How deceptive appearances can be, she thought suddenly, with an odd little shiver of foreboding.

Lisette knew very little about her sister's life in Edinburgh, but she guessed it must be grim. She watched Annie twirl dreamily in front of the mirror. Her delight was touching and almost drove Lisette to tears. But she would not cry. She knew her twin would consider pity an intolerable insult.

When Annie was safely tucked up in bed that night Lisette made her way to Madeleine's room.

'Mummy, Annie doesn't complain, but I'm sure money's a terrible problem. I gather they can only afford basic accommodation and food. Aunt Connie must be in dire straits now they've been told the little boy has asthma and needs special care. We *must* do something!'

Madeleine, a vigorous campaigner for many London charities, felt duty bound to help her adopted daughter's less fortunate family. Thoughtfully, she removed her jewellery and put it away in its case.

'I agree we should do all we can to help them, darling. What do you suggest?'

'I can persuade Annie to select some of my old costumes and dresses. I've more clothes than I need, since I bought my trousseau.'

'Good idea, *chérie*! Annie will benefit from smart new clothes. Meanwhile I'll plan a few surprises for her to take home with her, some luxuries and gifts for Connie and the children.'

'Thanks, Mummy. You're a gem!' Lisette

hugged her gratefully. 'I'll leave it to you.'

Lisette's happiness knew no bounds in the sunlit days prior to the wedding. She and Annie were together, and Freddie completed the happy trio. Most days, he drove them around in his sporty red MG, with Annie squeezed into the back seat. They would leave the city behind and speed out into the green countryside. Carefree, they laughed immoderately, hair tousled as Freddie drove like the wind. They ate hungrily in quiet English pubs, lay sunbathing beside quiet streams, returning home tired but happy through misty dusk and emerging starlight, to the bright artificial lights of London's nightlife.

Madeleine was left to fret over wedding details arranged weeks ago by a determined bride.

Alors! she thought. Imagine Freddie's best man, the Cockney aeroplane mechanic, nanny Ruth and her policeman fiancé, sitting at the top table with Lord and Lady Asherwood! It could be a clash of backgrounds *absolument horrible*! However, on the wedding day it all fell smoothly into place. The morning dawned mild and sunny, its calm broken by an army of hairdressers, dressmakers and florists.

The results, however, were more than worth it.

Much later, a hush descended upon the house. Madeleine and Dermot waited hand in hand in the hallway for bride and brides-maid to appear. When the two young women came slowly downstairs, Madeleine burst into tears. She could not help it.

She was proud, happy, and yet ... so sad.

The light of her life was leaving them. How dreary the house would seem without her, though a marble fountain played and exotic orchids bloomed!

But Madeleine smiled when she greeted Lisette, beautiful in white satin, and Annie, vibrant in red. Contrast between the two identical beauties was breathtaking and remarkable. Madeleine only wished their mother had been spared to see them.

'Ready, girls? The car is waiting,' Dermot beamed.

He took Lisette's hand proudly, leading the girl he regarded as his very own daughter out into the sunlight.

Afterwards, Annie found, the actual cere-mony passed like a dream, but she did re-member admiration and goodwill mirrored on every face in the large congregation as she walked down the aisle behind Lisette and her uncle. She did remember how her heart ached, wondering if she would ever know the happiness her sister had found with Freddie.

The reception was a joyful affair, and Madeleine's fears about the seating arrangements proved groundless. Lady Asherwood and the best man performed the Lambeth Walk, and nanny Ruth and Lord Asherwood attempted a spirited tango, much to the delight of the watching guests.

Annie found herself surrounded by admiring young men.

'I say, Lisette's a dark filly!' cried one. 'She never told us she had an absolutely stunning Scottish sister! Where have you been hiding all my life, darling?'

She smiled wickedly. 'Knee-deep in mud and up to my elbows in dishwater!'

Her admirers thought this a hilarious joke. She wondered what they would say if they knew it was perfectly true...

The twins bade each other a tearful farewell before Lisette and Freddie departed for a leisurely honeymoon on the French Riviera. Both sisters knew from past experience that despite fervent promises to meet again soon, the sad truth was that the parting could stretch into months, even years.

'Be happy, Lisette!' Annie cried, as she hugged her sister.

Freddie laughed and kissed his new sister-in-law. 'Don't worry, we will be, Annie dear.'

The couple left amidst a shower of confetti and a clamour of good wishes, a string of old shoes and tin cans clattering and bouncing behind Freddie's red sports car. Annie stood looking abstractedly down the street, lost in her own thoughts, long after the noisy crowd in the doorway had dispersed. Shivering in the chill air, she remained on the white marble steps, alone and broken-hearted.

Madeleine came outside to find her. One look was enough to arouse pity. Madeleine understood only too well this desolate sense of loss.

'Come, dear child,' she said compassionately, and led her niece inside, into the warmth.

Nothing brought home more forcibly the gulf between riches and poverty than Annie's return to Candlemakers Close. She left a household where money was lavished without thought upon expensive luxury, returning to a home where every penny was precious.

'And you hired a cab from the station. Fancy that!' Connie exclaimed, impressed.

'Aunt Madeleine slipped the fare into my pocket at King's Cross and wouldn't take no for an answer.' Annie was down on her knees, unpacking the large new suitcase she'd been given, bulging with clothes and gifts. To cries of joy from Leah and Benny, she began handing out her aunt's carefully selected presents, along with tinned foods, perfume and sweets. Connie was clutching a large crystal bottle of French perfume, speechless with pleasure.

Annie rummaged further down in the case and produced a fat brown envelope, which she handed to her aunt.

'Aunt Madeleine told me this was specially for you.'

Smiling, Connie opened it and pulled out a folded sheet of notepaper. As she did so a sheaf of banknotes escaped from the envelope and fluttered to the floor. Leah dropped to her knees and began counting. She glanced up in amazement. 'Fifty pounds, Ma! Fifty!'

The colour left Connie's cheeks as she slowly scanned Madeleine's note. Annie stood up, suddenly concerned.

'Ma, what's wrong?'

'All this money, that's what's wrong!' Connie cried bitterly. 'That woman says that she and your pampered sister hope it will comfort me for the loss of my dear husband. As if it could, Annie! As if it ever could!'

In a storm of anguished fury, Connie picked up the crystal flagon of perfume and flung it at the wall, where it shattered into a thousand pieces, filling the room with a strong, sickly scent. She turned upon Annie, eyes blazing, trampling banknotes underfoot.

'They think they can throw money at sorrow and it'll go away. But it never does, Annie, it never will, and I pray wi' heart and soul those two will learn that hard lesson for themselves one day!'

Then she whirled round and left the disordered room, pulling the door closed behind her.

It had all happened so quickly Annie felt stunned. How dare Lisette do this to Connie? she thought furiously. Couldn't she understand how hurtful it was, how heartlessly cruel?

Six

After a subdued family breakfast, Annie returned to work next morning.

The day had dawned with a blue haze on the river which promised warmth, and she hesitated beside the suitcase packed with a selection of her sister's cast-off clothes.

Annie had been wakened in the night by Connie's sobbing, and her thoughts that morning were bitterly resentful, but her only summer dress was much the worse for wear, while a smart green cotton outfit lay invitingly on top of the suitcase.

Lisette had tossed it in the waste paper basket, but Annie had rescued it.

'No, you don't! This'll do for work!'

Her sister had looked astonished. 'That old thing? The milkmaid look went out of fashion months ago!'

Annie had laughed. 'Not in Edinburgh, it didn't!'

So despite last night's ugly scene, she had decided to wear Lisette's dress. Connie noticed at once, but merely tightened her lips. Leah ate breakfast, eyeing Annie accusingly.

Sensing discord, Benny began wheezing and required Connie's attention with the bronchial kettle. City dust and family squabbles sparked off quite alarming asthmatic attacks in the little boy, and Annie was glad to escape.

Outside, the sun shone, the trees were fresh summer green, and the crisp cotton felt cool against her skin. She even felt young and light-hearted, for once. Heads turned as she passed by and a young man whistled appreciatively.

Scorning the servants' entrance, Annie walked boldly in at the hotel's front door, to find Conrad Whyte seated at the reception desk. He looked up.

'So you're back!' He studied her, frowning. 'I hope you don't intend to work dressed up to the nines? I'd better warn you, the kitchen's filthy. The temporary cleaning woman didn't see eye to eye with the chef and walked out after he threw a tantrum and a dish of rice pudding.'

'Don't worry. I shall be wearing greasy overalls, as usual!' She departed for the kitchen, head high.

He wasn't exaggerating about the filth, she thought, surveying it. The horrible mess brought her down to earth. She sighed resignedly and reached into the locker for the overalls.

They were pristine white and neatly folded. He must have had them laundered while she was away. She was quite touched, till another possibility presented itself. Had he assumed she would not be returning and taken steps to

141

entice an older woman into the job? It would be just like him to do it sneakily, she thought.

She had finished the kitchen and was emptying boxes of rubbish into the bins in the back yard when a van pulled up alongside and the driver climbed out. She clanged the bin lid shut and turned round.

'F-Fergus!'

He looked grimly triumphant. 'So! Found you at last!'

Annie had believed herself perfectly safe. John had assured her that while he was the van-man, Fergus processed the orders for farm produce.

'What are *you* doing here?' she demanded.

'Trying out McGills' latest enterprise.' With a flourish, Fergus waved a hand proudly towards the side of the van, which bore a colourful legend in large lettering.

McGILL'S REFRIGERATED DELIVERY
FOR FRESHEST FARM FARE

'I spent a couple of months in America studying refrigeration techniques. When I came back I fitted a refrigeration unit to the van. It's still at the experimental stage, so I'm doing the deliveries.'

He moved in closer, trapping her beside the bins.

'Lucky I did, or I might never have found you, Annie dear,' he said, his tone low and seductive.

There was a devastating look in his eyes

which Annie remembered. The bins gave no room for manoeuvre, and she could feel herself weakening.

'You shouldn't be here, dear girl. You belong in green pastures,' he said tenderly.

'Those days are over, Fergus, I'm a city girl now!'

'Farming isn't any fun these days. I miss having you around.' He had moved so close she knew that if he kissed her now, she'd be lost. Since childhood, he'd held the power to lead her blindly into all sorts of mischief. Nothing had changed. One kiss, and she'd follow him to the ends of the earth.

'You should see Kilmuckety now, Annie,' he was saying softly, his hands on her waist, lips brushing her hair. 'The house is restored to its former glory and the farm is flourishing. Please, darling, stop working in this third-rate hotel and come back where you belong.'

His attraction was so powerful that in her weakened state it sounded like the fulfilment of a wonderful dream. It was a moment or two before his words registered and sudden indignation crept in, and the famous Balfour temper flared. So the wealthy McGills were pouring money into the loving home Bob Balfour had worked so hard to create and had died struggling to preserve! Of course Annie would be overjoyed to see Kilmuckety restored, but by Balfours, not McGills! Besides, what right had Fergus to criticize the hotel? Conrad was doing his best with limited resources. Yesterday she'd seen for herself the hurt and humiliation careless wealth can cause, and now she too had nearly fallen victim to it. Angrily, she gave Fergus a hefty shove.

'Go away. Leave me alone!'

He staggered back against the van and stared in shocked surprise.

'I'm not interested, Fergus,' she told him, breathing hard. 'My future's here, helping Conrad turn this fine old house into a first-class hotel.'

'Ah-hah!' He scowled. 'I might have known there'd be a man involved. But you and Conrad Whyte? Good heavens, Annie, the man's old enough to be your father! That's scandalous!'

'No, no, I didn't mean that. Conrad and I...' she began in dismay.

He cut her short. 'Spare me the sordid details. I don't want to know.'

He opened the rear doors of the van and clambered inside. She could hear him crash around angrily within, assembling Conrad's order.

Annie retreated to the kitchen badly shaken. Perhaps a violent clash had been unavoidable, she thought tearfully. His family background ensured that conflict was inevitable every time they met. She crept out of hiding only once Fergus had made the delivery and driven off. Conrad was in the cold store examining the goods. He looked pleased.

'These fruit, vegetables and meat are first

class, even better than those delivered when you were in London. You'll be pleased to learn I told McGill I'd be placing a regular order from now on.'

Her heart sank. Good news for the kitchen, not so good for her peace of mind.

'What am I to do with this money, Annie?' Connie demanded, when they were alone together in the flat that afternoon. She glared at the notes stacked on the table. 'I'd like to fling it back in their smug faces, so I would!'

'You can hardly do that,' Annie said. 'Why not open a savings account for Benny? It would put the money to good use for his future.'

Connie looked thoughtful. 'That's no' a bad idea, love. I wouldn't touch a penny myself, but maybe it's only right the wee lad should benefit.'

So Connie paid a visit to the bank, and Benny became the proud owner of a brand new bank book. He lost no time showing his latest acquisition to Leah.

'If I don't spend it, Ma says I'll be rich when I'm old.'

Leah turned truculently to her mother, who was dealing with a heap of ironing.

'Why should Benny have it all, Mam? I need new clothes!'

'You're old enough to earn good wages, love. Benny's not so fortunate, bless 'im.'

'It's not fair!' Leah wailed. 'If I were better dressed the cinema manager might make me the ice-cream girl.'

Connie paused. She was ironing her daughter's uniform. Leah was a fully fledged usherette now, in a pert pillbox hat. The green uniform trimmed with brass buttons suited neat little Leah very well, though it was fiddly to iron.

'What's an ice-cream girl?' she asked.

Obligingly, Leah explained.

'The ice-cream girl comes out in the interval and stands in front of the curtain with a tray of choc ices and sweeties. A spotlight shines on her, just like a film star. You have to be smart to be an ice-cream girl.'

Annie laughed. 'And muscular! I bet that tray of goodies weighs a ton.'

'Stop making fun of me, Annie!' Leah wept.

Annie had forgotten fifteen is a sensitive age. She hastened to make amends.

'Sorry, Leah love, I didn't mean to upset you. If you want to look smart I'm sure some of Lisette's outfits would fit you. You're welcome to try them on.'

But Leah was much too offended to abandon the huff. 'I don't want your awful twin's nasty cast-offs!' she yelled, and flounced out, slamming the door.

Connie sighed and went on ironing. 'Poor wee lass. Lisette and that Gregory woman have brought nothing but grief to this family!'

Annie was disillusioned and angry. She and her sister had grown close in the days before the wedding, but it seemed Lisette would never understand how it felt to be poor.

146

There was so much pride involved, and great tact should be used to avoid humiliation. Thoughtful gifts of food and little luxuries could be thankfully received without loss of face, but obviously Lisette and Mrs Gregory could not imagine how hurtful it was to expect a fistful of cash to comfort a widow's grief.

And to think Lisette had gone off on honeymoon in complete ignorance of the misery she'd caused! Someone should tell her, Annie thought angrily.

That night, she sat down and wrote to Lisette, filling the pages with bitter accusations. Pausing to read the letter through, she was startled by the venom it had unleashed. Annie's childhood had been filled with love in a close-knit, hard-working family, but even so it seemed resentment had been simmering for years, hidden beneath the surface.

A nearby clock struck midnight as she picked up the pen to end with a few heartfelt words...

You are more than a sister to me, Lisette, because of the special bond we've shared from birth. I believed that could never change, after the wonderfully happy time we spent together before your wedding, but Mrs Gregory says in her note that it was your idea to send that large sum of money as comfort for Connie's grief. As if it could! Surely you must recall how proud Connie is, and how much she loved Uncle Bob? It has

caused her so much distress, I find it impossible to forgive you, Lisette. You must apologize, or I will never speak to you again. It is very late and I have to work tomorrow. This letter is all blotched with tears, and I am in tears now, remembering the happy days we spent together, gone forever now. I hope that you are crying too as you read this. Tears are something we can share, at least...
   Annie

Lisette was blissfully happy. The sun shone and a warm wind ruffled her hair as Freddie's sports car sped through peaceful French countryside. Laughing, she stretched tanned arms above her head.

'I'm a Frenchwoman today, Freddie! I even think in French! Isn't it odd?'

'Quite baffling, my darling. My grasp of the language is of the schoolboy variety.'

He gave his wife a smiling glance. She looked even more beautiful than on their wedding day, if that were possible. She leaned across and kissed his cheek.

'When our children are born I'll make sure they're bi-lingual, my love. You will have to learn the language to join in the fun.'

Freddie turned his attention silently to the road and Lisette settled back in the seat, closing her eyes dreamily. Her thoughts had been dwelling on family ties. They had left their honeymoon hotel in Antibes two days ago to begin a long leisurely drive through

France, to the Channel ports. A childhood spent as an only child had left its mark upon Lisette, and she wished she had belonged to a large family. Then she recalled her father saying once, long ago, that the twins must never forget they had family links with Normandy. They were in that region now. She opened her eyes and sat up.

'Darling, you remember the town I showed you on the map, Sainte-Claire-en-Bois? Could we go there?'

'Any special reason?'

'My mother and foster mother were born there. Mummy insists there are no Lefevre relatives left, but I'm not convinced. There might be second cousins, or even a black sheep. If there are, I'd love to meet them.'

Freddie pulled into the roadside and unfolded a map.

'It's a bit of a detour, but it could be an interesting trip. Plenty of vineyards, plenty of wine!'

Lisette laughed.

'Sorry to disappoint you, love. The green areas are onion fields. Mummy told me once that the area's noted for superb onions. This is where all the onion Johnnies come from who ride round Britain on bikes, selling strings of onions.'

'OK, I'll settle for steak and onions then.' Freddie folded the map and set off along the chosen route.

They drove into Sainte-Claire-en-Bois in late afternoon. The shadows were growing long, and a group of elders played boules in leafy shade. The players paused, staring at the red sports car.

Freddie and Lisette were accustomed by now to the interest their car attracted. He pulled into the kerb and they sat and took stock of the town. Lisette felt quite emotional. Suzanne, her Maman, was only a fond childhood memory now, but Suzanne and her elder sister Madeleine had once walked these streets.

And yet Lisette knew nothing at all about their family background. Both sisters had married foreigners and left France, never to return. Even that seemed odd. Why had all contact with their French family been severed? Madeleine had never mentioned her parents, except to tell Lisette they were dead. How strange! Lisette would never forget her own mother, nor her father living in the Far East. She and James Balfour kept in touch by letter, and she had even brought his medal with her on honeymoon, as a good luck token.

'Not a bad town, quite busy. Onions must be selling well,' Freddie remarked. On the way into town they had driven past onion fields, with men and women working in the hot sun.

'How do I track down my Lefevre relatives, though?' Lisette wondered.

Freddie glanced at the elderly spectators sitting in the shade, watching the game.

'If in doubt ask an old 'un. They're bound

to know everything and everybody.'

It was sound advice. Lisette left the car and walked towards the group. She selected the most venerable, a bearded old gentleman, eyes bright as blackberries set in a weather-beaten face, hard-worked hands resting on the crook of a stout stick. She smiled.

'*Pardon, monsieur,* I am searching for relatives. Do you know anyone named Lefevre?'

She sensed immediate heightened interest within the group. Even the boules players paused to study Lisette.

'It is not a usual name in these parts,' the old man said cannily.

Her face fell. She was surprised how disappointed she felt. The old man's bright little eyes watched her reaction. '*Cependant,* madame,' he went on, 'there *is* a person of that name in this district. You will find him in Rue de l'Hirondelle, at number thirteen.'

Lisette was overjoyed. She was given clear instructions to find the address and thanked the old man profusely before returning to the car. He called after her.

'I hope number thirteen may be lucky for you, madame!'

The sound of the old men's laughter followed her, as Freddie drove off.

Number thirteen was a tall town house, its front door leading straight from the pavement. The lower windows had windowboxes overflowing with scarlet geraniums. The bright colours cheered Lisette. She reached for a polished brass knocker and rapped

151

twice. Freddie had stayed in the car. She turned and smiled and he gave her the thumbs up.

The door was opened by a young man she judged to be in his early thirties. He was dark-haired and brown-eyed, and Lisette's heart leapt. She was sure she detected a family resemblance.

'*Monsieur* Lefevre?' she asked.

'*Oui,* I am Dominic Lefevre. What do you want?'

'I am searching for relatives, *monsieur.* My mother was Suzanne Lefevre before she married my Scottish father,' she explained eagerly. 'Sadly, she died young and I was brought up by her elder sister, Madeleine Lefevre...'

He had remained unsmiling and quite expressionless. She found his attitude so unnerving she faltered. A child's voice called to him from within the house.

'*Papa, Maman* and I are winning the game! You must come quickly!'

She heard a woman's laughter, and imagined she heard a baby's cry.

'In a moment, Jeanne!' he called, then turned back to Lisette. 'Those names mean nothing to me,' he said indifferently. 'I'm sorry, but I can't help you.'

The door closed and she retreated to the car close to tears.

'No luck?' Freddie said

'None at all.' She shivered. Somehow the meeting had caused a chill. 'I thought there was a family resemblance, but maybe I imagined it. He wasn't exactly rude, just … not interested.'

Her husband kissed her.

'Cheer up, my love. So you have no onion Johnnies in the family tree. It's not the end of the world. We'll head out of town and find a peaceful inn to spend the night. I still fancy steak and onions…'

Lisette had forgotten her disappointment by the time they were on the Channel ferry heading homewards. Freddie had rented a country cottage deep in the English countryside, in the small hamlet of Meeting Oak, not far from the airfield where he was taking an advanced flying course. Freddie was already a skilled pilot, but his aim was to be a test pilot for a new breed of faster aircraft, still at an experimental stage. He had turned down his father's offer of a house on the Asherwood estate, where he could live while learning how to run the estate.

'Maybe one day, Pa, but not at the moment,' he'd said.

Freddie carried Lisette over the threshold, banging his head on an overhead beam. He rubbed the bump ruefully.

'It's smaller than we're used to, darling.'

'It's quaint. I love it!'

She bent down to pick up post that had collected on the mat. 'There's a letter from Annie! How thoughtful of her to send a welcoming note.'

She put the letter unopened on the table

and ran to help Freddie unload the car. It wasn't till they'd enjoyed a meal in their new home and were curled up together on the sofa that Lisette read her sister's letter.

Her expression changed, the happy glow faded and colour left her cheeks. Freddie was concerned.

'Darling, what's wrong?'

'Everything!' she cried wildly. 'Such terrible accusations, Freddie! Mummy's gift of money offended Aunt Connie, and Annie blames me. We only wanted to help the family through a difficult time, Freddie. How dare my sister accuse me of cruelty, when stupid pride is to blame for all this fuss?'

He gathered her in his arms as she burst into tears. She rested her head wearily against his chest.

'When Annie came to our wedding I thought it was the beginning of happier times for us all, Freddie. How wrong I was! I love my sister, but why does she say such terrible things about us, when Mummy intended only to be kind and generous? It's heart-breaking! Annie must apologize, or I will never speak to her again!'

She was worn out with crying, and Freddie sat quietly as she drifted off to sleep in his arms.

He was angry. He had liked Annie, but was not blind to her faults, which were possibly the result of her upbringing. Prickly pride was one, impetuous behaviour another, judging by stories of past misdemeanours. He could well imagine Annie sitting down after a blazing family row to dash off a furious tirade to Lisette. But he couldn't imagine Annie apologizing, or Lisette forgiving. One thing the twins shared was a strong stubborn streak. Good job they're living so far apart, Freddie thought, or sparks would undoubtedly fly.

Annie waited for weeks for a response from her sister. When winter came and the trees in the gardens were stark and bare, she knew waiting for an apology was useless. Lisette had made her feelings plain. Annie must make the first move. She would never do it, she vowed. The wounds went much too deep. All the same, she could not deny that sometimes she felt desperately lonely with nobody to confide in. She had even considered reconciliation with Fergus, because he had left another empty space in her life, but Fergus took meticulous care that deliveries did not coincide with Annie's shifts.

The Balfours faced another bitter Edinburgh winter, and events at home and abroad were as gloomy as the weather. George V, the sailor king, died in January 1936 aged 70, just six months after celebrating the 25th anniversary of his reign.

Britain had acquired a new, controversial monarch, Edward Vlll, the former Prince of Wales. Although the prince was popular with the general public, the government was less enamoured. It was no secret that he had fallen in love with a married woman, the captivating American Wallis Warfield Simpson, who was seeking divorce from her husband, and quite unthinkable that the new King could take a divorcee as his queen. The wrangle between King and Parliament dragged on through the spring, summer and autumn of 1936. Meanwhile, German troops in their thousands, backed by armoured cars and tanks, marched unopposed into the Rhineland.

By the end of the year King Edward had informed the nation by wireless that he could not perform the onerous duties of state without the support of the woman he loved, and next day, newspapers proclaimed, in glaring headlines, ABDICATION!

Annie paused for a moment on her way to work to read the billboards, then hurried on. She was late. Today she wore a dark green coat trimmed with ocelot fur and a matching ocelot hat, much too dressy for a woman on her way to clean filthy kitchens. Benny had taken a wheezing turn that morning and by the time the little boy's breathing had eased, Annie had time only to grab the first warm coat that came to hand amongst Lisette's cast-offs and set off at a run.

She darted breathlessly through the hotel's front entrance, which was quicker than going round to the rear.

Conrad Whyte was sitting at the reception desk as she rushed past.

'Just a minute! I want to speak to you.'

'Sorry I'm late.'

'There's no hurry. I want to discuss your work.'

She stopped dead. Here it comes, she thought with dread, the sack!

It couldn't have happened at a worse time, either. Connie was not well. The strain of cleaning a large cinema to her own standards was telling, and she fell prey to every bug going the rounds. She had insisted on going to work, though she had a sore throat and should have been in bed.

'I know I'm late, Mr Whyte. It won't happen again, I promise.'

'It certainly won't! I intend to make changes.'

So it *was* definitely the sack! She stood with chin up, waiting for the axe to fall.

'You're too young and smart to be cleaning kitchens, Annie...'

She interrupted desperately. 'I could wear old clothes. I could look a mess.'

He laughed. 'I'm sure you could, but that's not what I had in mind. A smart receptionist sitting behind this desk would be a vast improvement, don't you think?'

She stared at him, hope slowly dawning. Colour returned to her cheeks.

'You want *me* to be a receptionist?'

He nodded. 'The job's yours if you want it. It'll mean longer hours, but much better pay.'

'Oh, Mr Whyte, I'd be daft not to jump at the chance!' Annie cried joyfully. A sudden thought occurred. 'But you'll have to find someone to clean the kitchen.'

He frowned. 'That's true. But where will I find somebody with your high standards?'

Annie smiled. The kitchen job would suit Connie down to the ground, and be much less stressful. Annie could keep an eye on her, to make sure she didn't overdo it.

'Leave it to me, Mr Whyte,' she said, beaming. 'I know the very person!'

Christmas was coming, and in her new capacity as receptionist, Annie was kept busy with bookings. Connie had accepted Conrad's offer of the kitchen job and had handed in her notice at the cinema. The hotel's restaurant had gained a reputation for good food, and there was peace and harmony in the kitchen for the moment, while the chef and his staff warily took stock of a more formidable opponent, Connie.

Seated at Reception, Annie looked around with pleasure. She'd persuaded Conrad to decorate the entrance hallway with garlands of holly tied with red ribbons. It looked festive, and she and Conrad had enjoyed doing it, while outside in the street little Edinburgh urchins had sung a popular version of the old Christmas carol:

Hark the herald angels sing,
Mrs Simpson's pinched our king!

Conrad had met her eye, and they'd laughed together, companionably. Smiling, Annie

158

returned to checking the hotel register. A shadow fell across the book.

'Well, well! Glad to see you've gone up in the world, Annie!'

'John!' She gave a cry of pleasure and hugged her cousin. 'Are you doing deliveries again? Where's Fergus?'

'He has – er – other commitments now, Annie,' John answered a little awkwardly.

'I expect the farm keeps him busy,' she said brightly, but she was disappointed. Recently, she had been hoping they might meet to talk over old times, now she'd changed her job. She really missed seeing Fergus. He'd been part of her life for so many years, and it was hard to forget him. John brought a newspaper cutting out of his pocket and laid it on the desk.

'Actually, Annie, I've a bit of news for you. I thought you'd be interested in this.'

She read it slowly, because she found it difficult to take in.

It was a snippet from a recent *Forfar Dispatch*, announcing the engagement of Fergus McGill to Lady Audrey Elizabeth Lambert. *The wedding will take place in July*, it finished. John had been watching her. 'I'm sorry, Annie. You were keen on Fergus, weren't you?'

'Once upon a time. It's over now.'

She folded the slip of paper and handed it back. Why did she feel so cheated, though she had never met the lady who had won Fergus's heart? Why had the festive season suddenly lost its cheer?

159

Seven

Annie found the news of Fergus's engagement unexpectedly shattering. Recently, she had been considering cautiously renewing the friendship, for old times' sake. Now that was impossible, and she was broken-hearted. She was forced to maintain a cheerful front, however, for the sake of others. John was the delivery man now, and Connie's delight at seeing her son more frequently was some consolation, at least.

Persuading Connie to leave the cinema and switch to Whyte House Hotel had been an inspired move on Annie's part. Her aunt's cleaning prowess had impressed Conrad Whyte right away. Connie's cleaning was not confined to the kitchen quarters, but encompassed areas of the hotel where Minnie the housemaid had formerly wielded a desultory duster and sloshed an occasional mop. Now there was no mistaking the rejuvenation of paintwork, floors and furniture.

Fortunately, Minnie did not mind. She followed in Connie's energetic wake, dreaming dreams of Clark Gable.

Conrad was not one to dish out praise, but he

had given his staff a generous bonus this year when the dining room had been fully booked for relays of turkey dinners. Connie planned a peaceful family Christmas in the flat, with John and the two younger ones, but Annie had other plans. She had volunteered to help organize the extra dining-room staff Conrad had hired to serve dinners.

Leah had Christmas Day off, though celebrating in the flat with her mother and brothers was not her idea of Merry Christmas. She glared at Annie, who was smartly dressed and preparing to leave for what Leah imagined must be more lively entertainment.

'You're keen on this Conrad man, aren't you?' she said.

Shocked, Annie stopped in her tracks. 'Certainly not! Whatever gave you that idea?'

'You dress up to the nines to catch his eye. That's how you got promoted.'

Connie came to the rescue, patting Annie's shoulder. 'Never you mind our Leah, lovey. Mr Whyte's a fine-looking gentleman with a business at his back. You could do worse.'

'For heaven's sake, Connie, he's old enough to be my father!' Annie protested.

She was glad to leave the flat and escape to the street. The incident had revived painful memories of the quarrel with Fergus. There were tears on her lashes, cold in the chilly air. Why did her thoughts keep straying to him? Fergus was history now.

Conrad was hovering in the hallway when she

arrived at the hotel. A crystal vase filled with Christmas roses and sprigs of holly adorned the reception desk. Annie glowered at it with angry suspicion.

'What's the meaning of this?'

He looked at her blandly.

'Whatever you want.'

'Merry Christmas, I – I suppose.' Her temper had abated quickly in the face of his detachment.

'Same to you, Miss Balfour. The arrangement is icy beauty and thorns. The language of flowers is appropriate, I think. One look at you, and I get the message.' He headed calmly for the dining room.

She watched him go, then took her place behind the desk. She studied the flower arrangement. It was really beautiful. Rainbow-coloured sparkles of light reflected from cut crystal onto delicate white flowers and dark glossy leaves.

Icy beauty and thorns!

She couldn't help smiling. That was a back-handed compliment, if ever there was one!

Soon after the New Year festivities in Edinburgh had ended, Annie received word that her father had arrived unexpectedly in London. He cabled that he would be visiting Lisette in England, then travelling north to meet Annie.

She was excited and happy, though news of James's arrival had upset Connie, who was ashamed to be found living in such poor accommodation. She'd done her best to make the tenement flat a home, but it was still sadly lacking in the comforts her brother-in-law would expect.

'He can't stay here, Annie!' she said anxiously.

Annie's smile was understanding.

'Don't worry, Connie. I'll ask Conrad to book Dad a hotel room.'

Several days later, Annie was waiting nervously in Waverley Station for the London train to arrive. She had not seen her father since she was ten, though they'd kept in constant touch by letter. Occasionally he had sent photographs from Johore, showing a black-haired woman, a little boy, and a beautiful long, low bungalow with a shady verandah, set amidst exotic surroundings.

Annie had examined mother and son with mixed feelings. Strange to think these distant strangers were her stepmother and half-brother!

When the train steamed in and passengers began to alight, Annie spotted her father right away. He looked older of course, grey-haired and tanned, but her heart lifted, the years fell away, and she ran to him with outstretched arms.

'Dad!'

She had not realized how much she had missed him, as they hugged each other with tears and laughter. She rested her head against his shoulder and cried like a baby.

'It's strange, you know...' James Balfour smiled a little shakily, looking down at his tearful daughter. 'Lisette cried too the moment I appeared.'

Annie wiped away tears.

'No wonder. It's been years!'

'That wasn't my choice, Annie dear.'

She looked away.

'We were very young, Dad. We – we didn't know then that...'

She paused and bit her lip. He smiled sadly.

'That if you stayed apart it would end in a bitter quarrel?'

'So Lisette told you?'

He nodded, looking around for a porter.

'Where's this famous hotel?'

Annie was pleased to change the subject. She linked an arm through his.

'It's in the Pleasance, Dad, not far from Holyrood Palace. There are super views of Arthur's Seat from your room.'

'Well, that beats jungle any day!'

For James Balfour, returning to Edinburgh was a bittersweet experience. In this city he had known some of the happiest days of his life, and had experienced the most heartbreaking sorrow. Sitting in the taxi with his daughter by his side, he looked out at a city which had not changed all that much.

Early summer in Scotland! James thought. The day was pleasantly cool, the sky filled with clouds every shade of grey, silver linings where sunlight inched through. Glimpses of familiar streets he'd walked along with a laughing young bride on his arm brought tears to his eyes.

But enough of that!

'How's Connie?' he asked. Annie laughed.

'Keeping us all in order, as usual. Including my boss, Conrad.'

Her father gave her a sideways glance.

'Hotel work suits you. You look very bonny, and so *chic*, my dear.'

She smiled.

'Thanks, but I'm nothing special really. Conrad tells me a good receptionist should look neat, pack up her own troubles in her old kitbag, and smile, smile, smile.'

He let that pass, but he would be interested to meet this Conrad fellow. Annie had mentioned him frequently in her letters, and just now James noted a secret smile on his daughter's lips and a sparkle in her remarkable dark eyes.

Conrad Whyte greeted James at Reception, and shook hands cordially. Now that James had met his daughter's boss, he did not know what to think. The man must be at least twenty years older than Annie...

The room was beautiful, and the view wonderful. James sat on the window seat, revelling in the sight of dark, craggy hills. His daughter sat opposite.

'Connie's dying to see you, Dad. She's laid on a feast in your honour tonight.'

He turned away from the view and looked at her.

'We must talk first, Annie. I'm so sorry you've had a hard time of it, what with Bob dying unexpectedly and Connie losing the farm. Maybe I should have done more to help.'

She sighed.

'It's not your fault. We didn't know Uncle Bob was in debt. The farm had to go, and Connie and I did the best we could, moving to the city. It was hard at first, but things are much better now.'

He looked serious.

'Not for much longer, I'm afraid, my dear! There's certain to be war in Europe very soon. It's inevitable.'

'Oh, we've heard those rumours too, Dad. Nobody believes them.'

He looked grim.

'Unfortunately, they aren't rumours! We've had such unprecedented orders from the British Government for rubber, I became curious and made inquiries. They're manufacturing gas masks, Annie. One for every man, woman and child in this country.'

She sat in silence as the awful implications sank in. Soldiers in the last war had suffered and died horribly from poison gas. Surely it would never be used to kill innocent civilians?

She looked at him seriously.

'Dad...' she began. 'This isn't just an ordinary visit, is it?'

He shook his head.

'No. I want you and Lisette to leave Britain and come to Johore before it's too late.

Lisette has already refused. I can't blame her. She's newly married, and won't leave her husband. But you are unattached, Annie. You could come.'

'And leave Connie and her bairns? That's poor repayment for the love and kindness she's shown me!'

He sighed.

'If Connie has any sense, she'll come too. There's plenty of room.'

She turned away, flustered.

'I'll have to think about it, Dad.'

'Of course. Take your time. I have to leave soon, but the offer stays open till you feel ready to join us.'

If her father was dismayed when they arrived at Candlemakers Close that evening, he gave no sign.

Connie's welcome was warm as ever, and a sumptuous meal was ready. She cried copiously while hugging her dead husband's brother, the resemblance reviving some of the heartbreak. She dried her eyes at last, and smiled.

'Why didn't you bring your bonny wife and big son with you, James? We're all dying to meet them.'

He laughed.

'I'm sure you are, Connie, but Teresa has to keep an eye on the house and plantation. It's not unknown for unoccupied houses to be emptied of their contents in our neck of the jungle. Kim is nearly thirteen and very keen to come with me, but he's sitting scholarship exams which can't be missed. Never mind, I've brought plenty of photos.'

After the meal, they sat relaxing by the fireside while James produced a wallet of photographs, and handed them round.

'So this is Teresa!' Connie said, fitting on her specs. 'She's really bonny, James.'

Smiling, James handed Benny the photo of a young lad.

'This is your cousin Kim, Benny. He's a bit older, but you two would be good chums.'

Benny studied a stocky, barefoot, black-haired boy, scantily dressed in shorts and vest.

He was not impressed, but Benny was a kind little boy who hated to hurt anyone's feelings. He looked at the photograph, casting around for an honest opinion which would not sound too wounding.

'He doesn't look very Scottish, Uncle James.'

James laughed.

'Maybe not, but Kim's proud to be a Balfour. He speaks Japanese and Malay, of course, and English with a Scottish accent, like his dad.'

'Fancy!' Connie said. She had a pretty shrewd idea what her brother-in-law was after. He would never abandon hope of getting his daughters back. He had failed with Lisette, and had come to try his luck with Annie. She studied a photo of James's bungalow with tightened lips. Her dear Bob had never aspired to such luxury, remaining loyal to the old family home that had been the death of him.

'It's a lovely house, James, and much too big for the three of you. You'll be hoping to encourage visitors?' She looked him straight in the eye.

'We could accommodate all the Balfours in comfort, Connie. You and your bairns would be very welcome to make a fresh start in Singapore. I've warned Annie that this country could be on the brink of war.'

'And you'll be well out of it as usual!' she said with a sudden flash of anger. 'History repeating itself. Off to sea at the first hint o' trouble and leave others to pick up the pieces!'

He flushed.

'That's not fair, Connie.'

'Maybe not, but it's how I feel. I hope for your sake your bonny daughter consents to go with you to share a life o' luxury, because that lass is pure gold and she deserves a break. But me and mine will stay here, where we belong. And if that means surviving another war, so be it!'

James stood up abruptly, gathering scattered photographs.

'Thanks for the meal, Connie, and for making your feelings plain. I'll thank you to remember it was not I who separated the twins, while I was struggling to build a secure future for my daughters.'

He turned to Annie, who was sitting

stunned by the sudden unexpected twist of events. He kissed her cheek.

'I'll see you tomorrow, Annie dear. We can talk then.'

Then he was gone.

John Balfour had been tempted to join the family gathering to welcome his uncle, but had decided against it. More responsibility for the farm rested upon John's shoulders these days. Now Fergus's engagement was official, he had seemingly lost interest in farming. Which suited John just fine.

There was only one wasp in the jam. Miss Marigold McGill kept a tight rein on everything he did. She would turn up unexpectedly in fields, on hillsides, in the woodlands, riding the large snorting black hunter she favoured.

Even today, John felt the ground tremble to the gallop which heralded her arrival, as he and the dog stood contemplating the old cottage by the main road. He didn't look round as she reined in behind him.

'What are you doing, Balfour?' she called.

'Thinking.'

'About pretty little Davina Williams?'

She dismounted, leading the big horse forward. He glanced at her coolly.

'Yes, as a matter of fact. If the old cottage became a farm shop, Davina would do very well behind the counter.'

She frowned, studying the stoutly built cottage while Barney grovelled shamelessly round her boots. The dog's antipathy to Fergus did not extend to his sister. Barney adored Marigold.

'How much do you reckon it would cost?' she said.

'Not far short of one hundred pounds to do it properly, with shop-fitting and refrigeration.'

She whistled. John laughed.

'Oh, come off it, Miss Marigold! That's peanuts to your pa.'

She patted the horse thoughtfully. Then made up her mind.

'It's a jolly good idea, Balfour. It'd take care of farm surplus. I'll see what I can do.'

John grinned.

'Tell your pa his only loss'll be a bonny housemaid promoted to shopkeeper.'

She gave him a cold look, shoved the fawning Barney aside with a boot, and swung herself into the saddle. Wheeling the hunter's head round, she urged the horse into a canter, riding off up the hillside without a backward glance.

John watched her go. She certainly was not bonny, with her tousled hair cut any-old-how. All the same, he liked her better than her snobby married sisters, whose shining coiffures rivalled the film stars'.

That Saturday, he and Davina went to the pictures in Kirriemuir. It had been a choice between dancing in the Town Hall or a film show at the Regal, and Davina had opted for the pictures, having been on her feet all week, she said, waiting on the McGills.

John felt restless, however, and would have preferred dancing. Watching Fred Astaire and Ginger Rogers in an energetic musical didn't help, but the Pathé News which followed made him sit up and take notice. Japan was at war with China, and closer to home in Europe there were scenes of incredibly vast German armies marching in triumphant rallies. It was a sight that brought a sudden chill.

What if there was a war, he wondered; would he be forced to fight, or stay on the land as a key worker producing food for the nation? John suspected he'd make a mediocre soldier, but had already proved he was a damn good farmer. No doubt time would tell, he thought grimly as the programme ended and the lights went up.

John and Davina held hands cosily on the bus going homewards. Reaching Kilmuckety road end, they set off arm-in-arm to walk to the house.

All thought of war set aside, John was feeling blissfully happy. He was walking with the girl he loved and his head was buzzing with ambitious plans for the new farm shop. John was quite confident Miss Marigold would persuade her father to provide the cash for the venture. It was bound to be a success, he thought, and as long as the farm ran smoothly and showed a healthy profit, Mr McGill was perfectly satisfied. He and his wife were too busy socializing to pay much attention to farming matters. They were content to leave that side of the business to their son and youngest daughter, and John, of course.

Davina glanced up at him curiously.

'You're awfully quiet tonight, Johnny.'

'Sorry, love. I've rather a lot on my mind.'

She laughed. 'No wonder. I saw you with Miss Marigold in the lower field. She's a bossy one. What was she after this time?'

He slipped an arm round her waist, eager to tell her what was on his mind.

'I was telling her about my plans for the old cottage. I've persuaded her to ask her pa to put up the cash for renovations.'

She whirled round with a delighted cry and flung her arms round his neck.

'Johnny, darling! How long before it'll be ready for us to move in? We'll have to set a date for our wedding!'

Chilled to the bone, he held her in his arms. He loved her dearly, but had no plans to marry her just yet. He wanted to work hard and save enough money to give them a better start in life. He'd had his sights set higher than living in the old cottage, and now he was in a fine pickle. It was cruel to disillusion her, but it had to be done.

'Davina, pet, the cottage isn't for us...' he began hesitantly, then reluctantly explained what was planned.

It broke his heart to watch her joy turn to humiliation. It was a heart-rending moment. He held her close.

'But you were always part of the plan, sweetheart. You'll do no more skivvying for the McGills; you'll be in charge of the shop.'

She broke loose furiously, and stared at him in the moonlight.

'So I'm supposed to be grateful for that crumb of consolation, am I? After being told you loved me and making me think you meant it! I bet you enjoyed watching me make a proper fool o' myself tonight. Well, it won't happen again, John Balfour, because you won't get the chance. We're finished! Find someone else to look after your shop, I'd rather be a skivvy.'

'No, Vina! Please listen to me—'

He tried desperately to reach out to her, but she avoided the embrace, gave him a withering look and hurried off along the smooth tarmac, her slim figure soon lost in darkness.

Connie turned up for her shift at the hotel next day, ready to give her brother-in-law a few home truths, if provoked. Conrad, finely tuned to moods, took one look at Connie's warlike demeanour and deduced that there had been an almighty family row. He gave Annie the day off.

'Take your father out for the day. Let him visit his old haunts,' he told her.

Delighted, she took his advice.

It was a delightful June day, warm but not too hot, a cool breeze stirring trees in Princes Street Gardens as father and daughter walked along, arm in arm. There were church bells ringing somewhere, and James Balfour paused to listen.

'That's St Andrew's in George Street, if I'm not mistaken! Your mother and I attended that kirk, when my ship was in dock in Leith.'

'I still treasure your war medal, Dad,' Annie said.

He looked pleased. 'Do you really, my dear? Lisette tells me she's kept hers safe too.'

They left the gardens and walked along busy Princes Street, then followed the sound of bells up a gradient towards the New Town, an area of beautiful Georgian terraces.

'Ahah! There's a wedding on. That explains the bells,' her father exclaimed as they approached the church.

Annie halted suddenly, filled with a horrible premonition. She knew Fergus intended marrying his Lady Audrey in June, in Edinburgh. What if...?

'Let's go to Leith. You'll want to visit the harbour, Dad,' she suggested hastily, tugging at his arm.

'I'll take a look at the kirk first, Annie. Your mother and I were married in France, but we exchanged vows in the vestry here because she wanted to be a Scottish bride. I'm glad there happens to be a wedding on today. Ours was a quiet wartime affair, but this will bring back happy memories.'

There was a tear in his eye, and Annie said no more.

They arrived at the edge of the crowd just as the bride and groom emerged from the ceremony. The bride was beautiful, the bridegroom handsome in full Highland dress.

But it wasn't Fergus.

Annie's reaction was revealing, however. It made her realize with a sickening sense of loss that she loved Fergus, had probably been in love with him for years, and had lost him because of her own foolishness. He'd offered her the chance to follow him to the ends of the earth, and she'd walked away. Secretly, she had been confident there would be a second chance.

But she was wrong.

Watching clouds of confetti fly in the breeze, Annie choked back tears. Her father glanced at her.

'Let's go on, shall we?'

They walked in silence, heading for the river. The fishy, oily harbour smell came to them on the wind as they entered the ancient port of Leith.

'Have you given any more thought to the future, my dear?' he asked.

'Yes, I have. I do intend to make my home with you and Teresa, Dad, but first I must see Connie and the family settled more comfortably. I have to move them out of Candlemakers Close somehow. The flat's cold and damp, and Connie shouldn't be taking her turn at scrubbing the stone stairs, down on her aching knees. I'm afraid it'll take time to find something suitable which she'll accept. She's so fussy and proud, bless her!'

'Annie, I'm in a much healthier financial

position these days. Please let me help her.'

'Heaven forbid!' she smiled ruefully. 'Sorry, Dad, but I had enough trouble dealing with Madeleine Gregory's heavy-handed charity!'

He sighed and shook his head.

'Connie's pride! It's admirable, I suppose, but I never dreamed it would be such a stumbling block. Don't wait too long, Annie dear. I won't rest till you're safe in Malaya with us.'

'Don't worry, Dad.' She stood on tiptoe to kiss his cheek. 'I agree it's time I moved on.'

And she meant it.

Lisette had expected married life to be blissfully happy.

But it wasn't.

Stuck in the tiny hamlet of Meeting Oak, Lisette was bored, friendless and lonely. Freddie left for the airfield at seven-thirty and didn't return till late evening. Weekends were not much better. He was tired and preoccupied and never wanted to take her out, and they had some stormy rows. Fortunately, the joy of making up was almost worth the heated arguments.

Lisette looked forward eagerly to her foster-mother's frequent visits. It was an opportunity to chatter endlessly in French, and catch up on London gossip.

Madeleine drove a little Morris coupé these days. Dermot had bought it for her, so that she could keep in touch with their daughter. Madeleine enjoyed driving the little car. It made her feel young, independent, and 'with it'. Besides, she was worried about Lisette, who seemed depressed and aimless and had lost all her sparkle.

Today, Madeleine studied her over the rim of the coffee cup, then replaced it carefully in the saucer.

'Is everything all right, darling?'

Lisette hesitated.

'Well, no, Mummy. It isn't.'

Tearfully, she revealed the full extent of the boredom and loneliness which was turning her into a discontented, nagging wife. No wonder Freddie stayed away!

Madeleine frowned.

'Are there no young women your own age in this place?'

'Yes, but they're either career women working in London, or young mothers with no conversation but babies. I don't fit in.'

Madeleine selected a biscuit.

'You could, if you were one of the group.'

'Mummy!'

She laughed. 'Oh, I know being a grand-mother makes one seem impossibly ancient, *chérie*, but I would simply adore it. I would spoil the little darlings most shamefully.'

Lisette had to laugh, visualizing this fashionable lady nursing sticky-fingered little rascals on her elegant lap. All the same, it was an appealing picture, worth considering. She and Freddie had grown up as only children despite the fact that she had a sister. It would be rather wonderful to have a large family one day, to redress the balance.

The idea lingered in Lisette's mind after her mother had gone. She became excited about it. Having a baby would change their lives completely. Freddie would make a wonderful, doting father. Arguments would magically cease. There would be children playing in the garden, a little group of mothers sitting chatting and laughing in the summerhouse, and she would be one of them. Loneliness would be a thing of the past.

She took special care with dinner that evening. Freddie was late, and looked exhausted, but she greeted him, radiant and smiling. He kissed her, a little startled.

'You look wonderful, darling. What's wrong?'

She laughed.

'Nothing, silly! I just feel happy. Mummy was here today.'

He smothered a yawn.

'Oh yes? What's for dinner? Smells good.'

After the meal, Freddie revived. He offered to help wash the dishes.

'No, darling, leave them for now. Let's talk.' She pulled him down onto the couch.

'What about?' He grinned and put an arm around her.

Lisette kissed him tenderly.

'Babies, Freddie. Don't you think it's time we had one?'

His expression changed.

'No, I don't. No babies, Lisette!'

She sat up and stared. His lips were set in a

grim, stubborn line, eyes dark and shadowed.

Lisette was indignant.

'How selfish can you get, Freddie Asher-wood?' she said cuttingly. 'It's all very well for you, going off to that wretched airfield every day, lazing around and boozing in the pub with your RAF chums. What about me? I sit here with nothing to do and nobody to speak to, bored to tears!'

He stood up suddenly, towering over her. She had never seen him so angry.

'You have absolutely no idea of the contribution these gifted designers and technicians are making to aeronautics, Lisette! They work round the clock with scarcely a break, perfecting this small, fast, fixed-wing aircraft. I feel privileged to be one of the test pilots.'

Lisette laughed scornfully. 'So they aim to win the Schneider Trophy for Britain, do they? What a waste of time and effort! Honestly, Freddie, aeroplanes are all you ever think about. My longing for a child takes second place with you, doesn't it?'

'Yes, my darling, I'm afraid it must.'

She stared at her husband in disbelief. Didn't he love her any more? Had he met someone else? Someone who understood his passion for flying – someone who didn't grumble and nag and long for babies?

'Oh, Freddie! What's happening to us?' she cried brokenly.

He stood looking down at her in silence, and she was shocked to find that her brave, laughing, loving Freddie, was in tears ...

Eight

Connie had decided a life of luxury in the Far East was not for them, but fortunately Leah had quickly overcome any feelings of disappointment. Edinburgh in the summer of 1938 was all set to outshine even the attractions of Singapore, and Leah was enjoying life.

However, her cousin was still swithering about leaving. Leah loved Annie like a sister, but was impatient with her dithering. Leah usually knew exactly what she wanted and set out to get it, but Annie had already lost a golden opportunity to marry rich, handsome Fergus McGill, and was stuck with Conrad Whyte, who was ancient, at least forty, and quite boring.

That was Annie's hard luck.

Leah's life had taken a decided turn for the better. The cinema was showing a selection of wonderful films this season, and audiences were huge. There were long queues for each performance of the Marx Brothers' *A Day At The Races*, and after that the auditorium was packed with parents and children for *Snow White And The Seven Dwarfs*, Walt Disney's first full-length cartoon film.

And to cap it all, the manager decided to make Leah the Eldorado ice-cream girl. This promotion was the height of her ambition.

He'd revealed he'd had doubts about the wisdom of his choice, at first. It had been a toss-up between Leah and Phyllis McLuskey. Phyllis had height and considerable bulk, but Leah was slender, wiry, and had won hands down on personality and charm. The manager had made his mind up to give the little lass a trial and see how she fared.

The fully loaded tray of choc-ices, ice cream cartons and goodies was heavier than Leah had bargained for, but she was determined to make a success of the unique opportunity and did not grumble. She endured weals on her shoulders and back inflicted by the harness and on the first night looked quite dazzling, enhanced by lipstick, rouge and eyeshadow bought secretly in Woolworths and applied liberally. Her mother would have half-murdered her, had she known.

But it was a dream come true, Leah thought ecstatically, as she stood in the proscenium that first evening, with a spotlight falling upon her while soft music played and every eye in the house fastened on her. The audience obviously thought she was the next best thing to a film star. Bathed in a golden glow, Leah moved dreamily forward to meet her customers, the admiring spotlight still in attendance...

'I'm worried sick about Leah, Annie,' Connie

admitted one evening, busy ironing soon after her daughter's debut.

Annie was engrossed in the Edinburgh *Evening News*, known affectionately as 'the pink' because of the unusual colour of newsprint. She glanced up at her aunt.

'Why? She seems perfectly happy.'

'I know. It's not like our Leah to be perfectly happy.' Connie folded a newly ironed pillowcase. 'And she's been wearing make-up, Annie. There were lipstick stains on this very pillowcase.'

'Connie, *I* use lipstick!'

'Och, yes, dearie, but you're not sweet sixteen! Do you think Leah's got a boyfriend?'

Annie laughed.

'We'd have heard all about it, if she had.'

'Not if the lad's unsuitable,' Connie retorted. 'She knows I'd raise the roof.'

Annie frowned. That was true. Connie's disapproval would be fearsome to behold. She did her best to add a word of reassurance.

'Maybe she doesn't want to talk about being in love; it's a sensitive subject at her age. Maybe she's shy.'

'Leah? Shy? Och, Annie...!' Her aunt snorted incredulously, iron arrested in mid-air. 'A lass who can face gawping rows of filmgoers wi' a tray of ice cream slung around her neck will not be bashful,' Connie declared emphatically.

Leah's elevation to ice-cream girl was an alarming development, in Connie's opinion.

When working in the cinema she had overheard hair-raising tales about flirting between bold young lads in the audience and ice-cream girls. The other usherettes had whispered and giggled about it. Shameful, it was!

'Well anyway, I don't think there *is* a boyfriend on the scene,' Annie said. 'Leah walks home every night with the other girls as usual. You can hear them laughing and carrying on a mile away, and I've never seen Leah so happy.'

Connie sighed.

'Aye. That's what worries me. There'll be a lad lurking somewhere behind this ice cream lark, you mark my words!'

Edinburgh had been one of the few Scottish towns to experience air-raids during the First World War, and when Annie heard the news that the City Engineer was inspecting basements and tunnels as locations for public air-raid shelters, her heart sank. Maybe the Corporation was taking the threat of war too seriously, but all the same she must soon make up her mind about joining her father in Singapore.

Connie was all for it. 'It's the chance o' a lifetime, lovey, what's stopping you?'

Annie hesitated. There were many reasons for her reluctance, mostly centred around concern for Connie, Leah and young Benny.

'I want to see you settled in a better place first, Connie. This flat's cold and damp.'

'Och, away! It's cosy once the fire's lit.'

Annie sighed. No mention of heaving buckets of coal from the cellar, up tenement stairs! This was an argument she could never win. Besides, deprived of the cash Annie contributed, Connie would struggle to pay rent even on this poor apartment.

She prepared for work, buttoning her jacket. The first hint of autumn was in the air, and the wind was chilly.

Conrad was hovering beside the reception desk when she arrived, a sure sign he had something to say.

'I've been thinking...' he began.

Annie took her place behind the desk and waited, admiring today's arrangement of fresh flowers, a heavy-headed second flush of late roses. Their perfume was gorgeous.

'The dining room's fully booked all week, isn't it, Annie?'

She nodded. 'We've had to turn dozens away.'

The volatile chef had fallen in love with the fishmonger's daughter. Love had exerted a calming influence upon the kitchen and wrought a magical improvement in the restaurant's menu. The chef's fish pie was out of this world.

'I've decided to enlarge the dining room,' Conrad said.

'But how?'

Annie was intrigued. She could see no possible room for expansion.

'I'll have the partition wall removed be-tween my living quarters and the dining room, that'll make the dining area twice as large.'

She stared at him in amazement. 'But where will you go?'

He smiled smugly.

'To the top of the house, my dear! I want to hire an architect to make the attic rooms habitable. No doubt Connie will be pleased to see the back of all the junk. She's been nagging me for months about the state of the third floor.'

His present quarters were to the rear of the hotel, overlooking the yard, and it would be much nicer for him living upstairs, Annie thought.

'That's a splendid idea!' she cried delightedly.

'Do you really think so?' he said softly.

Something in his voice made her pause.

'Why, yes ... of course...'

'I hoped you might.'

She met his eyes. She had grown to like Conrad, but had not learned to understand him. Then a thought struck her. Was it possible that Conrad nurtured warmer feelings for her? He was looking at her just a little too intently. She looked away, her gaze falling upon the latest flower arrangement.

'The ... the roses are red,' she noted blankly.

He smiled. 'Yes, my dear. The roses are remarkably red, a vivid and full-blown second flush. I thought it rather an apt choice, myself.'

Silently, she eyed the heavy blooms.

Unwelcome thoughts of her first love came leaping to mind, bringing pangs of regret which were still very painful. Would she ever forget Fergus and be able to move on? Could she face life with this attractive older man whom she did care for, but did not love? Was it fair to Conrad even to consider it?

She'd had no news of Fergus McGill for months. Even John had no idea where he was, though it was rumoured that Fergus and Lady Audrey had married quietly in London and were now living abroad.

Conrad was watching her closely. He was not surprised to see that Annie Balfour looked stunned. He felt stunned himself, to find he was in love with her. Love was something he had never expected to happen again, after his darling wife died eight years ago. He had been an officer serving with the army at that sorrowful, dreadful time. So Conrad had left the army and bought the Edinburgh hotel, mainly because he and his wife had made plans to run a small hotel together when he retired.

So he'd struggled on alone, morose and embittered, until a beautiful young girl walked in one day and captured his heart...

However, Conrad Whyte was not a man to spoil the first fragile moments of courtship with displays of emotion. He was satisfied he'd said enough for now. Holly had prickles and roses had thorns, and he knew Annie Balfour should be handled with kid gloves.

He stepped back and became businesslike.

'I've decided to close the hotel for a fortnight, Annie, starting next week, so please don't accept any more bookings. There'll be mess and disruption while builders remove walls and clear attics. I'll be on hand to keep an eye on everything, of course, but I've decided the hotel staff can take a holiday with pay.'

He looked at her, and his smile was tender. 'A fortnight without you will seem like an age, but it will give you a little breathing space. When you come back, you'll find the foundations for a fresh start for all of us will be in place.'

He turned away and went into the office, closing the door. Annie watched him go, the heady scent of mature roses drifting around her. He had made her aware of his feelings in a way that was typical of him, and rather endearing. All the same, knowing that he cared for her threw her into a panic.

She had enjoyed working at the hotel, and had been pleased to watch the business prosper. But that had been for Connie's sake, not her own. Annie had wanted to make sure her aunt had a steady job to look forward to.

As for herself, she could easily escape from this awkward situation by contacting her father and arranging to leave for Singapore...

Lisette and Freddie's marriage had struck a particularly bad patch that summer. A large happy family had been part of Lisette's plan for their future, and it was heart-rending to

188

discover that her husband did not share her dream.

Talking it over honestly might have resolved the difficulty, but conversation was guarded and skirted carefully around the real reason for frequent rows. Freddie spent more time at the airfield these days. An urgency had crept into these visits, and Lisette's imagination played jealous tricks. She was sure he'd become involved with another woman.

With that suspicion in mind one fine morning, she made a last desperate attempt to win him back.

'Couldn't you take time off, Freddie? It's a lovely day. We could drive somewhere and have a picnic.'

He paused for a minute, then shook his head.

'Sorry, Lisette. Can't be done. There's a problem with the plane which must be sorted.'

She lost control and screamed at him.

'I loathe that damn stupid plane of yours, Freddie Asherwood!'

He looked at her sadly. 'My darling, you don't know what you're saying. You've made no attempt to understand the importance of what I do.'

Then he drove off at dangerous speed in the sporty red car in which they had once been so happy. It was very late when he returned and she was in bed pretending to be asleep, the pillow wet with tears. Where had it all gone wrong?

The spell of fine warm weather ended and thick dark clouds drifted in. The sky turned bruise-black, there was not a breath of wind and the air lay heavy, hushed and still.

Lisette didn't mind the threat of an approaching storm, because Freddie couldn't fly in those conditions. He would come home early for once, and it would be a chance to make amends for her bad temper. She was busy all afternoon, preparing a special dinner.

Time passed as she waited impatiently. It was prematurely dark, thunder grumbled in the distance, lightning flashed far off. She ate a lonely meal, her annoyance so intense she could hardly taste it. She put the remnants in the oven to keep hot, and hoped they burned to cinders.

Freddie turned up after ten o'clock, weary and heavily coated in engine oil.

'Sorry, love. We stripped the engine down to the last nut and bolt. I'm pretty confident I know now why the plane stalls at awkward moments.'

She shrugged indifferently. 'I'm off to bed. You'll find the charred remains of dinner in the oven.'

She ran upstairs and cried herself to sleep. She did not stir when Freddie quietly joined her, much later.

The storm broke over Meeting Oak in the early hours, with a tremendous peal of thunder and a brilliant flash of lightning which wakened her suddenly, terrified. She had always hated thunderstorms. She screamed and reached out for her husband.

'Freddie...!'

She lay shaking and trembling in his arms. He kissed her and she clung to him as another thunderous peal shook the cottage. He silenced her frightened whimpers with kisses, and between kissing and the crash of thunder, she could talk to him at last, whispering in the eerie, flickering light.

'Freddie darling, I'm sorry, I've been so selfish and mean, thinking only of myself. Of course you couldn't stand sleepless nights with howling babies and demanding toddlers. No man could!'

He held her closer as the cottage shuddered to another mighty peal.

'Sweetheart, I do want a family, but is it fair to bring children into a world on the brink of war? Their father would be in the thick of it, too. The future's too uncertain, my darling!'

Lying cheek to cheek, Lisette's heart lifted. So that was the only reason for his reluctance! She smiled. 'Freddie dearest, the future's *always* uncertain, yet babies are born. Life must go on, my love.'

He was silent for a minute, then laughed outright. 'You're quite right, of course. I've been an idiot. Why be afraid of something that may never happen? Let's be reckless and let tomorrow take care of itself!'

'Yes! Oh, yes!'

She had found her brave laughing, loving Freddie again. Lisette threw back her head and laughed, as another vivid flash lit the room. How recklessly wild and beautiful she looked in the strange flickering light, Freddie thought in awe, and how much he loved her! Then the thunder pealed, the little cottage trembled in sudden darkness as he sought her mouth unerringly, and they kissed...

Lisette's new-found happiness gave her fresh zest for life. She made a determined effort to tame the overgrown garden, and in the process made friends with neighbours. As her energy and enthusiasm grew, she began to think seriously about offering her services to the local school next term, to teach French. It would be lovely working with children, till they had children of their own.

Meanwhile, the garden took up much of her time. The storm had cleared the air and the weather remained cloudy but dry. Perfect gardening weather. She was on her knees dealing with stubborn weeds when a distant rumble broke the afternoon peace. Lisette smiled and glanced up at the sky. She was not afraid of thunderstorms now, she welcomed them.

Freddie would be grounded, and might come home early.

But he did not come.

Lisette was not unduly worried. He'd told her about the problem with the fighter aircraft. It tended to be difficult to control during certain high-speed manoeuvres, and it was vital to get to the root of the difficulty.

She understood the importance of Freddie's work as a test pilot now, smiling to herself as she ate a solitary meal later on. He'd explained with a grin that her rival for his affection was a fast little lady called Miss Spitfire.

She was not perturbed when there was a tap at the door. She'd locked it as time went on, and Freddie often forgot his key. She ran to open it for him, laughing.

But it was not her husband. Puzzled, Lisette recognized George Morton, Freddie's Station Commander. She stared at him, wondering what on earth he was doing here at this time of night. And suddenly, she was afraid.

'Where's Freddie?'

He hesitated. 'May I come in, Mrs Asherwood?'

She stood aside.

He was a nice man, very kind. Gently, he told Lisette about the accident that had killed her husband. She listened quietly in the cosy sitting room, and could not cry.

Deeply concerned, the RAF man took her hand. It lay lifeless in his. This was a wretched business. He hated being the one to beak such awful news, but it was his duty to do so, and Freddie had been his good friend.

'He was the bravest of the brave, ma'am,' he told her. 'He dared to test the aircraft to the limit, and told us exactly where the fault lay. Now we can fix the problem for other pilots. When the plane failed, we urged him to bale out, but he deliberately stayed at the controls

193

to guide the aircraft safely past a densely populated area. He could've saved himself, Mrs Asherwood, but instead he chose to save many other lives.'

Perhaps it was not thunder she had heard that afternoon, she was thinking. Perhaps it had been the devastating final impact that had killed her husband.

Her life had spiralled from happiness to emptiness, all in the space of an afternoon.

The Station Commander was watching her anxiously. He had expected tears, but her calmness seemed unnatural and much more disturbing.

'Will you be all right? Can I arrange for any of your family to be with you?'

Family? What family? Lisette thought dully.

'Thank you. You're very kind, but I'd rather be alone,' she told him.

Days later, after all the necessary formalities had been completed, Lisette Asherwood cleared the rented cottage of personal items, packed a suitcase with bare essentials and stowed it in the car boot. Then she climbed into Freddie's sporty little red car and drove off without a backward glance...

Conrad's estimate of two weeks for demolition and reconstruction proved to be over-optimistic. Annie and the staff returned to the hotel to find builders still busy, a thick layer of dust over everything, and chaos. Conrad was unperturbed. He soothed the chef with promises of updated equipment and sent him off for another week in the company of the fishmonger's daughter.

Conrad grabbed Annie as she stood in the doorway.

'Come and see upstairs!'

He was as excited as a schoolboy. She had intended handing in her notice, but hadn't the heart to spoil his delight. Besides, there was less urgency about the trip to Singapore at the moment. Her father had cabled that he was scheduled to be in America for two months, discussing supplies with tyre distributors.

Recently, everyone had breathed a sigh of relief when Prime Minister Chamberlain signed a peace treaty with Herr Hitler, the German Chancellor. The threat of war had receded.

Annie had decided she could afford to wait a little longer, to see Connie and her family happily settled.

Following Conrad upstairs, she was amazed to see how spacious the third floor was, now that the junk had gone and walls and woodwork had been freshly papered and painted. The attic area had been split into two separate apartments, each with its own facilities and superb views of Arthur's Seat and the city. Conrad was installed in one and workmen were putting finishing touches to the other.

Annie was impressed.

'This is wonderful, Conrad!'

'I knew you'd like it.' He surveyed the view with satisfaction. 'It's peaceful and private up here among the clouds. It could be a love nest, don't you agree?'

She met his eyes, and was shocked to find herself blushing. She turned away in confusion.

'Now let me see the dining room, Conrad. I bet Connie will have her work cut out when she comes back, cleaning up the mess.'

Another week of hard work saw an amazing transformation, and Whyte House Hotel was ready to reopen. The refurbishment had created a great deal of interest, and Conrad's special opening offers ensured heavy bookings.

Annie was seated at the reception desk on the opening night when the phone rang.

It had been ringing steadily all day, but this time it was Madeleine Gregory, with the tragic news of Freddie's fatal accident.

Annie was distraught. She had liked Freddie immensely, and he and Lisette had been so much in love. How strange that she, an identical twin, had had no inkling of tragedy. Had she and Lisette really grown so far apart?

'Annie, have you seen Lisette?' Madeleine went on urgently. 'Is she with you?'

She was startled.

'No, of course not! Isn't she with you?'

Madeleine's reply was choked with tears.

'No. She does not want her mother and

father, who love her so dearly. We do not know what she wants, *la pauvre petite*. She says she will leave the cottage, and now we have no idea where she will go, or what she might do.'

The poor woman broke down, sobbing at the other end of the line.

Annie murmured awkward words of comfort. She was concerned and distressed. Once, she would have been allowed to share her sister's grief, been given some indication what her twin might do. Now there was nothing there but cold, blank emptiness.

John Balfour's plans for the farm shop were well advanced by spring 1939. The roadside cottage was painted inside and out, fitted with shelving, counters and a cold store.

An area of the lower field had been levelled and surfaced for car parking, surrounded by shrubs, hedges and wooden seating. John hoped customers might stop there for a while, to enjoy home baking and sweets for sale. There might be tea and coffee later, if John could find someone to dispense it.

He aimed to have the enterprise up and running soon. There was only one snag. He had not won back his lost love, Davina, who had been an integral part of the plan, an attractive, welcoming presence behind the counter.

Davina still worked at the big house, promoted to head housemaid. She was polite when they chanced to meet, but that was all.

John had not given up hope of a reconciliation, but the opening date wasn't far off, and he was growing desperate.

Miss Marigold had taken a keen interest in the project from the start. She had persuaded her father to fund the enterprise handsomely, by letting her parents assume the idea was hers alone.

Mrs McGill was pleased and proud, boasting to friends about her shrewd, gifted daughter.

'The dear girl is not interested in fashion like your modern misses,' she declared. 'She's much too busy running the estate, and is a fine horsewoman into the bargain. She would make such an admirable wife for some lucky man!' She would smile, casting hopeful glances towards any wealthy, titled landowners who happened to be listening.

Marigold was twenty-four. High time she caught somebody's eye!

She turned up in the farm shop while John was tinkering with the refrigeration unit in the cold room. He glanced up. Instead of the usual jodhpurs, hacking jacket and riding boots, she wore skirt, jersey, string of pearls, silk stockings and high heels. Her gingery hair was neatly brushed. She had neat legs and slim ankles, he noted with surprise.

'No horse? Or is it parked in the car park?' he asked.

'Of course not! I walked,' she snapped. She looked hot, bothered and ill at ease.

He set the controls and closed the cold

room door, before turning to her with raised brows.

'Walked, in those shoes. Why?'

She took a deep breath.

'Look here, Balfour, you have to accept Davina Williams is a lost cause. She's a brilliant housemaid and good housemaids are rare as hen's teeth. Mother would never let her go to serve in your shop.' She paused and then ended in a rush, 'So – so I'm offering my services behind the counter.'

He laughed outright. 'You?'

'Yes, me!' She scowled ferociously. 'I can count. I won't stand any nonsense from customers, and I'm reasonably presentable, aren't I?'

There was something quite fragile about her, which he found touching.

'Oh, yes, indeed. You clean up nicely and the pearls add a touch of class. But what will your ma say, Miss Marigold?'

She grinned. 'Nothing. She wants to curry favour with you.'

'What on earth for?' John was seriously alarmed. Mrs McGill was a formidable lady.

'She's been approached by the authorities to take in evacuees if the worst comes to the worst. Of course she doesn't want to take in any scruff from the slums. She asked me to sound you out about your little brother.'

He stared at her. 'Benny?'

'That's him.' She nodded. 'From what you've said about him, he could do with a little fresh air in his lungs.'

'Yes, so he could,' John agreed thoughtfully.

Benny had not had a good winter. The Edinburgh fogs did not agree with him, and he was pale and thin last time John saw him. But stay with the McGills in their showy palace? Poor wee lad! Wouldn't that be leaping off a midden into a bonfire?

He frowned doubtfully. 'I'll need to see what my mother says, Marigold.'

'But you will let me work in the shop, won't you, John?' she coaxed winningly.

'OK, if you must,' he agreed absently, having little idea of the trouble he was storing up for himself.

When the suggestion was put to Connie, she went nearly frantic. She voiced her doubts and fears to her niece.

'I know the Corporation's planning to evacuate bairns if there is a war, Annie,' she said worriedly. 'I wouldn't want Benny anywhere near the city if there are bombs falling, but I'd like a say in where he's to be sent.'

'Isn't Kilmuckety the perfect solution then, Connie?' Annie said. 'He'll remember his surroundings, and John can keep an eye on him.'

Her aunt wiped away a tear.

'Och, I know! But it's just I grudge my wee laddie to the rich McGills. It's you and Lizzie all over again.'

'Not really. Benny's older and he's an independent wee chap. His health is bound to improve in the country and he'll have friends in the Kirrie school who'll remember him.'

'Aye, there *is* that.' Connie looked more cheerful. 'They're saying some Edinburgh schools will close, if there aren't air-raid shelters for the bairns. What a to-do, Annie dear! Thank heavens you'll be safely out of it with your dad. But how will I manage without my wee Benny to keep me cheery?' Tears streamed down her cheeks.

Annie hugged her fiercely. 'Maybe it will never happen. Maybe the Germans will withdraw their forces. Maybe there won't be a war after all...'

Next day at work, Annie nibbled a sandwich at her lunch break. She was anxious and saddened after last night's conversation, and had no appetite for food. She threw the rest to the pigeons and went walking.

Workmen were digging deep holes in the park. Puzzled, she paused to watch. One of the men wiped sweat from his brow and rested his arms on the spade.

'Booking your place, are ye?'

Uncomprehending, she stared at him, and he laughed.

'In the shelter trench, lassie! This one'll take fifty if there's an air-raid. We've been digging at Pilrig, in the Meadows, and at Portobello. The cellars under the YMCA are fitted out to take two hundred.'

She walked on, upset by the encounter. Freddie's death had made the danger seem very real. How could she abandon Connie and those she loved, and keep an easy mind?

How could she leave Lisette to grieve alone? It would be impossible! And yet her father was urging her to come quickly. Time was running out.

Conrad was waiting when Annie returned to the hotel. He looked at her and frowned.

'What's wrong?'

She had to talk to somebody. Then, perhaps, she might know what to do for the best. So she told him of her fear, and the dilemma she faced, holding nothing back. When she'd finished, she was in tears.

He had said little, while listening intently. Now he put an arm around her, led her into the office and closed the door. He seated her at the desk and poured a small glass of brandy.

'Here. Drink it. Medicinal purposes. You're shivering. I suspect you've had no lunch.'

Ashamed, she wiped away tears and sipped the brandy. It soothed and warmed her. He perched on the edge of the desk and waited.

'So what's to be done about you?' he said quietly at last.

She shook her head hopelessly.

He leaned forward and took the empty glass from her.

'There is a simple solution, you know. Connie could act as hotel housekeeper and live rent free with her family in part of the third floor. I don't deny there may be a risk of air-raids, but we have cellars which should be safe, even with a direct hit. It all depends on you, Annie dear.'

She stared at him.

'Me?'

'Yes, of course. I love you so very much. Would you give up the idea of leaving Scotland, and marry me instead?'

He took her hand, raised it diffidently to his lips and kissed it. Annie was touched and startled by the unexpectedness of the proposal. Her thoughts were left in utter chaos.

She had suddenly realized that, whether intentional or not, what he was offering was a form of blackmail. If she refused to marry him, would Connie and her family be denied a wonderful chance to leave Candlemakers Close?

Nine

'I hadn't planned a whirlwind courtship, Annie dear,' Conrad said. 'But I love you, and I could lose you. Going to Singapore would be a disastrous move.'

She turned to him angrily.

'I thought you liked my father!'

'I do. It's the thought of you living there that scares me.'

She frowned.

'I can't imagine why! Dad says it's a fabulous place, and well defended.'

'I'll grant him that! Massive guns protect Keppel Harbour from attack by sea. But what if an enemy sneaks in the back door?'

Annie laughed.

'Let him try! There's nothing there but jungle and swamp.'

Conrad looked at her seriously.

'My dear girl, nothing could be farther from the truth! My regiment was stationed in Singapore for six months, and I'd plenty of time to explore the surrounding district. There are good roads linking rubber plantations to the major ports, and accessible jungle tracks which infantry could use. The island's vulnerability sent a shiver down my spine.'

'Nonsense! Dad wouldn't ask me to go out there if it was so dangerous.'

'But what if he and I see things differently? Your father's a seaman, on the lookout for attack by sea. I'm a soldier, looking at the possibility of assault by land. Germany and Japan signed a pact of mutual co-operation recently. Invasion of Singapore Island is a very real threat, Annie dear.'

She met Conrad's eyes uneasily. Despite politicians urging appeasement, the Nazi Party in Germany was growing ever more aggressive. If there was war, and Japan became involved, her father, stepmother and half-brother in the Far East could be in danger.

'Somebody should warn them!' she said.

He shook his head.

'They wouldn't listen. My CO asked me to draw up a detailed report outlining Singapore's weaknesses. He handed it to the naval authorities, but the regiment was warned to stop undermining public confidence.' He paused, and sighed. 'And now it's too late, my darling. I don't believe even you could convince your father of the danger. You'd be wasting your time.'

She faced him tearfully.

'Stop frightening me, Conrad! You're only saying this to make me marry you. If I refuse, I expect Connie and her family will get no help from you. It's a cruel form of blackmail!'

He stared at her in utter amazement.

'Whatever put that thought into your head?

Connie can have the rooms, no matter what you decide. Go to Singapore if you must, but do you really believe I'd lie to you?'

'You – you'd let me go?' she asked hesitantly.

He came round the desk and gathered her in his arms.

'My dearest girl, I love you. All I want is to marry you and spend the rest of my life with you. If you leave I'll be devastated, but it must be your decision, not mine.'

She rested her head against his shoulder.

Icy beauty and prickles, full-blown red roses and thorns! she thought. Had he found a pathway to her heart? Annie sighed. Ah, but she was weary, and his arms so warm and comforting!

She had spent sleepless nights worrying about Connie's future and Lisette's disappearance. So busy worrying about people she loved, she'd given no thought to her own future. After Fergus's rejection, it hadn't seemed to matter.

But of course it did! Time was passing, she would soon be twenty-four. She must make the most of life. Her father had loved her mother dearly, yet after she died he had sailed half round the world to find a new life and a new love.

However, that course did not appeal to Annie. Perhaps her reluctance to move to the Far East had been telling her so.

With a sudden optimistic lift of heart and spirit, she decided that happiness and contentment might yet be found, right here in Edinburgh, in the caring arms of an older man.

Conrad planted a light kiss on top of her head and she raised her eyes to look at him. His expression was not difficult to read today. It was warm and tender, softened with gentle humour. The look of love in his eyes made her feel breathless.

'So what do you say, sweetheart? Will you stay, and marry me?'

Annie answered without the slightest hesitation.

'Yes, darling Conrad, of course I will!'

He whooped like a schoolboy and whirled her crazily round the office. Then, giddily, Conrad Whyte and Annie Balfour sealed the momentous decision with a most satisfactory kiss...

Connie beamed when Annie told her.

'Best news I've heard for many a day!'

Leah too was delighted by the prospect of a wedding in the family.

'You'll be a gorgeous bride, Annie, and what about a bonnie wee bridesmaid?' She smiled hopefully.

'You'll be my first choice, Leah!' Annie promised, laughing.

But her thoughts had gone immediately to her twin. She wanted Lisette by her side when she married Conrad. A wedding without Lisette was unthinkable, but nobody knew where she was. Poor Madeleine Gregory was sick with worry.

'Have you chosen the ring yet?' Leah asked eagerly.

'Yes, it's a family heirloom. Conrad gave it to me this afternoon.'

She held out a hand, and they examined a beautiful antique diamond and ruby ring, set in heavy gold.

'Oh my, it's beautiful!' Connie breathed.

'Yes, isn't it?' Annie nodded happily. 'It belonged to Conrad's grandmother and mother. His wife wore it, too.'

Her aunt looked up, brows raised.

'And you don't mind?'

'Of course not. Why should I?'

Connie hesitated. 'I thought you'd choose your own. Start off as you mean to go on.'

'Conrad did offer to let me choose a ring, Connie.' Annie smiled. 'But why spend a fortune when there's a perfectly beautiful ring going begging?'

'Aye ... we-ell. True enough,' Connie said dubiously.

She busied herself setting the table. The ring's troubled past did bother her. Conrad's wife had worn the ring, and had died young. It was maybe a daft notion, but the thought sent a shiver down her spine. Connie would much rather the slate was wiped clean, but she would not spoil the dear lassie's pleasure by saying so...

When Connie returned to the refurbished Whyte House Hotel, she was shocked by the amount of cleaning to be done.

'Heaven help us, what a mess!'

Then Conrad led her upstairs to the third floor and revealed his plan for her family's future. She clasped her hands and stared at the transformation, quite overcome.

'Oh, Conrad, it's lovely!' she gasped, wiping away a tear. 'Self-contained and cosy, with a gas fire in every room. I don't know how to thank you.'

He smiled.

'Well, I'm hoping you'll accept the job of hotel housekeeper, so save the thanks till you see how we get on. I'm a dour devil and hard taskmaster, as Annie found out, bless her! Still there'll be no more lugging heavy buckets of coal for you, and your wee lad will breathe easier up here.'

Connie crossed to the window and looked out across the city. Some of Edinburgh's finest views were marred by the ugly blocks of brick and concrete public air-raid shelters. She shivered. Would her family be safe up here, if the bombers came?

'I'm thinking I'll still let Benny be evacuated though, if there's a war,' she said. 'They've told us parents that his school doesn't have air-raid shelters for the bairns.'

She turned to face her boss, soon to become one of the family. She was glad he was a mature older man, and not the young charmer Fergus Macgill Annie had set her heart on. True to type, Fergus had rejected her and left the lassie on the shelf. Typical!

'When were you thinking of getting married?' she asked.

'We haven't set a date. It's all been rather sudden, Connie, but I couldn't let her leave for Singapore without telling her how much she means to me. Fortunately, she wants to marry me, and I'm the luckiest man in Scotland.'

He smiled. Such a lovely warm, happy smile, Connie thought. Pity he didn't show that side of his nature more often.

'Aye, well, don't dilly-dally too long, dear. I don't believe in long engagements,' she said.

'Don't worry, I won't!'

Connie was reassured. The man loved Annie and would care for her and make her happy. The Balfour family's future had taken a turn for the better despite all the talk of another ghastly war, she thought...

On Friday 1st September 1939, the 11-inch guns of the German battleship *Schleswig Holstein* unleashed a devastating barrage of shells upon a Polish military transit depot at Westerplatte, an act of deliberate aggression which the British Government could no longer ignore. They issued an ultimatum to Herr Hitler: *Order the withdrawal of troops from Poland by the time stated, or face the consequences!*

That same Friday, as instructed by those in charge of the evacuation of children from danger zones, Connie took Benny to the station to send him off to Kilmuckety. Mrs

McGill had said she'd be delighted to have Benny, which had eased Connie's qualms somewhat. Transport had been arranged for him, on a train set aside for local evacuees bound for Forfarshire and the North.

Heart-rending scenes greeted mother and son when they arrived on the platform. Weeping mothers hugged crying, bewildered children. Teachers, volunteers and city officials bustled around, trying to bring order out of bedlam.

Benny, though paler than usual, remained calm, carrying his small case. He wore a luggage label strung around his neck, with identification and destination in large letters:

BENJAMIN BALFOUR
McGILL, KILMUCKETY ESTATE, by
KIRRIEMUIR, ANGUS.

Connie's heart was aching painfully, although she was outwardly cheerful.

'Did you put the sandwiches in your case, son?'

'Yes, Ma.'

'Keep the apple for after, lovey, and eat the sandwiches before you reach Dundee, 'cause you'll miss your dinner,' she instructed him. 'There's a clean hanky in your trouser pocket. Mind and use it, Benny!'

She hugged her son fiercely as a harassed schoolteacher bore down upon them. The woman read the label.

'This child's for Forfarshire. Come this

way, please.'

She led Benny towards a group of boys and girls being herded into a compartment.

Connie watched as Benny followed obediently. She saw him seated with the rest, clutching the small case on his knees. Apart from sandwiches, it contained camphorated oil to rub on his chest, toothbrush, pyjamas, underclothes, socks, gym shoes and a change of clothing. His little white face was turned towards her as the train started to move. Connie felt her heart break in small agonized pieces, but she swallowed heartbreak and smiled and waved as if she hadn't a care in the world.

She didn't start crying till the train had steamed out of the station and out of her sight...

Benny was relieved his mother hadn't made an embarrassing fuss, but would have felt more cherished if she'd shed a discreet tear or two. She'd seemed delighted to see the back of him.

Crushed tightly into a compartment with children of all ages, Benny comforted himself that maybe she was happy because she'd saved his life. Leah had told him that when German bombers came, Edinburgh would be blown to bits. She'd seen it happen to towns on film, in the Pathé News.

Consoled, he sucked the menthol lozenge his mother had popped in his mouth before departure to clear the airways, and looked around with interest.

He liked the train. The journey would be across two bridges, Ma had told him. The Forth Bridge was one, the Tay Bridge the other. Leah had told him the Tay Bridge fell down once upon a time when a train was crossing, and everyone drowned. Benny wished he'd been put nearer the door. The boys squashed next to him on either side gave him suspicious glances.

'What you chewin'?' one asked.

'It's medicine.'

'Toon Cooncil gave us biscuits. What you got?' another demanded.

'Sandwiches.'

There was a moment's startled silence.

'Are you posh, or somethin'?' a little girl asked curiously.

Benny shook his head.

'No, but I'm going to a posh place. Where are you going?'

'Dunno.'

Tears welled up and ran down the little girl's cheeks. She wiped them away dolefully on her sleeve. One of the boys muttered gloomily.

'It's a gamble who'll take us Cowgate scruff, my ma sez. We'll be the losers, she sez, like Pa on the horses.'

Benny's kind heart went out to his new-found friends. He longed to see them happy and settled like himself.

'You could come to the posh place with me,' he suggested eagerly. 'I'm sure they won't mind, 'cause it's a big farmhouse with plenty room. I know, 'cause I was born there,' he ended proudly.

Smiles broke out on grubby faces. It did his kind heart good to see it. The little girl dried her eyes, dug in a coat pocket and offered him a nibbled slice of limp bread, thinly spread with jam.

'You can tak' a bite o' my piece, if you want.'

Benny reached into the case and pulled out a lovingly wrapped package.

'Anyone like a sandwich?' he beamed, and was almost knocked over in the scramble...

Saturday 2nd September 1939 had been such a strange day, Leah thought as she made her way home that night. The news on the wireless that morning was depressing, and throughout the day cinema newsreels had shown guns and tanks advancing across Europe, and British Army reservists packed onto trains and sent off goodness knows where.

Yet in many ways it had been a perfectly ordinary Saturday.

That afternoon on the way to work, she'd pushed her way through crowds heading for the Hearts versus Motherwell football match. Outside the cinema, there had been long queues waiting to see John Wayne in *Stagecoach*.

All perfectly ordinary, except that the spotlights illuminating Leah and her tray of ice creams shone red, white and blue instead of warm gold. The bright colours confused her and she feared she might miss her footing and fall. Fortunately, the audience raised a loud patriotic cheer which steadied her. Then, later, an announcement flashed upon the screen. The firing of the one o'clock gun from Edinburgh Castle would be discontinued until further notice.

This was greeted by a moment of stunned silence, then uneasy muttering. For years the boom of the gun had been a reminder of the city's turbulent history. From now on, eerie lunchtime silence would mark the ending of peace.

A blackout was already in place as the usherettes walked home arm in arm. There wasn't the usual fun and laughter. They grumbled, stumbling over hidden obstacles.

'And the war hasn't even started yet!' Leah groaned, stubbing her toe.

'Don't worry, it will!' said one of her friends gloomily. 'Mr Hitler's grown too big for his boots. He's marching all over Europe.'

'Me and my boyfriend planned to get married next year,' another girl sighed. 'I s'pose it won't happen now. He'll have to go and fight.'

'Hard luck!' Leah said sympathetically. 'I suppose I'm jolly lucky to be fancy free.'

Her friends looked at one another, significantly.

'But you're not, Leah! Don't you know you

have a secret admirer?'

She stopped in her tracks, astonished.

'Who?'

'Ah, that would be telling!' they teased. 'Go on – work it out for yourself!'

'You're kidding! Fine chums, you are!' Leah feigned disgust.

Laughing, she linked arms with her friends, and continued through the darkened city streets towards Whyte House Hotel.

The move from Candlemakers Close to Conrad's hotel had earned Leah's hearty approval. The third floor flat was beautifully furnished, blackout blinds and curtains in place. Three comfortable bedrooms accommodated her mother, Annie and herself, and a quaint little turret room had been Benny's favoured eyrie. Leah furtively wiped away a tear. Her little brother had been packed off to Kirriemuir yesterday and she would miss him terribly. How she hated the horrible threat hanging over everyone!

Putting on a more cheerful face, Leah entered the sitting room. She found her mother in tears, and Annie providing comfort.

'I felt so hurt, Annie!' Connie was sobbing. 'Benny was as cheery as you like, while other bairns were breaking their hearts. You'd have thought he was glad to see the back of me!'

Annie hugged her. 'He was just putting a brave face on it, Connie. He wanted to protect you. You know what a thoughtful wee lad he is.'

Leah sat down on the sofa beside them. 'Annie's right, Ma. I bet Benny cried himself to sleep last night.'

Her mother let out a heartbreaking wail. Annie shot Leah a warning look.

'Of course he'll miss his ma, Connie dear,' she soothed. 'But maybe Mrs McGill told him a story and kissed him goodnight. She asked for Benny to come specially, so she must like little boys. No wonder, after all those daughters! Don't you remember how she doted on Fergus, when he was small?'

'I mind she dressed the poor wee mite like Harry Lauder, for the kirk,' Connie recalled with a watery smile. She dried her eyes, looking more cheerful. 'I wish you'd set a date for the wedding, Annie. That would give us something to look forward to, now the news is so awful.'

'I'm still trying to contact Lisette. I want my sister to be there.'

'Sister in name only!' her aunt declared indignantly. 'Not so much as a postcard since her poor man was killed! I don't deny it's a terrible tragedy, but Lisette should remember there's others involved besides herself. She was always a spoilt, selfish little madam!'

All those not sitting in a kirk pew in Edinburgh on the morning of Sunday 3rd September 1939 were glued to a wireless set. But the Prime Minister, Neville Chamberlain, did not have good news for the nation. The

217

ultimatum set for Germany's withdrawal from Poland had been ignored, and Britain was at war.

Up and down the old High Street, frantic mothers flung windows open and yelled to bairns on pavements below, 'The war's on! Come awa' home for your gasmasks!'

The German Luftwaffe took a great interest in areas around the River Forth, whose ports and harbours offered an anchorage for ships of the Home Fleet, and whose unique bridge provided a vital link between north and south. Scotland was considered a soft target, easily reached from Europe across the North Sea. Spitfires based at RAF Turnhouse retaliated quickly, however, and German bombers, out-manoeuvred by fast fighter aircraft, very soon dubbed the area 'Suicide Corner'.

Annie was growing anxious about Conrad's situation. She was afraid he might be called up because of his former military experience, and she didn't know how she would cope without him. The hotel, with its reputation for excellence, was heavily booked, but wartime restrictions were already causing problems. The seas were mined and dangerous, and some items of food were scarce already. News from British forces fighting in France was not good.

'You won't have to fight, will you, darling?' she asked Conrad worriedly.

He smiled and kissed her. 'No, sweetheart. I expect I'll be exempt this time because of my age, and having a business to run. Army and Navy top brass like dining here. It's handy for the harbour and barracks.'

Annie was reassured. Her affection for Conrad had developed into love, a gentler, less demanding passion than she had felt for Fergus, but love all the same. His dry humour amused her and his integrity and business flair were impressive. Conrad seemed content to wait till Annie felt the time was right to marry, but she knew that his love for her was true. After a stormy, heartbreaking 'affair' with Fergus, Conrad's quiet steadfast love was something Annie cherished.

With the outbreak of war, Conrad's staff problems eased. The Belgian chef, distraught by events in his homeland, married the fishmonger's pretty daughter and settled down to married life in Scotland. Connie's elevation to housekeeper ensured the hotel was spotless and customer service ran like clockwork. Even Minnie the cleaner was a reformed character. She abandoned rakish Errol Flynn in favour of the charismatic cowboy and soldier John Wayne. Minnie strode around upstairs rooms purposefully, wielding mop and duster, on the lookout for bad guys.

The first winter of war was exceptionally severe, bitter weather accompanying increasingly bad news from France. It seemed nothing could stop the Nazi *Blitzkrieg* or 'lightning war'. By May 1940, Belgium and the Netherlands were under Nazi control, and British and French forces were slowly retreating towards the Dunkirk beaches.

The only hopeful sign was news that a coalition British government had been formed, headed by Winston Churchill as Prime Minister.

Earlier, Glaswegians had raised a cheer when the unfinished ocean liner *Queen Elizabeth* slipped quietly out of Clydeside, painted the colour of the sea and with decks blacked out, racing safely across the Atlantic to Pier 90 in New York, another refugee from the tides of war.

Edinburgh and district suffered many air-raids that July, when the threat of invasion was at its height, after the evacuation of British and French troops from Dunkirk. There were fires and bomb damage throughout the city, and Connie was glad Benny was out of danger and thriving in the country air.

'He seems happy enough, bless him,' she remarked wistfully to Annie. 'And I've a better opinion of Mrs McGill, Annie. In fact, I take my hat off to her, taking in another six evacuees, as well as Benny. There's not many fine ladies would give house room to six of Edinburgh's roughest and toughest.'

Annie smiled.

'I believe they turned up on her doorstep, so she'd no option but to accept them, or lose face in the community. Apparently nobody had volunteered to take them so Benny took pity and brought them with him, John tells me. He says her grand house is a shambles.'

Smiling, Annie waved goodbye to her aunt and set out for the shops. She was searching for pepper and some other spices which had become scarce now that U-boats were disrupting convoys. It was a pleasant summer day with only thin cloud obscuring a hazy sun as she walked towards Princes Street. As she paused and glanced at the sky, air-raid sirens began their undulating wail.

'Drat!' Resignedly, she joined the rush for an air-raid shelter in Princes Street, and crowded into the concrete-smelling gloom along with many others. She managed to find a seat on the wooden slats. A soldier squeezed in beside her, uncomfortably close. She had opened her mouth to object when he spoke.

'I can hardly believe it! It's you, Annie!'

'Fergus!' The shock of recognition was so great she felt faint. 'What are you doing here?'

'Trying to pluck up courage to come and see you.'

He grabbed her left hand and stared at it. As it happened her fingers were ringless today. Conrad's engagement ring was much too precious to wear on shopping trips.

'So you didn't marry Mr Whyte!' he said. She pulled the hand away angrily.

'That's none of your business, Fergus! You're married.'

'As a matter of fact—' He stopped abruptly. They all heard the unmistakable whistling sound of a bomb descending. This one sounded too close for comfort. Fergus flung an arm round Annie protectively. The shelter shook to a resounding 'crrrump!' A woman screamed, a baby cried, and an older man remarked, 'That'll be Leith harbour again!'

Annie shoved Fergus aside.

'Get off me! I'll tell Lady Audrey!'

'You'll have a problem. She's in Australia, happily married to a sheep farmer.'

She stared at him in the grey gloom, noticing the change in his appearance for the first time. He was older, thinner, more grim, and his rank was not that of an officer, as she might have expected, but a private. She felt bewildered.

'She's not your wife?'

'No. She's a nice girl, but my heart wasn't in it and I told her so. She didn't mind. She'd already fallen for her Aussie bloke. They got married in London.'

Annie was suddenly angry. She wanted to pound her fists against his chest, hurt him somehow for the pain he'd caused. She gripped the coarse khaki of the battledress tunic.

'Why didn't you tell me?'

'Because I thought you would marry Mr Whyte. You led me to believe you might, and your cousin John seemed to think you'd be daft not to, so I volunteered to go to Spain to fight Franco and his fascist mob. We didn't win, of course. I was wounded, captured, and nearly died in a wretched prison camp. I was repatriated to hospital in Hastings with all the other poor crocks. I joined the army when war was declared and this is my first home leave. All I could think about when I reached Edinburgh was you.'

'How kind!' she said scathingly. 'Conrad and I will be married soon. If you hang around long enough, Fergus, you can come to the wedding.'

Revenge is sweet, they say, but this was bitter.

He looked at her gravely.

'Do you love him?'

'Of course I do! He's good, kind ... and faithful.'

Faithful! The word lingered between them, like an echo in the crowded, ugly space. Fergus sat motionless for a minute, then sighed.

'I can't claim goodness or kindness after my exploits in the Spanish civil war, but I *am* faithful after a fashion. I've never stopped loving you, Annie.'

Their eyes met, but she looked away quickly. They sat in silence, close together, yet far apart.

Presently, the All Clear sounded and there was a buzz of relieved conversation and even a little laughter. Everyone streamed outside into bright sunshine. Annie would have followed, but Fergus grabbed her arm.

'No. Wait!'

Soon they were alone. She turned to him, frowning.

'What is it? What do you want?'

'Only this!'

He crushed her in his arms and kissed her passionately. Shocked, she struggled at first, but it became impossible to fight the power of her own feelings for him. She shut her eyes and abandoned herself to the eager longing for his kiss. She had waited so long for this, so many months, so many years...

At last he broke away from her clinging arms and held her at arms' length. He looked down at her, breathing unevenly.

'So, Annie Balfour! Marry your faithful Conrad – if you dare!'

Then he was gone, leaving her distraught and shivering. Presently an ARP warden glanced in to check the shelter and found her there.

'You all right? The danger's over, lass.'

'I'm fine, thanks.'

She pushed past him, but she was anything but fine. She felt panic-stricken, not by the bombs that had brought destruction to Leith that afternoon, but by the irreparable damage done by one unfaithful kiss. How could she marry Conrad with a clear conscience?

She loved him dearly, and could not bear to hurt him, but she must tell him what she'd done. It was only fair.

Was it possible she loved both men, for very different reasons? she wondered. Conrad offered the stability and contentment she craved, but her love for Fergus had deep-seated roots stretching back into early childhood. She knew she could never forget his last soul-searching kiss. She shook her head in utter confusion. How could she choose between them?

Her immediate panicky reaction was to run away. Annie could understand now why her twin had chosen to disappear from a situation too heartbreaking to face. The difference was that Annie could think of nowhere to disappear to. She felt trapped.

Walking briskly, swallowing tears, Annie headed along Princes Street.

It was business as usual in the main street. Some shop windows had been boarded up since the outbreak of war, others disfigured with criss-cross tape. Many doorways were shielded from bomb blast by walls of sandbags, but one shop front in particular caught her eye and she stopped dead.

A recruitment centre! Could this be the answer? She pushed open the door and walked in.

The staff welcomed her with open arms. A smiling woman officer took her details.

'The way things are going after Dunkirk, your age group could be called up soon anyway, Miss Balfour, but we look very favourably upon volunteers. Are there any family connections with the Armed Forces, do you have any preference?'

'Only that my father served at sea during the Great War.'

'The Women's Royal Naval Service should be an obvious choice for you, then.' The recruiting officer consulted lists. 'There are vacancies for W.R.N.S. stewards and kitchen staff at the moment, and I note that you have catering experience. How would that suit you?'

'Perfectly!' Annie said with relief.

Later, having signed on the dotted line, Annie Balfour walked out into the street.

Joining up had been easy. Now came the harrowing task of telling Conrad that very soon she would be leaving him, to serve King and country with the Wrens.

Ten

Conrad was waiting for Annie when she returned to the hotel.

'I was worried when the raid started. They've bombed Leith again. Are you all right?'

'I took shelter. I'm fine.'

He studied her, frowning, and her heart sank. She'd forgotten how perceptive he could be.

'You don't look fine. What happened?'

'Nothing.'

She noticed an arrangement of fresh red rosebuds on her desk. He must have ordered them specially to surprise her. But even roses bought with love could not erase the memory of a kiss shared with Fergus. Red roses only made the betrayal seem worse, and her guilt almost unbearable.

'Oh, Conrad darling, you shouldn't give me roses!'

'Of course I should!' He smiled. 'Remember what the poet says, sweetheart? *Gather ye rosebuds while ye may ... this same flower that smiles today, tomorrow will be dying—!*'

She shuddered. 'Please – don't say that!'

The smile faded. He took her arm urgently.

'Something *is* wrong, Annie. Tell me!'

She looked around wildly. Reception was a busy area, with staff and customers coming and going.

'Not here!'

He hustled her into the office and locked the door. Then he took her in his arms. She rested her head against his shoulder and burst into tears.

'I don't deserve you, Conrad darling, I really don't!'

In anguish and tears, she told him about meeting Fergus unexpectedly, and the events culminating in one revealing kiss. He heard her out in silence.

'So you still have feelings for him?'

'But I love you, Conrad. I feel safe with you!'

He sighed.

'No doubt you do, my darling, but this young man offers danger and excitement, and that's tempting.'

Annie shivered. 'I've sampled Fergus's dangerous excitement, thanks. It always led to quarrels and misery. Who's to say it won't happen again?'

Conrad looked at her, so beautiful, and so troubled! His heart went out to her.

'Forget him!' he urged. 'We fell in love and we're going to be married. That's all that really matters, isn't it?'

'No, darling. It's not so simple,' she said sorrowfully. 'Fergus kissed me, but it wasn't his fault. I didn't resist, I – I *wanted* it, just as much as he did. Afterwards, I was devastated. I love you and I let you down. It will take time to come to terms with what I did.'

He kissed her tenderly and smiled. 'Don't worry, my love. We can work it out together.'

This was the moment she'd been dreading.

'We ... we can't, Conrad! I've volunteered to join the Wrens.'

'You *what*?'

For a moment he stood motionless, then stepped back and stared at her as if she were a complete stranger.

She let out a pitiful cry. 'Darling! Don't look at me like that, I can't bear it!'

He sighed wearily and shook his head. 'Annie dear, I was only thinking I can fight Fergus McGill, and keep you here with me, but I can't fight the Royal Navy!'

Fergus was heading home to Kirriemuir.

At Waverley Station, he'd picked up his kitbag from Left Luggage and caught a northbound train, which moved at a cautious snail's pace across the railway bridge. Heinkel bombers had given Leith a pasting and the driver and fireman were taking no chances. Fergus settled down in a corner, tipped the forage cap over his eyes and folded his arms across his chest to discourage conversation, then began to consider the afternoon's events.

He was sure Annie still loved him. His own feelings had never been in doubt. He'd loved her since she was a little girl, and had been too blind to see it...

Fighting in the Spanish civil war had given Fergus an insight into his strengths and weaknesses. A humbling experience. He wasn't the brave, jolly chap he'd thought he was. Most of the time he and his mates were scared, hungry, confused and filthy. Amateur soldiers fighting well-armed, Nazi-backed troops led by the charismatic General Franco.

Fergus had fondly imagined right would triumph, and evil be overcome. What a forlorn hope!

He and his disillusioned British companions had ended up hiding in a cellar in heavily bombed Barcelona. They were captured by Franco's victorious army and thrown into prison, suspected of spying.

Only dogged determination to survive had sustained Fergus till repatriation. That, and the thought of an innocent childhood sweetheart he'd loved and lost. Annie Balfour!

The train chugged on, gathering speed past coal mines, anxious to leave ugly coal bings behind and regain the green pastures of the Kingdom of Fife.

In his corner, Fergus stirred restlessly.

Just before joining up in an infantry regiment, he'd sent his parents a brief note assuring them he was OK. He had not divulged an address, still too fragile to face family concern and questions. But arriving in Edinburgh on his first home leave, the desire to see Annie once more had been overwhelming. He'd been struggling against temptation when, by an incredible twist of fate, they'd met. By some miracle, she was still single, and a sudden wild hope had aroused a positive volcano of emotion in his mind, the reunion ending with one amazing, unforgettable kiss.

So now he knew for sure she still loved him.

He should feel euphoric, but he just felt wretched, wishing they had never met and the kiss had never happened. She must love Conrad if she'd agreed to marry him. Honest Annie Balfour would not settle for a loveless marriage; that would be cheating in her book.

So, Fergus thought unhappily, he had kissed her on a sudden irresistible impulse and ruined everything for her.

Poor darling! He knew her so well. How guilty she must feel, how devastated!

He completed the journey to Kirriemuir by bus, arriving at Kilmuckety road end. The first significant change to catch his eye was the old roadside cottage, re-roofed and refurbished. A freshly painted sign above the door announced:

FARM SUPPLIES
Proprietor John Balfour

Well, well! Intrigued, Fergus left the kitbag outside and pushed open the door.

He found an interior lined with shelves packed with a vast variety of goods, tinned food, cooking utensils, tools, boxes of night-lights and candles. Neat lines of sacks containing everything from carrots and potatoes to dog biscuits and slabs of peat. Close by were bundles of kindling, jerry cans, and a large drum of paraffin. Well to the fore stood rows of stirrup pumps and sacks of sand, ready to deal with incendiary bombs.

Looking around, Fergus noted commercial refrigerators and the door to a large cold room, all very similar to the American models he'd admired on his travels.

A counter ran across one end of the store, and at that moment a door opened and his youngest sister appeared, very smart and businesslike in shirt and slacks.

'Can I help you?' she asked pleasantly then broke off and stared.

'Fergus!' she yelled and ran across the floor to hug him joyfully. 'We'd given up hope! We were told you and Audrey were in Australia, then there was a postcard saying you were off to Spain. After that, *total* silence, till a miserable little note arrives with an English postmark!'

He laughed and kissed her cheek.

'Pen and paper weren't to hand where I was, Marigold. I'll bore you with the details later.'

He held her at arms' length. She had always been his favourite, but the careless tomboy he remembered had gone, and she had blossomed into an attractive young woman. Her auburn hair was neatly styled, lips outlined with lipstick, and he caught a whiff of per-

fume. Fergus wondered if there was a boyfriend on the scene. He smiled at her fondly.

'How are Ma and Pa and the sisters? This
leave was unexpected and I'd no time to warn
anyone I was coming. As you can imagine,
everything's at sixes and sevens after Dunkirk.'

'You weren't there, were you?'

He smiled. 'No, I'm one of Mr Churchill's
raw recruits, ready for the blood, toil, tears
and sweat he's promised us.'

She studied him more closely, and was
shocked to note how much he had changed.
He was thin, with deep grim lines around the
mouth, but the greatest change was in the
eyes. Marigold struggled to hold back tears.
His expression was guarded, dark and sad,
and his eyes had lost their lively, mischievous
sparkle.

She swallowed tears and began blethering a
lot of bright nonsense.

'Mother and Pa are involved heart and soul
in the war effort, as you might expect.
Mother's a leading light in the Red Cross,
and helps run a canteen in Kirriemuir for
Polish soldiers. Everyone's sure the Germans
will invade, so Pa's joined the local Defence
Volunteers. He's out most days with a shot-
gun, keeping an eye open for German para-
chutists and warning kids to watch out for
spies handing out poisoned sweeties. And as
for our beautiful house! The windows are
criss-crossed with tape and every room over-
run with evacuees and Polish officers.' She

gave a nervous little giggle. 'Mother says it's her contribution to the sufferings of war. Thank heavens for Davina Williams; the woman's a saint! She's been promoted to housekeeper since the other servants rushed off to join the ATS. Dear Vinnie keeps house and occupants in order, and helps maintain our sanity...'

John Balfour had been checking accounts in the office. Hearing voices, he rose and went into the store to investigate. He stopped dead when he saw Fergus.

'You!'

There had not been much love lost between the two as schoolboys, although as adults they'd worked together amicably on the farm. But Fergus had been boss then. Now control of the estate had shifted to John, and he would not surrender command willingly.

Fergus sensed antagonism.

'Nice to see you too, John!' he said blandly.

Marigold glanced from one to the other apprehensively, and decided to make herself scarce.

'Well, I'll run and tell Ma and Pa the good news. You can bring Fergus up to date with what's been happening on the farm, John darling.'

The endearment was not lost upon Fergus. He frowned doubtfully. The door had no sooner closed behind her than John moved into the attack.

'You're in uniform! I gather you've no

intention of staying?'

'And you're in civvies! I presume you've no intention of going?' Fergus retorted.

A scathing reply trembled on John's lips, but he hesitated. What was the use of fighting? It wouldn't solve anything.

'I'm exempt from military service, Fergus,' he answered pleasantly. 'I may not be in the forces, but I'm just as involved. U-boats are a menace to shipping, and the estate can make a valuable contribution to food supplies. I've stepped up milk production and raised many more sheep, cattle and pigs. I've applied to the Ministry of Agriculture for a subsidy to reclaim moorland for additional root crops. To put it bluntly, Fergus, I'm a damn fine farmer, and a rotten soldier!'

Fergus was silent for a moment, then burst out laughing.

'Too true, old chum! I flattened you in the playground with one hand tied behind my back, but when it came to farming, you couldn't be beat!'

This was high praise. John beamed with pleasure. 'We were a good team, when we worked together on the land, Fergus.'

Fergus nodded. 'Aye, John. Those were good times.'

'So why did you leave? Did you lose interest, or did you and Annie quarrel?'

'Blame Barney. That dog never liked me,' Fergus said lightly.

John eyed him thoughtfully.

'Lady Audrey went to Australia before the

war. Did you two marry?'

'No, she married an Aussie sheep farmer.'

'Ah!' John was silent for a moment, then went on carefully, 'Did you know Annie is planning to marry Conrad Whyte?'

'Yes. I met her quite by chance in Edinburgh. She told me.'

'So what now?'

He shrugged. 'Who knows? I hope to survive the war, and you might have plans to marry my sister. Tell me, John, do you love her, or do you love the old family estate?'

John flushed. 'That's none of your business!'

'Oh, but it is, my friend!' Fergus said deliberately. 'Marigold's happiness is important to me, and you'd do well to remember that Kilmuckety is *my* inheritance now.'

With that said, he turned and left the store...

Like his brother John, eleven-year-old Benny Balfour did not welcome Fergus's sudden arrival in the McGill household. Benny stayed in the background while other evacuees clustered round the soldier hero and Polish Army officers greeted Fergus with heel-clicking deference. Mrs McGill was over the moon, kissing, hugging, and crying over the prodigal son.

Benny had nothing against Fergus; in fact, he liked and admired him as a man, but Fergus posed a serious threat which Benny knew he had to endure for at least fourteen days.

Benny was in daily terror that Davina Williams would fall in love with the soldier, or might even be prompted to join the ATS after listening to Fergus's exploits. He need not have worried. Fergus's leave ended, and Davina waved him off cheerfully.

Benny heaved a huge sigh of relief. Davina had been his guardian angel since his arrival in the house.

Benny had turned up on the white marble doorstep at the beginning of the war, along with a vanload of evacuees from the depths of Edinburgh's worst slums. Mrs McGill had turned paler than the pale pink carpets when she saw them, but Davina Williams had come good-humouredly to the rescue. She'd de-loused, bathed and fed them all in record time, organizing beds for boys in one large bedroom, girls in another. Benny had had an asthma attack during the night, brought on by guilt. He knew responsibility for bringing the whole unruly gang here was his alone.

It was a severe asthma attack, but Davina had eased his difficult breathing with steamy inhalations. She'd sat by his bedside, holding his hand, till morning. Strangely enough, since that awful night asthma attacks had been less frequent. He hardly ever had one now.

But Benny lived in constant fear that some-one would marry Davina and take her away. The Polish officers flirted shamelessly with the pretty girl and kissed her hand whenever they had a chance, but to Benny's relief neither Polish charm nor Fergus's battle-scarred good looks had attracted Davina.

The household returned to normal after Fergus's departure and Benny relaxed – until John announced that cousin Annie had joined the Wrens. Annie was about Davina's age, and Benny was terrified his heroine might be tempted to follow suit.

Fear of losing his guardian angel brought on the worst asthma attack Benny had suffered for months, and Davina was concerned. When it was over, the boy lay limp and exhausted in her arms as she put him to bed and sat holding his hand.

'What brought this on, lovey?' she asked gently. 'I thought you were growing out of it.'

'You – you won't join the Wrens, will you?' he whispered.

'Bless you, Benny love, of course not!' She laughed in surprise. 'I get seasick crossing the Gairie burn.'

He turned his head towards her on the pillow and smiled radiantly.

Such a lovely smile! Davina thought, as the lad drifted peacefully off to sleep. She brushed a damp curl from his brow, and kissed his smooth, flushed cheek tenderly.

What a kind, loving bairn, she thought with a tear in her eye. Such a pity his big brother wasn't more like him!

The Wrens lost no time calling upon Annette Balfour. Willing volunteers for cookhouse duty were in very short supply.

By mid-August, Annie had a travel warrant and instructions to present herself at a Royal Naval base near Balloch in Dunbartonshire for preliminary training. She was urged to appear no later than 14.30 hours on Wednesday 3rd September 1941.

Connie had wept, scolded and argued, ever since she'd been told of Annie's decision.

'You want your heid examined, Annie Balfour! A fine upstanding man with a thriving business at his back begging you to wed, me with material bought to make the bonniest wedding gown seen in this city, and you go off and join the Wrens! Would you mind telling me what bee got into your bonnet?'

'I just want to do my bit for the war effort, Connie,' Annie protested.

Connie snorted.

'You dinna fool me with the "King and country" lark, my girl! You're more use to His Majesty here in Edinburgh, keeping an eye on his Holyrood Palace down the road.'

Annie remained obstinately silent. She couldn't tell her aunt the real reason behind the decision. Any mention of Fergus McGill would drive Connie berserk.

Leah's distress was just as difficult to take.

'It's mean of you, Annie!' she sobbed tearfully. 'I was looking forward to being a bridesmaid, and now it won't happen. I hate this horrible war! I'll be all on my own when you go.'

Annie had to smile.

239

'No, you won't! You have masses of friends, Leah dear. The usherettes are a cheery lot, and isn't Phyllis McLuskey getting married soon? I bet she'll ask you to be a bridesmaid.'

'No, thanks! She says her bridesmaids will wear pink, 'cause pink makes the boys wink. I loathe pink; I look like a boiled lobster.'

Leah was having an anxious time at work, and this disappointment was the final blow. Ice cream supplies were drying up, sweets were on ration, and her job hung in the balance. The manager had decided the threat of incendiary bombs was bad enough, and refused to increase the fire hazard by sending Leah round selling cigarettes.

So she was to be reduced to the ranks. No film star status, no golden spotlight! Just a return to the dreary torch, lighting fumbling filmgoers down the aisles.

If she *did* have a secret admirer, a knight in shining armour, where was he? she wondered miserably. He was awfully backward in coming forward ...

When the time came for Annie's departure, Connie was inconsolable.

Annie was a dearly loved member of Connie's large family, and Connie had lost her husband and all her boys. Only Leah was left. She could hardly muster strength to say goodbye.

After a tearful farewell, Annie left her aunt sitting alone in the beautiful living room of the third-floor flat, comforted by a freshly brewed pot of tea and a packet of Rich Tea biscuits.

That experience had been heart-rending, but there was worse to come...

Conrad was waiting at Reception, all emotion hidden behind the professional smile reserved for customers. She could only guess how much he must be hurting inside. She hugged and kissed him tearfully.

'It's so hard to say goodbye, my darling!' she sobbed.

He kissed her lightly and stepped back smiling, though his eyes told a much sadder story.

'So you're off to Balloch, my dear! You'll have the bonny, bonny banks of Loch Lomond on your doorstep!'

She wished he hadn't said that. The words and music of the sad song went pounding through her thoughts like a heartbeat ... *Me and my true love will never meet again on the bonny, bonny banks of Loch Lomond!*

She held his hand. 'I love you, Conrad!'

'I know you do, my sweetheart. But maybe...'

He stopped himself in time, but she guessed what he could not bear to put into words.

Maybe not enough!

She drew the engagement ring off her finger, kissed it, and handed it to him.

'This is too precious to take with me, my darling. Keep it safe for me, till I come home.'

He nodded and stared at the ring lying on the palm of his hand. Maybe there were tears in his eyes, but when he looked up they were gone. He glanced at her small suit-case.

'You're travelling light!'

'I only need a toothbrush. The Navy sup-plies the rest.'

She tried to make light of leaving, but part-ing was breaking her heart. A car horn sound-ed. He picked up the case, took her hand and led her outside.

'I ordered a taxi to take you to the station, my love. I know we intended going together, but it's better to say goodbye now. We shouldn't prolong the agony.'

He held open the taxi door and looked at her for a long moment, before kissing her lightly on the lips.

'Goodbye, my darling, God bless!'

She clambered aboard unsteadily.

He raised a hand in farewell as the taxi drove off. Looking back, Conrad, the hotel and the hills beyond swam dizzily before Annie's eyes, awash in a blur of tears.

On her first full day in the Wrens, Annie had a medical examination and visited the quartermaster's stores to collect an armful of kit. Afterwards, she returned to a Nissen hut shared with twenty other recruits and sat on a hard narrow bed beside the locker assigned to her, feeling homesick and lost.

Jessie, her neighbour, was obviously made of sterner stuff. She began stowing vests, navy knickers, black stockings, uniform, and sensible low-heeled shoes inside the locker, singing cheerfully as she did so:

> There wis rats, rats,
> In spats an' bowler hats,
> In the store, in the store...

Catching Annie's eye, she broke off.
'Look busy, hen,' she advised, 'or they'll find ye somethin' nasty to do. An' for heaven's sake dinna catch an officer's eye if one looks in. This place is no' different frae the factory where I wis workin' in Cowcaddens. Women officers couldna be worse than our crabbit auld foreman...'
With a grin, she went on singing.

> There wis fleas, fleas,
> In a' the dungarees,
> In the quartermaster's store—!

Determined to make the best of it, Annie soon settled into the routine. She enjoyed drill, learning to march to the cookhouse with arms swinging like windmills. There the recruits received instruction on kitchen procedures and hygiene, and were told some of the complications of cooking vast quantities of food for large numbers of naval personnel.
The recruits rarely had an idle moment. The draughty corrugated-iron Nissen hut must be spotlessly clean and tidy at all times. It was autumn, and cold winds picked up

rubbish and a rustling scatter of fallen leaves, which mischievously infiltrated the hut, just as inspections were due. Discipline was on strict naval lines. Nothing escaped the Wren officer's eagle eye, and the recruits soon learned to dread a summons to her office. It usually meant a ticking off for some minor misdemeanour and a session spent scrubbing the cookhouse floor.

Annie had managed to avoid trouble so far, but her blood ran cold when Jessie popped her head round the hut door and announced sympathetically, 'You're wanted in the auld dragon's office, Annie. Hard luck. It'll be dust on top o' your locker. I kent thon long dreep o' misery wi' the hawk eyes had spotted somethin' this morning.'

Annie brushed her uniform, made sure not a strand of hair was touching her collar, and marched to the commandant's office, filled with trepidation. The office staff looked up from their desks.

'Took your time, didn't you, Balfour? Kept the officer waiting. You're for it!'

One of them rose and knocked on the office door.

'She's here now, ma'am.'

She beckoned to Annie, who took a deep breath, lifted her chin, flung back her shoulders and marched in. The door closed as she saluted, eyes fixed on a point somewhere to the right of the woman's left ear.

The officer laughed.

'Oh, come off it, Annie!'

Startled, Annie stared. 'Lisette!'

Annie rushed forward with a cry, Lisette bounded from behind the desk, and the twins hugged each other rapturously, laughing and crying. When they had recovered from their delight, Annie drew a chair up to the desk and she and Lisette sat down and looked at one another. Tears threatened.

'Lisette, what can I possibly say to you about dear Freddie? It was so tragic!'

'Don't say anything, dear. I – I understand.' She looked down at her hands, clenched tightly in her lap. 'I had a miscarriage not long after the accident, Annie. It was at an early stage, brought on by shock. Freddie never even knew he was to be a father. That made the heartbreak so much worse.'

Annie couldn't hide her sorrow. 'Why did you face that alone? I could have been there for you, dear, but I didn't know where you were. You didn't even tell the Gregorys!'

'It was better that way. I had to be alone, to find out who Lisette Balfour really is. We were parted at a formative age, Annie, and somewhere along the line I've lost my true identity. I love my foster parents dearly, and tried to be the daughter they'd always wanted. I became adept at acting a part, but all the time I think I was living a lie.' She paused and looked at her sister. 'I'm glad now that you wrote me that letter. It was cruel at the time, but it was true. I know it sounds daft, but after I lost Freddie and the baby, I became a different person, almost a complete stranger even to myself!'

'So what did you do?'

Lisette smiled. 'Retraced my steps, went back to the beginning, when you and I were four and Dad gave us each a medal. It seemed a significant point at which to start again, so I deposited my medal in the bank and joined the Wrens.'

Annie felt a sense of wonder. 'How astonishing, so did I! I needed space, time to think, so I joined up and gave *my* medal to Connie for safe keeping.'

'So the bond is still strong,' Lisette nodded. She was silent for a minute. 'How good is your command of French, by the way?'

The question was so unexpected, Annie laughed. 'Very poor! I left school at fourteen and we never had holidays on the French Riviera. Connie's idea of bliss was a day trip to Carnoustie!' She looked at Lisette, curiously. 'Why d'you want to know?'

'No particular reason!' Her sister looked away. 'The people I work with were intrigued when they heard I'd an identical twin. They wanted to know if your French was as fluent as mine. They thought it might come in useful.'

Annie smiled. 'Not unless the Navy wants Cordon Bleu menus.'

Lisette laughed. 'I couldn't believe it when I heard you'd signed on as a cook!'

Annie shrugged. 'It seemed a logical choice. I know all about cleaning kitchens and catering for large numbers, and I'm not chasing promotion, like some.'

Her sister winced whimsically. 'Ouch! Mind you, Annie, I had promotion thrust upon me. They need interpreters for French troops who escaped from Dunkirk. That's when I came to the attention of SOE.'

'What's that?'

'Oh! A branch of the FANYs ... the group everyone makes fun of, you know?' she said. 'We act as drivers for naval top brass, drive ambulances if needed, in fact we do any dirty work that needs doing.'

'I'll remember that when I'm scrubbing the cookhouse floor. Do the dirty work, if you want to get ahead,' Annie teased.

'Forget it, Annie, it's no joke,' Lisette said quietly.

Annie stared at her sister uneasily. There was something about her, some inexplicable change she couldn't put a finger on exactly...

'How did you know where I was? When I joined up I gave my next of kin as an aunt in Edinburgh, and a twin sister, status and address unknown. Nobody showed the slightest interest, yet you turn up a few weeks later. That seems an odd coincidence.'

'Oh, weird things happen in wartime, dear!' Lisette said airily. She glanced at her wrist-watch and stood up. 'I'm sorry it's been such a flying visit, Annie. I must be back in London tomorrow.'

'Yes, of course. You'll want to spend the rest of your leave with the Gregorys. Aunt Madeleine must be delighted to know you're OK.'

Lisette's eyes clouded. 'I worry about them. London's such an obvious target and Daddy has set up a first-aid post in the heart of the city. Mummy finds safe billets for French refugees and new homes for people's pets abandoned after air-raids.'

'Aunt Madeleine caring for cats and dogs? That stretches the imagination!'

'I told you war is weird!' Lisette laughed and hugged her twin. 'I have more training to do, but I had to come to see you, Annie, to say goodbye.'

Annie felt chilled. 'What do you mean – goodbye?'

'Well, pip-pip, if you'd rather.' She smiled nonchalantly.

'When shall I see you again?'

'That depends on whether they decide I've passed the test or not.'

'More dirty work?'

'You might say that.'

'Lisette, please tell me – who are "they"?'

'Nobody in particular,' she laughed. 'Connie would call them high heid yins, I suppose.' She kissed Annie fondly on the cheek. 'It's good to know I can always find you, thanks to the Wrens. Thank goodness the identical twin bond still flourishes!'

'Yes, of course...'

Annie sensed something was being kept hidden from her by her sister. Whatever it was, it just made her feel more anxious. Involuntarily, she took two paces backwards. By doing so, she was aware that naval discipline once more prevailed. She was one of the rank and file facing an officer.

'Now what do I do? Salute smartly, sharp left turn, and leave?' she asked.

Lisette laughed and held out her arms. 'Don't be such an idiot, Annie dear! Come and give your sister a big hug...'

Eleven

In the weeks following Lisette's visit, Annie worked hard to complete basic training, but the uneasiness persisted. Instinct told her that something Lisette had said did not ring true, though she could not say what.

The six o'clock news reported fleets of German bombers heading for London, which caused Annie much anxiety. There were reports of dogfights raging in the skies, and although heavily laden Heinkel bombers were no match for agile Spitfires and Hurricanes, some enemy aircraft did get through. Bulletins reported palls of black smoke obscuring London and other major cities, and a rising toll of casualties.

William Joyce, the British traitor dubbed 'Lord Haw-Haw' because of his plummy accent, broadcast from Radio Hamburg with exaggerated claims of the damage. Annie and her friends listened out of curiosity, but soon switched over to the cheerful music of Workers' Playtime or the fun of Tommy Handley's ITMA – It's That Man Again! This guaranteed a good laugh, and laughter was a valuable commodity these days.

Connie wrote reassuringly that although

the Gregorys were in London in the thick of the blitz, they were coping well, tending to the injured and homeless and sheltering in the safety of the Underground. But Connie had no word of Lisette.

Christmas came and went without so much as a postcard from her sister, and Annie's mood swung to despair. She was convinced she would know if her twin had been badly injured, or – heaven forbid – killed in the bombing, but of course she'd been wrong before, and could be wrong again. She tossed and turned restlessly in her sleep at night, sometimes wakening with a sudden jolt to sit upright in bed, sweating with fear.

Then startling news broke in December, which drove thoughts of Lisette momentarily from her mind.

Japanese planes launched an unprovoked attack upon the American naval base at Pearl Harbor, destroying the greater part of the American fleet, and America immediately declared war. Conflict in the Far East escalated rapidly. By mid-February 1942 the Japanese army had occupied Singapore. Annie discovered that Conrad's assessment of the island's vulnerability had proved only too accurate.

When news of the disaster was broadcast, she sought permission to leave the steamy heat of the cookhouse and went outside to clear her head, welcoming the icy wind whistling from snow-clad Ben Lomond.

There was a painful ache in her heart, and tears on her cheeks as she trudged along snowy pathways cleared around shrouded Nissen huts, worrying about her father, Teresa and young Kim. They must be in such danger! She should be out there with them! They had begged her to come, and she had refused. In her present mood, that refusal felt like betrayal.

Yet what could she have done to help, in such a terrible situation? Tearfully, Annie accepted that her father must be thankful his two daughters were comparatively safe, at home...

Far away in Johore, early morning mist lay over James Balfour's rubber plantation, close to conquered Singapore Island.

It was very early, before sunrise, and James Balfour saw the scene from the bungalow's verandah in shades of grey. His skin felt cold and clammy, whether from weather conditions or apprehension, it was hard to tell.

He had assembled his Malayan workers in the garden in front of the house, to meet their new masters. He had been assured by the Japanese that they intended to keep the plantation in full production, but James doubted he'd be left in charge.

Japanese soldiers had come swarming along jungle tracks on bicycles, a few startling weeks ago, fording streams and traversing marshes with incredible speed. No army could stand against the hordes.

James supposed the plantation had been fortunate. The soldiers had descended upon them like ants, grabbing every scrap of food, then sweeping on to Singapore. But the officer in charge had warned him they'd be back.

Teresa, his wife, was part Japanese, and had overheard officers discuss plans for this strategic spot. She could not determine exactly what the plan was, but it meant they had been granted a reprieve.

'You and Kim should go while the going's good, my darling,' James had urged her.

She'd looked at him with wry amusement.

'You know the going is not good, my love. So we will stay.'

He'd argued, but eventually had to admit defeat. She was proved correct. Singapore had fallen and there was no hope now of escape.

After two uneasy weeks, orders had arrived to make house and plantation ready for new occupants. On neighbouring plantations, opposition had cost lives, and James had decided it was wiser to avoid confrontation. His wife, his son and his loyal workers were his main concern.

Teresa and Kim waited patiently beside James on the verandah. His wife might be small and slender, but her courage was immense, he thought with a catch in his throat. If she was afraid, she hid it well. His worried gaze rested on their son Kim. The lad was sixteen, raven-haired and stocky, and could easily pass for Malay. He was clever, so bright, in fact, that his enthusiastic teachers had forecast a brilliant future for him. James felt a sudden fierce determination to secure that shining future for their gifted son.

Teresa turned to her husband urgently, as if reading his thoughts.

'Kim should not be seen with us, James. They must not know he's our son.'

Kim was startled. 'Mother, Father – you can't do this!'

But James agreed wholeheartedly with his wife. It was vital his son understood just how desperate their situation was.

'Listen, Kim, you've heard what's happened to other plantation owners and their families. They've either been killed or sent to prison camps. There's not a hope in hell that we'll be allowed to stay here.'

'But, Father, we must stick together!' the lad protested desperately.

'Son, there's no hope of that, I'm afraid! But we know they have plans for this place, and it would be interesting to find out what they are. You could stay here and pretend to be one of the workers. I'm very confident none of the staff would give you away. The Japs don't need to know you speak fluent Japanese and understand every word. You could keep eyes and ears open and send useful information to my friend Brigadier Osborne at Calcutta Army HQ. You know where the radio transmitter's hidden, don't you?'

Kim smiled briefly. 'You bet! They won't find that!'

James met his son's eyes. 'So – you'll do it?'

The lad nodded.

At that point James's resolve nearly failed. He knew the consequences for his son would be horrendous, should Kim's deception be discovered. Still, he calculated that the lad might stand a better chance of survival on the plantation, than condemned to forced labour in a Japanese prison camp. James could only pray Kim would use his initiative and take extra care. He delved into his pocket and brought out the medal he'd won for gallantry in the last dreadful war. If the worst came to the worst, he wanted his son to have it. He pressed the medal into Kim's hand.

'Here, son. Keep this safe for me, till we Balfours meet again.'

'Of course I will, Father.' Kim clutched the precious medal, struggling with tears.

James turned to Abri, the plantation foreman. James and Abri went back a long way. He would have trusted the Malaysian with his life. Now he was prepared to trust him with something infinitely more precious – his son's future.

The foreman nodded gravely when the situation had been explained to him.

'Do not worry, *tuan*, your son is my son now. It is a very great honour.'

There was no time to lose. Tearfully, Teresa kissed Kim, James hugged him silently, then they stood hand in hand as he was hustled away. Presently Kim reappeared, blending seamlessly into the crowd of plantation workers gathered in the misty garden.

And not a moment too soon.

A large staff car had appeared on the road stretching through rows of rubber trees. Covered trucks and a number of Japanese infantry on bicycles brought up the rear. The car drew up in front of the verandah. James and Teresa stepped down to meet the two Japanese officers and four dark-suited civilians who emerged.

The senior officer eyed them coldly. 'You will bow to these distinguished ones. You will have no more proud thoughts.'

Teresa inclined her head, James followed suit. The officer seemed satisfied.

'Now you will take what you need and go with soldiers.'

They stared at each other in dismay.

'So soon? But we can't possibly...' James began. The protest was curtly cut short.

'Argument from British will not be tolerated. You will go now!'

They had no choice but to obey. Hastily, they packed two small cases under the soldiers' watchful eyes, and were escorted to waiting trucks. Then came the final blow. Teresa was ordered to scramble into one while James was forced at gunpoint into another. There was no time for goodbyes, no farewell kiss, just clinging hands wrenched roughly apart, and a shared glance of loving desperation.

The shocked plantation workers watched as the trucks drove off. A heavy silence fell, broken only by the women's muffled sobbing and the uneasy shuffle of sandals. Kim found the treatment meted out to his parents almost too much to bear.

'No!' he muttered. He clenched his fists, trembling with rage. Abri's hand gripped his arm warningly, as the officer stalked across to the assembled workers.

The day was still young, an orange sun just beginning to rise through grey mist.

'Now you will face east,' the officer ordered in passable Malay. 'And you will bow, to honour the glorious Emperor Hirohito of the Rising Sun.'

Abri's fingers dug deep into Kim's arm.

'Do it!' he hissed.

Kim's head drooped in defeat. He bowed low with the others, the wide brim of the coolie hat hiding his shame – and his tears...

Annie's basic training ended and she was now a fully fledged Wren. To her delight, she was told Rosyth naval base had vacancies for kitchen staff, and she would be sent there. The base was on the banks of the River Forth not far from Edinburgh, and couldn't have suited Annie better. And before she took up the new posting, there was a fortnight's home leave to look forward to.

When Annie arrived at Whyte House Hotel some days later, she saw little change, apart from a wall of sandbags guarding the entrance. Inside, she found the solid barrier had made the interior seem dark and cold, but Conrad met her in the hallway with a warm bear hug that swept her off her feet.

'Welcome home, my darling!'

Connie hovered in the background.

'Oh, Annie dear, I'm heartsick about your father and his wife, and that poor young lad! What a blessing you didn't go out to that dangerous foreign place!'

'Has there been any more news?' Annie asked anxiously.

Connie shook her head. 'Not a chirp, but I'm still looking on the bright side, dear. Maybe they got away.'

Conrad squeezed Annie's hand. She knew he didn't hold out much hope of that, but the pressure was reassuring.

Connie led the way upstairs to the flat, where a feast of fine baking was prepared. It was only then that Annie noticed changes.

'I'll be mother,' Connie said, wielding the teapot.

She spooned precious sugar liberally into Annie's cup. Conrad protested.

'Hey, Connie, you've given her half my sugar ration, and she's sweet enough already!'

Connie wagged a finger at him.

'You and your sweet tooth! The lassie could do wi' a treat. She's skinny as a whippet!'

She passed the cup to Annie, who took a sip while studying her aunt thoughtfully over the rim.

Connie exuded confidence. Her hair was

nicely permed, manicured nails hinted at a minimum of housework. A well-cut navy dress suited her mature figure, and a string of pearls and black court shoes completed an elegant picture. She was much more than a mere housekeeper, Annie decided. 'Chatelaine' was the word which had sprung to mind. Queen of the castle, or in this case, the hotel!

She stole a curious glance at Conrad. He appeared relaxed, happy with the transformation and content to be bossed around.

'We've escaped bomb damage so far, thank goodness,' Connie was saying. 'Though there was a direct hit on the Caledonian Distillery at the end of September, a bit too close for comfort. I've never seen such a blaze, flames hundreds of feet high and folk nearby evacuated from their homes—'

'And a criminal waste of over one hundred gallons of neat whisky!' Conrad added.

'Trust you to mourn the booze and not the damage, my lad!' Connie said.

He looked at Annie and winked. Obviously, he thoroughly enjoyed teasing Connie, and she was only too pleased to retaliate.

Annie watched them with a catch in her throat. Two lonely people, deprived of those they loved, she thought. It seemed as if Conrad was willing to be mothered, and Connie delighted to adopt another son...

The hotel was busy that weekend, but Monday was quiet and Conrad grabbed the chance to have Annie to himself. They went out walking arm in arm, well wrapped up against a chilly breeze.

'So, has joining the Wrens cured an overactive conscience?' he asked, smiling, though his eyes revealed anxiety.

'Too soon to tell yet, darling,' she answered lightly. 'It's grand training for the catering trade, though. The Navy's fanatical about spit and polish, even more picky than you! I lost count of how often I scrubbed the cookhouse floor.'

'Any tips for cooking whale steaks?' he asked. 'Ours turn out – well – blubbery.'

'Sorry, love, whale's not on the Navy's menu. I can do perfect bangers and mash, though.'

They laughed together companionably.

The walk had brought them down the hilly street known as the Mound, to within sight of the air-raid shelters in Princes Street Gardens.

'Have you heard from him?' Conrad asked quietly.

'No.' She had wondered if Fergus would write, but there had been nothing. She met Conrad's eyes. 'It's over, Conrad. Fergus is history.'

'That's all I wanted to hear, my darling.'

He paused beneath the bare spreading branches of an old sycamore and fished in his pocket, bringing out the engagement ring she'd given him for safe keeping. He slipped it back on her finger, then took her in his arms and kissed her long and passionately. It was a most public display of loving, quite astonishing for such a reserved man.

Passers-by paused for a moment, smiled indulgently, then hurried on. War heightened emotion, partings were sorrowful and frequent. Nobody knew what the future might bring.

Annie's leave passed all too quickly, but departure was not such a wrench this time. Rosyth was within easy reach, and she could come home at weekends, when off duty. Conrad and Connie were happier about the situation. Leah, too, could see advantages.

'I could visit, and catch myself a handsome sailor boy, Annie!'

'Well, there's plenty of fine fish in the Forth!' Annie laughed, with a glance at her aunt, whose expression remained stony. Handsome sailor boys were not high on Connie's list of acceptable boyfriends.

Leah had abandoned all hope of finding a secret admirer, if indeed one had ever existed. The usherettes were notorious for practical jokes, and an ice-cream girl an obvious target. The joke foundered when Leah was once more reduced to the ranks. There had been no more talk of admirers.

Soon after Annie's departure, the cinema manager was on fire-watch duty, and Leah and two or three usherettes volunteered to stay behind after the evening performance. It had become necessary to clear cupboard space to install extra fire-fighting equipment, and they'd offered to help. Incendiary bombs were a menace and there had been air-raids and serious fires recently. As an added precaution, public buildings and offices had established nightly fire-watching rotas.

The task was soon finished and the others had gone on ahead while Leah stacked rubbish beside the bins in the back yard. She was preparing to catch up with her friends, when a man stepped out of the darkness, barring the way.

Leah gave a frightened gasp. The blackout held many dangers, not only from bombs!

'Go away! Let me pass, or – or I'll scream!' she cried.

'Please don't. I didn't mean to frighten you,' the man said.

Her eyes had grown accustomed to the dark, revealing more details. He was a young man, tall, broad-shouldered and strong-looking. She backed away nervously.

'What do you want?'

'To take you home.'

He's a nutcase, she thought in panic.

'You can't! Go away!'

Her friends couldn't have gone far. She tried to dodge round him, but he grabbed her.

'Let me go!' She struggled wildly. He hung on.

'Listen, I'm harmless. You know my father!'

'No, I don't! Stop it, you're hurting me!'

He released her at once. Her knees were weak, and she was so winded she didn't have the strength to run. He seemed just as badly shaken.

'Honestly, Leah, I didn't mean to hurt you. I'm sorry.'

'Who – who are you?' she demanded.

'I'm the manager's son, Andrew. I'm keeping my dad company fire-watching tonight. He said the other girls had gone, so I just wanted to make sure you got home safely.'

'You – you're not a nutcase?' she said.

He laughed.

'No, just a little light-headed. I know you, you see, but I forgot you don't know me. I operate the cinema lights for my dad in my spare time. I've been wanting to tell you for months how lovely you look, under the spotlight.'

Leah remembered the admiring golden spotlight following the ice-cream girl's every move, and suddenly the mystery was solved. '*You're* the secret admirer!'

He smiled. 'Well, it's no secret I was devastated when they stopped sales of ice cream. I couldn't watch you any more. It was only then that I began to realize...'

Andrew paused. He longed to tell her how much he'd missed her and dreamed about her, but he'd started off on the wrong foot already, rushing in like a fool. Better not push his luck.

'Ready to go, Leah? It's late. Your mother will be worrying,' he said.

He switched on a torch with a blinkered beam, shining it on the ground as they walked along dark deserted streets, arm in arm.

The night was moonless and quiet, but suddenly a searchlight pierced the black sky above them. There had been no siren to warn them anything was amiss, a single beam the only hint of danger, sweeping restlessly across the heavens.

They huddled together, looking upwards.

'Now that's what I call a light!' he remarked admiringly. 'I'm hoping to join the RAF soon, when I finish my apprenticeship as an electrician, Leah, but I wouldn't want to be caught in *that* spotlight, flying over Germany!'

She couldn't stop shivering. She imagined Andrew trapped like a helpless moth in the dazzling beam, while German anti-aircraft guns pounded the plane to pieces.

Andrew had his head to one side, listening.

'What is it?' she whispered.

'Listen! Can't you hear them?'

Then she made out the distant irregular droning of many Luftwaffe bombers, a distinctive sound very familiar to Edinburgh citizens by now. The lone searchlight snapped out as suddenly as it had appeared, leaving them in total darkness. He held her closer.

'You're shivering! Don't be scared. They're not coming here tonight, they're heading west. Looks as if Glasgow might be the target.'

They walked on soberly, Leah's emotions in a confused muddle. She had recognized the first stirrings of an amazing love. But if Andrew joined the Royal Air Force, it could be a love affair cut tragically short.

News of the disastrous air-raids on Clydeside soon reached Rosyth, causing consternation in the naval base. First reports told of severe damage and many casualties.

A group of Rosyth Wrens volunteered to leave for the devastated area, where staff were urgently needed to set up food centres for aid workers, civilians and the homeless. There was a queasiness in Annie's stomach as she sat with other volunteers in a truck heading for Glasgow. She wondered if Lisette had felt as scared when facing the horrors of the London blitz.

Annie had always thought a no-nonsense upbringing must make her a stronger person than her pampered twin. Now she wasn't so sure. She'd always had Connie's loving support when times were hard. Lisette had chosen to face tragedy alone. How incredibly brave!

The devastation the Wrens found when they reached their destination was beyond belief, but there was no time to stand around. An undamaged primary school nearby had been made the hub of rescue operations, with a first-aid post and feeding centre. There was ample sleeping accommodation in cellars and store rooms down below, where the Wrens left their kit.

Above ground, the schoolrooms smelled of

old chalk dust, musty schoolbooks, and a peculiar acrid, burning stench, from surrounding buildings torn apart by high explosives.

The civilian kitchen staff raised a cheer when the Wrens arrived.

'Here comes the Navy!' Glasgow voices cried joyfully.

'What's on the menu?' one of the Wrens asked.

The Clydesiders chortled, 'It's *cordon bleu*, luv! Tattie soup an' bangers an' mash. We'll leave youse to it, an' get wir heids down an' feet up.'

Dubiously, the new arrivals were left to eye the huge pile of potatoes awaiting attention, alongside strings of pallid sausages heaped high on platters.

Annie had never worked so hard before, for such long, demanding hours, but a weary smile or word of thanks from Red Cross workers and shocked civilians kept her going when she felt like dropping. At last the officer in charge caught her stumbling with fatigue, and called a halt.

'Get some rest, Balfour. You're excused duty till the morning watch.'

Thankfully, Annie removed the overalls and went to the canteen in search of food.

She'd had little more than a sandwich while preparing meals for others, and now she discovered she was starving. One of the helpers brought her a plate of meat and veg.

'It's oot o' a tin, lassie, but none the worse,

and here's a mug o' char an' a biscuit. You look all in,' she remarked kindly.

Annie cleaned the plate, and felt better. She was sitting dunking a ginger snap in tea, when there was a commotion at the doorway. The blackout curtains parted and several soldiers clattered into the canteen, their khaki fatigues stained and dusty from working in the ruins. They were remarkably cheerful, however, the old schoolroom resounding to loud banter and laughter.

Seated on her own, Annie was surprised to glance up and find one of the group had paused beside her table. Her heart gave a sudden, uncomfortable jolt.

'Fergus!'

'We must stop meeting in these odd places, you know, Annie,' he said.

He pulled out a chair and sat down as her heart returned to a more normal rhythm.

'What are you doing here?' she demanded.

'Digging through rubble, hoping to find more survivors. Officially billeted in Maryhill Barracks, on field exercises in the Campsie hills.'

'Come off it, Fergus!' she scoffed. 'The hills are feet deep in snow!'

'So what?' He shrugged. 'Last week we spent two nights in a snow-hole, courtesy of the Army.'

He fixed her with a piercing stare. 'John told me you'd joined the Wrens. Why?'

She ignored the question. 'How is John? He's worked wonders with the estate, since you went off to cultivate Lady Audrey.'

She'd touched a raw nerve. Fergus scowled at her.

'John's doing rather well. He's busy courting my sister Marigold, with a view to restoring the Balfour heritage.'

'Good luck to him! Marigold's the best of the McGill bunch.'

'Thanks!' he grunted caustically.

He removed a dusty khaki comforter from round his neck, revealing a stubbled jaw and cheeks grey with exhaustion and dust. His eyes were dark-rimmed and very tired. Struggling with a sudden warmth of pity, she drained the last few mouthfuls of cooling tea at the bottom of the tin mug.

'What on earth were you doing in Inverness last month?' Fergus demanded.

She looked up. 'You're blethering. I've never been there.'

'Come off it, Annie! I saw you with my own eyes when my platoon was returning from training on Loch Ness. You were in civvies, sitting beside an older chap driving a Morris. What's Conrad going to say about that, I wonder?'

'Nothing. Conrad knows I've never been anywhere near Inverness.'

He stared at her for a moment. The words held the ring of truth.

'Could it have been Lisette?' he said.

'I doubt it. She's down south. If she'd been in Scotland she'd have told us.'

'Not if she's going around with a man the

Balfours wouldn't approve of!'

Annie remained silent. Knowing Connie's formidabe prejudices, that was a possibility.

'OK,' he said resignedly at last. 'So you were a figment of my imagination in Inverness, but you appear real enough tonight. What brings you here?'

'I volunteered to help in the kitchen.'

He shook his head reprovingly. 'Never volunteer for anything, if you aim to stay healthy, my girl!'

'You're a fine one to talk! Sleeping in snow-holes in March! Honestly, Fergus, how daft is that?'

His expression darkened. 'Don't mock commando training, Annie! I was damn lucky to be accepted. It's tough going, but if I make the grade I'll be entitled to wear the red beret.'

Her eyes widened. She'd been in the Forces long enough to know that men deemed fit to wear the Commandos' coveted red beret were an elite band. They tackled the most danger-ous tasks facing the British Army, often behind enemy lines. She was suddenly so angry she could have hit him because of his foolish bravado – or wept for him because of his reckless bravery.

'You mean you've actually *volunteered* to get yourself killed?'

He stood up abruptly, looking down at her with hot angry eyes.

'What if I did? Here's a question for you, my dear! Why didn't you marry Conrad?'

Annie looked at him, lost for words.

His mates had downed mugs of tea and were preparing to leave. One of them called across.

'Stop chatting up that wee lass an' let's get a move on, Mac!'

Fergus bent down swiftly and planted a bruising, angry kiss on her mouth. When he drew back, the dust of ruined buildings and shattered lives lay gritty on her lips. She felt unbearably sad. Must it always end like this? For once, she longed to ease the pain of parting.

'Fergus, wait—' she began urgently.

'Wish me luck, as you wave me goodbye!' he said flippantly, turning away, and the chance was gone.

The others had been watching events unfold with broad grins, and launched into Vera Lynn's theme song, which had caught the nation's mood in an era of heroic good-byes: *Give me a smile I can keep all the while, in my heart, while I'm away...*

'Take care, Fergus, please take care!' she called after him.

But he had gone, the blackouts swinging shut behind him and his rowdy companions.

She doubted if he had heard her.

It was very late, the canteen almost empty, hollow echoes bouncing off dark-green walls as the tired women cleared the tables. Annie rose wearily and made her way downstairs to the muggy gloom of the cellars, lined with huddled shapes and resounding to snores and snuffles. Tired as she was, her thoughts were too disturbed for sleep.

Could Fergus have seen Lisette in Inverness? If so, what on earth was she doing there? Who was the man she'd been with, and why hadn't she got in touch?

There was no answer to the puzzle, of course, and eventually Annie slept...

Lisette sat in a colourless bedroom in a drab Edwardian house in an unfashionable London street. The district was well away from the East End in an area unimportant enough to warrant little bomb damage. She sat alone in the room in a creaking wickerwork chair, waiting patiently to be called.

She was already thinking in French in preparation for an epic journey.

Her administrator, Mr Brown, had told her in confidence that her French had impressed members of the Secret Service. Madeleine's roots lay in an agricultural region in northern France, and from her foster mother Lisette had picked up the distinctive local accent and turn of phrase of that area.

Which had made her a perfect choice for a simple task to be performed in that district, Mr Brown had informed her genially. He had spoken in the proud tones of a teacher whose star pupil had come top of the class.

'It's unfortunate your first mission as a courier should happen to be in northern France, Lisette. It's under German occupation at the moment, while Vichy France in the south hasn't had the enemy's full attention just yet,' he'd continued. 'Still, the south is treacherous with German sympathizers and Vichy police informers, so the north could well be safer, just so long as you remember your training and stay alert.'

He had smiled encouragingly and glanced into a folder of notes. 'Anyway, you'll be flown across the Channel to your destination and brought out again within ten days, providing moon phases and weather conditions remain OK. Piece of cake, as our RAF chappies say!' Mr Brown had chortled.

'Brown' wasn't his real name, of course. Nothing about this house, or the people in it, was as it seemed. You could walk past 'Mr Brown' in the street and be unable to recall a single detail of his appearance, he looked so ordinary. Yet not the minutest detail of Lisette's clothing, cover story, necessary documents and equipment had escaped Mr Brown's keenest scrutiny.

She studied her new image in the wardrobe mirror. Lisette Asherwood had disappeared. In her place sat Marie Duval, a rather plain, middle-aged widow.

Her dark hair, cut by a French hairdresser, was parted in the middle and dyed to introduce ageing signs of grey, then shampooed with coarse carbolic soap, all that was available in the occupied zone. Her teeth were good, but English fillings in back molars had been drilled out and replaced with French gold. She wore neither make-up nor nail polish, and her beautiful dark eyes seemed dull and insignificant behind cheap French spectacles with clever lenses creating the illusion, while also doubling as magnifying lenses for map-reading.

Beneath an ill-fitting greyish costume from a well-known French store, whose pockets contained traces of dusty French loaf crumbs and grains of Nantes soil, Lisette wore a black jumper hand-knitted with Paris wool. Vest and thick bloomers were of a type available at French markets and wide garters cinched thick brown stockings above the knees. A worn black beret and brown shoes bought in France, with Nantes mud engrained in the soles, completed the transformation.

Lisette had the cover story off by heart. Marie Duval was the widow of Armand Duval from Nantes, who had been a recent victim of TB. She was travelling to visit Armand's elderly cousin in the small village of Auberge-en-Amont. She wore a wedding ring of French design, which Armand had placed on her finger on their wedding day eight years ago. There were no children, but Marie worked as a kindergarten assistant. Every detail of the story could be checked and verified, should anyone be interested.

Lisette smiled at her changed image. Had Madeleine Gregory chanced to meet her beloved foster child in the street, she would have passed her by. Which was exactly what Mr Brown had intended.

'Special Operations executives are delighted

with you, my dear,' he'd told Lisette at the final briefing. 'It's jolly hard luck your sister's French isn't up to scratch. Identical twin agents would have been useful. Anyway, she could unwittingly provide useful cover for you in your absence, should any German Abwehr agents come snooping around.'

'Will it be a parachute drop?' she'd asked.

After gruelling fieldcraft training in mountains around Inverness, she'd had parachute training at Ringway near Manchester, before finally perfecting her spying skills at Group B finishing school in Beaulieu in the New Forest.

Mr Brown smiled and shook his head.

'Not this first time. You'll be flown in by a Lizzie – that's a Lysander, nice little crate. It'll land in a field, drop you off, pick up one or two bods and take off again within minutes. Your reception committee will provide a bicycle and safe house for the night. Next day you ride to the address in Auberge which you've memorized, and contact an RAF chap in hiding there. He was shot down recently, and has information we're very keen to have. Use your sketching skills, get him to help you draw maps and make detailed sketches. That's a very important precaution, mind. It's quite OK to look after yourself and save the drawings at all costs, should the chappie himself be – er – apprehended en route to the pick-up point. The bike frame is adapted to take rolled maps and sketches without arousing suspicion. His French is poor, so it's up to you to get him to the pick-up point on time and all in one piece, if humanly possible. One of our contacts will tell you when...'

Lisette tensed and stood up as she heard the click of high heels approaching in the corridor. The door opened and a fashionably dressed young lady looked in.

'Ready, my dear?'

Lisette picked up a scuffed brown case containing a change of underwear and a few toilet items, and followed her mentor to the waiting car. Very little was said on a journey timed to deliver Lisette to RAF Tangmere, near Chichester, as dusk was falling. Her companion, known only as Alice, shook hands when they reached the airfield.

'Good luck, and for heaven's sake don't blow your cover by asking for *café au lait*. Coffee's black. Milk's rationed.'

'I won't! Thanks for the tip.' Lisette smiled.

The waiting plane looked small and vulnerable to Lisette's eyes, but the Lysander's pilot exuded relaxed confidence which reminded her poignantly of Freddie. He carried a Michelin map as he helped Lisette aboard. It seemed to be the sole navigational aid, which he kept handy while completing routine take-off checks.

'We'll be flying low and slow, miss,' he told her. 'That's so I can keep track of rivers and fields below. Conditions are perfect, just enough moon to show the way. Don't fret if there's a little flak once we're over the French coast.'

'Isn't that dangerous?'

He laughed as the Lizzie shuddered and bounced across the grass towards the runway.

'Never been hit yet.'

The engine roared. After a remarkably short run Lisette felt a lift and release from solid ground which told her they were airborne. She tried to relax.

She knew she faced danger in France, but was prepared for that. She was afraid, and that was a good sign. 'They', the nameless ones of SOE, said fear kept you on your toes, made you wary and careful. Over-confidence was dangerous. She allowed her thoughts to stray to her family, and how much she loved and missed them. They must feel hurt and abandoned, she knew, but she could not do the work she had trained to do if restricted by ties of love and concern.

She glanced out as the Lizzie droned onwards across the Channel, and saw stars shining in the midnight sky over Normandy. Silver pinpoints of light gleamed with rainbow colours in a sudden blur of tears. She was doing this dangerous work because she could not stand the thought of a cruel regime occupying her dead mother's homeland. She could not bear the thought that an evil power possessed the beautiful sunlit land where she and Freddie had lived and loved and been blissfully happy...

The pilot glanced at her anxiously.

'Are you OK, miss?'

Lisette smiled. 'Fine, thanks. Just admiring the stars. It's a beautiful night.'

He nodded, glancing at the map folded on his knee. She could see pencilled crosses marking the field where lights would be lit for a landing, and just as swiftly extinguished.

He eased the little plane lower as they crossed the coastline. Soon a burst of flak came at them from the ground, seeming to travel slowly at first, then flashing by at tremendous speed. The Lizzie juddered and danced in the blast, then flew on steadily. The pilot chuckled.

'Bit too close for comfort. No worries. Piece of cake!'

With a lurch of the heart, Lisette could recognize the deftness of the clever hands on the controls, the cheerful, measured disregard of danger. It was almost as if Freddie sat there in the pilot's seat, approving what she was about to do, caring for her still.

She looked out at the midnight sky, smiling.

She thought she had never seen such a dazzling glory of stars...

Twelve

The Lysander's engine cut to a whisper. The small plane glided down through darkness towards a line of lights spaced out below. The pilot pulled out of a gentle dive and soared away. Lisette was startled.

'What's wrong?'

'Nothing. Can't be too careful, you know, but they've Morsed the correct code letter and everything's tickety-boo.' He glanced at her. 'Better have all your gear ready to hop out when we go in this time. I have two chaps to pick up, and I won't hang about.' He gave her a quick grin, then returned to the controls, turning in a wide arc back towards the lights.

The Lizzie touched down, bouncing across rough grass before coming to a restless halt. Lisette was aware of shadowy figures outside as the door opened.

'Good luck!' the pilot whispered.

Then she was outside in damp cool air, feet sinking in wet grass. Someone grabbed her arm, hustling her away. Two figures pushed past and disappeared into the Lysander. The little plane taxied, then turned. She held onto her beret as the slipstream tugged at her raincoat, then the plane lifted lightly into the wind and was soon lost in darkness. Lisette stared after it with a sudden feeling of isolation. The last link with home had gone!

A man swore softly, close by.

'We need weapons, and the English send women!'

'That will happen, one day,' said the man who had grabbed her arm.

There were others darting around, quickly dousing lights. He looked down at her. She could see only a gleam of dark eyes, but he was tall, his coat collar turned up over his chin.

'I'm Julius.'

'Marie.'

She felt a warm glow of relief. This was her contact. Not his real name, of course, any more than Marie was hers. They would work closely together and never know the real man and woman behind the names. It was safer that way.

'Come quickly. I don't think the plane attracted attention, but you never know.' He took her case, held her arm, and guided her across a stubble field, through a farm gate and onto a rough track. Once there, he released her.

'Follow me. It's not far.'

It was a silent walk and she stumbled once or twice, but he did not pause till the dark outline of a typical French farmhouse loomed up ahead. There were no lights visible behind shuttered windows, but Julius tapped on the nearest – three light taps, one heavy.

V in Morse code. V for Victory.

A dog barked inside, louder as a door opened. He took her arm, and bundled her inside.

She found herself in a dimly lit kitchen with
aromas of baked bread, onions and wood
smoke. A friendly mongrel sniffed her coat,
tail wagging, and a white-haired man seated
at the table gruffly ordered it away. The
elderly woman who had opened the door
glared at Lisette.

'This must stop, Julius. You involve us in too
much danger. What if the Germans get wind
of it?'

He laughed.

'They won't, *madame*. They invade towns
and cities and leave local gendarmes to police
the countryside.'

She shrugged. Her lips set in a thin line, she
eyed Lisette coldly.

'You'll be hungry. There's bread and cheese,
a little homemade wine. No coffee or tea.'

'Thank you, *madame*. Bread, cheese and
wine would be lovely.'

The woman looked surprised. She glanced
at Julius.

'This one's French is good, she could pass
for *une Amonteuse*.'

He shrugged. 'Perhaps. We shall see.'

The bread was homebaked, the cheese rich
and hearty, the wine harsh and dry. Lisette
ate every crumb and drained the glass, while
the elderly couple and Julius watched. He sat
with elbows resting on the table, a little wine

in a glass.

'What now?' Lisette asked him.

'You sleep here. Madame will show you to your room, and your bicycle waits in the stable. Tomorrow I'll show you the way to Auberge-en-Amont. You know the address? Good! But be careful. There are rumours that SS troops are coming here in force. Nobody knows why.'

She followed her hostess up creaking stairs to a simply furnished bedroom. Everything was spotlessly clean. The woman set the oil lamp down on a table.

'Don't open the shutters,' she warned. 'Someone might wonder who the visitor is. The bathroom is at the end of the landing.'

Lisette thanked her, and the farmer's wife relaxed a little.

'Why must you come to France, my dear, when it is so dangerous?'

'Because I was happy here once, *madame.*'

The farmer's wife sighed.

'Ah, we were all happy once!'

Lisette slept soundly and wakened at cock-crow. She could hear movement below and washed and dressed quickly, inspecting her appearance in the mirror to make sure she passed muster as a dowdy kindergarten teacher. Spectacles in place, she followed an appetizing smell of frying bacon and found her hostess busy at the stove. There was an aroma in the air resembling coffee.

'Bonjour,' Julius smiled. He sat as before,

elbows resting on the table. He caught her eyeing the coffee cup in his hand, and smiled.

'Roasted wheat grains make a passable substitute, *madame*.'

After breakfast, he told her to be ready to leave. She went upstairs and spent time removing traces of her occupancy. Pulling on the black beret, she picked up the battered case and left the room. Downstairs, the elderly couple were obviously relieved to see the back of her.

Mounted on a bicycle which had seen better days, Lisette found meticulous 'Mr Brown' had overlooked one important detail. It was almost impossible to judge where she was going when cycling, looking through distorted lenses. Julius, riding alongside, noticed nothing amiss. He was busily concocting a plausible story to explain their presence on the road this early.

'We've been visiting our grandparents, Marie. I'm your cousin, making sure you're on time to catch the early train. I trust your papers, permits, food vouchers et cetera are in order?'

She nodded, which was a mistake. The bicycle swerved sideways, narrowly avoiding a collision.

'What d'you think you're doing?' Julius demanded angrily.

'It's the spectacles. They're OK for normal use, but hopeless for cycling.'

She stopped and slipped the specs into her pocket. He had pulled up too, and she turned to him, smiling. 'I'm very sorry, Julius.'

His facial expressions were well-schooled, and did not reveal the impact her smiling dark eyes had upon him. He could understand the need for disguise. This woman was more than beautiful; she was memorable.

The warmth of her smile attacked the ice that had enclosed his heart since a British bomb killed his darling fiancée. It had happened when Germans were hounding the British out of France. The beaten army had scuttled homewards across the Channel in a fleet of little boats like rats leaving a doomed ship, deserting their French allies.

Afterwards, bitter and heartbroken, he had joined the Resistance movement and sworn to fight the German invaders, even if it meant working with the hated British. So he helped British secret agents come and go, in the hope that one day the British would send weapons for French patriots to drive the Nazis out of France.

And instead they send a beautiful woman with a tempting smile, he thought. To his dismay, an answering smile tugged reluctantly at the corners of his grim mouth.

He resisted the impulse and drew the hidden knife from his belt.

He stabbed her front tyre, which collapsed with a punctured hiss.

'Put on your specs, *madame*. We will walk,' he said.

After the first surge of outraged anger, Lisette saw the wisdom of the act. Spectacles

283

were an integral part of her disguise and she should not be seen without them. She couldn't ride, so she must walk, and there had to be good reason for walking. The flat tyre was perfect.

She looked at him with respect as she replaced the specs.

'Good thinking! I hope it isn't too far?'

'Only a couple of kilometres, *madame*.'

'Let's get going, then.'

The town was beginning to stir as they reached the outskirts, wheeling the bikes. The place felt to Lisette like a market town, with farm produce rattling past in horsedrawn carts, a few mud-spattered cattle trucks mingling with the cars. Nobody paid any attention, apart from a glance at the punctured tyre.

'It must be mended,' Lisette said.

'Don't worry, I'll see to it. Tell me the address of your contact.'

She told him. He obviously knew it well, and led the way unerringly to a narrow street lined with small dark shops with living quarters above. He stopped outside a shoe-maker's shop. Boots, shoes and wooden-soled leather sabots were displayed on shelves in a dusty shop window. Work was already underway in a busy workroom inside. Lisette's nose was assaulted by the smell of new leather, her ears deafened by hammering and the high-pitched whine of machines cutting and stitching. Glancing up at heavily screened windows, she judged this flat to be a perfect hideout for someone who did not care to be heard moving about above during the working day. Julius opened a scarred door beside the shop and left Lisette's bicycle in the gloomy hallway at the bottom of a flight of stone stairs.

He held out a hand.

'*Bonne chance, madame.* You'll find Chandelle upstairs.'

She was disconcerted, unwilling to let him go. Now she was really alone.

'Will I see you again?'

'I'll come and fetch you when conditions are suitable.'

She shook hands briefly. It was not much more than a quick pressure of her hand in his, but the effect upon him was electric. Julius went outside, appalled. First the smile, then the touch. What was happening?

Lisette climbed the stairs towards a door on the landing above. Taking a deep breath, she tapped on the panel. After a moment it was opened by a plump middle-aged woman with a frizz of salt and pepper hair and alert brown eyes.

'I am Marie Duval,' Lisette said.

'I grieve for Armand,' the woman answered.

'He was a good husband to me, Chandelle.'

The correct formula had been followed and the two women exchanged relieved smiles. Chandelle drew Lisette inside and locked the door.

'I'm very content to see a woman agent,

Marie. More men knocking at my door, and my good reputation, it is mud!'

She bustled around boiling a kettle while Lisette took stock of the apartment. It consisted of a living-room-cum-kitchen with a curtained bed recess, a bedroom and a small bathroom beyond. It would barely hide a mouse, let alone a British airman.

'I'll make some of the muck they call coffee these days,' Chandelle was saying cheerfully as she sliced a greyish, floury loaf and produced a jar of jam with a flourish which indicated this was a rare treat. 'No butter or milk, I'm afraid, my dear. I've used my ration.' They sat at the table drinking the potent black drink and eating bread and jam.

'I must leave you presently,' Chandelle said. 'I'm a cleaner, you understand. I clean everything – public lavatories, small houses, big houses, offices, hotels, even the town hall. It's amazing the information one picks up along with the rubbish.'

Lisette laughed.

'I can imagine!' She leaned forward. 'Where is he, Chandelle?'

The little woman rose and darted to a heavy old cabinet occupying one corner of the room. It was not as heavy as it looked, for she pushed it easily aside to reveal another door. She tapped out the code Julius had used at the farmhouse.

The door opened cautiously and a young man looked out. He wore the clothes of a French workman, but to Lisette's eyes looked unmistakably British, with tousled fair hair and very blue eyes.

He greeted her eagerly.

'I say, can you speak English? The dear old girl can't understand a word I say.'

'Maybe that's just as well,' Lisette said.

He gave her a serious glance.

'Yes, absolutely. Careless talk costs lives – mine probably, and hers.'

Chandelle had wrapped herself in a green apron and quelled her wild hair under a headscarf.

'I'll be off then, Marie. Don't answer the door, and don't be making more noise than you can help, even if the racket downstairs is enough to waken the dead.'

When she'd gone, Lisette introduced herself.

'Marie Duval.'

'Alex Morrison, late of 224 squadron, RAF Leuchars.'

Surprised, Lisette was caught off guard.

'Leuchars in Fife? Why, I can remember the Dundee train stopping at Leuchars station!'

'Now there's a coincidence!' He beamed delightedly. 'Do you come from Dundee?'

'Oh, no!' she said quickly. 'I was just passing through, visiting friends before the war.'

That was careless! she thought, annoyed with herself. She must be more careful.

She turned to the pot of ersatz coffee Chandelle had left simmering on the hob. He accepted a cup, and greeted the bread and jam with delight as they sat at the table. She decided she liked Alex Morrison. He was frank and friendly with an enthusiasm when talking about aircraft which reminded her of Freddie. She found she remembered her husband with love and great tenderness, but time was easing the dreadful pain of loss. She smiled at the young pilot.

'My people seem very keen to get you home, Alex. You don't speak French, and that's why I'm here. So what's all the fuss about?'

He frowned.

'I'm not sure, Marie. To put you in the picture, Leuchars airfield came under the control of Coastal Command just before the war, so when the Germans invaded Belgium and Holland in 1940, my squadron had to settle for routine patrols, leaving all the exciting stuff to the Brylcreem boys of Fighter Command.' He sighed and shook his head. 'Reconnaissance is deadly dull, you know, just keeping an eye open for enemy ships hour after hour. Sometimes it pays off, of course. One of our chaps spotted the German prison ship *Altmark* and tipped off HMS *Cossack*. The Navy freed over two hundred British prisoners that day – a jolly good show.'

'It does make boredom seem worth while,' Lisette remarked.

'Yes, it does,' he agreed. 'Anyway, there's a place called Peenemunde on the north German Baltic coast, right by the border with Poland. I happened to take a different route

288

home after my last mission and was amazed to find this place boasted an airfield and was a hive of activity. Also, there were strange circular emplacements on the ground, the like of which I've never seen before, with one or two long cylindrical objects lying alongside. I went down lower, to have a closer look, but the Germans didn't welcome the intrusion and sent up a terrific barrage. The plane was hit, and I was in deep trouble.'

He took a sip of coffee, grimaced, then went on, 'I've never fancied ditching at sea, so I turned inland over Germany, hoping to keep the kite flying for as long as possible. After a while I noticed something else that struck me as odd. There were new roadworks down below in open countryside, fresh railway tracks being laid, ending in scattered areas of construction. The sites resembled ski runs, all angled in one direction, towards London and southern England. Then the plane started to fail and I had to get out. Fortunately, Belgian resistance fighters picked me up. When I told them what I'd seen, they became excited and contacted London. I was smuggled off to a safe house, and here I am!'

'What do you think is going on?' Lisette asked.

'Whatever it is has stirred up a wasps' nest. The Germans found the wreckage of the plane, so they know I'm still around. They seem determined to prevent me escaping to Blighty. There have been rumours they're developing a secret weapon, so maybe it could be to do with that. Anyway, I've marked all the sites on a map. The boffins in Whitehall can work it out for themselves,' Alex said, finishing the last slice of bread and jam.

Lisette's battered brown case was actually a cunning box of tricks devised by Mr Brown's colleagues, containing a full set of drawing materials. Over the next week, she transferred the information Alex had gleaned onto paper as delicate as tissue and strong as parachute silk.

'Gosh, you're a fine artist, aren't you?' he said admiringly, studying the meticulous plans, sketches and diagrams she'd produced.

She laughed, remembering the ladylike subjects the school art mistress had favoured.

'This beats fussy watercolours any day, Alex. Much more rewarding!'

They had established a warm rapport. He was an attractive man with a keen sense of humour and they enjoyed their daily sessions around Chandelle's table, Alex talking and studying the dog-eared map while Lisette committed his conclusions to paper.

She sensed he found her attractive, and couldn't help feeling flattered. She had discarded the specs when they were alone, and caught him staring at her with a warmth in his blue eyes which made her heart beat faster.

Lisette had not ventured outside, but as time went by and there was no word from Julius, she grew restless. Surely they should have heard from him by now?

And then one evening Chandelle came home with alarming news. She had been cleaning the Town Hall offices that day, often a source of valuable information.

'The Mayor, he waddles around, flapping like the Christmas goose! Maybe he hears goose-steps in our streets!' she said, digging in her overall pockets and producing crumpled scraps of paper salvaged from wastepaper baskets.

Lisette smoothed out discarded copies of inter-office memos and her blood ran cold.

'Bad news, Chandelle! The councillors are ordered to commandeer suitable billets for an SS Panzer division, arriving in Auberge within the next few days. The soldiers are to conduct a house-to-house search for so-called 'undesirables', and the Mayor has instructions from German High Command to provide a quota of able-bodied men from this district. The men are to be transported to the Pas de Calais for vital construction work. No wonder *Monsieur le Maire* is flapping!'

Chandelle let out a wail and wrung her hands. 'But this is terrible, Marie! The SS has left us alone so far, but now they are here on our doorsteps. Julius must be told!'

He arrived silently after curfew that night, looking grim.

'The first convoy of trucks and motorcycles is not far away,' he told Lisette. 'This couldn't have happened at a worse time. The plane from London is due in two days and I've had to tell it not to come. The whole district will soon be swarming with German SS.'

'What will happen to Chandelle, if they search the house and find Alex?'

'It doesn't bear thinking about, but we will leave immediately and take him with us, and then she should be safe enough.'

'Where will we go?'

'If we cycle north-west towards the coast, keeping to minor tracks, we should keep one jump ahead of the Germans. In that area we have only Vichy police and their informers to worry about. When I can find a safe place for a landing, I'll contact London and arrange for them to send a plane for you and the airman.'

She studied him in silence. He was a hard case, unpredictable. Yet strangely enough she trusted him. She even felt concern for his safety.

'But what will happen to *you* afterwards, Julius?'

He shrugged.

'I won't stay in Auberge, that's for sure, *madame!*' he said. 'I have been a lawyer in this town, and an outspoken *avocat* always gains enemies who will be glad to see him in a German labour camp.'

Chandelle had shooed Alex out of his room with a torrent of French. He hadn't understood a word, but the urgency was obvious.

'What's up?' he asked Lisette.

She explained the situation. 'We have to

move at once, Alex. It'll give Chandelle a chance to return the flat to its original state before the Germans come. Julius says he'll take us somewhere the plane can land more safely.'

Alex studied the Frenchman and didn't like what he saw.

'Can we trust this chap? If looks could kill, I'd be a goner.'

Julius smiled faintly.

'My English is good, *monsieur* – and yes, if looks could kill, you would certainly die. I do not like British airmen.' He turned to Lisette in disgust, reverting to French. 'This man will be a constant danger to us, Marie. He speaks no French and looks too English.'

When Julius judged it was safe to venture out, they hugged tearful Chandelle and set off on bicycles along dark, deserted streets. Alex's map had been reduced to white ash in Chandelle's living-room fire, his fair hair and pale skin darkened with coal dust and boot polish. Lisette's maps and sketches were concealed in cardboard cylinders hidden within the bicycle frame.

Julius had a sob story ready to cover their disregard of curfew. They were hastening through the night to be at their dying mother's bedside...

Lisette's rigorous training had prepared her for dangerous situations, but this was the most hazardous she could imagine. Yet she wasn't afraid. There was magic abroad, she thought, as she cycled along, following Alex and Julius along dark shadowy tracks, relishing fresh air and exercise after days of confinement. She felt almost euphoric. A crescent moon hid behind misty cloud, and there were no stars, only the black tracery of branches and leaves, like a cathedral roof arching over their heads.

After three hours without a break, Alex's condition began to give cause for concern. Julius had kept up a gruelling pace, perhaps forgetting that Alex's plane crash, followed by weeks of inactivity, must inevitably have an adverse affect upon his stamina. The airman struggled on bravely, but began showing serious signs of exhaustion and finally collapsed. Julius was forced to call a halt to let Alex recover in the shelter of the hedgerow.

They found themselves on the outskirts of a dark, silent town. Lisette raised her face to the night air blowing across the fields. She sat up suddenly.

'Do you smell onions, Julius? Where are we?'

He gave her a keen glance. 'Sainte-Claire-en-Bois is the only sizeable town in this region, Marie, but I've no contacts here.'

'I do. I have relatives!'

He frowned thoughtfully. 'The airman is not fit to reach the safe house I have in mind. We must lie low somewhere till he recovers. Can you trust these relatives?'

'I don't know.'

They looked at one another. Already the sky

294

seemed lighter; wisps of morning mist were gathering over the onion fields. She put a hand on his arm.

'Let me go to them and assess the situation, Julius. If they raise the alarm, I'll create such a rumpus you and Alex will have time to get away. Then you must get Alex and all his information back safely to London.'

He stared down at the hand on his arm.

'What about you?'

She laughed softly.

'I'm not important.'

Ah, but she was to him! he thought. She was becoming the most important being in the whole treacherous world, and there was nothing he could do to protect her. The airman's vital information *must* reach Whitehall soon. Julius had learned from Dutch patriots about Hitler's secret weapon. He hardly dared imagine what might happen to south-east England when the missile launching sites became operational.

He looked at her impassively, hiding his anguish.

'Very well, Marie. Go ahead.'

They waited till it was light and the town had wakened. Rest had revived Alex and they walked boldly into town wheeling their bicycles, mingling freely with field workers and citizens in the market square. Lisette recognized with a lurch of the heart the spot where the old men had played boules in happier times. The shrubbery was overgrown and neglected today, but the bench was still there, beneath the tree.

'Wait here,' she told her companions. 'If it's safe, I'll come for you. If not, I'll scream the place down.'

She found 13 Rue de l'Hirondelle without much difficulty. The tall town house looked much the same. Heart thudding, she raised the brass knocker and tapped boldly. Moments passed before the door opened cautiously. She recognized Dominic Lefevre at once. His hair had grown grey, but the family resemblance was even more striking. She decided to take a chance.

'Dominic, I'm Suzanne Lefevre's daughter Lisette. Madeleine is my foster mother...'

'I know who you are,' he broke in. 'I've done more research since last time.' He glanced up and down the street. It was deserted, apart from one or two children trailing slowly to school.

'What in heaven's name are you doing here, Lisette?' he demanded softly.

'Not Lisette, please. Marie Duval.'

He drew back suspiciously. 'So! You're an English spy?'

Suddenly the man's allegiance seemed questionable. She kept smiling.

'No, just someone who loves France. I only need somewhere to rest for a few hours, Dominic, that's all, but if it's not convenient, I'll go.'

He opened the door wider. 'No, wait! Please come inside.'

She hesitated, debating for a moment.

'I should warn you, I have two friends with me.'

He shrugged. 'No matter. Tell them to come.'

Lisette lingered doubtfully on the doorstep. She still wasn't convinced Dominic Lefevre was a safe bet. Dare they risk it?

Wren Annie Balfour's fortunes had taken a turn for the better since the Clydeside blitz. She had apparently won high favour with somebody in the War Office.

Annie assumed this must be because she had applied Conrad's stringent standards to the naval storerooms and cookhouse, waging unrelenting war upon cockroach, mite and vermin infestations. Perhaps her efforts had not gone unnoticed.

The result was swift elevation to Leading Wren, followed a few months later by a glowing recommendation for promotion to Petty Officer.

There was only one snag. The promotion involved a posting to Southsea, which, as Connie remarked in disgust, was just about as far south in England as you can go without getting your feet wet.

Worriedly, Annie talked it over with Conrad. He was quiet for a moment.

'I'll miss you terribly, darling,' he admitted at last. 'But golden opportunities don't grow on trees, and in my experience you should never turn down promotion. If you do, you could be left peeling spuds for the duration.

They've obviously recognized your ability, and I'm very proud. Of course you must go! Never mind about me.'

'I don't deserve you, Conrad darling, really I don't!' she said, kissing him tenderly. His generosity was all the more humbling because she'd noticed the strain of running a wartime hotel was taking its toll. He looked tired and thin, and she suffered pangs of guilt. They should have been married. As his wife, she could have helped to cope with the worry and stress of work. She sighed. Fergus had a lot to answer for, with his sudden appearances and wild, unsettling kisses!

Connie grumbled furiously of course. She was in a bad mood anyway, despite the fact that Leah had clicked with the cinema manager's son, a young man who met with Connie's hearty approval. There had been a lull in air-raids on Scotland's east coast, and Connie had decided it was safe to bring young Benny back to Edinburgh. She'd had a quiet word with John when he'd brought the hotel's weekly order, but the outcome was that Benny had flatly refused to leave the McGills.

'I'm sorry, Ma,' John had told her apologetically. 'He says he likes school, has lots of pals, and loves life on the farm. He insists he doesn't want to return to the city just yet.'

He did not add that his young brother had a serious crush on Davina Williams, the McGills' housekeeper. Wild horses wouldn't drag Benny away from her side at the moment – a situation which John found disturbing. He wished he could speak to Davina about the youngster's infatuation, but she was always surrounded by a crowd of child evacuees, or an adoring group of Italian prisoners of war, recently drafted in to replace farmworkers who'd been called up.

John hadn't been keen to take the prisoners, but Marigold had overruled him. Fortunately, the Italians were delighted to be out of the war and were determined to be no bother to anyone.

There had been no more news from Singapore concerning the fate of John Balfour, his wife and son, and this was a constant worry for all the family. It was no wonder that Annie was quite glad to leave Scotland and occupy her thoughts with fresh challenges down south. Being Petty Officer in charge of staff and storerooms on the naval base carried considerable weight, and she was determined to make a success of it. After the first few frantically busy weeks, she had reorganized the stores and storerooms to her satisfaction, and found that by keeping a watchful eye on supply and demand, administering the job was, as the popular saying went, 'a piece of cake'.

'Your fame's spread, PO,' the Leading Wren announced breathlessly one day, appearing in the office at the double. 'There's an inspector from the Ministry of Food snooping around, wanting to inspect the stores. You never know, could be Lord Woolton!'

Annie wasn't unduly concerned. The department had been running like clockwork for several weeks, with only a few minor hiccups due to enemy action. She was confident the Minister of Food himself couldn't find fault with the orderly store cupboards. She went on with her work serenely.

The inspector appeared in her office a little later. This was certainly not His Lordship, Annie decided. This was a mildly apologetic little man, who introduced himself diffidently as Mr Brown.

Seated opposite her with a cup of tea and biscuits to hand, he beamed approval.

'All ship-shape and Bristol fashion, Petty Officer Balfour. Jolly good show!'

He dunked the biscuit neatly in the tea and smiled in a friendly fashion. 'Settled in well down south, have you? Good. And I believe you have an identical twin, who is also a Wren? How fascinating!'

'Yes, we-ell...' she replied. 'We're not all that close, sir, I'm afraid. My sister hasn't been in touch for months. I've no idea where she is.'

He sighed. 'Sad how families lose touch in wartime! I was rather hoping you might throw a little light on her whereabouts at the moment?'

Annie frowned, wondering why on earth the Ministry of Food should be interested in Lisette.

'All I can tell you is that she was seen with a man friend months ago, in Inverness,' she said tersely, unwilling to remember any part of the last painful conversation with Fergus.

Mr Brown flicked a crumb off his waistcoat and glanced up. She suddenly noticed how keen the mild gaze was behind the bookish spectacles.

'Are you quite sure it was her? Who spotted them?'

'A – a friend of mine, Fergus McGill, was in the district doing commando training. He wouldn't be mistaken, Mr Brown. He's known both of us since we were little girls.'

'Interesting!' he murmured thoughtfully.

She had the impression every word had been committed to this man's memory, and it made her nervous. She leaned forward.

'Why do you want to know? Has – has something happened to my sister?'

'Nothing to be alarmed about, I'm sure,' he said heartily. 'But I'm afraid your sister has gone – er – absent without leave.'

Annie sat bolt upright. This was awful. Desertion in wartime! It could mean Lisette's dismissal from the Wrens in disgrace. Maybe even worse!

'AWOL? Surely not. She wouldn't do that without good reason!'

'That's what I think.' The shrewd, bright eyes fastened upon her. 'They do say twins have a sort of strange affinity, don't they?'

'Yes, but I already told you – I haven't a clue where she is.'

Mr Brown hesitated a moment.

'We can hazard a guess *where* she might be, my dear, it's *how* she is that worries us.'

301

An icy chill ran down Annie's spine. She stared at the ordinary little man, and didn't trust him. The keen eyes didn't match the insignificance.

'I know my sister isn't dead, if that's what you're hinting!' she said coldly.

He stared at her with narrowed eyes, as if assessing the implications of Lisette's survival, then relaxed, smiling.

'Good-oh! We can assume she's OK then, my dear? Jolly good show!'

He rose, congratulated her upon running a tidy ship, and departed as silently as he'd arrived.

AWOL? Annie thought anxiously. Had her sister fallen in love with some dangerous stranger, and disappeared with him?

She sat staring into space, wondering why the man from the Ministry had left her with such an alarming sense of fear for Lisette's safety...

Thirteen

Lisette knew she was taking an appalling risk asking the Lefevres for sanctuary, but the situation was desperate and whom can you trust, if you can't trust relatives?

Trust nobody, Julius would say!

Her indecision had not escaped Dominic Lefevre's attention, and he was not so willing to welcome strangers.

'You know what I think?' he said. 'You and your friends are saboteurs on the run. I have two young children, and I will not involve children in your dangerous game. Thank God they left for school before you turned up! They need never know you were here.'

He was ready to slam the door in Lisette's face, but she cried out desperately.

'Dominic, please! We just need somewhere to rest for an hour or two. We'll be gone long before your children come home.'

Dominic hesitated, eyeing her doubtfully. He suddenly saw in the young woman an unmistakable resemblance to his own little daughter. Against his better judgement, his resolve weakened.

'Oh, very well!' he agreed reluctantly. 'Go fetch your friends while I have a word with Eva, my wife.'

Lisette returned to the bench beneath the tree and told Julius what had happened. He had serious doubts.

'I don't like this mention of children, Marie. You can't trust them.'

'So you'd do away with childish innocence, would you?'

'Innocence is dangerous in wartime,' he said.

She turned her back on him pointedly and mounted the bike, leading the way. There were cyclists still thronging the streets, mostly office workers heading for work. When they reached the house, Dominic hustled them inside, bikes and all.

Eva Lefevre stood watching in the hallway and her attitude was far from welcoming. Lisette gave the unwilling hostess a wary glance. Eva caught her eye and her expression hardened.

'I won't pretend you're welcome,' she cried angrily. 'There were whispers in the bread queue that the Gestapo are in town, on the lookout for a British airman accompanied by a dark-haired woman. If I had my way, I would not let you set foot in this house. I am not partisan where my children are concerned. I want you out of here before they come home from school. So you may rest for an hour or two, and count on my prayers for your safety when you leave'

'Thank you, *madame*. That's all we ask,' Julius said, quite kindly.

The bicycles were cluttering the narrow hallway. Dominic opened a door leading to kitchen premises and stowed them inside a stone-flagged scullery.

'Nobody will see them there,' he said casually, shutting the door. Lisette was unwilling to let hers out of her sight, and opened her mouth to say so, till Julius caught her eye warningly.

Eva Lefevre provided bread and cheese and ersatz coffee. Julius and Lisette ate every crumb, but Alex only sipped a little coffee. Their hostess revealed that there were three unused bedrooms and a bathroom in the attics at the top of the house.

'The *domestiques* slept there, when we could afford such luxuries,' she shrugged. 'The beds are not the best, but you can rest undisturbed.'

Lisette lingered behind talking to Dominic, while the others went upstairs.

Having established that they were indeed first cousins, Dominic relaxed.

'I'm sorry I wasn't much help when you visited me before the war, Lisette, but I honestly thought past history was best forgotten.'

'That's what our Aunt Madeleine thinks too!' Lisette remarked. 'She's been my foster mother since my own mother died, but she refuses to talk about the family.'

'Not surprising, since Madeleine was the ruin of it,' he said drily.

She was shocked. 'What did she do?'

'I don't know, but it must have brought disaster. I always knew Madeleine was the black sheep nobody mentioned, so your last visit set me thinking, and I became curious to find out more. Eventually I located an elderly woman who'd lived next door to the Lefevre family years ago. She told me it was whispered that Madeleine Lefevre had committed a wicked crime which was quickly hushed up. The old lady remembered hearing shouted arguments, quarrels and weeping coming from next door. That upset her, because before the tragedy they had been a happy family with never a cross word. Soon afterwards they all left town and never returned.' He looked at Lisette. 'That's quite true. My father was the eldest son and he went to southern France, where he met and married my mother. I was an only child, born and brought up in Marseilles.'

'But you came back!'

'I think my father was always homesick for Normandy. After my parents died, I felt the same urge to return to my roots.'

He glanced hurriedly at the clock ticking on the wall.

'I'm sorry, Lisette, I must go. I'm manager of the local bank – a law-abiding citizen, you understand, but a partisan at heart. God go with you and your friends, little cousin!'

Emotionally, he hugged her and kissed her on both cheeks.

★ ★ ★

306

Lisette dozed in the attic room, wakening with a start to find Julius standing by the bed. She stretched and yawned.

'Is it time to leave?'

'Yes, but there is bad news. The British pilot is ill.'

She sat up. 'What's wrong with him?'

'He's feverish and talking nonsense. When he tries to stand, he cannot.'

They looked at each other. This was serious.

'Have you told Eva?' she asked.

He nodded. 'She's with him now. This is dangerous, Marie. We must get out of here before those children come. They must not see us.'

Lisette followed Julius to the neighbouring room. Eva was bending over the sick man, persuading him to sip liquid from a cup. Alex looked very ill, eyes feverishly bright, muttering gibberish.

Eva straightened, glancing at them, and Lisette saw terror in her eyes.

'His throat is badly swollen. I've made a *tisane* of herbs, which will reduce the inflammation and make him sleep.'

Julius frowned. 'You mean he can't travel today?' he demanded.

Agonized, she nodded. 'If he leaves the house in this state, he will attract too much attention. He cannot be moved.'

They stared at her aghast.

'What about the children?' Lisette said.

She was distraught, wringing her hands. 'They mustn't come home! They might

307

mention your presence to their friends. Word gets around, and there are informers and Nazi sympathizers everywhere. We could all be shot for harbouring saboteurs!'

Lisette moved closer to Julius. They stood in silence as the frantic mother paced the floor. It was heartbreaking to watch Eva Lefevre's anguish. She stopped suddenly.

'I have an idea! I will paper and paint the children's bedrooms. Dominic will help. I'll tell the children they must stay with Tante Mathilde, and not come home till the work is done. My aunt lives on the other side of town, and I know she'll be pleased to look after them for a few days. That will give time for this man to recover, and the children will not be suspicious. Their father took them to the shop weeks ago, to choose paper and paint. Fortunately, my husband is a reluctant decorator. Rolls of paper and pots of paint are still untouched in a cupboard. But now the job must be done!' she cried with desperate determination.

She turned to Lisette.

'You will stay here while I run to Tante Mathilde and ask her to take Jeanne and Pierre. It will be safer if she is not told the truth. Then I'll meet the children after school and tell them what's planned. God grant that it will work!'

Overcome, she covered her face with her hands and sobbed. 'Poor little ones! They will be so happy to hear their rooms are to be decorated at last, and they will never suspect they are in appalling danger!'

'It's the perfect solution, Eva,' Julius told her gently. 'Show me the rooms, and I'll make a start on the preparation.'

Gentle co-operation seemed out of place with ruthlessness. It made Lisette stare.

Eva gave him a grateful smile, drying her eyes. 'Remember, stay away from the windows, Julius. You must not be seen.'

Left on her own with Alex, Lisette found the silence oppressive. A weak shaft of sunlight slanting dustily through drawn curtains did nothing to cheer the attic room. She sank down on a chair at the bedside and listened to Alex's quiet breathing. Presently, he stirred restlessly, waving his arms around wildly and muttering.

Concerned, Lisette grabbed his hands. The skin felt dry and hot, his grip tightening so that she couldn't let go even if she tried.

He began to talk more lucidly, but the tone was tense.

'Ten thousand feet ... losing height ... nose heavy, controls sluggish,' he reported, as if talking to some imaginary controller. His voice rose suddenly. 'Airspeed three hundred and rising! Must pull her out of this damned dive, but ... *controls not responding*!' he yelled.

He struggled to sit up and Lisette held him down. She knew he could not win this nightmare battle to save his plane.

But Alex had strength fuelled by feverish

desperation, and struggled frantically. Unwillingly, Lisette found herself being drawn into a nightmarish situation which was beginning to seem all too real.

Freddie! she thought suddenly. This must be how it had been for Freddie, wedged in the narrow cockpit with the plane hurtling uncontrollably towards the ground in a screaming dive. The thought made her feel disorientated, dizzy, close to fainting, as if speed were whipping her breath away. But it was not yet too late – there was still time...

'Get out, Freddie! You must get out!' she panted.

'Not yet!' he said impatiently, warding her off, sweat glistening on his brow, hands steady on unseen controls.

'Haul back the stick, boot the rudder bars ... levelling out. Hell! The ruddy altimeter's gone haywire!' For the first time there was a hint of panic as he yelled, 'Come on, old girl, we'll make it past the town. Green fields ahead, but ... smoke in the cockpit – flames!' He began to cough and choke, struggling to sit up, struggling to remove oxygen mask and radio-transmitter leads attached to the headset, one hand still steady, guiding the plunging aircraft...

Lost in her own nightmare, Lisette screamed.

'Get out, Freddie darling! For my sake, please! *Get out!*'

She pushed him down with all her strength, and watched him fall away from her, arms outstretched, free-falling ... safe!

She closed her eyes, weak with relief, then focused dazedly on the man whose life she had saved. She stared in disbelief.

Not Freddie, it could never be Freddie. This was Alex!

Lisette collapsed in tears. Her sorrow dug so deep she was afraid it would break her heart and spirit and leave nothing but emptiness. She had no sense of the passage of time, but presently became aware that she was not alone. Still drifting on the fringe of reality, she turned and clung blindly to the shadowy presence haunting the nightmare.

'Freddie darling!'

His smiling image slowly faded, but strangely enough, when it had gone she felt more at peace. She raised her head with a sudden start, and found herself clinging to Julius. He looked down at her gravely.

'Freddie was someone you loved, Marie?'

She nodded.

'My husband. He was a test pilot for Spitfires, just before the war. A fatal flaw developed in a plane during a test flight...' Shakily, she went on to tell Julius about the crash, the vital contribution Freddie had made to the fighter aircraft's development, and the civilian lives he'd saved quite deliberately, at the cost of his own.

He listened in silence. Her eyes were red and swollen, face all blotched and tear-stained, but to him she was beautiful. He loved her, though he knew only too well it was a love with no future. He pondered on the British husband who had loved her too, yet made the deliberate choice between love, duty and the lives of strangers. Julius remembered, with a wrench of the heart, his own young fiancée, killed by British bombs. Strange! he thought, but somehow a balance had been restored. The hatred had left him.

Lisette regained her composure.

'I'm sorry, Julius. Alex was delirious and started reliving the plane crash. Somehow I became involved.' She paused a moment, then went on hesitantly, 'You see, I couldn't cry when Freddie was killed. Even afterwards, when I lost our baby, I couldn't cry. But just then I believed for an instant I really could save my husband's life. When I realized it was all a dream, I couldn't stop crying. You – you must think I'm quite mad.'

'No,' he said seriously. 'I think it was good for you to cry.'

She laughed, embarrassed. 'Oh, nonsense, Julius! I'm trained to be cold as ice and tough as old boots, just like you!'

He looked at her, saddened by her false vision of the true Julius. She'd no inkling of the warmth and tenderness of his love ... but maybe that was just as well.

Lisette had not noticed the emotion Julius couldn't hide. She turned away to check on Alex, who was snoring peacefully with mouth wide open, dead to the world.

Julius was a meticulous decorator. His attention to detail drove Eva up the wall. She was in a fever of impatience to get the job done, the unwelcome visitors out of her house, and her children back home.

'Do you think children will notice, if patterns don't match and edges don't abut?' she cried. 'And for heaven's sake, Julius, stay away from that window!' she screamed at her helper.

Lisette found great pleasure in the transformation of the two shabby rooms, and it was a revelation to her, watching Julius work. His hands were strong and square, fingers sensitive to any imperfection in walls and woodwork. She liked to watch his absorption with each piece of wallpaper, carefully easing it to fit perfectly beside its neighbour. Sometimes he would turn and smile at her when it was done to his satisfaction. A special smile, younger, warmer. She liked that, too...

Alex was better, but still not fit to travel. Lisette stayed with him in her spare time, making sure he drained the herbal potion Eva prepared. He swore it tasted vile but did him good.

'Please stay, Marie,' he begged one afternoon, as she prepared to get on with the job. 'You're on my mind, night and day, you know. I consider it's wonderful luck that we met, even in this peculiar fashion.'

She laughed. 'You're right! I didn't expect to find a good friend hidden away in Chandelle's secret room.'

He reached for her hand, a light in his eye.

'More than a friend I hope, my darling, if we come through this OK!'

She didn't know what to say. She knew she could easily fall in love with Alex, but wasn't sure if she was ready to take that step. He reminded her of Freddie in so many endearing ways, but...

'What on earth did Eva put in that potion?' she teased him lightly.

He grinned wickedly. 'A love potion? I say! What fun!' He would have grabbed her, but she dodged the embrace. Pausing laughingly in the doorway, she blew her disappointed lover a kiss, which she reckoned was ample encouragement for one day.

By Thursday morning, Alex was pronounced fit to travel and the children's rooms were finished. Eva was overcome with relief.

'I told Tante Mathilde the rooms were ready, and the children could come home at four o'clock this afternoon after school. Oh, I'm so glad this terrible time is over!' She wiped away tears.

Julius was eager to get going. He had assembled their few possessions in the hallway along with the bicycles, blowing up tyres, making ready for the journey. Eva prepared a repast to take with them, bread and cheese laced with the region's famous sliced onions.

Lisette was sad to leave her relatives, yet impatient to be gone. Waiting made her edgy.

'We'll leave during *déjeuner*,' Julius decided.

'The streets are busier at lunchtime and three more cyclists won't be noticed.'

The clock hands seemed to crawl past midday, but at last it was safe to leave. Eva embraced them, opened the door and stepped outside, looking cautiously up and down the street. The road was busy enough with lunchtime traffic, and she turned to them, smiling...

Suddenly, they heard the sound they had all been dreading. Excited childish voices echoed down the street, shouting, *'Maman! Maman – we're home!'*

Eva froze; the blood left her cheeks. She swayed, putting a hand to the wall to steady herself as a dark-haired little girl and a small boy flung themselves into their mother's arms.

'Maman,' the girl said breathlessly, 'Mademoiselle Leclerc gave us permission to come home for *déjeuner*. She says we can tell the class all about our beautiful new bedrooms this afternoon!'

'And me!' added the little chap. 'I can do a drawing, Mam'selle says...'

Children are notoriously perceptive, and these two bright sparks were no exception. They sensed something was amiss. The girl caught sight of strangers in the hallway.

'Who are these people?' she asked curiously.

Lisette shivered. All their efforts, all in vain!

But Eva quickly gathered her wits. 'Oh, they are just good friends who helped with the

315

painting, my dears.' She forced a smile. 'Don't you want to see your rooms?'

They didn't need a second bidding and rushed into the hallway. As they clattered past, the little girl glanced at Lisette and smiled, then stared curiously at Alex, who hadn't had time to pull the black beret over the tell-tale fair hair. Then the children lost interest in the strangers and raced upstairs. Delighted cries and happy laughter echoed down to those standing listening below. Eva turned to them, pale and shaking, her expression grim.

'Quickly! Get out of here. God grant they will think nothing of it!' she said tersely.

They bumped the bikes recklessly down the steps into the street and cycled off. Lisette was badly shaken by the speed of events, and Julius's expression was grim. They both knew that lives were at the mercy of the innocent indiscretion of young children...

Soberly, the three mingled with other cyclists leaving town for outlying districts. Alex had pulled the black beret well down around his ears. Lisette prayed the sickroom pallor would go unnoticed. The traffic thinned out on the main road outside town and cyclists were more conspicuous. Julius seemed to know exactly where he was going, and turned off onto less frequented sidetracks. They continued for some miles without a break, but the going was rougher. Lisette had lagged a little behind, keeping an eye on Alex, but she

316

put on a spurt and caught up with Julius, in the lead.

'How much farther? Alex is tiring.'

'We'll stop shortly for a rest. It's not too far. We should be there some time after curfew.'

'Where are we going?'

'To the safest house in Normandy,' he said, an amused gleam in his dark eyes.

They sheltered presently in thick forest. Julius walked to the edge of the trees and stood studying the sky. Lisette followed, leaving Alex to rest. It was a peaceful, beautiful day. She took a deep breath of fresh air. They were hunted fugitives and nowhere was safe, but for a few fleeting moments she was happy, standing with Julius on the edge of green fields.

'How beautiful it is!' she said softly.

He shrugged. 'Conditions are perfect for a plane to land.'

She felt chilled by the remark. For a moment she had felt drawn to him and had longed to know the real man behind the alias, but Julius obviously wanted to be rid of her. Rebuffed, she returned to Alex.

They cycled on, keeping to farm tracks as the hours passed. Night came and Alex kept going bravely. He was on the point of collapse when Julius announced that they had reached their final destination.

This was a village of dark, huddled houses, very old and rural. There wasn't a light to be seen, nor a sound to be heard. Julius dismounted outside an official-looking building.

Lisette took one look at the dimly lit sign above the doorway, and stared incredulously.

'You – you're joking!'

He smiled faintly. 'Did I not promise you the safest house in Normandy?'

Lisette was suddenly afraid. She had trusted him, but hadn't he warned her to trust nobody? Maybe he wanted to have the glory of capturing two wanted fugitives, and keep on good terms with the Nazis.

Alex was leaning on the handlebars, exhausted.

'What's up, Marie? Where are we?'

'Outside a police station,' she told him flatly.

He lifted his head. 'I knew we couldn't trust this damn Frenchman!'

Julius scowled at him. 'Keep your voice down and bring the bikes inside,' he ordered.

An elderly gendarme dozing behind a desk awoke with a start, blinking sleepily. Recognition dawned after a moment and his moustache quivered into a broad smile.

'Julius, *mon brave*! You're late!'

'We were delayed,' he said brusquely. He glanced at his two silent companions. 'Is the reception committee ready for these two, Grégoire?'

The policeman studied Lisette and Alex with heightened interest.

'It will be – given a few hours.'

Lisette was afraid then, heart beating fast. There was no hope of escape, and she'd no doubt she'd been betrayed.

'What do you intend to do with us now, Julius?' she demanded with contempt.

'Clap you in jail, my dear!'

He grinned. The policeman chuckled.

'This man is not *galant*, *madame*, but it's true we can only offer a prison cell.'

Julius had lost interest in the subject of their accommodation. 'So what's the situation here, Grégoire?' he asked.

The older man shrugged. 'Peaceful and law-abiding, as always. The Vichy police will take over the Commissariat soon. François and I will be retired. There are plans to build massive gun emplacements in this region, using forced labour and malcontents. Life here will change, for everyone.'

The prison cell was not too uncomfortable, Lisette discovered. Rather to her surprise, she slept soundly once the cell door had clanged shut. She rested all the next day and ate the plain fare the gendarmes provided. Food and rest revived her, but did not lift her spirits. Julius's betrayal had been a cruel blow. She was surprised how hurtful it was.

It was growing dark when the cell door opened and he appeared. He sat down beside her on the trestle bed. His tone was abrupt.

'A plane will land tonight to take you and Alex to England, Marie, weather permitting. Coastal fog might be the only hazard.'

Relief washed over her. She could have hugged him.

'So you don't intend handing us over to the

Gestapo?'

He was deeply hurt and turned to her angrily.

'You really believed I'd do that? I would rather die, Marie!'

'Julius, I'm sorry!' she apologized, shamed and miserable. 'But you *did* tell me to trust nobody, not even someone I love—' She broke off, shocked. Loving Julius was a revelation to her. Obviously, it had no significance for him. He made no response.

'I taught you well!' was all he said.

Julius was adept at hiding his feelings, but that had been a difficult moment. He loved her and now she had indicated that perhaps she too had feelings for him, yet he must let her go, for her own safety. But he knew that when the plane took her away from him tonight, he would not care what happened to him afterwards.

'It's been quite an adventure, hasn't it, Julius?' she ventured hesitantly. 'What will you do, when we've gone?' She was too close to tears to look at him.

He shrugged guardedly. 'Maybe join a group of freedom fighters called the Maquis. They're based in hills and copses farther south, a wild undisciplined bunch of desperate men with few weapons. I believe I could help them form a more effective resistance movement.'

'That will be dangerous!'

He smiled mirthlessly. 'Yes, my dear. Very dangerous – for the enemy.'

'I – I'll miss you so much, Julius,' she said.
He stood up abruptly.

'No, you won't! You will have Alex to comfort you, a good man, one of your own kind.'

Showing formidable willpower, he kissed her chastely on the brow, and left.

Conditions remained perfect that night as they wheeled the bikes out of the police station. They set off by the back way, riding silently through the sleeping village into the countryside beyond. After a mile or so they reached a field prepared for the landing, a scene quite familiar to Lisette. The shadowy figures of the 'reception committee' darted around in darkness laying the flare path in the shape of an inverted L.

When that was done, it was just a question of waiting.

Julius had removed the saddle of Lisette's cycle and retrieved the precious maps and drawings in cardboard tubes hidden within the frame. He handed them to Alex with a smile.

'A job well done, *mon ami*! Make sure the British make good use of the information. Perhaps you will make our lovely Marie happy, one day.'

'Thanks, Julius, I intend to try.'

Lisette was shivering uncontrollably, and Alex put an arm round her, drawing her close. They stood in darkness on the edge of the field, listening.

The drone of the Lysander could be heard

a long way off in the still night. There was a flurry of activity from the reception committee, as they lit the flares. The lamps seemed dangerously bright, lighting up the field. The Lizzie came whispering cautiously down to check, then soared away to circle before coming in gently to land.

Alex grabbed Lisette's hand, dragging her forward, but she looked round wildly for Julius. He had disappeared into the shadows without a word.

'Come on, old girl. No time to waste,' Alex cried impatiently.

Together, they ran to the plane. The door was open. Alex scrambled in and placed the precious cardboard rolls carefully inside, then turned to help her aboard. The plane was already preparing to leave, the whole operation taking no more than minutes. Alex held out a hand.

'Hop in, my love! The pilot says hurry up!'

All of a sudden, something told her this was wrong for her. She stepped back.

'No, Alex. I'm staying.'

'What?' He was stunned with disbelief. 'You can't, Marie! You *must* come back to London, you said those were your orders!'

Yes, she knew that!

If she disobeyed orders, she could expect no further help from the Special Operations Executive. They would wash their hands of her. As far as Whitehall was concerned, she would cease to exist. But the door still stood open, she could change her mind. The Lizzie had barely paused since touching down. The engine gave an impatient, throaty roar.

Alex forgot the need for silence and shouted at the pitch of his lungs.

'Marie, please! Don't do this!'

But it was already too late, the Lizzie was on the move, bumping and lurching across the grass, turning into position for takeoff. Alex gave one last despairing cry: 'What am I to tell London?'

'Tell them I've joined the French Resistance!' Lisette yelled, hair blowing in the slipstream as the Lysander picked up speed and made its short leap upwards into the night sky.

She was surprised to find how liberated she felt, and how isolated, as the flares were doused and darkness closed around her. There was a stench of smoke and kerosene, mingled with a sweet smell of crushed grass and disturbed earth.

Her arm was grabbed none too gently, and she was whirled around to face Julius.

'Are you quite mad?' he demanded.

'Possibly!' She laughed breathlessly. 'But how could I leave you? I'd spend sleepless nights wondering where you were, what you were doing, praying you were safe...'

He looked down at her in the darkness, but a glint of moonlight reflected in his eyes.

'Why me?'

The answer was simple. 'Because I love you. I know I have to stay with you, Julius, for better or worse.'

'My darling, crazy girl!' He laughed. 'Don't you know it's more likely to be till death us do part, with me?'

'That's quite a commitment, Julius!'

'Yes, it is, my darling,' he agreed seriously. He put his arm around her. 'Let's get out of here. It's too dangerous. Poor rejected Alex did not go quietly!'

Together, they ran, joining other dark shadows scurrying across the empty field. Behind them, the faint whispering sounds of Lisette's last link with London faded into silence.

Annie Balfour's rapid promotions had ceased abruptly. She didn't mind. She enjoyed being PO in charge of stores. There had been no word from Lisette, but of course there wouldn't be, Annie reasoned. She'd gone AWOL and was officially a deserter. Annie hoped her sister was hiding somewhere safe in the Highlands, with the mysterious lover.

There was definitely something odd in the wind, down in southern England. There were large concentrations of shipping and small craft moored in secluded harbours, and more military personnel and vehicles than usual, camped around quiet, out-of-the-way places.

With large concentrations of troops around, Annie was not too surprised to receive a visit from Fergus McGill, now sporting a red beret. He trapped her in the storerooms, and as usual the atmosphere immediately became highly charged.

She eyed the insignia on his uniform. Pegasus, the winged warhorse of the Greek gods!

'Fergus, don't tell me you've joined the Paras!' she said despairingly.

'Yes dear. I'm a country boy at heart, I like fresh air.'

'Well, it don't get much fresher than ten thousand feet up,' she said.

Or more dangerous! she thought, suppressing a shudder.

She shook off her trepidation and looked at him.

'So what can I do for you? And you can take your eyes off those boxes of Cadbury's, they're strictly NAAFI.'

He eyed her thoughtfully.

'Bossyboots! I knew promotion would go to your head. This has nothing to do with chocolate, though a bar or two would be welcome, mind! I want to know why someone is leaning on me to swear it was you I saw in Inverness, not Lisette.'

'Why would they do that?' She was mystified.

'You tell me. This civilian chap followed me and my mates into a pub. Insignificant little bloke, but quite chatty. We began talking, and when I told him I came from Kirriemuir, he claimed to know a girl from the same neck of the woods. Said he'd met her some months ago in an Inverness hotel. She was called Annie Balfour, on leave from the Wrens, obviously in love with some unknown man. I chipped in with the twin sister angle, but he would have none of it. Insisted it was you.'

'He was blethering. I told you it wasn't!'

'And I believe you,' Fergus said seriously. 'I went along with his story, in order to get rid of him, but I reckon he'd found out I'd seen Lisette, and was trying to convince me it was you. The question is, why? That bothers me.'

It bothered Annie. She often had nightmares about her sister. From Fergus's account, the man in the pub bore a striking resemblance to Mr Brown. She recalled mentioning Fergus's name to the Government snooper, and Fergus could be easily traced within the select band of Commandos.

There was a simple explanation, of course. 'Lisette went absent without leave weeks ago, Fergus,' she told him. 'Officially, she's a deserter, and that's bad for morale. I've tried every official channel for news, but my sister has vanished off the face of this earth. The official line is, she doesn't exist!' She bit her lip, tears welled up. He squeezed her hand comfortingly.

'But *we* know she does, my dear! Don't give up hope, the war will end one day, Lisette will turn up with her mystery man, your cousin John will marry my sister, and you'll be happy ever after with long-suffering Conrad.'

She stared at him sadly. 'And what about you, Fergus? Will you be happy ever after?'

He laughed. 'Let's see if I'll have a future to look forward to, shall we?'

He released her and stepped back. Why

must he be so flippant? she wondered sadly. An emotional barrier of unspoken words lay between them. It seemed insurmountable.

'You can have a bar of chocolate, if you want one,' she said awkwardly.

'No thanks, love. Give it to the NAAFI.'

He sketched a vague salute and left. He made no attempt to kiss her. She stood alone, in tears, wishing he had...

Winter had not been kind to Conrad Whyte. Rationing and wartime restrictions made it difficult to maintain high standards in the restaurant and hotel. Months of chilly fog, ice and snow had an adverse effect upon Conrad's health. By the time spring sunshine promised to make life more bearable in 1944, he'd become totally dependent upon Connie's help.

As if she didn't have enough on her plate, worrying about her own scattered family.

Leah was the most immediate concern. The cinema manager's son Andrew was the love of Leah's life, a fine upstanding lad who had Connie's unqualified approval. But Andrew had joined the RAF and aimed to be a fighter pilot, much to Connie's consternation. Everyone knew that was a dangerous, risky business. Och, poor Leah!

Not that the little lass moped. Far from it! In between shifts at the cinema, Leah joined the Red Cross, learned to drive in no time, and took turns driving ambulances across the city at breakneck speeds which made her mother's hair curl.

Connie had given up persuading Benny to return home, which was just as well, since the Luftwaffe turned its attention to Edinburgh once more, due to false rumours that a British invasion of Europe was assembling in Scottish ports, aimed at the Norwegian coast. However, raids had tapered off recently, since the West Pilton battery, manned by the Home Guard, had brought down four Junkers 88 bombers in quick succession.

Another worry was her son John, by an odd twist of fate, now virtual boss of the old Balfour estate. She saw John most weeks, when he arrived with the hotel's order. Connie was relieved John hadn't gone to war, unlike Fergus McGill, who had always been in the thick of a fight. But John was nearly thirty-four and still a bachelor, despite courting the youngest McGill lassie for years. Connie had no time for the McGills, but was willing to welcome Marigold with open arms if only she'd marry John.

Connie sighed as she climbed the stairs to inspect the second-floor rooms. The cleaning required close supervision again. Minnie was in love with one of the American GIs to be found everywhere on Edinburgh's streets these days. She drifted around in a dreamy haze, idly flicking a duster here and there while chewing gum.

But apart from worries concerning the fate of James Balfour, his wife and young lad in Singapore, Connie's greatest concern was

328

Conrad's health. He'd an annoying dry cough which he couldn't shake off, and after weeks of nagging had reluctantly agreed to see a doctor, if only to shut Connie up.

When she'd sorted Minnie out, Connie returned downstairs to greet Conrad, after his latest doctor's appointment.

She found him sitting in the office.

'Did the doc prescribe a stronger cough mixture, dear?'

He looked up and her heart contracted when she saw how pale he was.

'Cough mixture won't help me, Connie,' he told her quietly. 'I've to go into hospital right away. The doctor's had the result of the X-rays, and I'm afraid it's bad news...'

Fourteen

Connie phoned Annie straight away to tell her about Conrad's illness.

'It's tuberculosis, dear, TB. I'd hardly time to pack a bag before an ambulance was at the door, whisking him off to hospital.'

Annie's instinct was to rush to Conrad's side, but leave for naval personnel on the south coast had been cancelled till further notice. She could have wept with frustration.

'I feel helpless, Connie. I want to be with him, but only weekend passes are being issued.'

'Well, not to worry, dear. Conrad will understand, bless 'im,' Connie said. 'There's nothing any of us can do anyway, but pray he'll get over it. He's in hospital for tests, then he'll be sent to a sanatorium to continue treatment. You can visit him there when he's feeling better.'

'What about the hotel? How will you manage on your own?'

'I'll manage fine,' Connie declared confidently. No point telling the poor lass she'd been in virtual charge of the place for months. It would only upset her.

The reason for cancelled leave soon became

apparent. A narrow window of opportunity for the planned invasion of Normandy must be seized while weather conditions were favourable. On the morning of 6th June 1944, the British public awoke to the news that the invasion of Europe was underway.

First reports indicated the landings had been successful, despite heavy resistance in some areas. It was reported that British paratroopers had landed behind enemy lines, catching the enemy by surprise and securing a vital bridgehead. The news only served to increase Annie's worries. She was certain Fergus would be in the thick of the action, and had no way of knowing what had happened to him.

The first German unmanned flying bombs hit London barely a week after the Allies landed on French soil. V1s were Hitler's secret weapon of revenge for the invasion. He had already boasted that the missiles would win the war for Germany, as hundreds were launched from sites on the Pas de Calais, aimed at London and the south. Annie's base remained under constant alert and it was a dangerous, nerve-racking time for everyone in the vicinity. The Germans had originally constructed ninety-six operational launch sites, but thanks to information provided by Alex and others, British and American bombing raids had reduced that number to a mere twenty-three. Even so, those remaining caused misery and heartache to long-suffering civilians as the 'doodlebugs' rained down upon London.

As news of casualties and random destruction filtered through, Annie became increasingly anxious about her aunt and uncle, Madeleine and Dermot Gregory. She applied for a weekend pass and set off for the capital to assess the situation. When the train arrived, she was met by boarded-up shops, ominous gaps in terraces, and large areas of devastation. Heavy with apprehension, she boarded a London bus heading for the suburbs.

Her spirits revived after she left the double-decker and walked along peaceful avenues, lined with large mansions similar to the Gregorys' and she saw no signs of bomb damage. She began looking forward to a night of luxury in her aunt's elegant surroundings, most welcome after the rigours of Navy air-raid shelters. As an added bonus, Madeleine might have heard from Lisette, she thought, quickening her pace.

The only change Annie could see as she approached her aunt's house was an absence of gates and railings, but this was not unusual. These features had been sacrificed the length and breadth of the country, to combat a shortage of iron.

But when Annie reached the empty gateway, she stopped and stared in disbelief.

The house had suffered a direct hit. Only one wing of the palatial mansion remained standing. Blackened joists and rafters poked from shattered brickwork, twisted lathes and crumbling plaster clung to broken walls. It was a chilling sight.

No wonder there had been no answers to recent phonecalls! She felt a sudden, sickening panic. What had happened to her aunt and uncle?

Annie made a closer inspection of the ruin, picking a precarious path through rubble before returning to the roadway, wondering what to do next. She was bracing herself to contact neighbours for news, which she feared could only be bad, when she heard someone call, 'Coo-eee! I'm over here!'

A dishevelled old woman was scrambling towards her past blocks of fallen masonry. Annie realized, with a shock of recognition, that this was her Aunt Madeleine.

Though the day was warm, Madeleine wore an ancient cardigan buttoned to the chin, a thick tweed skirt, black wool stockings and large dusty boots. A green knitted 'pixie' hood – popular wartime headgear – completed the unlikely picture.

Her aunt seized her, hugged her to her breast and sobbed emotionally.

'Lisette, *ma belle*! I knew you'd come back to us one day!'

Dismayed, Annie tried to struggle free. 'Aunt Madeleine, I'm Annie!'

Madeleine Gregory stared blankly at her for a moment, then released her sadly.

'Annie, of course! Please forgive me, my dear.' She retrieved a crumpled hanky from the cardigan sleeve and mopped her eyes.

'Haven't you heard from Lisette yet?' Annie asked.

Her aunt shook her head. 'Not since she joined the Wrens. I'm so sorry for the *faux pas*, my dear It was the Wren uniform, you see.' She made a valiant effort to smile. 'But now we must make the celebration, Annie dear, because I am so glad you have come.'

She linked an arm through Annie's, guiding her niece along a tortuous track past heaps of fallen brickwork and shattered fragments of marble.

'It's so terrible to see your beautiful home in ruins,' Annie remarked.

Madeleine shrugged. 'It is only bricks! I'm just thankful your uncle and I were working at the Red Cross depot at the time. Luckily for us, Dermot much prefers tending air-raid casualties to sitting behind a desk in Harley Street.'

They had reached a side door in the remaining wing, leading to the kitchen premises. A chorus of barking heralded the arrival of an elderly black labrador, a slender grey whippet and two perky little terriers, bounding to the door to greet a visitor. The only sign of damage Annie could see as she looked around the large kitchen was a collection of buckets and basins placed under a gaping hole in the ceiling, over in one corner. The room was very warm, a huddle of assorted cats snoozing on a rug beside an Aga cooker going full blast. The kitchen smelled pleasantly of baking, and faintly of fish. Madeleine patted the dogs and gestured towards the cats.

'Meet my little war orphans. Their owners are either dead or cannot be traced. These abandoned ones will soon be happy in new homes in the countryside. I keep them safe meantime.'

Doubtfully, Annie eyed the devastation outside the kitchen window.

'You call this safe?'

'Of course, dear! Lightning rarely strikes twice. Neither will doodlebugs.'

She untied the pixie hood, fluffed out her grey hair and removed the old cardigan. Now she bore some resemblance to the elegant lady Annie remembered.

Madeleine slid a simmering kettle onto the hotplate. 'We'll sit in the kitchen, if you don't mind, Annie. The other rooms are cold, and draughts whistle through.'

Seated at the table with the dogs ranged around, scrounging for scraps of a flattish yellow sponge cake – made, Madeleine explained, with powdered egg – there was a chance to talk. Annie frowned.

'I can't understand why Lisette hasn't been in touch. She must be so worried about you!'

Madeleine lowered her gaze for a minute, carefully cutting slices of cake.

'Annie ... did your father ever tell you why I left France?'

'He said you and Uncle Dermot met on holiday in Paris. It was love at first sight, and you married him and settled in London where he was working as a GP.'

Madeleine sighed softly. *'Mon Dieu,* such a pack of lies!'

Annie was indignant.

'My dad wouldn't lie! Why should he?'

'Because maybe he was not told the whole truth. Perhaps your mother did not want him to know it.'

The dogs wolfed down titbits of cake and lost interest, except for the elderly labrador. The dog rested its head on Madeleine's lap and looked up at her with sad old eyes. She stroked its heavy head pensively with a soothing hand. The kitchen was suddenly so quiet you could hear the cats purr.

'So what *is* the truth?' Annie said quietly.

Madeleine hesitated. She preferred to live with the lies, the past buried mercifully deep, but she sensed she could expect a sympathetic hearing from Annette Balfour. The true facts were painful, but maybe they should be known. She took a deep breath, steadying herself.

'Dermot was not on holiday when we met, Annie. He was a newly qualified doctor, gaining experience working in Paris with a mission caring for the poor. He found me beside the River Seine one cold, miserable evening. I was destitute, and in my desperate state had lost the will to live. I had just climbed onto the parapet of the bridge and was plucking up courage to jump when Dermot grabbed me. He saved my life. Afterwards, he took me to the mission hospital, and cared for me there. Your papa was right in only one detail. For us, it was love at first sight.'

Annie stared incredulously. This was a shocking revelation.

'But how could you be in such a state? Dad said my mother's French relations were quite well off. Why didn't they help you?'

'I was too ashamed to ask, after what I'd done.'

'Nonsense! What could possibly be so bad?'

'Try deceit, lies, vanity and greed, my dear!'

'Those are just standard human failings!'

'Ah, but package those four together, and see the distress they can cause!'

'I still say your family should've helped, no matter what!' her niece argued stubbornly.

Sadly, Madeleine Gregory shook her head.

'It was too late, Annie, the damage was already done. My father was a prosperous merchant in a town called Sainte-Claire-en-Bois, and my older brothers worked in the family firm. I was sixteen at the time, much admired as something of a beauty, and insufferably vain in consequence! I despised my father's trade of exporting onions, and turned up my nose at the farmers' sons who came courting with their onion breaths. And then, one summer, Henri Dupont arrived in our town.'

Madeleine's expression softened at the memory.

'Ah, but he was handsome and debonair, Annie, a true son of Paris! When he stopped me in the street and confessed he was captivated by my beauty, I thought it was a dream come true. We sat in a café and talked for hours. I boasted about my wealthy father and Henri revealed that his rich father planned to buy a country estate in the district, and had sent him to investigate the area. After that, we met every day, and he made no secret that he loved me as much as I adored him.

'Naturally, my parents were alarmed by the intensity of Henri's whirlwind courtship. They said it must stop, that I was too young to contemplate marrying a man I scarcely knew.'

She paused, absently chasing cake crumbs around the plate with a fingertip. The dog padded off to lap rainwater noisily from a bucket under the damaged ceiling.

'Did you elope with him?' Annie asked eagerly, sensing a romance.

Her aunt sighed.

'It was not so simple! Henri *did* ask me to marry him, but my parents remained adamant and refused to give their consent. So Henri suggested that he should buy me an engagement ring, something beautiful and costly, to show them just how much he cared.'

'A good idea!' Annie nodded approvingly.

'We went hand-in-hand to the jeweller's,' Madeleine continued. 'Once inside, I was in heaven, seated at the counter like a *comtesse,* surrounded by trays of fabulous diamonds, while the jeweller fawned over me. I was hard to please, of course, but at last I made my choice and turned to Henri for approval – but my lover had gone, vanished like morning mist, along with a pocketful of the shop's finest gems.'

'The rotten thief!' Annie exclaimed angrily.

'Yes,' her aunt agreed bitterly. 'The shrewd confidence trickster had taken my measure very accurately – a greedy, spoiled brat, puffed up with selfish conceit!'

'You were only a young girl, he was a hardened criminal! You weren't to blame!'

'Maybe not, but the shopkeeper wanted me arrested as an accomplice, till my dear papa stepped in. Since the real culprit had vanished, Papa offered to pay full compensation for the theft, if the jeweller dropped the charge against me. The man agreed, but the huge sum he demanded bankrupted my father. He was ruined, the business failed, my brothers were thrown out of work, and it was my fault. I could not face them, Annie! The shame and guilt were too great, so I ran away from home and went to Paris, taking with me a small amount of money I had saved. How naïve I was! I had intended to confront Henri Dupont, to force him to recompense my father, but of course that was not his real name, and he couldn't be found. I searched till my money ran out, then lived a miserable existence which led inevitably to the banks of the Seine.'

For a moment, Madeleine sat staring sadly at her niece. 'So, Annie, now that I have told you how I met my darling husband, you will think I do not deserve such good luck!'

'I think nothing of the kind!' she declared briskly. 'You were cheated by a crook, who'd probably used the same mean trick on other pretty young girls with wealthy fathers. Besides, you did your best to rectify matters, which was recklessly brave. Goodness knows what the heartless wretch would have done to you, if you'd caught up with him!'

Madeleine fished for a hanky and dabbed her eyes.

'Maybe so, Annie, but I can't help wondering if Lisette has found out what I did. Perhaps she despises me now. Maybe that's why she never comes.'

'No, Lisette would think as I do, that the tragedy wasn't your fault,' Annie said positively.

She hesitated a moment, then decided against telling her aunt what Annie believed to be the real reason, that Lisette was in hiding as a deserter. 'Maybe she can't reveal where she is at the moment; maybe it's too sensitive and hush-hush. Careless talk costs lives, you know.'

She reached for the teapot and refilled her aunt's cup, spooning in a liberal spoonful of precious sugar.

'Aunt Madeleine,' she went on. 'Why don't you and Uncle Dermot leave this ruin and find a peaceful place in the country? Don't worry about Lisette turning up here and finding you've gone. If she contacts me I promise you'll be the first to know.'

★ ★ ★

In northern France the night was pitch black and moonless. Lisette rested a cheek against the bruised grass where she lay keeping watch, one ear pressed to the ground. Thankfully, no vibrations of vehicle or footfall disturbed the sensitive earth. The wide river rippled and flowed not too far away, but that sound was muffled by the high railway embankment.

Julius appeared out of the dark, slithering down the embankment, searching for her hand.

'OK?' she whispered.

'All set, my darling.' His lips brushed her cheek briefly, and she knew he smiled. The night's work of sabotage had gone well, the explosive charges were laid and ready. An approaching trainload of components, destined for flying-bomb launch sites, would end up sunk irretrievably in the river. Another small victory for besieged Londoners!

When news of the Normandy landings had reached France six weeks ago, Lisette's initial elation had turned to grief when V1s began targeting London. She had no way of knowing what had happened to her beloved foster parents, and lay crying helplessly in Julius's comforting arms, in their bedroom above the cycle shop.

The couple had settled months ago in a small village in the *bocage*, a district of hedges and copses which bred recklessly brave patriots called Maquis. Julius and Marie were accepted as Monsieur and Madame Lamontine, identities as false as their forged papers and marriage documents. They had kept their real personae secret even from each other. It was safer that way, in case the Gestapo captured one or the other.

Julius mended bicycles, even German ones. His 'wife', Marie Lamontine, taught tiny tots ABC and 1-2-3 at the village school. To the occupying German forces they appeared a dull, docile couple, not worth bothering about.

If they only knew! Lisette twined her arms around Julius's neck for a quick, exultant kiss. How she loved this man, and how he loved her! Neither could imagine life without the other, yet the possibility of sharing a future together after the war had never been discussed. Life was too precarious, the danger too real. But now Allied armies had captured Cherbourg and were driving the Germans back, Lisette knew it was necessary to plan a future, after the war was won.

'Better get going, sweetheart.' Julius helped her to her feet, then froze suddenly, head turned towards the roadway.

'*Zut!* A German truck, what bad luck! It'll pass close to the track and they could spot the explosives. There would still be time for them to stop that train.'

He gave Lisette a push in the opposite direction. 'Run! I'll warn the others and create a diversion. Follow the railway line till you reach the old quarry, then head into the *bocage* and go straight home. With luck, I'll be back before dawn.'

She was terrified for him.

'Julius, take care!'

'Don't I always?' She felt the quick pressure of his hand, then he was gone.

Lisette ran, following the narrow path below the railway embankment. All was quiet behind her. Maybe the truck had passed and there had been no need for a diversion, she thought thankfully. Maybe...

A stutter of machine-gun fire turned her blood cold. She stopped and looked back, then went on running. She must be home in bed, innocently waiting for Julius to return from inspecting rabbit snares, should the Vichy police come banging on their door.

The disused quarry was an overgrown gash in a green hillside by day; by night it was a black and menacing hole. Opposite the quarry, an access tunnel ran under the railway embankment, leading to fields and the river beyond. Lisette stopped anxiously in the shelter of the tunnel to listen for gunfire and get her breath back. Resting against the stonework, she felt a faint thrumming come from the track above her head, first indication that the train was on its way. That must mean the diversion had worked, but what had happened to Julius and the others?

Suddenly the peace was shattered by a deafening explosion. Even at this distance, the railway embankment shuddered violently, rails buckled, wrenching bolts from sleepers with a crack like pistol shots and hurtling stones and gravel in all directions. All these sounds were magnified a hundredfold in the confines of the tunnel.

Lisette huddled at the tunnel mouth, deafened but jubilant. She imagined tons of sheet metal casings, engines, propellers, gyrometric compasses, timers and warheads, vital components of flying bombs, which would now be useless scrap plunged deep in the river. Nobody was more skilled at sabotage than Julius Lamontine!

She did not realize her immediate danger till the keystone of the archway thudded to the ground only feet from where she crouched. Its stability breached, the arch began to fail. Masonry, rubble and earth tumbled around her as she attempted desperately to dodge outside. With a supreme effort, she flung her body onto the path just as the tunnel collapsed behind her. She screamed as earth loosened from above rained down onto her legs, her cries silenced as a falling rock caught her a stunning blow.

She roused slowly to torchlight shining in her eyes. The light hurt, but she could just make out a circle of boots gathered round. Her fuzzy brain registered that at least these were not German jackboots.

'Is the puir wumman deid, Jock?' a man's voice asked.

'No' far off,' replied the torch holder, bending closer. 'Her heid's hurt. Gie's a hand to shift the earth off her, lads.'

Scottish? she puzzled, too dazed to be astonished. The men soon freed her and dragged her free of the debris. The pain in one leg was so agonizing as they moved her, she nearly fainted, screaming. The man they called Jock clapped a hand over her mouth.

'Wheest, lassie! You'll bring the Germans down on us.'

'Save your breath, Jock! It's a French wumman. She'll no' understand,' someone muttered.

Lisette's lips felt gritty and unresponsive, but she managed to whisper.

'Not French. I'm ... British agent, helping French resistance...'

'Well, I'll be damned! It must be your mates that blew up the supply line to the launch sites!' exclaimed Jock admiringly.

'Look, we'd better get oot o' here,' one of his mates said anxiously. 'But what'll we do wi' the lassie?'

'Leave me!' she wanted to tell them. 'Let me hide in the quarry till Julius comes. Please, please, just leave me!' But her head spun sickeningly, and the words wouldn't come.

The soldier stood up. 'We'll tak' her wi' us, lads. She says she's a British agent. If the Germans find her here, she'll be shot, for sure.'

In panic, she tried to protest, telling them she mustn't leave. She couldn't possibly leave Julius. Not now...

But distraught mumblings were all she could manage, and her rescuers paid no attention. Someone produced an army blanket. Lisette was lifted gently onto it and borne away, hammock-fashion, towards the British lines...

The winter of 1944 had been bitter. War-weary civilians struggled with shortages, food rationing, blackout and, in the south, a fearsome bombardment of V2 rockets which came silently with no warning, out of nowhere. Everyone was heartily sick of war. An end was in sight, but fighting in Europe still took worrying ups and downs.

Petty Officer Annie Balfour sat at her desk one morning in February 1945. Her mind kept wandering from lists she was checking. She had taken time off recently to see the Gregorys and their orphan animals safely settled in a quiet English village, a satisfactory arrangement whereby her Uncle Dermot could act as locum for the local GP and her aunt could continue to dote upon the elderly labrador. Annie still intended to apply for an extended leave later, in order to visit Conrad and her family in Scotland.

She had kept in constant touch with Conrad by phone and letter, of course, and he had assured her the TB sanatorium situated in the Angus hills was doing a splendid job of rehabilitation. Eventually, he hoped to make a complete recovery.

Annie frowned. Knowing Conrad's reticence where his health and well-being were concerned, she was not entirely convinced. She would reserve judgement till she saw him.

Her second in command appeared in the doorway at that moment.

'Red alert, PO!' she hissed. 'The little snooper from the Ministry's back, sampling cake in the NAAFI. He's heading this way. Thought I'd better warn you.'

'Thanks, Polly.' Annie abandoned the list of stores and folded her arms on the desk.

Mr Brown turned up at her door presently, knocking and entering diffidently.

'We meet again, Petty Officer Balfour, how nice!' he said, shaking hands, mild blue eyes guileless behind horn-rimmed spectacles.

Inviting him to take a seat, she eyed tell-tale cake crumbs clinging to his lapels.

'I hope our NAAFI fare meets with your approval, Mr Brown?'

'Oh, absolutely! Jolly good show,' he said, unabashed. There was a pause, then he cleared his throat. 'Umm ... Miss Balfour, this visit is off the record. I'm here unofficially, just to see you, actually.'

Her heart gave a sudden lurch.

'It's my sister, isn't it?'

'Your sister?' he repeated in puzzled fashion, raising his brows.

'My twin sister, Lisette. She went AWOL, remember?' she reminded him icily.

'Oh, *that*! We're no longer interested in *that*,' he said offhandedly. 'No, I came to tell you we've had word from reliable contacts in Malaya that your father, stepmother and brother are surviving reasonably well in captivity. I thought it would take a weight off your mind.'

She stared at him, her thoughts chaotic. The news was very welcome, but raised disturbing questions.

'Why are you so interested in my family, Mr Brown? I believe you even approached my friend Fergus McGill!'

'McGill?' He frowned thoughtfully, then his brow cleared. 'Oh yes, the commando paratrooper!' He nodded approvingly. 'Shrewd fellow. Didn't believe a word I said.'

Annie felt horribly confused. Her family, and Fergus too, seemed to be directly linked in some way to this insignificant little man. Who on earth *was* he?

'I don't know what's going on, Mr Brown, but please – *please* – make it stop!' she pleaded tearfully.

He leaned across the desk and took her hand, speaking in gentler tones. 'Don't worry, my dear girl. It's all over now, I promise you.' Resuming his former breezy manner, he stood up, preparing to leave.

'Well, Petty Officer, must be off. I've thoroughly enjoyed my visit. When I see the Admiral I'll tell him everything in your department's absolutely tickety-boo. Jolly good show!'

He crossed to the doorway then turned to her, grinning. 'Mind you, Annie – off the record – it's been absolutely fascinating, getting to know the Balfours!'

She sat staring at the door after it had closed behind him. What had happened to Lisette? Mr Brown had dismissed her so offhandedly, it was almost as if Lisette didn't exist any more. Returning to her work with a heavy heart, she comforted herself with the wonderful relief of knowing that her father, stepmother and Kim had survived the fall of Singapore and were doing as well as could be expected, in Japanese captivity...

Actually, had Annie but known it, the re-assuring report from Malaya had been ill-timed. Kim Balfour was in serious trouble at the rubber plantation.

It was early morning, the sun's first scarlet rays filtering through damp grey mist. The plantation workers were gathered shivering in the chilly garden, waiting for the Japanese occupants of James Balfour's bungalow to appear for a daily ceremony.

Kim stood beside the tall flagpole from which the Scottish saltire had once flown. It was Kim's task to hoist the Japanese flag embodying the rising sun to the top of the mast at sunrise, while the assembled guests and workforce paid homage to the Emperor.

Usually Kim took some satisfaction from the daily ritual. Unknown to the Japanese, the flagpole served as an excellent aerial for a hidden radio transmitter, Kim's secret link with military authorities in India.

The radio lay in a tiny space beneath a loose flagstone in the floor of the ruined dragon pagoda, a small garden folly which had been dear to his mother's heart. Water gushed from the dragon's gaping jaws into a lily pond when a pump was activated, and the busy gurgling of falling water effectively drowned sounds of radio activity.

It was fortunate that the Japanese had few sources of rubber, and consequently did not interfere in the running of the plantation, which continued to function as before, with a loyal workforce under the leadership of Abri, the foreman.

James Balfour's palatial bungalow was now used as a guest house for high-ranking Japanese officials visiting Singapore, and Kim had gleaned valuable information from these distinguished guests while going about his duties as house-servant. Malay servants understood only a few orders and commands delivered in Japanese, but their masters had not realized that Kim had a fluent grasp of their language and took note of everything discussed at table, when *sake* flowed freely and tongues were loosened unwisely.

But this morning Kim was worried. A new guest had arrived, a stocky, high-ranking officer with keen cruel eyes. When General Haku Sagura entered the house yesterday, a lingering scrutiny had terrified the house-boys, and made even Kim quail.

They knew this ruthless person was in charge of a project once deemed too complex and costly in human life to contemplate – the construction of a railway line across mountain, jungle and swamp, from Thailand to Burma. The railway was now well under way, another step in the plan for a Japanese invasion of India, driven forward relentlessly by an expendable workforce of thousands of prisoners of war.

Kim stiffened as the general appeared in full dress uniform with battle honours. That in itself was unusual. Guests more often than not attended the obligatory ceremony sleepily, in night attire. As usual, Kim wore his father's decoration for gallantry pinned defiantly to his vest beneath his jacket. The general came too close to the flagpole for comfort, but noticed nothing amiss. He gave the signal, Kim released the breath he'd been holding and hoisted the flag. The assembled company bowed.

Abri's wife Selina cooked for the visitors, aided by her daughters. Her younger sons helped Kim serve meals. More guests than usual had arrived from Singapore that evening, to hear what the famous general had to say. Kim noticed that while the other guests were loud and talkative after copious draughts of rice beer, Sagura sipped only green tea. When the general was questioned at last about progress on the Thai-Burma Railway, the room fell respectfully silent.

'Work is progressing fairly well,' he answered idly. 'But you must appreciate that it is difficult to secure a good day's hard labour from these lazy British cowards. They are weedy specimens, sickly men with poor physique and no stamina.'

Kim fumed at the unwarranted slur. It was well known prisoners were starved, and in no fit state for such demanding work. He was so angry he could have struck the man. He forgot caution for an instant and doubled his fists.

Realizing the mistake at once, he glanced cautiously sideways and found the general's narrow black gaze fixed upon him. Kim grew cold, waiting for disaster to strike, but Sagura merely raised the teacup.

'You, boy!' he called. 'More tea!'

Eyes lowered respectfully as etiquette demanded, Kim took the empty cup and scuttled off. But he remained badly shaken and apprehensive. Had the evil man noted the angry gesture and decided to play cat and mouse? Was the general biding his time before he pounced?

Only time, Kim thought dejectedly, would tell...

Annie phoned Connie shortly after Mr Brown's visit, to tell her she'd been granted fourteen days' leave and was leaving for Scotland right away.

'About time!' her aunt retorted.

'Is everything OK?' Annie asked tentatively.

'Oh aye, everything in the garden's lovely, dear,' Connie answered grimly. 'Conrad's decided to sell the hotel. That's me homeless and unemployed at a single stroke.'

Annie's heart missed a beat. There had been no word of that in Conrad's letters.

'What's brought this on? Has his health deteriorated?' she demanded anxiously.

Connie sighed. 'He was fine when John and Benny visited last week. I don't know what's got into the man. It's high time you came home and sorted him out...'

Annie began the journey north next day, with this new worry looming large. London looked grey and grimy in drizzling rain as she reached King's Cross and boarded a crowded Edinburgh train, packed to the luggage racks with service personnel and depressed-looking civilians. Nobody made any pretence at cheer on this gloomy morning. Annie secured an uncomfortable seat squashed in the middle of an overcrowded compartment, and dozed fitfully all the long journey, till the Pentland Hills came into view through the steamy carriage windows. Edinburgh wasn't far away. She sat up eagerly. She was going home!

Connie was waiting on the platform when the train steamed into Waverley. They greeted one another with delighted cries and tearful hugs. Clasped tightly to her aunt's bosom, Annie caught a whiff of Yardley lavender perfume, rare as hen's teeth down south.

They left the platform, arm in arm, and Connie summoned a taxicab with practised ease which made Annie stare. Her aunt had always been capable, but now she exuded brisk confidence. Changed days indeed!

'So how's the hotel doing?' Annie said, once they were seated in the back seat.

'Fine!' She sighed heavily. 'Heaven knows why he wants to sell such a wee goldmine, Annie. Army and navy top brass always stay at the Whyte House, and their families too. John's farm produce has been a godsend and the chef goes from strength to strength now he's a father. There's not a restaurant in the city can beat us for food.'

'Has John married Marigold McGill yet?'

'Not him!' Connie said in disgust. 'I never met such a pair for draggin' their feet!'

The taxi drove slowly along familiar streets. It was growing dark; masked headlights in the blackout didn't speed a rush-hour traffic jam. Annie stared out of the window.

'And what about Fergus?' she said.

Connie gave her niece a concerned glance. 'There's been no word about the poor lad since he was at Arnhem, and that battle was a terrible disaster for our lads. I'm so sorry, Annie.'

Annie felt choked with tears. Since childhood she'd known that Fergus would always be to the forefront of battle. She should have been prepared for bad news sooner or later, but this hit her hard. People talked about heartbreak. Now she knew how painful it felt.

At last the taxi accomplished the short journey to the hotel. Annie studied the familiar façade with affection while Connie paid the

354

driver. It seemed inconceivable that Conrad would part with it. Was his illness worse than she'd thought?

There was an elderly lady in charge of the reception desk, younger men and women being in short supply. She glanced up as they entered.

'You have a visitor waiting in the public lounge, Connie.'

Connie sighed. 'Och, it's sure to be a salesman trying to sell me something. What a pest!'

Marching briskly into the lounge, she stopped short and stared.

'Bless my soul, it – it's you!'

Annie's curiosity was aroused. She followed her aunt into the lounge. It was a comfortable room with deep armchairs and sofas spread around low coffee tables, and the lighting was dim and restful. The room was empty except for the woman who was struggling to rise from an armchair. Annie's heart missed a beat.

'Lisette? Liz, is it really you?' she said, hardly daring to trust her eyes.

Lisette laughed and held out her arms. 'Of course it is, silly! Don't you recognize your own twin?'

Annie hurtled across the room with a yell and the sisters hugged ecstatically, laughing, crying, both talking at once, each trying to convince the other of their joy and happiness. It seemed like an age, but at last they were together again. The bond was still there, the love strong as ever.

Annie held Lisette at arm's length, a smile fading as she studied her sister more closely. Such a haunting sadness in Lisette's dark eyes! And there was a long, fading scar on her brow, two sticks propped beside her on the chair. But more than that…

'You're expecting a baby!'

'Yes, quite soon. I was determined it would be born in Scotland.'

'Is your husband – er – around?' Annie ventured.

Lisette hesitated momentarily.

'No. He's fighting, in France.'

Lisette thought about Julius with the aching longing which rarely left her. The marriage document might be false, but they were truly husband and wife, and always would be. Their parting had been so unexpected and sudden, there had been no chance to tell Julius she was expecting his child. It had been early in the pregnancy then, and she had hugged the wonderful secret to herself, still anxiously fearing a miscarriage, like last time. She need not have worried. When the tunnel fell, even the serious injuries Lisette suffered had not loosened this strong little baby's tenacious grip on life.

After the army flew her home from France, she had lain in a private nursing home in England for months, recovering from concussion and a badly broken leg, carefully guarded by members of the Special Operations Executive as she lay immobile. They had explained that she knew too much about British agents, methods and their French contacts to be allowed freedom of movement just yet. Wait a while, be patient, they told her.

Lisette had accepted the wisdom of such restrictions, but no matter how desperately she pleaded, they refused to tell her what had happened to Julius. She was tormented by the fear that he had been killed or captured. In any case, she knew that Julius Lamontine would not be his real name, any more that Marie Duval was hers. If he were still alive, it might be impossible to find one another again, when the war ended.

Annie had sensed Lisette's anguish, which she found understandable, since her sister faced the birth of her baby without her husband. But she also sensed that there was something deeper, something her sister kept hidden, which Annie could not fathom. She only knew that Lisette's reserve blighted some of the joy of the reunion.

Fortunately, Connie, bless her, was beaming with all the delight of a thwarted grandmother. True, this baby would be great-nephew or niece, not grandchild, but a baby was a baby, and Connie's arms longed to hold the wee one. She noticed how wan and sad the expectant mother looked. She'd obviously been in the wars, poor soul! Connie beamed fondly upon Lisette, whose wish to have her bairn born in Scotland met with her hearty approval.

'Your news is just what the Balfour family needs, Lizzie dear. This wee baby will bring a hope o' happier times ahead, for all of us,' Connie declared, emphatically.

Fifteen

Annie set off by train early next morning to visit Conrad, leaving Connie to pamper Lisette with rest and tender loving care.

The sanatorium was situated in the Angus hills, an area Connie had chosen so that John could visit and keep an eye on Conrad's progress. Annie wasn't sure what to expect. Why had he decided to sell the hotel? Was he as fit as his amusing, loving letters claimed? Sitting in the train, she was anxious and tense.

But leaving Edinburgh's damp morning mist behind, her spirits lifted when she reached Dundee in mild sunshine. She boarded an ancient bus which trundled towards the sanatorium at a leisurely pace through countryside fresh with signs of spring. She grew more optimistic. Conrad couldn't fail to get better, breathing such fresh, exhilarating air.

The sanatorium had been a rich man's residence once. Entering the large building, she saw traces of original splendour in large airy rooms converted to hospital wards. A faint scent of floor polish drifted in high-ceilinged corridors.

Conrad was waiting in the entrance hallway, alerted by a phone call from Connie. He kissed her warmly, smiling his delight.

'Annie, my darling, you're here at last! It's a dream come true.'

'You look so well, Conrad. Thank goodness! I was worried.'

'Didn't I tell you I'm fine?'

They laughed together, and she hugged him. Conrad did look fit, unchanged, except for more silver in his dark hair than she remembered. He tucked her hand under his elbow and led her towards the doorway.

'Let's walk. We'll have something to eat later on.'

They passed through well-kept grounds out into the countryside, and he told her he walked miles every day and exercised in the gym three times a week.

'I'm much fitter than ever I was living in Auld Reekie,' he said.

'Connie tells me you've decided to sell the hotel. Is it true?'

'Yes, but don't worry, my love. The deal won't be done till I'm discharged with a clean bill of health.'

So his mind was made up, she thought. Where did *she* fit in? Did he still want to marry her?

'Connie says the hotel's a goldmine, darling. Why sell it?' she asked.

'The specialist warns I must breathe fresh mountain air, if there's any hope of my surviving to a ripe old age, Annie. I can't live in cities any more.'

This was an unexpected complication, she

thought. He had been gravely ill, of course, surviving against all the odds, so she smiled cheerfully, hanging onto his arm.

'No problem, love! We'll look for a picturesque small hotel, in the Scottish Highlands.'

'No, Annie dear. Not Scotland. Canada.'

She stopped abruptly and looked at him blankly.

'Canada?'

He nodded. 'My mother was Canadian. We had wonderful holidays with the Canadian grandparents when I was a boy. They lived near the Rockies and the cool dry climate suited me down to the ground then. It would be ideal for me now.' He turned to her eagerly. 'Looks as if the war could be over soon, Annie. Let's get married after you're demobbed and make a fresh start in Canada. I plan to buy a small hotel with views of the Rockies. There's bound to be an increase in tourism after the war, and we'll make a fortune. What do you say, my darling?'

The prospect had taken her breath away. She looked stunned, and he laughed.

'I'm not asking you to fly to the moon, my dear, only across the Atlantic! But take your time to get used to the idea, consider the advantages!'

He kissed her lightly. She had recovered from the shock, but this was a momentous decision. She loved Conrad. He was kind and considerate and she had treated him so badly, all because of one unforgettable kiss. But Fergus had gone, lost forever in the battle for

Arnhem.

Time to move on at last, she thought.

Annie lifted her head to face a chill wind blowing from snow-flecked Grampians. It must be the icy wind that had brought tears to her eyes...

She had arranged to stay that night with her Balfour cousins, John and Benny, before returning to Edinburgh next day. The estate could be reached easily by bus, which had given her more precious time to spend with Conrad that afternoon.

It was dark when she reached Kilmuckety, but Benny was waiting patiently at the road end. A Benny she scarcely recognized, a small boy grown into a tall, lanky youth. Annie hugged him.

'Benny, you're a man!'

He grinned. 'Tell that to brother John, will you? He treats me like a bairn still. He's worse than Ma.'

He carried Annie's small case for her. They walked in the pitch-black dark along a smooth tarmac driveway edged with trimmed privet, much changed from the pot-holed track small twin girls had stumbled along with their grieving father, so many years ago. The memory brought her fresh sorrow. Where was her father now?

John had combined bothy, byre and stables into a comfortable and stylish home, well furnished with old and new pieces he'd picked up cheaply in salerooms. Annie was impressed. Her two cousins produced a simple meal, beautifully cooked.

'John, this is lovely!' she enthused, relaxing afterwards before a roaring fire. They were alone. Benny had departed to his study bedroom to finish his homework.

'Marigold's a lucky woman!' she added artfully. Connie had given strict instructions to move the sluggish love affair along, whenever possible.

'Marigold doesn't visit here; she's too busy keeping the big house from falling to bits.'

She was surprised. 'I understood Mrs McGill had restored the dear old homestead to its former glory?'

'So she did, before the war, but fuel's scarce now and the house is unheated. It has dry rot and God knows what else, and last winter burst pipes ruined Mrs McGill's expensive wallpaper and carpets. Water damage was the last straw after the ravages inflicted by evacuees, Polish infantry and Home Guard. The lady took a scunner at the house. She and her husband moved to a warmer, more suitable residence in Kirriemuir.'

'That wouldn't have happened if Fergus had been around,' Annie said.

John shrugged. 'It was *his* choice, and now the house is a war victim, like Fergus himself. *I* chose to stay around, and the farm has never looked back, despite red tape and rationing. This country is self-sufficient, thanks to us farmers. Who served the nation best, Annie, the conscript or the stay-at-home?'

'Both play an important part,' she said diplomatically. 'But what of the future, John? Did you know Conrad is selling the hotel?'

'Yes, he told me. He says he'll look kindly upon any reasonable offer I may make. That would be an ideal solution for my mother, but...'

He paused, gazing moodily into the fire.

'You don't have the cash!' Annie said knowingly.

'Not at the moment, but I could get it when I marry Marigold. My dad told me the quickest way to get rich is to marry a rich wife.'

'So what are you waiting for?'

John sighed. 'I've often wondered that, myself.'

Annie declined a visit to the big house next morning. She would find it too painful. Besides, she wanted to return to Edinburgh and spend time with her sister. Benny said goodbye to her and left for the bus taking him to Forfar Academy. He had admitted modestly that he was doing well at school, close to top of the class in maths. Annie promised to pass on a good report to his mother.

Later, John waited at the roadside with her till her bus arrived. He kissed her cheek.

'Let me know when Lizzie produces the new member of the Balfour clan, won't you?'

'Don't worry, I will,' she promised, waving

goodbye.

Trudging back to the farm, John felt unaccountably depressed. Talk of marrying Marigold was unsettling. His older brothers lived far away, in distant lands, happily married with growing families, getting on with their lives. Now Annie and Conrad planned to emigrate to Canada, while he, John, was stuck in the same old rut. It was high time he snapped out of it!

John never set foot in the big house which had once been his home, but today he headed for the front entrance. He noticed the stone steps had been scrubbed and brass door furniture polished, and was touched. No doubt his old flame, Davina Williams, was struggling to keep up standards – a thankless task. He wondered why she bothered to stay, now that the evacuees had gone home and the Poles were fighting valiantly in Europe and Italy.

As for Marigold, his intended bride, she was always busy. Marigold worked in the farm shop, and tended to horses, chickens and other livestock, besides keeping an eye on the welfare of the Italian prisoners of war working on the land. These men were comfortably settled in the former gamekeeper's cottage.

It was too early to open the shop, and he knew Marigold would still be at home. John walked boldly into the hallway and came face to face with Davina, trundling a wheezy old vacuum cleaner over water-stained carpets. She turned the machine off and looked at him.

'Marigold's not here, John. She's helping Giuseppe feed the hens and collect the eggs.'

It was many months since John and Davina had been alone together. She was usually surrounded by yelling evacuees or admiring Polish officers.

She prepared to restart the vac, ending the need for conversation. It annoyed him. He grabbed her arm, forcing her to turn and look at him.

'Why do you always ignore me?'

'I don't!' She struggled. 'Let go, you're hurting!'

He released her. To his dismay the touch had evoked tender memories. He didn't want it to end like this in an unfriendly silence. Once, it had been so good.

'Couldn't we be friends, Vina?'

She averted her face, but a tear slid furtively down one cheek.

'Maybe you could be friends, John. I can't.'

The sight disturbed, and yet in some odd way, encouraged him to persevere.

'Tell me why you don't leave this place, now the children have gone,' he demanded.

'Benny needs me. He's delicate.'

'No, he isn't! He's outgrown his asthma and is strong as a horse. Try again, my dear. Why don't you leave?' He forced her round to face him. She glared at him, tear-stained and wild-eyed.

'Stop it, John! I don't want to tell you why!'

He wasn't sure how it happened, but suddenly they were clinging together, her angry breath warm against his cheek. He had an almost overwhelming desire to kiss her, but first, he had to make her answer...

'Tell me!'

She let out a sobbing wail. 'I can't leave *you*, John Balfour! Heaven knows, I've tried dozens of times since you took up with Marigold, but I just – can't!'

He kissed her then, and after a startled moment she returned his kiss just as eagerly. Even as he floated in a dreamy ecstasy, John knew he would never marry Marigold. He was very fond of her, but Marigold deserved better than someone whose aim was to grow rich at her expense. A man whose heart belonged elsewhere.

If only Davina would agree to marry him, John resolved, he would use the brains God had given him to work hard and make a decent home for wife and family. But already he suspected that loving the girl in his arms would make life rich beyond his wildest dreams.

He kissed the warm curve of her cheek. 'Darling, now I know why I was reluctant to marry Marigold. I'm still in love with you! It broke my heart when it all went so wrong.'

'It wasn't your fault, John,' she said. 'I wanted us to be married, and my impatience ruined everything. You naturally turned to Marigold, and all I could do was watch.'

She looked up at him, suddenly concerned. 'Oh, John darling, what about poor Marigold!

She'll be devastated when she finds out about us!'

'I'll have to tell her, and the sooner the better. In fact, I'll go and find her now, before she leaves for the shop,' he said, bracing himself. He kissed Davina, to give himself strength and purpose for the ordeal ahead, and went outside, heading for the henhouse.

Marigold would feel bitterly hurt and rejected, and who could blame her? John thought wretchedly. He hated hurting her, but it had to be done...

Hens ranged freely around the farmyard and paddock by day, but an old wooden barn fitted with roosts and straw-filled nesting boxes served as a henhouse, providing the flock with warmth and shelter.

The barn was strictly Marigold's province. Eggs were rationed and quotas controlled by the Ministry of Food. A certain quantity must be collected, cleaned and graded daily, and sent off to various distribution centres. It was a taxing, time-consuming job, judging by the time Marigold spent in the barn when not serving in the shop. It was also a vitally important commodity. Fresh eggs in wartime were, quite literally, scarce as hens' teeth.

John took a deep breath and pushed open the barn door. It was gloomy inside and there was a clucking and rustling from nests and perches as morning light pierced the interior. The barn smelled of fresh straw and faintly of Marigold's perfume. He looked around, but couldn't see her.

'Are you there, Marigold?' he called.

Two figures cuddled together on bales of straw sprang guiltily apart. John's jaw dropped in astonishment. Marigold and Giuseppe clung to one another and looked absolutely terrified. She let out a sorrowful wail.

'Oh, John dear, I didn't mean you to find out about Giuseppe and me like this! I've been trying to pluck up courage for months to tell you we've fallen in love, and we plan to be married in Italy, when Giuseppe's repatriated after the war. Oh, I'm so terribly sorry, John!'

She broke down and sobbed on Giuseppe's shoulder.

The young Italian faced John defiantly.

'Maybe you think I justa take my chance with this lovely lady, love her and leave her? This is not true! I not want to fight in this bad war, but war has brought my *bella scozzese carissima* to me. It is fate, and now we will be together and in love for always!'

Recovered from the initial shock, John studied the couple. Somehow they seemed right together. He could imagine Marigold bathed in Italian sunshine, helping this hard-working man rebuild his life after the ravages of war. She was a feisty young woman, and she would relish the challenge. There would be hard times ahead for Marigold and her Giuseppe, he thought compassionately, but they must realize that, and be willing to take the risk, because they knew their love was strong. He smiled. Good luck to them!

'I believe you, Giuseppe,' John said aloud. 'I just want Marigold to be happy. That's all I really care about.'

And he meant it, wholeheartedly.

Annie had Lisette all to herself while Connie was busy in the hotel. The twins had spoken to Leah at breakfast, but Leah had left soon after to meet her fiancé, who was on leave from his work as an aircraft mechanic at RAF Turnhouse.

'Of course, Andrew really wanted to be a fighter pilot,' Leah had told them. 'Dead keen he was, but they turned him down and you'll never guess why!' she giggled. 'Hay fever! The mere hint of dust or pollen sets him off sneezing, poor darling, and of course you can't risk a fit of sneezing when you're flying a Hurricane at four hundred miles an hour. So Andrew settled for ground crew. I was so relieved and happy when he told me, I danced in the cinema aisle. Everyone ended up in the wrong seats, and it was an awful muddle!'

Laughing and quite unrepentant, Leah had gone dancing off downstairs, to spend the day with the love of her life...

Lisette was stretched out comfortably on the sofa in Connie's sitting room. Annie relaxed opposite, in an armchair.

'So what happened with Conrad?' Lisette asked.

'After we're married and the hotel's sold, he

wants us to settle in Canada.'

'Will you?'

'I'd much rather stay home in Scotland, to be quite honest.'

'Do you love him?'

'Of course I do!'

Lisette studied her sister thoughtfully.

'I can only speak for myself, of course, but if Julius were to say to me, come to Antarctica and study polar bears with me, my darling, I'd reach for the winter woollies and go with him like a shot.'

'This man, Julius...' Annie frowned. 'Did you meet in Inverness?'

'Heavens, no! In France.' She hesitated a moment, then shrugged. 'You may as well know the truth, Annie, it doesn't matter now. Julius was with the French Resistance, and I was a British secret agent with a mission in France. We fell madly in love and the Special Operations Executive will never forgive me for what they see as an indiscretion. Love is frowned upon, in the SOE.'

'You were a spy?' Annie stared in shocked disbelief, but this extraordinary revelation solved the puzzle surrounding Lisette's disappearance. It had to be true. 'So that's why that insignificant little man from the Ministry took such an unusual interest in me!'

Lisette grinned. 'Mr Brown used you to cover for my absence, did he? That would put German agents off the scent. The cunning old fox!' she said admiringly.

★ ★ ★

371

After a fascinating day spent with her sister, Annie wakened suddenly that night. She couldn't tell what had roused her, not any sound, more an alert, heightened awareness. She lay still for a minute, then suddenly sat up.

The baby!

She was out of bed in an instant, hurrying to her sister's room. Lisette sat on the side of the bed, looking quite calm.

'Is it time?' Annie asked.

She nodded. 'No need to panic yet, you know. First babies can take hours to put in an appearance. Time enough to phone the doctor in the morning, Annie dear.'

But by morning, Connie and Annie were seriously alarmed. The doctor and midwife came at once, and after a cursory examination, the nurse smiled and rolled up her sleeves.

'This little one's in a remarkable hurry!'

Lisette and Julius's strong little son was born shortly afterwards, announcing his arrival with loud, indignant cries. Later, Annie and Connie were ushered in to visit mother and baby. Lisette lay propped against the pillows, dazed by the speed of events but sublimely happy. Her son, wrapped in a Balfour shawl, lay peacefully in the crook of her arm. Predictably, Connie went into raptures.

'Oh my, what a bonny bairn, Lizzie dear, sleeping like a wee cherub, bless 'im!'

Annie had known turmoils of anguish while

her sister laboured, and was utterly exhausted. She kissed Lisette's cheek.

'Well done, Liz, jolly well done!'

Together, the twins examined the sleeping baby. He *was* bonny, Annie thought, or should that be 'handsome'? He had such a boyish wee face, and quite a thatch of dark hair.

Lisette heaved a wistful sigh. 'He looks just like his father!'

'Have you thought about a name, lovey?' Connie asked.

'Yes. He is Julien.'

Connie frowned doubtfully. 'That's a bit foreign-like, isn't it?'

Lisette laughed and hugged her son.

'He will be Julien Balfour Lamontine, Connie. Do you approve of that?'

'Better!' she beamed. 'I like the Balfour.'

The remainder of Annie's leave flew past while attending to her sister and the demands of a newborn baby. Julien was a contented baby and seldom cried, as if he preferred to save energy for growth. Lisette was back on her feet, although Connie insisted that she rest every afternoon. Despite protests, Lisette was secretly glad to take weight off her injured leg. It was an opportunity for the twins to spend the last few precious days of Annie's leave together, while Julien slept angelically in the cot.

'He's unbelievably good! I bet he'll be a wee terror when he's toddling,' Annie remarked.

'Yes, he will be, if he's anything like his daddy!'

Lisette smiled, but Annie guessed there was sadness behind the smile. It was hard to believe that her sister, brought up in luxury, had risked her life as a British secret agent, let alone fallen in love with a member of the French Resistance. Lisette's exploits made Annie's wartime contribution seem pathetic. It was a depressing thought.

She sighed. 'You live dangerously behind enemy lines, Liz, while I sit behind a desk handing out NAAFI rations. You deserve a medal!'

'Thanks, but I already have one. So do you – our Dad's!' Lisette reminded her.

The twins looked at one another, remembering the night their father gave both his little daughters one of his medals as a keepsake.

'I wonder where the third medal is now?' Annie said.

Not with Dad in a Japanese prison camp, she thought sadly. No doubt his captors would have found it and taken it from him, years ago...

James Balfour's medal for bravery lay safe in the secret cache beneath the ruined dragon pagoda in the bungalow garden. Kim Balfour had hidden it there hastily, while the soldiers searched the rubber plantation on General Sagura's orders. They had made everyone's life a misery, but had not discovered the radio transmitter, nor the flagstaff aerial. It seemed the general had a sixth sense for detecting mutinous thoughts, Kim thought gloomily.

Why else was he sitting in a filthy truck that morning, packed shoulder to shoulder with twenty other plantation workers? They were all fit young men, with no idea where they were being sent. The truck was completely enclosed, hot as an oven, and had jolted and shuddered its way along an unseen roadway for hours.

It would be the Thai-Burma railway, of course! Kim thought despairingly. General Sagura would find such punishment amusing under the circumstances. The thought of slaving on that infamous project filled Kim with dread.

He had drifted into an uneasy doze, but wakened with a start after what seemed like an age. The truck had rattled to a stop. Blinding daylight poured in as the rear doors swung open. A voice yelled orders in Malay.

'Out! Outside, you men. Get out now!'

They tumbled out and stood in a dishevelled group. As Kim's eyes grew accustomed to daylight, he found to his bewilderment that they stood in a building site on the outskirts of Singapore. The ruins of a fine old mansion, commanding views across the island, stood nearby. There was not a Japanese soldier in sight and the truck driver was Malay. He grinned at the confused young men.

'General Sagura requires this bomb-damaged old heap to be restored to its former glory. You'll be shown what to do, but he insists the project must be kept secret. No-one must know. This is why he will have only Malay workers under minimum supervision. He plans to govern Singapore from this house when Japan wins the war.' The builder's shoulders shook with suppressed mirth. 'He should be so lucky! It is whispered the Americans have gained the upper hand in the Philippines, and have already recaptured Manila.'

Kim breathed a sigh of relief. So the angry fists had gone unnoticed after all! The only reason he and the others had been selected was for their youth and fitness. He'd no illusions about the job facing them, however. It would be no picnic if Sagura had anything to do with it, but infinitely preferable to working on the Thai-Burma railway...

The war in Europe ended on 6th May 1945.

Conrad was discharged from the sanatorium and returned to the hotel to find Connie in a flutter of anxiety about her family's future. Lisette judged the time was right to leave them to work things out. She planned to return home to her foster mother and father, now that the Special Operations Executive had given her permission to resume contact with the Gregorys. Those responsible for training agents had considered Dermot Gregory's high profile as a lecturer and Harley Street consultant too much of a threat to his foster daughter's anonymity.

'They' had decided Lisette should 'disappear' from family life for the duration. Now that the war was over, that was no longer necessary.

Julien was three months old and Lisette had regained her strength. The baby's bright dark-eyed gaze followed everything with intense interest. He had a gappy grin that would melt ice. Connie doted on the bairn and could hardly bear to let him go. However, she did agree it was only fair that he should meet his English great-aunt and uncle. So Lisette stood misty-eyed at the carriage window with Julien in her arms, as the London express picked up speed, leaving Connie's forlorn little figure standing all alone on the Waverley platform.

Madeleine and Dermot had made an onerous train journey from their village home to King's Cross station, to meet mother and baby.

Bomb-damaged and battered London was still in the grip of peace celebrations, but nobody on the crowded streets was happier than Madeleine Gregory, as she flung her arms around Lisette and Julien, crying and laughing like a child.

'You have come home, my darlings! I could dance in the street, I could sing for joy!'

The thought of elegant Madeleine dancing and singing 'Roll out the Barrel' made Lisette smile. Then to her surprise she noticed dog hairs on her foster mother's coat, and her reddened hands and broken nails, tell-tale signs of a dedicated gardener. Madeleine's hat had tilted over one ear and she made no effort to straighten it. Dermot came forward to kiss Lisette and admire the baby. The elderly doctor looked relaxed, happy, tweedy, the epitome of a well-loved country GP. Lisette hugged her foster parents with a tear in her eyes and an ache in her heart. She owed them so much, and had been forced to treat them so badly.

Once settled in the Gregorys' comfortable old rambling house, Lisette did her best to make up for the neglectful years. She told them as much as she dared about her work with the Secret Service during the war. Madeleine grew agitated when Lisette mentioned Dominic and Eva Lefevre and their children.

'They would tell you how my bad deeds ruined my family! Do you hate me now, *chérie*?' she asked wistfully.

'No, Mummy, of course I don't!' Lisette assured her with a hug. 'Annie told me the whole story when she was on leave. Dominic and Eva were not concerned with the past, the present was much too dangerous.'

Prompted by thoughts of Dominic and Eva, and desperate for news of Julius, Lisette sat down and wrote to them that evening, while Julien slept peacefully beside her in his cot. She wrote, praying they'd been spared the horrors of war and telling them what had happened to herself and Julius. She begged them to find out if he had survived and, if so, to tell him that she loved him devotedly, and that they had a fine son. She wrote tearfully, for how can anyone find a man who lived under a false name? And yet, when Lisette posted the letter next day, she couldn't help hoping...

Annie was demobbed from the Wrens shortly after Japanese troops in Singapore surrendered to Lord Mountbatten in August 1945.

She was jubilant. She'd had a telegram from Kim informing her that her father and Teresa had been released from the prison camp and that young Kim was caring for his parents at the plantation. They were half-starved after their ordeal, but would recover well, the telegram assured her.

So Annie had a demob gratuity in her purse and a fistful of clothing coupons to spend on a wardrobe of civvies. It felt wonderful.

The jubilation lasted till the train crossed the border into Scotland. Then glimpses of hills guarding the ancient stronghold of Stirling, trees with the first golden tints of autumn, brought sudden melancholy tears. She was home again in her beloved Scotland, but for how long?

Conrad was waiting on the platform to greet her when the train reached Edinburgh. He looked very well, she thought, as they kissed and hugged. She stretched out her arms to embrace the smoky old city she had grown to love.

'Oh, it's wonderful to be home!'

He picked up her case and took her arm. 'Connie's prepared a feast, or as close to one as she can get. Rationing is worse than ever.'

'Have you sold the hotel?'

'Yes. I'm just waiting for the deal to go through '

She glanced at him. His tone was not forthcoming and she did not pursue the subject.

'That's good,' she said. There would be time to talk, later.

However, her aunt had organized a welcome-home party which left little room for conversation. Leah and her fiancé Andrew were there, and Benny, who'd grown a good inch since they last met, and to Annie's surprise, John was holding hands with Davina Williams whom Annie remembered from schooldays in Kirriemuir. She cornered Connie in the kitchen for an explanation.

'Marigold?' Connie lifted the lid on a large saucepan, inspecting the contents. 'Och, Marigold's history, Annie. She fell head over heels for an Italian prisoner of war working on the farm. She's away to Italy to meet her future in-laws, and good luck to the lassie. Davina's much more my cup o' tea!'

'Conrad says he's sold the hotel, but he didn't tell me who'd bought it,' Annie said.

'No, I don't suppose he would. He's keeping it close to his chest.' Connie replaced the pan lid with a grim clang. 'Anyway, I'm told my job's secure, so we'll wait an' see.'

Considerate as ever, Conrad allowed Annie time to settle back into civilian life before broaching plans for the future. He was content just to have her home again, he told her. Wedding plans could wait until he had settled one or two details with the Scottish businessman who had bought the hotel. Annie found her return to the familiar routine soothing, although she soon realized that rationing and food quotas were making life difficult. Fresh vegetables from Kilmuckety estate were a godsend, helping to maintain standards in the restaurant.

When Annie noticed the farm van arrive with a delivery later that week, she hurried out to the yard to have a word with John.

But it wasn't John who came clambering out of the cab. This driver was tall and auburn-haired. The driver was—

'Fergus!'

The shock of seeing him alive and well was so incredible, she stumbled and nearly fell. He caught her in time, steadying her. She looked up at him.

'They told me you were missing ... I thought you were dead!'

Her overwhelming joy illuminated her. Her heart raced, telling her over and over *he's alive!*

Fergus grinned. 'Taken prisoner – again, Annie! Next time I'll be sensible, and stay home, like John.' He studied her guardedly, the grin fading. 'When's the wedding?'

'Wedding?' She stared blankly for a moment, trying to gather her thoughts.

'You and Conrad.' He frowned. 'Didn't Conrad tell you about my wedding gift?'

She shook her head in bewilderment.

'The hotel, Annie dear!' Fergus explained patiently. 'It's a first-class small hotel, an ideal outlet for farm produce and a good business prospect for the future. So I bought it for you.'

'*You* did?' She looked at him, stunned.

'Yes. You see...' He paused awkwardly, refusing to meet her eyes. 'I – I wanted to give you peace of mind when you marry Conrad and leave for Canada. This way you can be sure Connie will have a job for as long as she needs it, and a home for life for herself and her family. You'll find it's all written into the sale contract.'

She should be grateful, but she was overcome with grief.

'Fergus – why are you doing this for me?'

He looked at her sorrowfully.

'Because I love you, Annie darling. I've always loved you, only somehow or other it all went wrong.'

'Fergus, why must you tell me this now, when it's much too late?'

Annie stared at him in despair. This was the boy, the man, she'd loved and lost, ever since she was a little girl following eagerly in his heroic footsteps. Tearfully, she remembered Lisette vowing to follow her Julius willingly, no matter where he led. That was true love!

'Forget about me, Annie dear. Be happy,' Fergus said sadly.

He raised her chin with a gentle hand, and kissed her goodbye. This would be the last time, he thought. The very last time...

Conrad had walked into the hotel kitchen at that moment and stopped dead after glancing into the yard. He could hardly believe his eyes. Annie – kissing Fergus!

'Well I'll be—' he exclaimed in utter dismay, chilled by the sight.

He hurried outside, but they were so absorbed in one another they did not hear the door open and close. More slowly, with a heavy heart, Conrad walked towards the young couple. They broke apart guiltily.

Annie cried out, distraught, 'Conrad darling! I'm sorry. I – I didn't want you to see!'

'I'm glad I did,' he said quietly.

'I love you, Conrad. I really do!' she wept.

He sighed. 'I know you do. But not the way you love this young man. I admit I was afraid this might happen when you met. So afraid, I couldn't pluck up courage to tell you Fergus had bought the hotel for you and Connie. I honestly thought that you could forget him, when we were married and living in Canada. I dreamed it would be all moonlight and red roses for us.' He looked at her steadily. 'But that was *my* dream, my darling, and I don't believe you share it wholeheartedly. Oh, I know you'd do your very best to make our marriage work, because that's the wonderful, loyal girl you are, but sooner or later it could fall apart, and I dare not take that risk. I love you and I'm heartbroken, but the dream's over, Annie dear.'

She hugged him in tears, woefully confused.

'Conrad ... I don't know what to say – what to do!'

He kissed her lightly. 'Don't say anything, my dear girl. Go back to Balfour land today with Fergus. That's where you really belong. Plan a future together, make up for lost time. When you come back in a week or two, I'll be gone.' He smiled faintly. 'You know how I hate goodbyes, Annie, especially this one.'

He turned to the younger man and held out a hand. 'You win, Fergus. Take care of her. She's a wonderful girl, a star.'

'I will, Conrad, don't worry.' Emotionally, Fergus gripped the older man's hand. He looked at him with concern. 'But what will you do?'

He shrugged. 'There's still Canada, and a hotel to find near the Rockies. I'll enjoy that challenge, and maybe you and Annie will visit one day, when you're an old married couple.'

And Conrad smiled, the rare generous smile that Connie wished he'd show more often...

The war was over, and rationing was even more stringent. However, that had not put a damper upon Christmas preparations at Kil-

384

muckety in the winter of 1945. The old Balfour family home, grown shabby in wartime and rejected by Mr and Mrs McGill in favour of their son, glowed warmly with candlelight and holly. A magnificent Christmas tree stood in the hallway, decked with family trinkets from Christmases past and chocolates selflessly donated from sweet rations. This first peacetime Christmas was a double celebration. Annie Balfour and Fergus McGill had announced their engagement.

'About time!' Connie said to family assembled in the farmhouse kitchen to stir the Christmas pudding for luck. 'Those two were made for each other, and too pig-headed to see it!'

Which raised a smile from those recalling a certain disastrous incident involving piglets.

The Balfour twins were reunited for the occasion. Madeleine and Dermot had sent Lisette and Julien north, insisting this was a Balfour family occasion not to be missed. Lisette and the baby had arrived a few days earlier, leaving time for the sisters to reminisce.

'Look! I'm wearing my medal,' Lisette said. 'Nicer than yours, mine has two rainbows!'

Annie grinned. 'Ah, but mine has the King's head, yours only has a lady in a nightie!'

And the two of them collapsed, laughing.

Annie handed Lisette a slip of paper. 'Dad sent us a telegram, Liz.'

She read it eagerly. *All well. Wear your medals, dear girls, you deserve them! Much love, Dad,*

Teresa and Kim.

Lisette sighed. 'That's lovely! But how I wish Dad could see Julien, his first grand-child.'

But she'd no intention of spoiling the first peacetime Christmas with sad regrets, though there had been no reply from France, and still no news of Julius. Maybe none of the French relatives had survived. Every time she looked at Julius's bright little son, she was reminded of the pain and loneliness. Only Annie knew the heartbreak behind Lisette's brave smile.

Everyone had brought a present, small gifts, plainly wrapped because Christmas paper was impossible to find. These parcels were piled beneath the tree, a magnet for the baby, who was already an agile crawler. Lisette took her eyes off him for a few minutes while chatting with Annie, and off he went, gaining speed on the hallway's polished wooden floor. The twins went in pursuit, Lisette scooping her son into her arms as he reached for the parcels under the tree. 'No, you don't, you rascal!' She laughed.

The doorbell pealed at that moment.

'That'll be the post. More parcels, Julien!' Annie opened the door merrily.

But a complete stranger stood on the doorstep, a stocky young man with black hair and very dark eyes. A foreigner, and yet, when he smiled, impossible as it seemed, Annie knew at once who he must be...

'You're Kim!'

'Hi! I guess you must be my sister.' He

beamed. 'My father sent me. He says to tell you, I'm his Christmas present.' The smile broadened, the black eyes twinkled. 'Mind you, I suppose you folks might appreciate a bunch of bananas, rather than a long-lost brother, but bananas don't travel so good.'

'Kim, how absolutely wonderful!' Annie hustled her half-brother inside. His arrival was more than wonderful, she thought. It seemed like a miracle.

'I'm Annie, this is Lisette,' she said.

'Father's famous twins!' he declared enthusiastically, hugging them both. 'And you're wearing his medals. Father said you might, so I wore mine.' Kim pulled aside a large tartan muffler to reveal James Balfour's third medal. The ribbon was well-worn, but the silver was bright – For Bravery – for saving life. It was fitting that Kim should wear it, the twins thought. It was hard to imagine the dangers he'd faced.

So James's children stood in a close circle, his grandchild in Lisette's arms. Candlelight struck glints of silver and bronze from three medals worn with pride. A truly miraculous moment – together again at last.

On the morning of Christmas Eve, Annie and Fergus went on a sentimental journey, hand in hand. They were visiting scenes from the past, redolent of mischief and mayhem, anger, jealousy and anguish. Montgomery the sheepdog, one of Barney's descendants, accompanied them.

'All this was once Balfour land, Annie,' Fergus said, surveying it pensively. 'I never wanted my family to have it, you know! Didn't seem right, somehow. But the Balfours will have it back, sweetheart, when you and I are married. The parents have retired to the town, John and I will run the estate together, and you, my love, will be lady of the dear old shabby manor. Perfect spot to raise a brood of spirited Balfour-McGills,' he grinned.

Annie laughed. 'That's the décor settled then, my darling. Mud-coloured carpets!' She nestled closer to him, out of the icy wind.

They stopped by the old bridge by the stream.

'This is where I would've declared undying love, Annie, if Barney hadn't attacked me. To think that blasted dog caused years of quarrels and misunderstanding!' Fergus sighed. 'Barney never liked me. Nipped my ankles, every chance he had. I just hope that Monty...'

Fergus took Annie in his arms and kissed her, one eye warily on the dog.

But Montgomery had settled down at the entrance to the footbridge, head down watchfully on front paws. Monty had sensed he would be on guard for some considerable time, judging by the way these two were behaving...

Lisette had also gone walking that bright, frosty morning, pushing Julien in the pram.

She paused when she came across the engrossed lovers and the patient dog, turning tactfully off the farm track and headed along the driveway. It was easier pushing the pram along the tarmac, the smooth going lulling the baby to sleep. She walked dreamily, remembering Christmases spent in France in deadly danger, but so happily, with Julius by her side. She could see him in her mind's eye, quick-thinking and clever, dark eyes that could light with anger at sight of cruelty or injustice, and warm with such devoted love for her alone.

Looking dreamily ahead, she could imagine she was seeing his tall, lean figure walking towards her, recognize the easy, athletic stride...

Lisette stopped dead. She had gone mad! Driven herself crazy with waiting and longing.

She could hardly believe it was not imagination. He was there. Julius was coming striding towards her. It was Julius!

The winter landscape whirled around her, then steadied as he caught her in his arms.

'A dream!' She murmured against the darkness of his coat. 'I must be dreaming...'

He laughed and she felt the warmth of his kiss on her lips. 'No dream, my darling. Madeleine and Dermot sent me north, when I went to the address on your letter.'

She looked up, still dazed. 'I don't understand, Julius. For months I thought I'd lost you forever, and now you're here.'

'It was the war, my love. Dominic and Eva's house was badly damaged in hand-to-hand fighting during the liberation, but they and the children are safe. They fled to Tante Mathilde when the fighting began, and her house was spared. Your letter was not found till Dominic started repairing the house after the war. Then it became easier. I was searching for news of you, while they searched for me.'

She frowned. 'How on earth could they find you when you went under a false name?'

He laughed delightedly. 'I am not the man to hide behind a lie, *chérie*! My parents had me baptized Julius Lamontine, and *that* is my name! And now I too have a son!' Julius said exultantly.

'I called him Julien Balfour Lamontine,' Lisette said proudly. Hand in hand, they bent over the pram. Julius spoke in a choked whisper.

'Our son is wonderful!'

She laughed. 'Handsome, strong, clever, bold – and full of mischief, like his *papa*.'

Julius kissed her tenderly. 'Brave and beautiful, like his *maman*, you mean! But Marie Duval served her country well and is gone forever. If you agree, we will renew our marriage vows before the priest, Lisette my love.'

She turned to him joyfully. 'Oh yes, Julius! Let's arrange a quiet ceremony with all the family present, before Julien and I go home with you, to France.'

The baby wakened suddenly, studying with bright, curious gaze the tall man bending over the pram. Lisette held her breath anxiously, but it was all right. Julien had greeted his father with a wide, welcoming grin...